SHAKESPEARE'S OTHER LIVES

An Anthology of Fictional Depictions of the Bard

Edited by
MAURICE J. O'SULLIVAN, JR.

McFarland & Company, Inc., Publishers
Jefferson, North Carolina, and London

The editor is grateful to the following permission grantors: "Bingo," from *Bingo and the Sea*, © 1975 by Edward Bond; reprinted by permission of Reed Consumer Books Ltd. "Everything and Nothing," from *A Personal Anthology*, © 1978 by Jorge Luis Borges; reprinted by permission of Grove/Atlantic Inc. "The Muse," from *Enderby's Dark Lady*, © 1984 by Anthony Burgess; reprinted by permission of Artellus Limited. *Will Shakespeare*, © 1977 by John Mortimer; reprinted by permission of the Peters Fraser & Dunlop Group Ltd. *Shakespeare's Dog*, © 1983 by Leon Rooke; reprinted by permission of Alfred A. Knopf, Inc. "Proofs of Holy Writ," © 1932 by Rudyard Kipling; reprinted by permission of A.P. Watt, Ltd., on behalf of the National Trust. *A Myth of Shakespeare*, © 1928 by Charles Williams; reprinted by permission of David Higham Associates Limited. The editor also thanks the editors of *Shakespeare Quarterly*, which published an earlier version of the essay "Shakespeare's Other Lives" in vol. 38, no. 2 (1987).

992522

British Library Cataloguing-in-Publication data are available

Library of Congress Cataloguing-in-Publication Data

Shakespeare's other lives : an anthology of fictional depictions of
   the Bard / edited by Maurice J. O'Sullivan, Jr.
     p. cm.
   Includes bibliographical references and index.
   ISBN 0-7864-0335-7 (library binding : 50# alkaline paper) ∞
   1. Shakespeare, William, 1564–1616—Literary collections.
2. Dramatists, English—Early modern, 1500–1700—Literary
collections. I. O'Sullivan, Maurice, 1944–   .
PR2935.S48 1997
822.3'3—dc21   97-1050
                                       CIP

Manufactured in the United States of America

McFarland & Company, Inc., Publishers
  Box 611, Jefferson, North Carolina 28640

SHAKESPEARE'S OTHER LIVES

To my parents, Dr. Maurice J. O'Sullivan
and Agnes Brady O'Sullivan

TABLE OF CONTENTS

PREFACE

During the summer of 1983 I found myself in Stratford upon Avon working on a series of research projects. While my wife explored the back roads to Warwick Castle and my sons tried to master the codes of cricket, I spent my days working through seventeenth and eighteenth-century texts in the Shakespeare Centre Library. One afternoon one of the librarians commented, "You Yanks really take this much more seriously than Will would have," and handed me a copy of John Mortimer's *Will Shakespeare*.

With Mortimer I quickly discovered the library's extraordinarily rich collection of novels, plays, and poems about Shakespeare, as I spent the rest of the summer lost in an entire universe I had not realized existed. From Robert Folkstone Williams' massive epics and H.F. Rubinstein's hermetic puzzles to Walter Savage Landor's erudite wit and George Bernard Shaw's politically tinged attacks, these works share a fascination with the biographical mysteries and a desire to discover the true Shakespeare.

Long before Samuel Schoenbaum and Gary Taylor traced the ways each generation unconsciously reinvented Shakespeare in its own image, these writers had consciously recreated him. Like an improvisational troupe of widely differing talents, they took the same locations and the same cast of characters to create Shakespeares ranging from distracted adolescence to anxious retirement and from a country pedant instructing a lightly talented band of scholars to an urban socialite exchanging quips with royalty.

My goal in this collection has been to gather together those works I found most interesting and entertaining. They include stories, plays, and poems from England, Ireland, the United States, France, and Argentina. Among the works are Alexandre Duval's domestic romance, Walter Savage Landor's courtroom drama, Edward Bond's political manifesto, Anthony Burgess' science fiction, and Jorge Luis Borges' postmodernist meditation.

Throughout my life I have been fortunate to work with scholars whose fascination with Shakespeare inspired both their students and colleagues: Albert Reddy, S.J., and Donald Lynch, S.J., of Fairfield University; Robert Ornstein of Case Western Reserve University; Levi Fox, director of the Shakespeare Birthplace Trust; Alan Nordstrom of Rollins College; and Stuart Omans of the Orlando Shakespeare Festival. I must also thank Barbara

Mowat and Andrea Loewenwarter of *Shakespeare Quarterly* for their help on an earlier version of the introduction which appeared in *Shakespeare Quarterly* 38.2 (Summer 1987) and Wyatt Benner for his suggestions about revisions.

On a practical level, I owe deep debts to my family's patience, my colleagues' forbearance, my students' insights, and, especially, our department's administrative assistant, Karen Slater, who handles all the practical matters with a graceful ease. No work like this would be possible without understanding librarians; I especially thank those at the Birthplace Library, the British Library, and the Winter Park and Orlando public libraries. Lynne Phillips, whose legendary genius at tracking down the most obscure request through interlibrary loans, deserves special recognition.

Above all, I owe my love for reading to my parents, Dr. Maurice O'Sullivan and Agnes Brady O'Sullivan. To them I dedicate this work.

INTRODUCTION

My life stands in the level of your dreams....
The Winter's Tale III.ii.80.

For the generations of scholars who have devoted their lives to check-
ing Baconian gambits and slogging through Oxford marshes in order to separate the facts of Shakespeare's life and career from the myths that have entan-
gled them, fictions about Shakespeare create a curious dilemma. On the one
hand, such fictions often invoke—and even embrace—the very legends that
scholarship has sought to discredit. On the other, scholars share with the
authors of such work a kinship of interest. Like theologians fascinated by sin,
many Shakespeareans develop an affection for even the most arcane or misleading piece of Shakespeareana. The ambivalence towards conscious fictions
on the part of those who have devoted their lives to identifying and correct-
ing the biographical fictions may explain why the large collection of novels,
stories, and plays is so rarely discussed.

Although questions of intentional fallacies occasionally arise, few readers have trouble distinguishing between conscious and unconscious fictions.
The large body of conscious fictions involving Shakespeare offers a rich variety, ranging from anachronistic fantasy to scrupulous fidelity, from bardola-
trous flights to Marxian dialectics, and from Catholic apologetics to an
attempt to establish Ulysses S. Grant as head of a state-governed Church of
America. Most authors have larger ambitions than mere art. They offer solutions to the identities of W.H. and the Dark Lady, suggest Shakespeare's role
in shaping the King James Bible, and trace his relationships with Sir Thomas
Lucy, Francis Bacon, Elizabeth I, Kit Marlowe, and Ben Jonson. They celebrate, mourn, and demean Anne. And they speculate endlessly about Shakespeare's pets and poaching, his sources and inspirations, his melancholy and
death.

For the most part, these "other lives" reinforce patterns that have emerged
in studies of the biographies. In a few cases, they also offer interesting experiments in fiction or drama, works worth reading for their own sake. I have
divided the material into seven broad categories, discussing under each some

1

representative examples. The first five categories involve differing approaches to Shakespeare himself. Cygnets and Daytrippers, the first two categories, provide younger or less experienced readers an entrance to his world. Approaching more sophisticated audiences, Domestics and Players, the third and fourth categories, attempt to identify "the essential man," the former at home and the latter in the theater. The last of the categories includes those for whom relevance is a prime consideration, those who seek to show Shakespeare as a contemporary of their audiences. Two other categories overlap these first five but can be distinguished by attitudes or achievement: the Obsessed, who devote an extraordinary amount of time or space in turning the search for Shakespeare into a quest; and the Wits, who succeed where so many fail.

I

Perhaps the most successful category of fictions about Shakespeare is that of the Cygnets, works written directly or indirectly for children. They avoid much of the pretentiousness and posturing so frequent in other categories and find a more appropriate audience for the sentimentality ubiquitous in Shakespearean fictions. Generally, these works pretend to offer nothing more than a rudimentary introduction to Shakespeare and the Elizabethan age. Their tendency to flatten characters and to fatten morals seems, for better or worse, endemic to children's literature.

Within the Cygnet category are two groups. In the first, Shakespeare is a tangential, occasionally shadowy figure. Typically, these stories focus on youngsters traveling to London and becoming involved with the actors. John Bennett appears to have established the prototype with his *Master Skylark: A Story of Shakspere's Time* (1898), an account of Nicholas Attwood's heroic experiences in Stratford and London. H.M. Anderson's *Golden Lads* (1928) and Marchette Chute's *The Wonderful Winter* (1956) follow Bennett's model closely. T.H. Porter offers an interesting variation with *A Maid of the Malverns* (1912) by providing not only a heroine but one attracted to Jonson's company rather than Shakespeare's. In all of these works Shakespeare plays a secondary role, although he often proves the catalyst for a protagonist's moment of insight or realization of his quest. In the second group of Cygnets, Shakespeare appears center stage. Even though John Brougham's very brief *Shakspeare's Dream: An Historical Pageant* (1858) was not written explicitly for children, it has the simple, vivid effectiveness of good school plays. After a masquelike production in which Chronos, Fancy, Genius, and Fame inspire the sleeping Shakespeare, all the principal characters from his plays appear in a pageant. Katherine Lord takes a similar approach in "The Day Will Shakspere Went to Kenilworth" (1926). In it the young Will captures Robin Goodfellow and is, in turn, adopted by fairyland and given visions which will become the plots of his plays. More conventional are biographical novels of the young would-be playwright, like Mrs. George Madden Martin's *A Warwickshire Lad* (1916) and Rosemary Anne Sisson's *The Young Shakespeare* (1959). Sisson's novel ends with a "Letter to the Reader," which sorts the facts from the fictions—though some readers may find her distinctions suspect. She claims, for example, "Another of the 'facts' [in this novel] is that our William remained all of his life very faithful to his home and his family." Finally, one of the most interesting of the Cygnets is a novel that perfectly embodies Victorian sentimentality, Imogen Clark's *Will Shakespeare's Little Lad* (1897), the story of Hamnet.

Like many of the Cygnets, the Daytrippers take a fairly relaxed view of distinctions between fact and fiction. In illustrating typical days in Shakespeare's life, they appear to assume that history becomes more palatable when fictionalized. And fiction offers possibilities for embellishment that are rarely denied. Mrs. Constance Rose, for example, provides a series of formal tableaux and songs in *Shakespeare's Day* (1927), while E. Hamilton Gruner's *With Golden Quill* (1936) becomes a cavalcade for over 120 actors, one lap dog, and one horse.

Like the Cygnets also, these fictions offer a curiously childlike prose ("'Whither away, sweet Will?' asks Ben Jonson. 'Where my feet take me—a wandering fit is on me,' says the great William"), or an equally childlike certainty about character ("His dress was not like many of his fellows, thrown negligently upon his person, but was scrupulously arranged with almost puritanical neatness…"). All agree that his characters derive from his character; in a typical scene he stands aloof, quietly accepting congratulations on the publication of *Hamlet*, "clad in a somber dark doublet."

These Daytrippers have two virtues. As an introduction for younger readers, they evoke a strong sense of the age's cultural context. Even more appealing are their illustrations, especially the color prints in *My Magazines'* "A Day with England's Greatest Man," the color plates of the plays in Maurice Clare's *A Day with Shakespeare*, and the portraits and views of England in Gruner's *With Golden Quill*.

II

While the Daytrippers appear primarily interested in easing our absorption of social or cultural history, the Domestics have more serious fictional intentions. They focus on Shakespeare's family life, primarily, as might be expected, on his relationship with Anne. The earliest of these works, Nathan Drake's "Montchesney, a Tale of the Days of Shakspere" (1824), introduces a dilemma that many of those following him were to puzzle over. The tale is conveyed by a series of very long, very descriptive letters from a young girl.

Although Drake, author of *Shakspeare and His Times* (1817), promises to present the "moral and domestic feelings of" the poet, his inability to realize Shakespeare as a character leads him to shift the story quickly to others. It leaves Shakespeare a constantly retiring figure, a reclusive Prospero hovering around the edges of the story.

In 1845 Emma Severn took a very different approach from Drake in her novel *Anne Hathaway; Or, Shakspeare in Love*. Attempting to integrate all the emerging myths, she presents him as both a young genius and an unsullied child of nature. Her initial description of the young lovers suggests how difficult such an approach proved:

> Young and fair were the twain who threaded the mazes of that rude path. The girl had the grace and beauty of Venus, blended with the sprightliness of Hebe. It would be difficult,—perhaps impossible,—to describe her companion. A statuary might have modelled that figure for a youthful Apollo,—a painter have studied the head for a copy of Christ's boyhood,—yet in both, even a Canova, and a Da Vinci, must verily have utterly failed—not, perhaps, in embodying the form, and accurately sketching the features, but in representing the lofty expression of intelligence that emanated from every glance, movement, and attitude, of that fair forest boy; yet these two young people were only rustic villagers ... [I, 3].

Severn also takes a clear position on the Hathaway controversy. As the opening paragraph suggests, throughout the book Anne symbolizes both Hellenistic and Christian conceptions of the ideal. Appropriately, William often addresses her in quasi-religious terms:

> "How could I have suffered existence without you, Anne?" replied Shakespeare with animation. "You first taught me to know the soul of virtue, to experience the feelings of true-hearted honour; and it is in your presence alone I live, in your society alone I move and breathe, and have a being" [III, 62].

Such idealization, of course, makes for awkward prose and more awkward plotting.

On one side of the Domestics are the anti–Annians, a group especially prominent in the twentieth century. C.E. Lawrence's *The Hour of Prospero* (1927), for example, offers a damning portrait of the older Anne: "She is fifty-four years of age, but looks ten years older. Her expression is vacuous; her face that of a peasant-woman grown coarse with time; but her clothing is neat. She sits with her eyes shut, and is a picture of wornout womanhood." In the play Anne wavers between senility and craftiness while plotting to inherit the second-best bed, the bed Hamnet died in. An even more typical, bourgeois view of Anne appeared two years later in Roy S. Sensabaugh's *The Favor of the Queen.* Anne spends much of her time in this play puzzled about her marriage and her husband's values. He, of course, concerns himself with far more lofty thoughts:

> SHAKESPEARE. Thou art my wife, Nan, my own good wife; for whom I care, but none can share my soul.
>
> ANNE. I understand thee not. In the three weeks I spend with thee each year, thou scarce dost notice me. T'would seem thou didst belong to some far player world and gave it all thy sympathy. If I were thee, I'd never write again—it does but worry thee and keep thee from our company [p. 110].

Eric Milpass' *Sweet Will* (1973) provides a similarly loving but not overbright Anne confused about Will's longings. The novel, with its melodramatic view of Shakespeare fleeing Stratford after his early version of *Hamlet* offends the Earl of Leicester, leaves relatively little to the imagination: "Onomatopoetically, he clip-clopped and clattered over the cobbles of Clopton Bridge, followed the road along into Bridge Street, then turned left at High Cross into High Street" (p. 185).

Supporters of Anne, however, outnumber her critics. Sarah Sterling's *Shakespeare's Sweetheart* (1905), told in the first person by Anne, borrows from the Cygnets by having her follow Will to London in male disguise, fool the Dark Lady, play Juliet to Will's Romeo before the Queen, and save him from a plot concocted by Marlowe. She even dies with Will's name on her lips. In 1907 William T. Saward's play *William Shakespeare* also sends Anne to London seeking a husband, this time one who has fled from Sir Thomas Lucy's writ. The lovers finally meet at a masque where Sir Thomas also appears, still trying to prosecute Will. Salvation comes from a *deus ex machina* when the Queen blesses Will with her praise and absolves him from all youthful errors. Grace Carlton's *The Wooing of Anne Hathaway* (1938) and Cornel Adam Lengyel's *Will of Stratford* (n.d.) offer similarly sympathetic views of Anne. C.A. Somerset's *Shakespeare's Early Days*, first performed on 29 October 1829 at the Theater Royal with Charles Kemble as Shakespeare, features Sir Thomas prominently. Somerset appears principally interested in pleading the poet's case against charges of criminal activity. In lines that would provide solid evidence for those who would deny him authorship of the plays, Shakespeare justifies his poaching by describing a needy family he encountered in his solitary ramblings, a family for whom he sought food:

> His wretched wife, his helpless babes, himself,
> On the bare earth lay stretched!—their pallid cheeks,
> Their sunken eyes, proclaimed the ruthless war,
> Which hunger then was waging 'gainst disease,
> Hunger, and cold! her mortal enemies!

"Have you no food?" quoth I—
"None, for the last two days," was their reply [pp. 22–3].

Sir Thomas ("a second Sir John Falstaff for corpulence" [p. 19]) shows no compassion for such a crime of mercy and fines him fifty crowns, which John Shakespeare conveniently has with him.

Clemence Dane's play *Will Shakespeare* (1921) takes sympathy for Anne a step further. It shows an egocentric Will moping around Stratford before shadows of characters from the plays seduce him away from a stately, caring Anne:

> SHAKESPEARE. How long since we two married?
>
> ANNE.   Why,
>   Four months.
>
> SHAKESPEARE. And are you happy?
>
> ANNE.   Will, aren't you?
>
> SHAKESPEARE. I asked my wife.
>
> ANNE.   I am! I am! I am!
>   Oh, how can I be happy when I read
>   Your eyes, and read—what is it that I read?
>
> SHAKESPEARE. God knows!
>
> ANNE.   Yes, God He knows, but He's so far away—
>   Tell Anne!
>
> SHAKESPEARE. Touch not these cellar thoughts, half worm,
>   half weed:
>   Give them no light, no air: be warned in time:
>   Break not the seal nor roll away the stone,
>   Lest the blind evil writhe itself heart-high
>   And its breath stale us! [p. 4].

Most of the play, which opened at the Shaftesbury Theater on 17 November 1921 with Philip Merivale as Shakespeare and Claude Rains as Marlowe, centers on Anne's waiting. In fact, the last line has Anne's voice in the background saying, while Will writes, "I wait."

Edward Fisher makes the most extensive contribution to this genre in his trilogy *The Silver Falcon: Shakespeare and Son* (1962), *Love's Labour Won* (1963), and *The Best House in Stratford* (1965). As the titles suggest, Fisher's interest revolves around Shakespeare's domestic relationships. At the core of his stories is Fisher's vision of Anne:

> My Anne Hathaway is not so much the daughter of a Shottery farmer, who married suddenly, at an out-of-town church, in a forbidden season, with no time for the banns, a boy with no money or prospects who was eight years younger than herself. My Anne is rather the bright vision he

carried in his mind which made it so difficult to appreciate the wise, kind, incredibly patient woman he inadvertently married [Preface, unpag.].

Not all nineteenth-century writers concerned with Shakespeare's domestic life focus on his marriage. In Christopher Brooke Bradshaw's *Shakspere and Company* (1845), the playwright is involved in marrying off his three sisters: Eleanor, Susanna, and Katharine. And in William Black's *Judith Shakespeare: A Romance* (1884), he becomes enmeshed in his daughter's courtship. One of the more curious works from the nineteenth century is C.E.D. Phelps and Leigh North's *The Baliff of Tewkesbury* (1893), the story of William Helpes' rise from Shakespeare's fellow poacher to bailiff. His friendship and loyalty to the playwright lead ultimately to the sonnets' dedication to Mr. W.H. Although the idea is a promising one, Phelps and North let their prose stumble over their bardolatry. Thus, when the young poet is called forward by the ubiquitous Sir Thomas Lucy, "Slowly Shakespeare raised his head, and looked full at his judge with those wondrous eyes—the brightest, deepest, wisest, that ever shone under mortal brows" (p. 21).

A far less bright, deep, and wise figure appears in Alexandre-Vincent Pineu Duval's *Shakespeare Amoureaux* (1804). In this eighteenth-century French romantic's vision of Elizabethan life, Shakespeare courts the Globe's leading actress. (In Duval's version of the British Renaissance, women play women's roles.) A mixture of Hamlet's moods, Richard III's ruthlessness, and Othello's jealousy, this French Shakespeare must deal in an Anne-less world with a duplicitous maid, a powerful rival, and a coy mistress.

In addition to reflections on his marriage and other relationships, Domestics also find themselves fascinated by Shakespeare's death. Sir Edward Hamley set the model in his play "Shakespeare's Funeral" (1878) by showing Michael Drayton and Walter Raleigh, eldest son of Sir Walter, in Stratford for the funeral. They meet the citizens, who are clearly sources for the plays (e.g., a Master Sherlock who lends money), and hear the minister's funeral sermon, a sermon which belittles poetry and, by extension, Shakespeare's achievement. Wilfred Blair attempts a slightly more elevated chronicle play in *The Death of Shakespeare* (1916), but he shows much the same reverence as his peers. His characters all speak in prose except when Shakespeare speaks or is spoken to. Then all speak verse.

A recent play provides perhaps the most interesting interpretation of Shakespeare's last day. In *Bingo: Scenes of Money and Death* (1974), Edward Bond provides a Marxian critique of the poet's life and death. Bond wrote *Bingo* because he found "the contradictions in Shakespeare's life ... similar to the contradictions in us. He was a 'corrupt seer'" (p. xiii) who wrote about poverty and injustice in *King Lear*, yet whose "behaviour as a property-owner made him closer to Goneril than Lear" (p. ix). The play shows him supporting and benefiting from "the Goneril-society—with its prisons, workhouses,

whipping, starvation ... and all the rest of it" (p. ix)—and then in the final
scene, poisoning himself and dying in despair. An alternative approach to
Shakespeare's apparent materialism was offered near the beginning of the
century by Conal O'Riordan [Norreys Connell] in his play *Shakespear's End*
(1912). As Drayton, Jonson and other poets celebrate Shakespeare's birthday,
a sailor and an Irish Jesuit come upon them. The Jesuit acts as a catalyst, let-
ting Shakespeare see how shallow his concern with objects is and how much
he needs the true faith. Feeling empty, Shakespeare finally mutters, "In man-
uas tuas Domine" (p. 166) and dies.

Even after his death Shakespeare's bones continued to attract writers.
M.Y. Halidom's adventure *The Poet's Curse* (1911), with Shakespeare's epitaph
stamped boldly on its cover, offers the story of an American millionaire
attempting to steal the skeleton for his museum. Highly predictably—and
accompanied by language like "dastardly" and "foul play"—the American dies
after seeing the death of his only son. "A Warwickshire Man" (C.J. Langston)
had taken a similar approach in the story "How Shakespeare's Skull Was
Stolen" (1879), a mystery in which the skull is offered for sale to Horace Walpole. Although Walpole rejects the offer, Langston leaves open the question
of whether the skull was ever returned. Such larcenous phrenologists will
inevitably continue to appear, spurred on by that wonderful promise in the
epitaph.

III

Just as the Domestics think to catch the essential Shakespeare in his village, marriage, or death, the Players, with a bit more success, seek him in the
theater. Maurice Baring's "The Rehearsal" (1911), for example, offers a witty
burlesque of a rehearsal of *Macbeth* in 1606 at the Globe. Baring sees a gentle playwright awash in a sea of actors' egos:

Enter Mr. BURBAGE, *who plays* MACBETH

MR. BURBAGE. That scene doesn't go. Now don't you think Macbeth
   had better walk in his sleep instead of Lady Macbeth?

THE STAGE MANAGER. That's an idea.

THE PRODUCER. I think the whole scene might be cut. It's quite
   unnecessary.

LADY MACBETH. Then I shan't come on in the whole of the fifth act.
   If that scene's cut I shan't play all.

THE STAGE MANAGER. We're thinking of transferring the scene to
   Macbeth. [*To the* AUTHOR] It wouldn't need much altering.
   Would you mind rewriting that scene, Mr. Shakespeare? It wouldn't
   want much alteration. You'd have to change that line about Arabia.

Instead of "this little hand," you might say: "All the perfumes of
Arabia will not sweeten this horny hand." I'm not sure it isn't more
effective.

THE AUTHOR. I'm afraid it might get a laugh.

MR. BURBAGE. Not if I play it.

THE AUTHOR. I think it's more likely that Lady Macbeth would walk
in her sleep, but—

MR. BURBAGE. That doesn't signify. I can make a great hit in that
scene.

LADY MACBETH. If you take that scene from me, I shan't play Juliet tonight [pp. 242–3].

In a more ambitious attempt to define the artist, Charles Williams attempts
both performances and story in his *A Myth of Shakespeare* (1928). This blank-
verse drama, written "to provide a momently credible framework for representative scenes and speeches from the Plays ... contains," wrote Williams,
"no thesis of Shakespeare's life, character, or genius, except that he was born
poet and a working dramatist" (p. 7). Designed to be produced on a double
stage, with the inner "separated from the outer by curtains which could be
withdrawn whenever an actual scene from the Play was given" (p. 8), the *Myth*
varies its blank verse to accord with the Shakespearean speeches it is sur-
rounding or introducing. Marlowe and Mary Fitton play significant roles in
this "myth" of Shakespeare's life, and Williams' own power shows through in
such lines as the one he gives to Burbage, who answers Ben Jonson's words
about Shakespeare with "It is his poetry/ Searches our hearts out" (p. 108).

Norbert Krieger used a rehearsal of *Hamlet* in his story "Prologue to
Shakespeare's *Hamlet*" (1942) for a bit of literary criticism. When Burbage
questions the author about his play, he finds out that it is really a bit of Protes-
tant apologetics with Hamlet representing Martin Luther, his mother the
True Church, and Claudius the pope who has usurped power in the Church.
Thus, Hamlet arrives from Wittenburg and sends Polonius to his Diet at
Worms. Krieger's clever if slightly didactic reading balances D.H. Fruehe's
bland *Swan of Avon* (1924), in which Shakespeare plays Hamlet in that play's
premiere and later is knighted by the Queen. When he asks how he can serve
her, her response reflects the awkward dialogue Fruehe's admiration gener-
ates:

You—serve.—You jest. Who might demand
Worship of earthly women from the man
Upon whose high-arched thinker's forehead
The Muse's consecrating kiss is glowing? [unpag.].

Both Clara Longworth, the Comtesse de Chambrun, and John Mortimer
allow Shakespeare's fellow actors to tell his story. Longworth's *My Shakespeare,*

Rise (1935) offers the fictional reminiscences of John Lacy as told to John Aubrey. Mortimer's *Will Shakespeare* (1977) has John Rice, onetime boy actor, recount his life among the players. He does so in witty, energetic prose:

> Now my reader, if times should change by the Grace of God and men suddenly remember that they have an ear for verse and a taste for pleasure, and I have a reader, let me tell you how I shall go to work. Something I saw of Will when he was at the Theater, when he was with his pot-girls, and that I can set down of my own knowledge. A lot more I learnt of Dick Burbage and the other actors and of the servants of my Lord Southampton. (It's a wonder what men will do before their servants who, by and large, they regard but as chairs and tables who will not mind their leching, or weeping or quarrelling before them.) Some more I learnt at Stratford when I visited there as an actor and et the neighbours and his wife (he called her the "She-Dragon" but when I saw her she had grown old and patient and somewhat lacking in her Dragon's teeth). And some, perforce, I must invent, keeping in my head all I knew of Will and his probable manner at the Court and in the Ale house, of his adventures with Royalty and Harlotry. So as I write out the scenes that follow shall I become, like himself, a playmaker but in secret [p. 13].

Focusing more narrowly, Martin Holmes' "Shakespeare at Whitehall" (1957) describes a production of a Christmas play and Alan Woods' "Playing Days at Stratford" (1964) offers an account of the players appearing at Stratford in 1576 with an abridgement of *The Famous Victories of Henry V*. In it the young William is recruited for the role of Queen Katharine. In a similar vein, W. Rendle's "Shakespeare at the Tabard Inn: A Phantasy" (c. 1880) finds the poet visiting Chaucer's Tabard Inn and transforming its owner, Isabel Mabb, into the fairies' midwife, Queen Mab.

Transformations also characterize works about Shakespeare and Bacon. Most of these books try to answer the Baconians by showing a personal and ideological sympathy between the two figures. But the subject is such a quagmire that most who venture into it tend to sink quickly. Easily the most confusing of these works is Tresham Gregg's *Queen Elizabeth, or the Origin of Shakespeare* (1872), an attempt to show the necessity for an established church through a series of strangely disjointed discussions between Elizabeth and Mary, Queen of Scots. The future glory of England and its church are adumbrated at the end of the play when Elizabeth quizzes the young Shakespeare and Bacon and crowns both with laurels. The play may have a special interest for American audiences because it is dedicated to Ulysses S. Grant, with the hope that he will establish a Church of America, for "without a religion established by law no Commonwealth can be viewed as perfect." Far more secular are David Graham Adee's *Bacon and Shakespeare* (1896), a play more about Shakespeare and his actors than about Bacon, and Samuel Alfred Cox's *Shakespeare Converted into Bacon* (1899), in which the two protagonists, aware of their "twin-like mystic nature," consider switching roles in life. The most extensive—and the wittiest—entry into the gammonite camp is Caryl Brahms and S.J. Simon's *No Bed for Bacon* (1941). The book focuses on Sir Francis' sleepless attempts to convince Shakespeare to write a play for the Queen's Revels. In this broadly comic novel, Bacon eventually succeeds and brings the Queen *Twelfth Night*.

IV

Shakespeare's earliest appearances as a fictional character occurred in the guise of a contemporary of his audiences. At first, the eighteenth century, with its fairly limited understanding of the possibilities of historical fiction, resurrected him as a ghost, often appearing spectrally in prologues to comment on his own plays. An example is John Dennis' patriotic prologue to a subscription performance of *Julius Caesar* at Drury Lane (14 January 1706/7), in which Shakespeare says:

> Hail, my lov'd Britons! how I'm pleas'd to see
> The great assertors of fair Liberty,
> Assembled here upon this solemn day,
> To see this *Roman* and this *English* play!
> This tragedy in great Eliza's reign,
> Was writ, when Philip plagu'd both land and main,
> To subjugate the western world to Spain.
> Then I brought mighty Julius on the stage,
> Then Britain heard my godlike Roman's rage,
> And came in crowds, with rapture came, to see
> The world from its proud tyrant freed by me [Prologue, pp. 1–2].

Such nationalism was to mark a number of the ghost's reappearances.

An unsigned poem in *The London Magazine*, "Shakespeare's Ghost" (1750), set the tone for the remainder of the century. Beseeching the reader, "Guard me, ye Britons, from the pedant's page," Shakespeare goes on to praise David Garrick and to hope he will prevail against Cibber and Tate. As the most visible Shakespearean of his age, Garrick inevitably became the focus of many of Shakespeare's fictional appearances. In *Garrick in the Shades; or A Peep into Elysium, a Farce* (1779), a play "[n]ever offered to the managers of the Theater-Royal," the author goes one step beyond representing Shakespeare as a character and has other characters describe the bard's cold reception of the newly dead Garrick. Shakespeare is reported as accusing Garrick of "filthy love of lucre" (p.48) in his Stratford Festival:

> ... thy fam'd Jubilee, was a mean device
> To gull the people—and to cram thy well-fill'd purse [p. 25].

Two decades earlier, a slightly more sympathetic writer challenged Garrick on other grounds. As manager of the Drury Lane Theater, Garrick had attempted to expand his militantly chauvinistic audience's taste to include a wider variety of theatrical forms. Criticism reached a climax with his staging of the French choreographer Jean George Noverre's ballet, *The Chinese Festival*, in 1755. Its premiere, at a time when war with France seemed increasingly probable, led to riots at Drury Lane. When Garrick appeared on stage to calm his audience, they screamed, "Monsieur," at him and hissed. In *The Visitation; or, an Interview Between the Ghost of Shakespear and D–V–D G–RR-- K, Esq.*, the ghost joins the chorus of criticism and accuses Garrick of helping to undermine the martial spirit of the British:

> You have of late, why best you know,
> Deserted those, that serv'd you so;
> Contemn'd that Pow'r, you lately priz'd,
> And follow'd Arts you once despis'd;
> O'erbearing all, with haughty Spirit,
> Buoy'd up by *self-sufficient Merit*,
> Preferr'd Tom Loll, and what's akin,
> Compar'd with *Drama—Harlequin* … [p. 7].

The work ends with Shakespeare forgiving Garrick (if he promises to perform "My fifth Harry") and praising England's military might.

The same sort of jingoism animates G.A. Loessel's "A Midnight-Vision in Westminster Abbey" (1930), in which Shakespeare's statue speaks in praise of George V:

> Times, threatening the world with wreck and ruin,
> Prove Britons still, who ever, as of aye,
> Fight but to conquer, used, in rougher sea
> To hold our fleets or wreck and ruin free,
> Our throne it held and will yet ever hold—
> The acme of this glorious monarchy [unpag.].

To ensure that no nuances are lost, the poem ends with directions for an orchestra to play "Rule Britannia." Shakespeare's statue in New York's Central Park speaks more gently, sentimentally, and earnestly in Lawton Campbell's *Shakespeare Smiles* (1924). The statue tries to inspire a young playwright to look at life. And in W.F. Vandervell's *The Tercentenary; or, A Night with Shakespeare* (1864), Shakespeare and his characters form a pageant in the mind of Mulberry Mugs, Beadle of St. Anthony the Good.

Two important literary figures of the early twentieth century wrote curiously disjointed and derivative books about Shakespeare as their contemporary. William Dean Howells' *The Seen and the Unseen at Stratford-on-Avon* (1914) has an American visitor encounter Shakespeare and Bacon. Apparently influenced by Twain's *A Connecticut Yankee at King Arthur's Court*—there is even a mention of Twain early on—the book eventually settles into a travelogue of the Shakespeare country with Shakespeare as tour guide. Hugh Kingsmill's *The Return of William Shakespeare* (1929) has the playwright returning to London through a process of reintegrating life. Despite obvious allusions to H.G. Wells, the story lacks the conflict and development Wells' fantasies have.

That those who see Shakespeare as a contemporary often find his relevance universal is apparent in Douglas Jerrold's "Shakespeare in China" (1837), Edward H. Warren's *Shakespeare on Wall Street* (1929), and Morris Chariton's *Conversations with Shakespeare* (1969). Jerrold, in a parody of Shakespeare criticism, quotes a letter from Ching the Mandarin to a fellow artist about Shakespeare's and Falstaff's lives. The result is an exotic expansion of Shakespeareana. Warren, in the midst of the financial crisis of '29, calls on the market bulls ("May Their Courage Never Wilt") in a play that brings about Shakespeare's metamorphosis into a New York investor with three sons: Hamlet, a bond salesman; Macbeth, a timid bull; and Falstaff, an anti-prohibitionist. All are saved by the wisdom of Anne, who counsels aggressive policies for an uncertain market. Only the brave survive the battle of bears and bulls. Behind it all is a note of ironic ambivalence, probably best captured in the opening scene when the three witches appear near a blast furnace in New Jersey:

> FIRST WITCH. The sky is blue, the weather fair,
> And business prospers everywhere.
>
> SECOND WITCH. I'm looking here, and looking there,
> I do not find a prosperous bear.
>
> THIRD WITCH. There is a Turn to every fate.
> Who buys them now, buys far too late.
>
> FIRST WITCH. That's not what I heard.
>
> SECOND WITCH. What did you hear?
>
> FIRST WITCH. What all the speculators say:
> The market wings its upward way,
> That Radio will sell more high;
> Than eagle's flight across the sky.
>
> THIRD WITCH. There'll be an end to all this winning;
> The bears will play the final inning.
>
> FIRST WITCH. When Radio is thirty-two
> What the Hell will people do?
>
> THIRD WITCH. Come, sisters, we shall meet again
> When prices fall like showers of rain.
>
> ALL. When the market's set to crack,
> To this foul spot we'll all come back.
>
> *Exeunt* [pp. 1–2].

Warren's humor provides a balance for such works as Chariton's *Conversations with Shakespeare*. Chariton promises to offer "a present-day situation, of people, ordinary people in conversation with Shakespeare." Although he does begin with a wife, a husband, a school teacher, and a skilled worker, his attempt to combine Shakespeare our contemporary, Shakespeare the common man, and Shakespeare the sublime collapses when he replaces ordinary people with Beethoven and Socrates. Even the simpler dialogues begin on a pretentious note; the wife opens her speech with the line, "Your works, Oh great demolisher of mortal baseness...." Chariton has so much confidence in "this booklet that I am sure will be read extensively" that he lists other books he is willing to write for a sympathetic audience.

V

Readers of the plays have long recognized how easily an interest in the works can spark an interest in the life. For some, that interest becomes an obsession. The truly obsessed tend to share at least one of three characteristics—idolatry, volubility, or perseverance. The middle of the nineteenth century saw two of the more remarkable of these figures. In 1848 Henry Curling ("Captain Curling") published the rather comprehensively titled *Shakspere; The Poet, the Lover, the Actor, the Man: A Romance* in three volumes of almost a thousand pages. In 1853 he republished it with a slightly more romantic title, *The Forest Youth; or Shakspere as He Lived: An Historical Tale*. With proper Victorian thoroughness, Curling's subtitles make certain his readers recognize that his romanticism is tempered with the truth of history. The following year, Curling, apparently not completely satisfied by his alteration, published a play, *The Merry Wags of Warwickshire: or, the Early Days of Shakspere*, which covers the same territory. Much of the play focuses on the twin forces which conspired to drive the young would-be poet to London: deer poaching and Anne's shrewish nature:

> SHAKESPEARE. Well, good mother, your reproof is just.
> Would I had consulted thee ere I made this rash
> marriage.
> MISTRESS SHAKSPERE. Alas! William, 'tis useless to grieve
> for that which is beyond remedy. I could have told
> thee that Anne Hathaway was unsuited to thee in
> years as in disposition [p. 27].

The last scene shows Shakespeare, now a favorite of the Queen, interceding with her on behalf of Sir Thomas.

Even more obsessed was Robert Folkstone Williams, author of three massive novels between 1838 and 1844. The first, *Shakspeare and His Friends* uses three volumes and 1126 pages to describe Shakespeare as a young writer. In attempting to create an epic view, Williams rarely uses a single word if he can find three, a trait his opening paragraph reflects:

> I prythee have patience, courteous reader! the whilst I describe a cer- tain chamber well worthy of most minute delineation—as thou wilt see anon—from its having been the retreat, or closet, or place retired from the public eye, in which the master spirit of his age, and the glory of all times to come, did first develope those right famous qualities from which the world hath received such infinite profit and delight. I will not trou- ble thee with a vain show of phrases architectural, which crabbed anti- quarians do much affect; for I am not learned in the mystery of stone and timber; but what true heart and simple skill can do with language, will I essay, to give thee an accurate conception of a place that hath so many admirable recommendations to thy attention [pp. 1–2].

The Youth of Shakspeare appeared the next year and recounted the poet's days in school with Tom Greene, Jack Hemmings, Rich Burbage, and Harry Con- dell. It has the same baroque prose as the earlier novel, but it is balanced at times by a breathtaking compression of action (e.g., "Time passed on, and in due time the young husband was made a father" [p. 268]). The final volume, *The Secret Passion* (1844), set a standard for bardolatry which has never been surpassed. When Shakespeare dies, for example, an extraordinary, cosmic epiphany occurs:

> Suddenly there arose a low wail; it was not easy to pronounce its cause, for it partook of the moan of the wind among the trees, and the just audi- ble diapason of the church-organ heard afar off. It gathered force and character every moment, and grew into a solemn chant, or lament, so touching, so subduing, it might have passed for a Miserere, sung by a company of spectral monks in some ruined abbey....
>
> As the innumerable multitude approached, the attentive spectator could not fail of observing that, in the midst, was a sort of circle, at the head of which two figures might have been noticed, so far like the rest in wear- ing black cloaks, but differing from them in this important matter—each wore on its head what looked to be a golden crown. In the centre, thus surrounded, it was difficult to make out what had a place—it bore the appearance of a thin gray film, having much the resemblance—though too indistinct to pronounce decidedly—of a human figure and countenance, floating upon the air. Afterwards came a countless crowd of the same small figures, in their inky garments, and the doleful wail of their numer- ous voices sounded like a funeral dirge.
>
> Presently a huge mass of clouds came upon the moon, and when she emerged from behind this black shield, the same deep stillness reigned that had a moment since wrapped the whole neighbourhood as closely as if the place formed a sepulchre in the midst of a mighty desert [III, 322–5].

Harold Frederick Rubinstein's works offer slightly more muted epiphanies dealing with the celebration of a granddaughter or the burning of the Globe. From 1921 to 1965 Rubinstein published a series of plays illustrating his view of Shakespeare as an unfulfilled playwright who seeks salvation through art only to find it is not a completely adequate medium. Although plays written over nearly half a century will inevitably have some inconsistencies—in *Shakespeare* (1921), a play he wrote with Clifford Bax, Judith appears barely literate, while in *Unearthly Gentleman* (1965) she discusses the hermetic mysteries with her father—all of Rubinstein's works suggest Shakespeare's frustration with the impossibility of reconciling opposites and achieving unity while constantly surrounded by people with little interest in his quest. His true love, the Dark Lady, for example, falls asleep during a rehearsal of *Hamlet*.

Rubinstein's essential optimism appears when he gives us a glimpse of Shakespeare in a minor role within a play that examines George Bernard Shaw, another writer obsessed with the playwright. In *Bernard Shaw in Heaven* (1954), Shaw, predictably surprised to find himself in heaven after his death, is less surprised to discover, through a series of dialogues, that art is a code. What he learns, however, is that the code can be represented in many ways:

> SHAW. Then we are in agreement that man is asleep and
>   life is dangerous. I made it my business to wake the
>   sleeper up, brother Shakespeare.
>
> SHAKESPEARE. That was my business, too. But we went
>   about it in different ways. Yours was the more direct.
>
> SHAW. It was the time-honoured method of Chanticleer!
>   with a few variations, perhaps. Your method was
>   certainly less crude.
>
> SHAKESPEARE. Less energetic, shall we say? Mostly a
>   whispering in the sleeper's ear—the inner ear [p. 27].

It is ironic that Shakespeare becomes Shaw's guide in heaven because, in fact, the twentieth-century writer had a lifelong sense of rivalry with the Elizabethan. Shaw's reservations about Shakespeare work their way through many letters, prefaces, and miscellaneous writings but, surprisingly, only two short plays—one for puppets—and a brief sketch. In Shaw's "The Dark Lady of the Sonnets" (1911), Shakespeare lurks about, Hamletlike, copying everything he hears in his tablets. The opening lines of the Queen, who appears at first incognito, give some sense of Shaw's whimsical view of his rival's use of sources:

> THE LADY (rubbing her hands as if washing them). Out,
>   damned spot. You will mar all with these cosmetics.
>   God made you one face; and you make yourself

another. Think of your grave, woman, not ever of being
beautified. 'Twill not out. All the perfumes of Arabia
will not wash away these freckles [p. 260].

The Dark Lady appears as a jealous, self-centered figure; she proves less important to the play than discussions of the need for a national theater. In a brief sketch, "A Dressing Room Secret," for the Haymarket program of "The Dark Lady" (1910), a bust of Shakespeare talks to several of his characters, revealing some frustration that most of them turned out not quite as he had planned. Echoes of the bourgeois qualities Shaw finds in Shakespeare's characters abound. The story ends on a malicious note when the bust falls to the ground and shatters.

In 1949 Shaw wrote a puppet play for the Lanchester Marionettes to perform at the Malvern Festival, *Shakes* versus *Shav*. After an initial boxing match, which Shav wins with what Shakes admits is a "heavier punch than mine," Shav points out other writers who have surpassed Shakes. When Shakes responds by charging Shav with borrowing liberally from his plays, Shaw chooses to end the play on a slightly ambiguous note that epitomizes the relationship between the two:

SHAV.   Peace, jealous Bard:
          We both are mortal. For a moment suffer
          My glimmering light to shine.
          [*A light appears between them*].
SHAKES. Out, out, brief candle! [He puffs it out].
          [*Darkness. The play ends.*] [p. 9].

Shaw's questions about Shakespeare and his achievements fall short of the anti–Stratfordians' vigor. Their obsession stems not from aesthetic reservations or professional jealousy but from the need to reveal the true begetter of the plays and poems. Louis Alexander's *The Autobiography of Shakespeare: A Fragment* (1911), purposely designed to look unfinished, has the playwright originate in Warwick of Dutch stock and begin his career by writing *The Tempest*. Rhoda Henry Messner's *Absent Thee from Felicity* (1975) offers the story of another true author of Shakespeare's plays, Edward de Vere, seventeenth Earl of Oxford. As a wittier alternative to such suggestions, William Jordan's *Elizabeth's Immortal Son: Part Three: His Autobiography* (1960) presents his hero as Proteus. There is more promise than realization in this story of Shakespeare—a Tudor prince, twin brother of Marlowe and half-brother of Bacon—staging a mock funeral at Stratford so he can get on with the business of writing *Paradise Lost*.

VI

If the least successful attempts to fictionalize Shakespeare spring from
his idolaters, the most successful ones arise from those who approach him
with a twinkle in their eyes. William and Samuel Ireland's additions to the
Shakespeare canon called forth one of the earliest responses from a wit. The
most notorious and perhaps most successful forger of Shakespeareana was
William Henry Ireland (1775–1835). Attempting to please his father, Samuel,
who had turned their home into a museum of rare books and curiosities,
William began in late 1794 to "discover" papers for his father's collection.
Searching out old paper and parchment, William started modestly by forg-
ing legal documents. As his father's interest and demands grew, the son created correspondence, including a love letter to Anna Hatherrewaye with a
lock of Willy's hair, a profession of faith, and eventually two unknown plays,
Vortigern and Rowena and *Henry VII*.

Even though skeptics had appeared from the very beginning, many
prominent figures from the literary world visited the Irelands' home on Nor-
folk Street in the Strand. James Boswell, for example, with his usual extrav-
agance came, knelt, and kissed the documents. The debate over their authen-
ticity continued, however, with many writers questioning the works' naive
sentiments and odd spelling, especially the almost comically doubled conso-
nants (e.g., bllossommes).

In March of 1796 Edmund Malone, the most respected Shakespeare
scholar of his age, published an inquiry which permanently discredited the
Ireland papers. The month before Malone's book, George Moutard Wood-
ward had published anonymously his *Familiar Verses from the Ghost of Willy
Shakspeare to Sammy Ireland*. In the tradition of the eighteenth century, it is
the ghost who speaks and sets Ireland's discoveries in perspective:

> When late to STRATFORD you incog. came down,
> Peeping for relics through each lane in town,
> I guess'd that something fresh was in the wind,
> And thus to DAVY GARRICK spoke my mind:
> "Since you call'd forth the wond'ring nobles round
> To see my JUBILEE on Fairy ground,
> To chaunt my praises in harmonious strain,
> And strut in Pageants through a shower of rain,
> Ne'er has mine eye in *Warwick's* county scann'd
> So learn'd a wight as SAMMY IRELAND!"
> The chair, the kitchen, room where I was born,
> All from old Time's mysterious veil were torn;
> I often thought—so steady were his pains,
> And from his work, so certain were his gains—
> He'd never give his deep researches up,
> Until he found my spoon and christ'ning cup:

Some curious remnants of my mother's spinning;
My little shoes, and all the child-bed linen!" [pp. 7–8].

If Ireland's poaching proved an attractive target, Shakespeare's own poaching of Sir Thomas Lucy's deer was an irresistible one. Walter Savage Landor's anonymously published *Citation and Examination of William Shakspeare, Euseby Treen, Joseph Carnaby, and Silas Gough, Clerk, before the Worshipful Sir Thomas Lucy, Knight, Touching Deer-Stealing, on the 19th Day of September in the Year of Grace 1582; Now First Published from Original Papers* (1834) offers an account of the hearing by Sir Thomas' clerk, Ephraim Barnett. Barnett describes discussions ranging from theology and literature to pedagogy and ethics. The main problem with the work is that the speakers enjoy hearing themselves talk a bit too much; if anything, Landor could have used an editor to tighten his prose. Too often extraneous characters debate at length about material already more than adequately presented. Quoting his friend, Sir Everard Starkeye, Sir Thomas cautions the young Shakespeare to avoid the fictions of drama:

> "Our people," said Sir Everard, "must see upon the stage what they never could have imagined; so the best men in the world would earnestly take a peep of hell through a chink, whereas the worser would skulk away.
>
> "Do not thou be their caterer William! Avoid the writing of comedies and tragedies. To make people laugh is uncivil, and to make people cry is unkind. And what, after all, are these comedies and these tragedies.... We Englishmen cannot find it in our hearts to murder a man without much difficulty, hesitation, and delay. We have little or no invention for pains and penalties; it is only our acutest lawyers who have wit enough to frame them. Therefore it behoveth your tragedy man to provide a rich assortment of them, in order to strike the auditor with awe and wonder. And a tragedy-man, in our country, who cannot afford a fair dozen of stabbed males, and a trifle under that mask of poisoned females, and chains enow to moor a whole navy in dock, is but a scurvy fellow at the best. Thou wilt find trouble in purveying these necessaries; and then must come the gim-cracks for the second course; gods, goddesses, fates, furies, battles, marriages, music, and the maypole. Hast thou within thee wherewithal?"
>
> "Sir!" replied Billy, with great modesty, "I am most grateful for these ripe fruits of your experience. To admit delightful visions into my own twilight chamber, is not dangerous or forbidden. Believe me, sir, he who indulges in them will abstain from injuring his neighbour: he will see no glory in peril, and no delight in strife" [pp. 170–1].

Landor's interest in penning such passages appears to stem from simple pleasure in playing with ideas and language. And, despite the book's wandering narrative, Landor's wit makes it enjoyable reading. Near the end, Sir Thomas, presented more sympathetically than in most Shakespeare fictions, expresses his belief that the examination has helped the young poacher:

> Thou art grown discreet and dutiful: I am fain to command thy release, taking thy promise on oath, and some reasonable security, that thou will abstain and withhold in future from that idle and silly slut, that sly and scoffing giggler, Hannah Hathaway, with whom, to the heart-ache of thy poor worthy father, thou wantonly keepest company [p. 233].

But William declares his love for Anne, heaves away the Bible on which he is to swear his oath, steals a horse, and rides off.

A tighter and even wittier version of the legend appears in Richard Garnett's *William Shakespeare: Pedagogue and Poacher* (1904). The story is a simple one. Shakespeare, brought to trial as a thief, has his sentence annulled by the Earl of Leicester because Elizabeth admires his *Taming of the Shrew*, a play based on the poet's home life. At the end, Shakespeare leaves with Leicester for court. Much of the pleasure in Garnett's play arises from its clever blank verse and marvelously traditional portrait of Sir Thomas. In the opening scene, for example, Sir Thomas confronts his pragmatic forester, Moles, about the disappearance of deer from his land:

SIR THOMAS.   Know, rude forester,
          There's something rotten in the state of Charlecote
                    • • • • • • • • •
                    Where the troops
          Of stag and doe and delicate fawn that erst
          Did gambol in these groves?....
          Storms the wild huntsman with his swarthy pack
          Along my woodland alleys? Do the hounds
          That erst with horrid fangs Actaeon tore
          Seek in these shades a quadrupedal prey?
          [Moles scratches his head]
MOLES.   Sir Thomas, I be thinking it be thieves [pp. 11–5].

Franklin H. Head, in a parody of deductive biography, moves from Shakespeare's hobbies to his relationships in *Shakespeare's Insomnia and the Causes Thereof* (1886). The book begins with lines from the plays praising sleep and notes that such images do not appear in Shakespeare's sources: "These are jewels of his own; transcripts from his own mournful experience" (p. 23). From that start, Head introduces a series of letters that shed a crepuscular light on the poet's preoccupation with sleep. They include letters to Shakespeare from Mordecai Shylock, an investor, and from lawyers for Mistress Anne Page, claiming a false promise of marriage. Perhaps the most intriguing are those from Bacon admitting that Shakespeare is the true author of poems Bacon gave the Queen. Head's *jeu d'esprit* offers an entertaining commentary on Oliver Wendell Holmes' belief that "no man writes other than his own experience: that consciously or otherwise an author describes himself in the characters he draws" (p. 8).

Recent years have seen two of the more successful novels about Shakespeare's loves. Anthony Burgess' *Nothing Like the Sun* (1964) and Leon Rooke's *Shakespeare's Dog* (1983) both combine sprawling vigor with solutions to classic Shakespearean conundra. *Nothing Like the Sun* is a kaleidoscopic journey through the world of Shakespearean fact and fantasy. Told in a Nabokovian variety of voices, it has become justly famous for the ways Burgess toys with both language and critics. Burgess' interest threatens to evolve into obsession, for, after completing his novel, Burgess has returned to the same subject in two later stories. The first, "Will and Testament," has Will revise the new translation of the forty-sixth psalm during his forty-sixth year by substituting "shake" for "tremble" as the forty-sixth word from the beginning and "spear" for "sword" as the forty-sixth word from the end. The story, originally published in 1976, became the prologue to *Enderby's Dark Lady* (1984). Its epilogue, "The Muse," is a science fiction tale in which a space traveler, bearing a copy of the plays, voyages to a parallel earth (and, in effect, back in time) to visit Shakespeare. The Shakespeare he meets, a writer of questionable ability, has the traveler arrested and sets about plagiarizing (self-plagiarizing?) *The Merchant of Venice*. He copies the play, "not blotting a line."

Leon Rooke's *Shakespeare's Dog* has a canine named Mr. Hooker tell the story of the war between "the noxious Hathaway" and "my wordy Shaksbier":

> "This Avon's a pimple!" Will would rail, croaking his fury at the unbending Hathaway, his face blazing as the great actor Alleyn's would, rapping her with sauce pots to show that his rage matched her ire and that a Henley Street son could better a Shottery wench even on the worst of days. "You twilight hump," he'd screech. "Old woman! Cradle snatcher! Apple-john, Barbary hen, you drumbling, letharged, pizzle-minder. To become the laced mutton, you'd have betrothed your patch even to the wheelwright's crass boy" [pp. 14–5].

Functioning as a fairy dogfather, with traces of Hamlet's melancholy and Macbeth's bloodlust, Hooker teaches his master about human nature, rescues him from drowning, receives a promise of the best bed in the house, and finally frees Shakespeare from Stratford. The young poet's frustrations are mirrored in a dog who rules his turf, with its leafless elm, while dreaming of London and bursting into frequent rages at rivals and would-be rivals:

> "I'm sorry, Mr. Hooker," the potato-head whined. "Don't go believing all you see. No, I wouldn't do nothing wrong either to your sister Terry or to your love's breath Marr, from whom I was only juicing fleas."

"Aye," I said, "and here's fleas for you, nasty hedgehog, thou jouncing hen's dung and bawdy-basket. I'll soon have your bones dusted and ready for the charnel house." And I hit him again, this time from one side to the other of his gorbellied flanks and on his noodle, and with rich venom quaking fullway down my spine, I kept on throttling and maiming the sodden piece [p. 4].

Will's release occurs when he must save Hooker by taking him to London, for, in a nice turn on tradition, the dog has been discovered poaching Sir Thomas' deer. By creating a fresh perspective, along with a series of newly minted facts, Rooke's narrator, Mr. Hooker, offers, through his energetic language and canine sensibility, one of the more exuberant assessments of life in Stratford.

VII

From the Cygnets' innocent visions to Mr. Hooker's snarling portrait, all of these "other lives" attempt to offer insights into England's most celebrated and elusive writer. But why add even greater confusion to the murky depths of Shakespearean biography? Why bring together these admittedly fictional lives when even attempts at serious biography seem to shed so little light on the figure behind the plays and when the very idea of approaching Shakespeare biographically raises such a wide range of questions and objections?

Almost a century and a half ago Ralph Waldo Emerson outlined five of the major objections to any attempt at Shakespearean biography:

1. *Such biographies are unnecessary*: "So far from Shakspeare's being the least known, he is the one person, in all modern history, known to us" ["Shakspeare," p. 120].

2. *They are impossible*: "Shakspeare is the only biographer of Shakspeare; and even he can tell us nothing, except to the Shakspeare in us..." [p. 119].

3. *They are arbitrary*: "But whatever scraps of information [research] may have rescued, they can shed no light upon that infinite invention which is the concealed magnet of his attraction for us.... [It] seems as if, had we dipped at random into the "Modern Plutarch," and read any other life there, it would have fitted the poems as well [as those biographical facts we know]" [p. 118].

4. *They are irrelevant*: "Can any biography [of Shakespeare] shed light on the localities into which the Midsummer Night's Dream admits me?" [p. 119].

5. *They are misleading*, because they represent Shakespeare as an extraordinary figure unlike us: "Perhaps if we should meet Shakspeare, we should

not be conscious of any steep inferiority; no: but of a great equality,—only that he possessed a strange skill of using, of classifying his facts, which we lacked" ["Intellect," p. 197].

And, of course, Emerson is right. Shakespeare's true biography continues to lie in his work.

Not all of the writers included in *Shakespeare's Other Lives*, however, would agree with Emerson, especially on his last point. Duval's *Shakespeare Amoureaux*, Landor's *Citation and Examination*, Brougham's *Shakespeare's Dream*, and Kipling's "Proofs of Holy Writ" all present an extraordinary rather than an ordinary man. And although many of the other authors might agree that attempting to recapture Shakespeare's life is impossible and arbitrary, few would acknowledge their work as either unnecessary or irrelevant.

But if these works offer us little about the historical figure of Shakespeare, they tell us a great deal about ourselves, at least the ways we have viewed the man and his work. Ever since people began discussing Shakespeare the man, they began discovering how much he appeared to resemble them. In fact, two of the most valuable studies in recent years, Samuel Schoenbaum's *Shakespeare's Lives* (1970) and Gary Taylor's *Reinventing Shakespeare* (1989), offer histories of how the study of Shakespeare "tends towards oblique self-portraiture" (Schoenbaum, pp. viii–ix).

The following nineteen attempts to portray Shakespeare at home, at work and at play reveal writers shaping a character as much from themselves and their ages as for themselves and their ages. From the childlike pageant of John Brougham to the personally and politically charged obsession of George Bernard Shaw, and from Edward Bond's picture of Shakespeare's domestic dilemmas to the professional challenges described by William Rendle, Maurice Baring, Charles Williams, and John Mortimer, all of these writers offer fascinating examples of self-portraiture. When Edward Warren, for example, resurrects Shakespeare as a New York broker, the Harvard lawyer has less to say about Renaissance England and its theater than about twentieth-century Wall Street and its practices. And the Wits, the most entertaining of these writers working on the fringe of Shakespearean biography, add their own idiosyncratic visions. Walter Savage Landor and Richard Garnett show a witty provocateur, Franklin Harvey Head a besieged insomniac, Rudyard Kipling a classical scholar, Leon Rooke an untamed post-adolescent, and Anthony Burgess a self-centered alien.

Just as Warren and Burgess break time barriers, the opening and closing pieces suggest Shakespeare's capacity to shatter the boundaries of language and geography, his ability to appeal to Napoleonic France as well as contemporary Latin America. Alexandre Duval's Romantic description of a love struck voyeur, *Shakespeare Amoureaux*, and Jorge Luis Borges story/essay,

"Everything and Nothing," as unclassifiable as so much of his work, reflect the breadth of that appeal. Two works from the eighteenth century appear as Appendices to give an idea of that century's emerging sense of Shakespeare's potential not only as an author but as a character as well.

Alexandre-Vincent Pineu Duval
(1767–1842)

Alexandre Duval's life reflects the radically changing world in which he lived. The son of a successful French lawyer in Rennes, he convinced his parents to let him leave school in his early teens to fight as a volunteer sailor in the American War of Independence. Returning home to join the army, Duval began writing comedies. Eventually he spent time as an engineer, architect, painter, and actor, before becoming librarian at the Bibliothèque de l'Arsenal and a member of the Académie Française.

Shakespeare Amoureux, which premiered at the Théâtre Français on 24 January 1804, reflects Duval's melodramatic taste and apparently sketchy knowledge of his hero's life and Renaissance England's theatrical customs. Shakespeare's desire to marry the actress Clarence ignores both the existence of Anne and the all male culture of the Elizabethan and Jacobean stage. The play's climax, with Shakespeare's message to his rival, Lord Wilson, suggests that Duval's primary inspiration was an anecdote from an Elizabethan lawyer. In his domesticated version of Shakespeare's love life, Duval has eliminated the risque implications in this nugget of theatrical gossip.

Shakespeare's interest in concealment, his willingness to risk all for his goal, and his moods—especially the twinges of melancholy and flashes of jealousy—clearly indicate that Duval found the man in his characters. Richard Penn Smith (1799–1854), a Philadelphia lawyer and playwright, left an abbreviated, rather wooden adaptation of the play as *Shakespeare in Love* in an undated manuscript, which has been published in *The Sentinels & Other Plays*, edited by Ralph H. Ware and H.W. Schoenberger (Vol. XIII of *America's Lost Plays* [Princeton: Princeton University Press, 1941]). The following translation is by the editor.

Shakespeare Amoureaux
(1804)

The stage represents an Elizabethan salon; a window is on the side, two doors face the window, a third is in the back; some candles on a table light the room.

SCENE I

SHAKESPEARE [*entering by the door in the back and speaking to a servant*]. Tell Anna I wish to speak to her.... What devil draws me back to this house? What devil? Ah, it is love. Can anything make us more foolish? O Shakespeare! Why cannot you protect yourself from those passions and follies you describe so well?

SCENE II
ANNA, SHAKESPEARE

ANNA. Oh, sir, is it you? Tonight? Here? At my mistress'?

SHAKESPEARE. Yes. I have come. Ah well, what is she doing at this moment?

ANNA. She is studying her role in your wonderful tragedy of Richard III.

SHAKESPEARE. Wonderful tragedy? At least hold your praise until it has been performed.

ANNA. But everyone says it is magnificent.

SHAKESPEARE. After its failure, everyone will call it terrible.

ANNA. In a few days you will know its fate. Until then, my mistress is studying her role. Oh! She will be lovely.

SHAKESPEARE [*with enthusiasm*]. Lovely! Charming! Divine! What a ravishing voice! She can move, disturb, overwhelm an audience. On her lips, all my verses seem perfect, my ideas have more power, more energy. When she speaks, my soul is captivated. I fear to lose a sound, a gesture, a look. Everything she does appears to me sublime. And like a modern Pygmalion, I adore my own work.

ANNA. But the beauty is your play. Your "Richard III."

SHAKESPEARE. "Richard III"! Fool that I am! I deserve that title.... Anna, I wish to see your mistress.

ANNA. Impossible.

SHAKESPEARE. Why? Is she rehearsing?

ANNA. Yes. But she rehearses ... what all women generally rehearse. Her role is at her vanity. And as I fix her hair, she constantly studies herself.

SHAKESPEARE. She is very happy?

ANNA. Yes, sir. She even said that it has lasted a long time.

SHAKESPEARE. But why this care tonight? Is she going to the theater? To a meeting?

ANNA. No, sir. It is a care born of habit or of precaution, whichever you wish.

SHAKESPEARE. O women! So much time spent on folly.... And I, am I any more reasonable after all.... Will she be ready soon?

ANNA. Yes, sir, if we do not start over.

SHAKESPEARE [*aside*]. I will wait. I must speak to her; she must explain herself. I cannot live in this torment, in this uncertainty. Since I had the bad luck to fall in love, each day dawns with new agony. My personality has changed; I have become gloomy, impatient, distracted; I cannot concentrate; I do not hear what people say to me. Can I write? My pen has run dry; words fail me. If I go out to distract myself, everyone I see irritates me. I even irritate myself. And at the end of the day I return as bothered, as tired of others as I am of myself.

ANNA. That astonishes me. You should be the happiest of men.

SHAKESPEARE. Me! Happy! How could I be happy!

ANNA. It is your fault if you are not. When one has the advantage of spirit....

SHAKESPEARE. Everyone has that.

ANNA. Talent.

SHAKESPEARE. The envious deny it.

ANNA. The great search you out and love you.

SHAKESPEARE. They make us come and they protect us.

ANNA. You are always in the midst of feasts, of pleasures....

SHAKESPEARE. Of work and of boredom. But, Anna, what does my life matter to you? At this moment life has become unbearable ... I love, but I love with all my soul, and I wish....

ANNA. Oh! I know that you are very gallant; everyone says so.... You even have a reputation for seeking adventures....

SHAKESPEARE. Yes, I might have in my youth.... The desire to know the world, dangerous society ... a fiery imagination, always above reality....

ANNA. And you have, no doubt, often been happy? An author has so many resources to please us.... First his reputation makes us want to know him; his smallest cares touch us; his eloquence charms us; his style inflames us; his least line....

SHAKESPEARE. Which might not always be so terrible....

ANNA. Which charms us irresistibly.

SHAKESPEARE. By St. George! Forget my poetry and my affairs.... I am talking to you about me, about my love for Clarence. She knows my feelings. What does she say? What does she think?

ANNA. She says that one day you will be the pillar of the English theater and the glory of your country.

SHAKESPEARE. But what does she say about my love? Do I have a rival? Is he preferred? What is the state of her heart?

ANNA. Very peaceful.

SHAKESPEARE. Has she found nothing about me that she dislikes?

ANNA. Nothing.

SHAKESPEARE. Could she get used to my manners, my habits? What does she think of my conversation?

ANNA. Charming.

SHAKESPEARE. You delight me, Anna. So I can hope that the tenderness of love will overcome her coldness, that she will consent to our marriage, since you assure me....

ANNA. But she does not love you.

SHAKESPEARE. What?

ANNA. No, I am certain of it. But you are the Englishman she admires and honors the most.

SHAKESPEARE. Why must you tell me this? ... I can no longer contain myself and my despair....

ANNA. Ah, my God! But this is a tragedy. And since I am neither an actor nor the author, I shall leave.

SHAKESPEARE. No, no. Stay. Now I am master of myself. You can see that I am very calm. [*He says the word calm with fury. Anna, frightened, moves away.*] O treachery! To have seduced me to this point.... But I will not lower myself to reproaches.... She will never again find me in this house, and I curse the moment when I first entered it.

ANNA. Very well, sir, I will show you out.

SHAKESPEARE [*sitting on the front of the stage*]. Oh! Be calm. Soon I will leave.

ANNA. That is enough, sir. I go to announce your despair, your composure, and your departure. [*Aside, while leaving*] Ah, my Lord Wilson, I have served you well.

SCENE III

SHAKESPEARE [*alone*]. Finally, I know my fate. I am not loved ... and I, who flattered myself with hope.... Let us calm our anger. We must do more, take a drastic course of action. First I must ... see her and speak with her. But no. I would do better to flee from her, to run to the end of the earth.... Her vanity would welcome that. No, let us stay and see her every day ... with indifference. I believe myself capable of speaking to her without emotion, even of laughing at her thoughtlessness.... Yes, I already feel more free, more content. But what if Anna has deceived me? If they are protecting some unknown rival, she would.... I hear something! They are coming, speaking of me. I would give everything I have to hear their conversation.... Good! This closet is open.... What would I risk? ... Ah! If love is indiscreet and jealous, I must prove even more so.

[*He enters the closet leaving the doors open; he can only be seen by the audience.*]

SCENE IV
ANNA, CLARENCE, SHAKESPEARE [*hidden*]

ANNA. Yes, Madame, he was here, he wished to see you.... But he is undoubtedly gone.

CLARENCE [*whispering*]. He is gone.

ANNA. Furious, probably.

CLARENCE. For some time he has fallen easily into rages, but his love ought to excuse him in my eyes.

ANNA. Him, Madame! He does not love you. I am certain.

SHAKESPEARE [*aside*]. The traitor!

ANNA. And then all these authors who are so glittering in society, so gallant around young ladies, prove hollow dreamers with their dear wives. And when they return home from being the spirit of the party, more often than not they bring back merely distaste and ennui.

CLARENCE. Ah! That shows itself every day.

ANNA. And it must be so. He would only see in marriage a tiresome bond. The simplest household chores bore them. Their heads always filled with dreams, they neglect reality. Some words, some compliments, and finally vapors attract them rather than money; and the little that they have acquired, often the beautiful product of spirit and imagination, become, thanks to their carefree attitude, the inheritance of rogues and fools.

SHAKESPEARE [*aside*]. She has more spirit than I thought.

CLARENCE. It is less his small fortune than his moods, violent, fiery....

ANNA. Ah, if you would only follow my counsel. Novelty draws you to the theater. You shine there through your talents and well deserved reputation.... But everything passes, Madame. The future is unpredictable, another's talent eclipses ours. The public, ignoring the past, mercilessly rejects the idol who was long the object of its admiration.

CLARENCE. So, I can only hope for a career in which today's success cannot often compensate for tomorrow's pain.

ANNA. Marriage could make you independent, if you wish it.

SHAKESPEARE [*aside*]. Marriage! ... I fear I will explode!

CLARENCE. Ah! You are going to speak of Lord Wilson? He is amiable and his personal advantages....

ANNA. He is rich. Consider. He demands only that you leave the theater. That condition agrees with your wishes. And you will commit the greatest folly if you do not consent to a marriage that guarantees your happiness and your future.

CLARENCE. I know he loves me. And I would confess that my heart, my thoughts.... We will see.... But I fear that Shakespeare, that poor William....

ANNA. Ah! That poor William is the most fickle rogue alive. I would wager that at this very moment he is at some rendezvous. Above all, he loves adventures and I have heard of thousands of them.

SHAKESPEARE [*aside*]. That woman is a devil!

ANNA. If you do not decide tonight, you must give him up.

CLARENCE. What?

ANNA. Yes, without doubt. Lord Wilson has been called to Windsor and must leave tonight. He wishes to propose to you and begs an audience.

CLARENCE. But how can I? Shakespeare will undoubtedly come back. He needs to rehearse my new role in his play....

ANNA. Ah well! Refuse to see him.

SHAKESPEARE [*aside*]. O damnable maid!

CLARENCE. No. He is distrustful, jealous. If he sees Wilson's carriage, his men, his livery at my door, he will be suspicious.

ANNA. Bah! Our author will not know. Besides, are you not your own woman? Are you not free to start a relationship? What do you fear from him?

CLARENCE. His jealousy, his rages.

ANNA. There is one way so that nothing will be known. Listen.... I will go to let Lord Wilson know the hour of the rendezvous. Eleven o clock! That is early enough. He must come alone, wrapped in a cloak.... I will give orders to the servant.... No one else will be admitted. Lord Wilson will need a signal, a password.... But what word?

CLARENCE. What foolishness! ... Leave me alone so that I can learn my lines from "Richard III."

ANNA. So be it. *Richard III.* The password is excellent. He comes; he knocks; you question him; he responds, "*Richard III*"; and the door opens.

SHAKESPEARE [*aside*]. I will be at that rendezvous.... Then my rival will tremble!

CLARENCE. What is your plan? What? What are you saying?

ANNA. I said that I read your soul, that I will triumph over the last trace of your weakness, that you will marry a lord, and that I will make you happy in spite of yourself. Adieu. I will go to notify the honest Lord Wilson and to prepare everything for your meeting.   [*She leaves.*]

SCENE V
CLARENCE, SHAKESPEARE [*still hidden*]

CLARENCE. Stop, Anna! She cannot hear me. Besides, I see no danger in this meeting. Am I not always mistress of my feelings? Let me make use of my solitude to study... O my celebrated friend! I only hope that I can be a worthy organ of your sublime thoughts!

[*She rises and goes to look for her script which is on a table across the room; Shakespeare leaves the closet and crosses to the entrance.*]

SCENE VI
SHAKESPEARE, CLARENCE

SHAKESPEARE [*after knocking on the door*]. Excuse me, dear Clarence, if I come into your home like this without ceremony.

CLARENCE. What! You! ... Oh, I am delighted!

SHAKESPEARE [*ironically*]. You are delighted to see me. Oh! I believe it.... [*aside*] Let me hide my anger so that my rival will not escape me! ... Then you have some feelings for me? ...

CLARENCE. What you have earned. No one is more interested in you, in your fame.... With respect to that, are you still working on your *Othello*? What a magnificent character! He is so jealous! How far are you on it?

SHAKESPEARE. I am, I am ... in the fourth act.

CLARENCE. The fourth act! If I remember your plot, it is the moment when the furious lover bursts in on Desdemona, when he threatens to strike his rival. You have so often spoken to me about that beautiful scene on jealousy....

SHAKESPEARE. Ah well! I have worked on it all day. But let us stop talking about my tragedy....

CLARENCE. You look troubled.... Your eyes are glowing.... Your lips are trembling....

SHAKESPEARE [*very excited*]. Do you think so? . . No. It is nothing. I was never very happy.

CLARENCE. No, something is certainly wrong.

SHAKESPEARE. On the contrary, I should be delighted. I have just discovered something of the greatest importance.

CLARENCE. How wonderful!

SHAKESPEARE. Ah, you say that it is wonderful!

CLARENCE. Certainly. If it is something that can contribute to your happiness, I must rejoice in it. And what is this great news?

SHAKESPEARE. It is.... [*aside*] Let me probe for a weakness.... My dear

Clarence, I am going to speak to you frankly. Today I discovered a young woman destined for the theater.

CLARENCE. A young woman?

SHAKESPEARE. Beautiful as an angel! … And such expressiveness in her face, such mobility in her features.…

CLARENCE. And she looks promising?

SHAKESPEARE. Oh! A great talent! … Her diction is pure, her voice grave, her step noble, imposing, and majestic.

CLARENCE. I am delighted to hear it.

SHAKESPEARE [*aside*]. She is enraged.

CLARENCE. And on what foreign stage did you find this Phoenix?

SHAKESPEARE. She is not yet a Phoenix, but she could become one. Some very important people are interested in her.

CLARENCE. A wonderful recommendation in the eyes of the public!

SHAKESPEARE. They engaged me to give her some roles.

CLARENCE. Mine, perhaps? … And you could not refuse?

SHAKESPEARE. To some extent. Such requests are sometimes orders. And I am in a position to….

CLARENCE. To grant everything…. To the roles which you must give her, I beg you add "Richard III."

SHAKESPEARE. Come now, you are teasing me. So soon jealous?

CLARENCE. You insult me…. I have never felt jealousy, and I hope never to feel it.

SHAKESPEARE [*aside*]. An actress and not jealous?

CLARENCE. What did you say?

SHAKESPEARE. I said that I know my own interests too well to allow you to leave a play which owes its success to your performance.

CLARENCE. Shakespeare! … You affect a modesty which you do not have…. You know too well that we actors can add something to a play, but we can never assure its success.

SHAKESPEARE. Oh! I believe that we have something to do with it.

CLARENCE. You believe that? … And yet you have promised roles to this new actress?

SHAKESPEARE. I could perhaps give her some roles unsuited to you. For example, you have little skill in those roles which require dissimulation. Your face, full of candor, has difficulty disguising, without a struggle, betrayal and falsehood.

CLARENCE. Perhaps?

SHAKESPEARE. I will imagine you in the role of a princess who wishes to betray her lover. In that instant when her inconstant soul considers the most frightening betrayal, could you swear to him that you love him, that you only breathe for him? Then you affect a necessary calmness, you turn your head, your eyes fill with tears....

CLARENCE [*troubled*]. But ... I ... assure you ...

SHAKESPEARE. No. Your voice stammers a few words, and that same confusion, even more eloquent now, will drive into the soul of that unhappy prince the conviction of your crime.

CLARENCE [*aside*]. Let us leave this. I will blush so much that he will know....

SHAKESPEARE [*aside*]. I believe I am betrayed.

CLARENCE. In truth, I do not understand you. You know that every actor is obliged to take the tone and the language of her character. It would be very unpleasant for anyone who only played villains if, by the skill of her acting, audiences believed that the role reflected her true self.

SHAKESPEARE. I am not saying that.... But I believe that at least art and habit have to give the possibility of acting dishonestly.... You, you do not have that habit. You dissimulate badly; you deceive awkwardly; and the truth paints itself every moment on your features and in your looks.

CLARENCE [*casually*]. My looks have deceived you, sir. I can dissemble as well as anyone.

SHAKESPEARE [*piqued*]. From the way you are talking now, I am beginning to believe it.

CLARENCE. Let us drop this topic. It is surely not your only reason for visiting me. Why have you come?

SHAKESPEARE. I came to hear you rehearse your new role.

CLARENCE. It is beautiful. What eloquence! What energy in the details! What truth in the dialogue! Each new production adds to your fame!

SHAKESPEARE. Ah! What does fame mean to me? Can fame make me happy while robbing me of hope? Am I not aware of all the prejudices against the life of an author? Do not people fear his dissipation, his carefreeness?

[*The actors can eliminate some of the following lines if they find them tedious.*]

CLARENCE. Your behavior can overcome such fears. And are not famous men often guilty?

SHAKESPEARE. Yes, those grand celebrities of the salon, worn out in spirit and jealous of compliments they must fish for, pass all their time as lively guests, elegant in dress and wit. In pitying the fate of their efforts, I will excuse them, perhaps, if they would not destroy by malicious pamphlets and impotent epigrams that talent which they cannot acquire.

CLARENCE. Oh! I know it. This is not your character.

SHAKESPEARE. Oh, that my hand would wither the instant that, by an abusive line, it brings sadness to the heart of an honest man. It is to an enthusiasm for art, to the sensitivity of my heart, to love alone perhaps that I owe my first plays. Having married a woman I adored, my desire to make her happy drove me to my success. Scarcely entered into my career, I walked there with cautious steps. But soon eager to surpass my rivals, no effort was too much. Perhaps one day I would dare, with a bold pen, to wrest from history all its famous figures and bring them to life before the eyes of my fellow citizens so that I might leave a warning to the ambitious and the unscrupulous. If success has rewarded my hope, if fame has been the prize for my painful efforts, would I not then have made enough for my family by leaving it, rather than an estate, some rights to national recognition and the heritage of a name cherished by posterity?

CLARENCE. Oh! A thousand times happy she who will bear the beautiful name of Shakespeare!

SHAKESPEARE. I must not lose myself in these shimmering dreams. Ah, the heart so fiery....

CLARENCE. You suffer, Shakespeare!

SHAKESPEARE. Oh, no. Nothing.... Where is the man that is happy here? ... But, dear Clarence, pardon me, pay no attention to all my extravagances. My head is always filled with my works.... Besides, you know that a poet.... But we would do better to rehearse.

[*He takes the script and sits.*]

CLARENCE. I agree. I will begin.
        "I called thee then vain flourish of my fortune;

> I called thee then poor shadow, painted queen,
> The presentation of but what I was,
> The flattering index of a direful pageant,
> One heaved a-high to be hurled down below,
> A mother only mocked with two fair babes,
> A dream of what thou wast, a garish flag,
> To be the aim of every dangerous shot,
> A sign of dignity, a breath, a bubble,
> A queen in jest, only to fill a scene."

SHAKESPEARE [*aside*]. What inflections!

CLARENCE [*continuing*]:

> "Decline all this and see what now thou art:
> For happy wife, a most distressed widow;
> For joyful mother, one that wails the name;
> For one being sued to, one that humbly sues;
> For queen, a very caitiff crowned with care;
> For she that scorned at me, now scorned of me;
> For she being feared of all, now fearing one;
> For she commanding all, obeyed of none."

SHAKESPEARE. Frightful! Pitiful! Detestable!

CLARENCE. What! You are not satisfied?

SHAKESPEARE. Enough of warmth, enough of feeling, enough of soul! When the heart is touched by true passion, it does not express itself like this.

CLARENCE [*intimidated*]. Yet I thought I had captured....

SHAKESPEARE. Love! Anyone can easily see that you have never felt the effects of that terrible passion. The words, "*I love you*," cannot express it by themselves. It is the instrument: it is the eye which paints it; it is the expression which alone can carry the energy. "*I love you*" in the mouth of a person truly inflamed can be heard by strangers, by all people, by the most barbarous savage. Nature is never limited only to language; it belongs to the soul. And as this love shows itself to us in the air we breathe, in the sounds echoing in our ear, in all objects which capture our attention, "*I love you*" can also say: I see only you; I hear only you; I breathe only by you; and I will die at your feet if I cannot share your existence.

CLARENCE. Oh! I see it now. You alone know how to love. You alone know how to express it.

SHAKESPEARE. Can I believe it? Great God! ... But let us continue with the rehearsing ... and pardon the restlessness of spirit which carries me away in spite of myself.

CLARENCE. Yes, I will continue.

> "Thus hath the course of justice whirled about
> And left thee but a very prey to time,
> Having no more thought of what thou wast
> To torture thee the more, being what thou art.
> Thou didst usurp my place, and dost thou not
> Usurp the just proportion of my sorrow?"

What is wrong? You are looking dissatisfied again.

SHAKESPEARE [*lost in his reflections*]. Yes, I am dissatisfied, but it is with myself. How could I have created that miserable description? ... It is cold, colorless, feebly expressed, without movement, without ideas, without force! Yes, how could I have written like that about jealousy? Oh! Now I can express it perfectly! O jealousy! A searing weight which presses the....

CLARENCE [*aside*]. These reflections on jealousy remind him of his Othello, and his soaring imagination....

SHAKESPEARE [*rising quickly, aside*]. My heart has been hidden so long, I wish to disclose everything to this treacherous woman and confound her at that very moment.

CLARENCE. He is writing a scene.

SHAKESPEARE [*to Clarence, while glancing furiously around the theater*]. You think you have hidden your plot from me, unnatural and cruel woman, but these indiscreet walls have revealed all. Yes, I know that you have deceived me. I have a rival, I know him. You wish to give him that heart which belongs to me, that deceitful heart which will pay me in blood.

CLARENCE [*coldly*]. Ah. Well! I would like the chance to say....

SHAKESPEARE [*in a great fury*]. What could you say? Will you deny that you have betrayed me? It is useless to affect the calm of innocence; I can read the confusion in your heart. This studied silence only adds to my anger. I no longer know myself; I no longer have reason, love pity! I go where vengeance calls me. I will find my rival, attack him, fight him, harm him. Covered with his blood, I will present myself to you. You will tremble then. And soon before your very eyes your unhappy victims will testify to the universe about my crime, your lies, and your infidelity.

CLARENCE [*with an air of satisfaction*]. It is perfect!

SCENE VII
ANNA, CLARENCE, SHAKESPEARE

ANNA. What is this noise, this commotion! Are you rehearsing a tragedy?

CLARENCE. O Lord! ... You are interrupting at the most interesting point.

SHAKESPEARE. What! What are you saying?

CLARENCE. It is a magnificent scene!

SHAKESPEARE. So, you think it only a scene?

CLARENCE. Full of energy and passion.

ANNA [*to Shakespeare*]. Ah! Begin it again for me.

SHAKESPEARE. Begin it again? What the devil?

CLARENCE. There is a power, a strength....

SHAKESPEARE [*aside*]. She has mistaken the truth for a fiction.... I will not disabuse her.... At least we can avoid ridicule.

ANNA. And it was around jealousy that the scene turned?

CLARENCE. Oh! But what expressiveness! What truth in the dialogue!

SHAKESPEARE. Yes, I should have captured a note of truth.

CLARENCE. With what art you have orchestrated it! How well you have questioned her infidelity! She does not answer you, but such obstinate silence again stirs your fury.

SHAKESPEARE. Oh! All that would be very interesting.

CLARENCE. And then you attack your rival. He falls beneath your sword. And covered with his blood you come to present yourself to one who betrayed you.... That gradation is sublime.

ANNA. But is it then a tragic scene?

CLARENCE. Oh, a terrifying tragedy! You know the subject! ... After killing his supposed rival, the lover would finish by suffocating his mistress.

ANNA. Happily, such things only happen in the theater.

SHAKESPEARE. I wish I were a hundred feet under the earth.

CLARENCE. You will give me the role of the lover, won't you? She is not guilty, I think?

SHAKESPEARE. No.

CLARENCE. I will do my best to play it well.

ANNA. I advise our author to go and write the scene as quickly as possible. [*aside*] It is also time we were free of him.

CLARENCE. She is right. He must not lose his ideas. And it is in the moment of inspiration that he must capture it on paper.

SHAKESPEARE. I will follow your sound advice. [*aside*] I am suffocating with anger.

CLARENCE. Go, my dear friend. Lose no time…. As soon as you finish your tragedy, come back and read it to me. Will you promise?

SHAKESPEARE. Yes. Yes. The denouement will surprise you.

CLARENCE. But I know it already. She is an innocent woman, victim of a man's mad jealousy.

SHAKESPEARE [*with great anger*]. No! No! A thousand times no! … It is the woman who is guilty.; I am certain of it. But I am losing my head. Until later, Clarence.

CLARENCE. Think more about your scene!

SHAKESPEARE [*furious*]. I go to write it in strokes of blood.

[*He leaves.*]

SCENE VIII
CLARENCE, ANNA

ANNA. My word, it was time that he left.

CLARENCE. He has left but his wonderful images have carried all of us away.

ANNA. Madame, Lord Wilson has answered me. He is overcome with joy.

CLARENCE [*without hearing*]. What enthusiasm! What love for his art!

[*She daydreams.*]

ANNA. He will be at the rendezvous at the stroke of 11…. She is not listening…. Madame, I am speaking to you of Lord Wilson.

CLARENCE [*still dreaming*]. Ah! Yes, Lord Wilson. I know him well.

ANNA. He burns with desire to tell you that he adores you.

CLARENCE [*still dreaming*]. That he adores me? … Oh, I have already heard him speak about love, Anna. What brilliance! What fervor!

ANNA. I believe it. He is young, amiable, and with those qualities….

CLARENCE. Oh! If you heard him say, "*I love you*," with a force that renders everything new for me!

ANNA. That is not surprising…. It is a lovely phrase.

CLARENCE. But it is necessary to hear it from his lips!

ANNA. Each person says it in a special way. But everyone says it well.

CLARENCE. Ah! His voice is still engraved in my heart and in my memory. I have good reason to reproach myself.

ANNA. You are going to atone…. You will soon see this amiable Lord Wilson. He is noble, generous, honest. Oh! He has nothing in common with our other suitors.

CLARENCE. Oh! I shall do him justice.

ANNA. For a moment I feared that our poet had seduced us. Those people have such beautiful phrases, such elegant words that it is sometimes difficult to resist them.

CLARENCE [*whispering*]. Without doubt.

ANNA. But it is the hour when our lover is due. [*She approaches the window.*] Truly, I see a man under the window. He is covered in a long cloak … as if he is walking with a purpose.

CLARENCE. Oh, my God! … Could it be Wilson?

ANNA. It could only be he…. See how much he loves you! It is thirty minutes early and he is already at the rendezvous.

CLARENCE. I know all that I owe to his love, to his generous proposal. But I cannot accept it. I will not receive him.

ANNA. Why this timidity? You are trembling…. But what are we going to do?

CLARENCE. I will write to him.

[*She sits at her desk.*]

ANNA. What caprice! Ah, I see…. She fears her own weakness.—You are going to write that you love him?

CLARENCE. I will write what is necessary…. Now let us address it: To my Lord Wilson.

ANNA [*running to the window*]. Ah! This time someone is knocking on the door.

CLARENCE [*rising*]. It is he no doubt.

ANNA. Yes, Madame, it is he. Listen…. Good! The servant is questioning him…. He responds, "Richard III." It is he…. The door is opening, and soon he will be in this room.

CLARENCE. Let me withdraw quickly into my room. You, my dear Anna, you must bring him this letter. You must then send him away, but politely, respectfully....

ANNA. Oh, leave it to me ...

CLARENCE. And come back immediately after he leaves.

[*She takes the candles from the table and enters her room.*]

SCENE IX

[*Night*]

ANNA [*alone*]. Oh dear! Oh dear! You have left me in the dark. Poor woman! She has lost her wits.... The more I consult my heart, the more I sense that she is right to flee from danger.... In a tete-a-tete these men are so pressing, so reckless that we can never triumph over them, only fly from them.... I hear a sound. Someone is climbing the stairs. Let me hurry and find a lamp. But he is here.

SCENE X
SHAKESPEARE, ANNA

ANNA [*approaching Shakespeare whom she mistakes for Lord Wilson*]. Ah, my Lord, you are exactly on time for your rendezvous! ... Come in. First I must tell you that my mistress refuses to see you.

SHAKESPEARE [*aside*]. Ah! What good luck!

ANNA. I see that frustrates you. But do not be annoyed. Before you leave, take this letter in which you will find proof of her love for you.

SHAKESPEARE. Oh, Lord!

ANNA. And then she has been tormented all evening by Shakespeare, your rival. He is a very somber man. If he appeared to us this moment, we would think him the ghost in his own *Hamlet*.

SHAKESPEARE [*aside*]. I can pretend no longer. [*drawing himself up furiously*] Yes. Yes. It is a ghost! An avenging ghost! ... Do you know me?

ANNA. Oh heavens! It is Shakespeare! Where can I hide?

[*She cries out while backing away and falls in an armchair.*]

SHAKESPEARE [*furious*]. In hell, demon! I condemn you and your mistress to the furies. May you both....

SCENE XI
ANNA, CLARENCE, SHAKESPEARE

[*Day*]

CLARENCE [*entering with candles*]. What is this noise? Ah, my Lord, I have been thinking.... Heavens! [*She calms herself.*] It is you, my dear William!

SHAKESPEARE. It is a lover in despair who has come to punish two treacherous monsters.

CLARENCE [*cheerful*]. How could you understand? ... Oh! How shrewd and ingenious jealousy can become!

SHAKESPEARE. Jealous? I? Oh, I am no longer jealous.... It is suspicion which nourishes jealousy.

CLARENCE. And you have no more suspicions?

SHAKESPEARE. None....—You love a lord. And this letter....

CLARENCE [*aside, with joy*]. He has my letter! ... [*proudly*] Containing the secrets of my heart.

SHAKESPEARE. She dares to confess it....

CLARENCE. Ah well! You have not read it? ...

SHAKESPEARE. This calmness redoubles my rage.... I want to meet him here, this fortunate rival of mine. He will not enjoy his triumph.... [*While speaking, he opens the letter.*]

CLARENCE [*calmly*]. Shakespeare, read.

SHAKESPEARE. Yes, o faithless one, I will read it. The more your infidelity shows itself, the easier it will be to forget. It will purge my bad humor as I wait for some respite from my pain.

[*He reads the letter.*]

"The proposal which you deign to offer me, my Lord, ought to flatter my vanity. I feel the deepest pleasure in expressing to you my gratitude. However, it is the only sentiment which I can give you in exchange, because my hand and heart belong only to Shakespeare." [*He throws himself on his knees before Clarence.*] O Clarence, Clarence! How can you ever forgive a man so unjust and reprehensible! ...

CLARENCE. Ah! How can your proving my love offend me?

[*A loud knock without*]

ANNA. It is the other one. He has certainly taken his time!

SHAKESPEARE [*on his knees*]. Anna, do you hear? Answer....

ANNA [*embarrassed*]. It is the denouement.... [*in a trembling voice*] Who is there?

OFF STAGE VOICE. Richard III.

SHAKESPEARE [*crossing quickly to the window*]. Richard III has come too late. William the Conqueror has seized the fortress.* [*He closes the window.*]

ANNA. Ah, sir, I believe now in your genius. Why? A lady won, a servant outwitted, a rival vanquished. And all that in an instant. Superb! Now, I do not fear to admit that, although a woman and a maidservant, I have less wit ... than a man of wit.

SHAKESPEARE. I can only claim to be a happy man. Poet, lover, husband of the woman I adore. What else could I wish?

CLARENCE. Wise friends and applause.

Shakespeare's line is clearly a play on the anecdote which John Manningham, a London lawyer, entered in his diary for March 13, 1602: "... Upon a tyme when Burbidge played Rich. 3. there was a citizen greue soe farr in liking with him, that before shee went from the play shee appointed him to come that night unto hir by the name of Ri: the 3. Shakespeare overhearing their conclusion went before, was intertained, and at his game ere Burbidge came. Then message being brought that Rich, the 3.d was at the dore, Shakespeare caused returne to be made that William the Conquerour was before Rich. the 3. Shakespeare's name was William."

Walter Savage Landor
(1775–1864)

When Charles Dickens gently caricatured Walter Savage Landor as the choleric yet magnanimous Boythorn in *Bleak House*, he effectively captured the paradoxical nature of this complex, passionate eccentric. After a troubled childhood, including a pressured withdrawal from Rugby and "rustication" from Oxford, where he was known as the "mad Jacobin," Landor devoted his life to farming, literature, and a series of crusades large and small, which all too often resembled quarrels. His temper, which led to a long estrangement from his wife, was balanced by a capacity for friendships that lasted throughout his life.

Although his experiments in farming had mixed success, his writings gained the admiration of contemporaries from Coleridge and Shelley to Browning. The most substantial part of those writings was his series of about 150 dialogues, which he published as *Imaginary Conversations*. Largely a vehicle for his own views on a variety of subjects, Landor uses a wide range of writers, statesmen, and classical figures. Among the more notable conversations are those between La Fontaine and La Rochefoucault, Diogenes and Plato, and Cicero and his brother. Landor's *Citation and Examination of William Shakspeare ... Touching Deer-Stealing* (1834) reflects both the strengths and weaknesses of the dialogues. His witty, realistic conception of character allows him to create the mildly pretentious Sir Thomas Lucy, a knight longing for the good old days when classes knew their place; the earthly, skeptical chaplain, Sir Silas Gough; and the meticulous clerk, Ephraim Barnett, who captures the entire scene with a sly, cautious humor. But the work also has long digressions on a variety of topics having little to do with the characters. Landor has a tendency to allow his speakers to wander either directly or obliquely into the maze of his own political, economic, moral, and artistic views. The following selections from the *Examination and Citation* focus on the knight's slightly confused legal and dramatic reflections, and the young poacher's ambiguous responses.

Citation and Examination of William Shakspeare

Euseby Treen, Joseph Carnaby, and Silas Gough, Clerk, Before the Worshipful Sir Thomas Lucy, Knight, Touching Deer-Stealing on the 19th Day of September in the Year of Grace 1582 Now First Published from Original Papers

(1834)

About one hour before noontide, the youth William Shakspeare, accused of deer-stealing, and apprehended for that offense, was brought into the great hall at Charlecote, where, having made his obeisance, it was most graciously permitted him to stand.

The worshipful Sir Thomas Lucy, Knight, seeing him right opposite, on the farther side of the long table, and fearing no disadvantage, did frown upon him with great dignity; then, deigning ne'er a word to the culprit, turned he his face towards his chaplain, Sir Silas Gough, who stood beside him, and said unto him most courteously, and unlike unto one who in his own right commandeth,

"Stand out of the way! What are those two varlets bringing into the room?"

"The table, sir," replied Master Silas, "upon the which the consumption of the venison was perpetrated."

The youth, William Shakspeare, did thereupon play and beseech his lordship most fervently, in this guise:

"O, sir! Do not let him turn the tables against me, who am only a simple stripling, and he an old cogger."

But Master Silas did bite his nether lip, and did cry aloud,

"Look upon those deadly spots!"

And his worship did look thereupon most staidly, and did say in the ear of Master Silas, but in such wise that it reached even unto mine,

"Good honest chandlery, methinks!"

"God grant it may turn out so!" ejaculated Master Silas.

The youth, hearing these words, said unto him,

"I fear, Master Silas, gentry like you often pray God to grant what he would rather not; and now and then what you would rather not."

Sir Silas was wroth at this rudeness of speech about God in the face of a preacher, and said reprovingly,

"Out upon thy foul mouth, knave! upon which lie slaughter and venison."

Whereupon did William Shakspeare sit mute awhile and discomfited; then, turning toward Sir Thomas, and looking and speaking as one submiss and contrite, he thus appealed unto him:

"Worshipful sir! were there any signs of venison on my mouth, Master Silas could not for his life cry out upon it, nor help kissing it as 'twere a wench's."

Sir Thomas looked upon him with most lordly gravity and wisdom, and said unto him, in a voice that might have come from the bench,

"Youth! thou speakest irreverently;" and then unto Master Silas,—"Silas! to the business on hand. Taste the fat upon yon boor's table, which the constable hath brought hither, good Master Silas! And declare upon oath, being sworn in my presence, first, whether said fat do proceed of venison; secondly, whether said venison be of buck or doe."

Whereupon the reverend Sir Silas did go incontinently, and did bend forward his head, shoulders, and body, and did severally taste four white solid substances upon an oaken board; said board being about two yards long, and one yard four inches wide; found in or brought hither from, the tenement or messuage of Andrew Haggit, who hath absconded. Of these four white solid substances, two were somewhat larger than a groat [a silver coin], and thicker; one about the size of King Henry the Eighth's shilling, when our late sovereign lord of blessed memory was towards the lustiest; and the other, that is to say the middlemost, did resemble in some sort a mushroom, not over fresh, turned upward on its stalk.

"And what sayest thou, Master Silas?" quoth the knight.

In reply whereunto Sir Silas thus averred:

"Venison! o' my conscience!

Buck! or burn me alive!

The three splashes in the circumference are verily and indeed venison; buck, moreover,—and Charlecote buck, upon my oath!"

Then carefully tasting the protuberance in the centre, he spat it out crying,

"Pho! pho! villain! villain!" and shaking his fist at the culprit.

Whereat the said culprit smiled and winked, and said off-hand,

"Save thy spittle, Silas! It would supply a gaudy mess to the hungriest litter; but it would turn them from whelps into wolvets. 'Tis pity to throw the best of thee away. Nothing comes out of thy mouth that is not savoury and solid, bating thy wit, thy sermons, and thy promises."

It was my duty to write down the very words, irreverent as they are, being so commanded. More of the like, it is to be feared, would have ensued, but that Sir Thomas did check him, saying shrewdly,

"Young man! I perceive that if I do not stop thee in thy courses, thy name, being involved in thy company's, may one day or other reach across the county; and folks may handle it and turn it about, as it deserveth, from Coleshill to Nuneaton, from Bromwicham to Brownsover. And who knoweth but that, years after thy death, the very house wherein thou wert born may be pointed at, and commented on, by knots of people, gentle and simple! What a shame for an honest man's son! Thanks to me, who consider of measures to prevent it! Posterity shall laud and glorify me for plucking thee clean out of her head, and for picking up timely a ticklish skittle, that might overthrow with it a power of others just as light. I will rid the hundred of thee, with God's blessing!—nay, the whole shire. We will have none such in our county: we justices are agreed upon it, and we will keep our word now and for evermore. Woe betide any that resemble thee in any part of him!"

Whereunto Sir Silas added,

"We will dog him, and worry him, and haunt him, and bedevil him; and if ever he hear a comfortable word, it shall be in a language very different from his own."

"As different as thine is from a Christian's," said the youth.

"Boy! thou art slow of apprehension," said Sir Thomas....

"In God's name, where did he gather all this?" whispered his worship to the chaplain, by whose side I was sitting. "Why, he talks like a man of forty-seven, or more!"

"I doubt his sincerity, sir!" replied the chaplain. "His words are fairer now...."

"Devil choke him for them!" interjected he with an undervoice.

"...and almost book-worthy; but out of place. What the scurvy cur yelped against me, I forgive him as a Christian. Murrain upon such varlet vermin! It is but of late years that dignities have come to be reviled; the other parts of the Gospel were broken long before; this was left us; and now this likewise is to be kicked out of doors, amidst the mutterings of such mooncalves as him yonder."

"Too true, Silas!" said the knight, sighing deeply. "Things are not as they were in our glorious wars of York and Lancaster. The knaves were thinned then; two or three crops a year of that rank bent grass which it has become the fashion of late to call the people. There was some difference then between buff doublets and iron mail; and the rogues felt it. Well-a-day! we must bear

what God willeth, and never repine, although it gives a man the heart-ache.
We are bound in duty to keep these things for the closet, and to tell God of
them only when we call upon his holy name, and have him quite by ourselves...."

To save paper and time, I shall now, for the most part, write only what
they all said, not saying that they said it, and just copying out in my clearest
hand what fell respectively from their mouths.

Sir Thomas

"Ay, indeed, we are losing the day: it wastes towards noon, and nothing
done. Call the witnesses. How are they called by name? Give me the paper."

The paper being forthwith delivered into his worship's hand by the
learned clerk, his worship did read aloud the name of Euseby Treen. Whereupon did Euseby Treen come forth through the great hall-door, which was
ajar, and answer most audibly,

"Your worship!"

Straightway did Sir Thomas read aloud, in like form and manner, the
name of Joseph Carnaby; and in like manner as aforesaid did Joseph Carnaby make answer and say,

"Your worship!"

Lastly did Sir Thomas turn the light of his countenance on William
Shakspeare, saying,

"Thou seest these good men deponents against thee, William Shakspeare."

And then did Sir Thomas pause. And pending this pause did William
Shakspeare look steadfastly in the faces of both; and, stroking down his own
with the hollow of his hand from the jaw-bone to the chin-point, said unto
his honour,

"Faith! it would give me much pleasure, and the neighbourhood much
vantage, to see these two fellows good men. Joseph Carnaby and Euseby Treen!
Why! your worship! they know every hare's form in Luddingtonfield better
than their own beds, and as well pretty nigh as any wench's in the parish."

Then turned he, with jocular scoff, unto Joseph Carnaby, thus accosting
him, whom his shirt, being made stiffer than usual for the occasion, rubbed
and frayed.

"Ay, Joseph! smoothen and soothe thy collar-piece again and again! Hark-
ye! I know what smock that was knavishly cut from."

Master Silas rose up in high choler, and said unto Sir Thomas,

"Sir! do not listen to that lewd reviler: I wager ten groats I prove him
to be wrong in his scent. Joseph Carnaby is righteous and discreet."

William Shakspeare

"By daylight and before the parson. Bears and boars are tame creatures,
and volubly discreet, in the sunshine and after dinner."

EUSEBY TREEN

"I do know his down-goings and up-risings."

WILLIAM SHAKSPEARE

"The man and his wife are one, saith holy Scripture."

EUSEBY TREEN

"A sober-paced and rigid man, if such there be. Few keep Lent like unto him."

WILLIAM SHAKSPEARE

"I warrant him, both lent and stolen."

SIR THOMAS

"Peace and silence! Now, Joseph Carnaby, do thou depose on particulars."

JOSEPH CARNABY

"May it please your worship! I was returning from Hampton upon All-hallowmass eve, between the hours of ten and eleven at night, in company with Master Euseby Treen; and when we came to the bottom of Mickle Meadow, we heard several men in discourse. I plucked Euseby Treen by the doublet, and whispered in his ear, 'Euseby! Euseby! let us slink along in the shadow of the elms and willows.'"

EUSEBY TREEN

"Willows and elm-trees were the words."

WILLIAM SHAKSPEARE

"See, your worship! what discordances! They cannot agree in their own story."

SIR SILAS

"The same thing, the same thing, in the main."

WILLIAM SHAKSPEARE

"By less differences than this estates have been lost, hearts broken, and England, our country, filled with homeless, helpless, destitute orphans. I protest against it!"

SIR SILAS

"Protest, indeed! He talks as if he were a member of the House of Lords. They alone can protest."

SIR THOMAS

"Your attorney may object, not protest, before the lord judge.
"Proceed you, Joseph Carnaby."

JOSEPH CARNABY

"In the shadow of the willows and elm-trees, then—"

WILLIAM SHAKSPEARE

"No hints, no conspiracies! Keep to your own story, man, and do not borrow his."

SIR SILAS

"I over-rule the objection. Nothing can be more futile and frivolous."

WILLIAM SHAKSPEARE

"So learned a magistrate as your worship will surely do me justice by hearing me attentively. I am young: nevertheless, having more than one year written in the office of an attorney, and having heard and listened to many discourses and questions on law, I cannot but remember the heavy fine inflicted on a gentleman of this county who committed a poor man to prison for being in possession of a hare, it being proved that the hare was in his possession, and not he in the hare's."

SIR SILAS

"Synonymous term! synonymous term!"

SIR THOMAS

"In what term sayest thou was it? I do not remember the case."

SIR SILAS

"Mere quibble! mere equivocation! Jesuitical! Jesuitical!

WILLIAM SHAKSPEARE

"It would be Jesuitical, Sir Silas, if it dragged the law by its perversions to the side of oppression and cruelty. The order of Jesuits, I fear, is as numerous as its tenets are lax and comprehensive. I am sorry to see their frocks flounced with English serge."

SIR SILAS

"I don't understand thee, viper!"

SIR THOMAS

"Cease thou, Will Shakespare! Know thy place...."

JOSEPH CARNABY

"At this moment one of the accomplices cried, 'Willy! Willy! prythee stop! enough in all conscience! First thou divertedst us from our undertaking with thy strange vagaries; thy Italian girls' nursery sighs; thy Pucks and pinchings, and thy Windsor whimsies. No kitten upon a bed of marum ever played such antics. It was summer and winter, night and day with us within the hour; and with such religion did we think and feel it, we would have broken the man's jaw that gainsayed it. We have slept with thee under the oaks in the ancient forest of Arden, and we have wakened from our sleep in the tempest far at sea. Now art thou for frightening us again out of all the senses thou hadst given us, with witches and women more murderous than they.'

"Then followed a deeper voice: 'Stouter men and more resolute are few; but thou, my lad, hast words too weighty for flesh and bones to bear up against. And who knows but these creatures may pop amongst us at last, as the wolf did, sure enough, upon him, the noisy rogue, who so long had been crying wolf! and wolf!'"

SIR THOMAS

"Well spoken, for two thieves; albeit I miss the meaning of the most part. Did they prevail with the scapegrace and stop him?"

JOSEPH CARNABY

"The last who had spoken did slap him on the shoulder, saying, 'Jump into the punt, lad, and across.' Thereupon did Will Shakspeare jump into said punt, and begin to sing a song about a mermaid."

WILLIAM SHAKSPEARE

"Sir! is this credible? I will be sworn I never saw one; and verily do believe that scarcely one in a hundred years doth venture so far up the Avon."

SIR THOMAS

"There is something in this. Thou mayest have sung about one, nevertheless. Young poets take great liberties with all female kind; not that mermaids are such very unlawful game for them, and there be songs even about worse and staler fish. Mind ye that! Thou hast written songs, and hast sung them, and lewd enough they be, God wot! ...

"William Shakspeare! we live in a Christian land, a land of great toleration and forbearance. Threescore cartsful of faggots a year are fully sufficient to clear our English air from every pestilence of heresy and witchcraft. It hath not always been so, God wot! Innocent and guilty took their turns before the fire, like geese and capons. The spit was never cold; the cook's sleeve was ever above the elbow. Countrymen came down from distant villages, into towns and cities, to see perverters whom they had never heard of, and to learn the righteousness of hatred. When heretics waxed fewer, the religious began to grumble, that god, in losing his enemies, has also lost his avengers.

"Do not thou, William Shakspeare, dig the hole for thy own stake. If thou canst not make men wise, do not make them merry at thy cost. We are not to be paganised any more. Having struck from our calendars, and unnailed from our chapels, many dozens of decent saints, with as little compunction and remorse as unlucky lads throw frog-spawn and tadpoles out of stagnant ditches, never let us think of bringing back amongst us the daintier divinities they ousted. All these are the devil's imps, beautiful as they appear in what we falsely call works of genius, which really and truly are the devil's own—statues more graceful than humanity, pictures more living than life,

eloquence that raised single cities above empires, poor men above kings. If
these are not Satan's works, where are they? I will tell thee where they are
likewise. In holding vain converse with false gods. The utmost we can allow
in propriety is to call a knight Phoebus, and a dame Diana. They are not meat
for every trencher.

"We must now proceed straightforward with the business on which thou
comest before us....

"Youth! I never thought thee so staid. Thou hast, for these many months,
been represented to me as one dissolute and light, much given unto mum-
meries and mysteries, wakes and carousals, cudgel-fighters and mountebanks,
and wanton women. They do also represent of thee—I hope it may be without foundation—that thou enactest the parts, not simply of foresters and
fairies, girls in the green-sickness and friars, lawyers and outlaws, but likewise, having small reverence for station, of kings and queens, knights and
privy-counsellors, in all their glory. It hath been whispered, moreover,and the
testimony of these two witnesses doth appear in some measure to countenance and confirm it, that thou hast at divers times this last summer been
seen and heard alone, inasmuch as human eye may discover, on the narrow
slip of greensward between the Avon and the chancel, distorting thy body
like one possessed, and uttering strange language, like unto incantation. This,
however, cometh not before me. Take heed! take heed unto thy ways: there
are graver things in law even than homicide and deer-stealing."

Sir Silas

"And strong against him. Folks have been consumed at the stake for pet-
tier felonies and upon weaker evidence."

Sir Thomas

"To that anon."

William Shakspeare did hold down his head, answering nought. And
Sir Thomas spake again unto him, as one mild and fatherly, if so be that such
a word may be spoken of a knight and parliament-man. And these are the
words he spake:

"Reason and ruminate with thyself now. To pass over and pretermit the
danger of representing the actions of the others, and mainly of lawyers and
churchmen, the former of whom do pardon no offences, and the latter those
only against God, having no warrant for more, canst thou believe it innocent
to counterfeit kings and queens? Supposest thou that if the impression of their
faces on a farthing be felonious and rope-worthy, the imitation of head and
body, voice and bearing, plume and strut, crown and mantle, and every thing
else that maketh them royal and glorious, be aught less? Perpend, young man,
perpend! Consider who among inferior mortals shall imitate them becom-
ingly? Dreamest thou they talk and act like checkmen at Banbury fair? How
can thy shallow brain suffice for their vast conceptions? How darest thou say,

as they do, hang this fellow—quarter that—flay—mutilate—stab—shoot—
press—hook—torture—burn alive? These are royalties. Who appointed thee
to such office? The Holy Ghost? He alone can confer it; but when wert thou
anointed?"

William was so zealous in storing up these verities, that he looked as
though he were unconscious that the pouring-out was over. He started, which
he had not done before, at the voice of Master Silas; but soon recovered his
complacency, and smiled with much serenity at being called a low-minded
varlet.

"Low-minded varlet!" cried Master Silas, most contemptuously, "dost
thou imagine that king calleth king, like thy chums, filcher and fibber,
whirligig and nincompoop? Instead of this low vulgarity and sordid idleness,
ending in nothing, they throw at one another such fellows as thee by the
thousand, and when they have cleared the land, render God thanks and make
peace."

Willy did now sigh out his ignorance of these matters; and he sighed,
mayhap, too, at the recollection of the peril he had run into, and had ne'er a
word on the nail.

The bowels of Sir Thomas waxed tenderer and tenderer; and he opened
his lips in this fashion:

"Stripling! I would now communicate unto thee, on finding thee docile
and assentaneous, the instruction thou needest on the signification of the
words *natural cause*, if thy duty towards thy neighbour had been first instilled
into thee."

Whereupon Master Silas did interpose, for the dinner-hour was drawing nigh.

"We cannot do all at once," quoth he. "Coming out of order, it might
harm him. Malt before hops, the world over, or the beer muddies."

But Sir Thomas was not to be pricked out of his form even by so shrewd
a pricker; and, like unto one who heareth not, he continued to look most graciously on the homely vessel that stood ready to receive his wisdom:

"Thy mind," said he, "being unprepared for higher cogitations, and the
groundwork and religious duty not being well rammer-beaten and flinted, I
do pass over this supererogatory point, and inform thee rather, that bucks
and swans and herons have something in their very names announcing them
of knightly appurtenance. And (God forfend that evil do ensue therefrom!)
that a goose on the common, or a game-cock on the loft of a cottager or vil-
lager, may be seized, bagged, and abducted, with far less offence to the laws.
In a buck there is something so gainly and so grand, he treadeth the earth
with such ease and such agility, he abstaineth from all other animals with
such punctilious avoidance, one would imagine God created him when he created knighthood..... .

"William, it is well at thy time of life that thou shouldst know the customs of far countries, particularly if it should be the will of God to place thee in a company of players. Of all nations in the world, the French best understand the stage. If thou shouldst ever write for it, which God forbid, copy them very carefully. Murders on their stage are quite decorous and cleanly. For gentlemen and ladies die by violence who would not have died by exhaustion. 'For they rant and rave until their voice fails them, one after another; and those who do not die of it, die consumptive. These cannot bear to see cruelty: they would rather see any image than their own.' These are not my observations, but were made by Sir Everard Starkeye, who likewise did remark … that 'cats, if you hold them up to the looking-glass, will scratch you terribly; and that the same fierce animal, as if proud of its cleanly coat and its velvety paw, doth carefully put aside what other animals of more estimation take no trouble to conceal.

"'Our people,' said Sir Everard, 'must see upon the stage what they never could have imagined; so the best men in the world would earnestly take a peep of hell through a chink, whereas the worser would skulk away.'

"Do not thou be their caterer, William! Avoid the writing of comedies and tragedies. To make people laugh is uncivil, and to make people cry is unkind. And what, after all, are these comedies and tragedies? They are what, for the benefit of all future generations, I have myself described them,

> The whimsies of wantons and stories of dread,
> That make the stout-hearted look under the bed.

Furthermore, let me warn thee against the same on account of the vast charges thou must stand at. We Englishmen cannot find it in our hearts to murder a man without much difficulty, hesitation, and delay. We have little or no invention for pains and penalties; it is only our acutest lawyers who have wit enough to frame them. Therefore it behoveth your tragedy-man to provide a rich assortment of them, in order to strike the auditor with awe and wonder. And a tragedy-man, in our country, who cannot afford a fair dozen of stabbed males, and a trifle under that mask of poisoned females, and chains enow to moor a whole navy in dock, is but a scurvy fellow at the best. Thou wilt find trouble in purveying these necessaries; and then must come the gim-cracks for the second course: gods, goddesses, fates, furies, battles, marriages, music, and the maypole. Hast thou within thee wherewithal?"

"Sir," replied Billy, with great modesty, "I am most grateful for these ripe fruits of your experience. To admit delightful visions into my own twilight chamber, is not dangerous nor forbidden. Believe me, sir, he who indulges in them will abstain from injuring his neighbour: he will see no glory in peril and no delight in strife.

"The world shall never be troubled by any battles and marriages of mine, and I desire no other music and no other maypole than have lightened my heart at Stratford."

Sir Thomas finding him well-conditioned and manageable, proceeded:

"Although I have admonished thee of sundry and insurmountable imped-iments, yet more are lying in the pathway. We have no verse for tragedy. One in his hurry hath dropped rhyme, and walketh like unto the man who wan-teth the left-leg stocking. Others can give us rhyme indeed, but can hold no longer after the tenth or eleventh syllable. Now Sir Everard Starkeye, who is a pretty poet, did confess to Monsieur Dubois the potency of the French tragic verse, which thou never canst hope to bring over.

"'I wonder, Monsieur Dubois!' said Sir Everard, 'that your countrymen should have thought it necessary to transport their heavy artillery into Italy. No Italian could stand a volley of your heroic verses from the best and biggest pieces....'"

SIR THOMAS

"I will do what thy own father would, and cannot. Thou shalt follow his business."

"I cannot do better, may it please your worship!" said the lad.

"It shall lead thee unto wealth and respectability," said the knight, some-what appeased by his ready compliancy and low gentle voice. "Yea, but not here; no witches, no wantons (this word fell gravely and at full-length upon the ear), no spells hereabout.

"Gloucestershire is within a measured mile of thy dwelling. There is one at Bristol, formerly a parish-boy, or little better, who now writeth himself gentleman in large round letters, and hath been elected, I hear, to serve as burgess in parliament for his native city; just as though he had eaten a capon or turkey-poult in his youth, and had actually been at grammar-school and college. When he began, he had not credit for a goat-skin; and now, behold ye! this very coat upon my back did cost me eight shillings the dearer for him, he bought up wool so largely."

WILLIAM SHAKSPEARE

"May it please your worship! if my father so ordereth, I go cheerfully."

SIR THOMAS

"Thou art grown discreet and dutiful: I am fain to command thy release, taking thy promise on oath, and some reasonable security, that thou wilt abstain and withhold in future from that idle and silly slut, Hannah Hath-away, with whom, to the heart-ache of thy poor worthy father, thou wantonly keepest company."

Then did Sir Thomas ask Master Silas Gough for the Book of Life, bid-ding him to deliver it to the right hand of Billy, with an eye upon him that he touch it with both lips; it being taught by the Jesuits, and caught too greedily out of their society and communion, that whoso touch it with one lip only, and thereafter sweareth falsely, cannot be called a perjurer, since perjury is breaking an oath. But breaking half an oath, as he doth who toucheth the Bible or crucifix with one lip only, is no more perjury than breaking an eggshell is breaking an egg, the shell being a part, and the egg being an integral.

William did take the Holy Book with all due reverence the instant it was offered to his hand. His stature seemed to rise therefrom as from a pulpit, and Sir Thomas was quite edified.

"Obedient and conducible youth!" said he. "See there, Master Silas! what hast thou now to say against him? who sees farthest?"

"The man from the gallows is the most likely, bating his nightcap and blinker," said Master Silas peevishly. "He hath not outwitted me yet...."

WILLIAM SHAKSPEARE

"I await the further orders of your worship from the chair."

SIR THOMAS

"I return and seat myself."

And then did Sir Thomas say with great complacency and satisfaction in the ear of Master Silas,

"What civility, and deference, and sedateness of mind, Silas!"

But Master Silas answered not.

WILLIAM SHAKSPEARE

"Must I swear, sir?"

SIR THOMAS

"Yea, swear; be of good courage. I protest to thee by my honour and knighthood, no ill shall come unto thee therefrom. Thou shalt not be circumvented in thy simpleness and inexperience."

Willy, having taken the Book of Life, did kiss it piously, and did press it unto his breast, saying,

"Tenderest love is the growth of my heart, as is the grass of Alvescote mead.

"May I lose my life or my friends, or my memory, or my reason; may I be viler in my own eyes than those men are...."

Here he was interrupted, most lovingly by Sir Thomas, who said unto him,

"Nay, nay, nay! poor youth! do not tell me so! they are not such very bad men; since thou appealest unto Caesar; that is, unto the judgment-seat."

Now his worship did mean the two witnesses, Joseph and Euseby; and soothe to say, there be many worse. But William had them not in his eye; his thoughts were elsewhere, as will be evident,—for he went on thus:—

"... If ever I forget or desert thee, or ever cease to worship* and cherish thee, my Hannah!"

SIR SILAS

"The madman! the audacious, desperate, outrageous villain! Look-ye, sir! where he flung the Holy Gospel! Behold it on the holly and box boughs in the chimney-place, spreaden it all abroad, like a lad about to be whipt!"

SIR THOMAS

"Miscreant knave! I will send after him forthwith! Ho, there! is the caitiff at hand, or running off?"

Jonas Greenfield the butler did budge forward after a while, and say, on being questioned,

"Surely, that was he! Was his nag tied to the iron gate at the lodge, Master Silas?"

SIR SILAS

"What should I know about a thief's nag, Jonas Greenfield?"

"And didst thou let him go, Jonas? even thou?" said Sir Thomas. "What! are none found faithful?"

"Lord love your worship," said Jonas Greenfield; "a man of threescore and two may miss catching a kite upon wing. Fleetness doth not make folks the faithfuller, or that youth yonder beats us all in faithfulness.

"Look! he darts on like a greyhound whelp after a leveret. He sure enough, it was! I now remember the sorrel mare his father bought of John Kinderley last Lammas, swift as he threaded the trees along the park. He must have reached Wellesbourne ere now at that gallop, and pretty nigh Walton-hill."

SIR THOMAS

"Merciful Christ! grant the country be rid of him for ever! What dishonour upon his friends and native town! A reputable woolstapler's son turned gipsy and poet for life."

SIR SILAS

"A Beelzebub; he spake as bigly and fiercely as a soaken yeoman at an election feast, this obedient and conducible youth!"

"It was so written. Hold thy peace, Silas!"

LAUS DEO.

E.B.

POST-SCRIPTUM
By Me Ephraim Barnett.

Twelve days are over and gone since William Shakspeare did leave our parts. And the spinster, Hannah Hathaway, is in sad doleful plight about him; forasmuch as Master Silas Gough went yesterday unto her, in her mother's house at Shottery, and did desire both her and her mother to take heed and be admonished, that if ever she, Hannah, threw away one thought after the runagate William Shakspeare, he should swing.

The girl could do nothing but weep; while as the mother did give her solemn promise that her daughter should never more think about him all her natural life, reckoning from the moment of her promise.

And the maiden, now growing more reasonable, did promise the same. But Master Silas said,

"I doubt you will, though."

"No," said the mother, "I answer for her she shall not think of him, even if she see his ghost."

Hannah screamed, and swooned, the better to forget him. And Master Silas went home easier and contenteder. For now all the worst of his hard duty was accomplished; he having been, on the Wednesday of last week, at the speech of Master John Shakspeare, Will's father, to inquire whether the sorrel mare was his. To which question the said Master John Shakspeare did answer, "Yea."

"Enough said!" rejoined Master Silas.

"Horse-stealing is capital. We shall bind thee over to appear against the culprit, as prosecutor, at the next assizes."

May the Lord in his mercy give the lad a good deliverance, if so be it be no sin to wish it!

October 1, A.D. 1582

John Brougham
(1810–1880)

Born in Dublin to an Irish-French family, John Brougham set out to study medicine in London. When family economic problems made him search for a quicker route to his fortune, he moved to the theater. An actor, playwright, and theatrical entrepreneur, Brougham appeared at and wrote for Covent Garden and the Olympic and managed the London Lyceum. In 1842 he moved to the United States where, except for a five year return to London in the early 1860's, he found fame in comic Irish roles, cleverly constructed burlesques, and adaptations of others' works.

Shakspeare's Dream (?1858) is a fairly simple homage to the genius of the young yet-to-be poet. It is a pageant in which Chronos (Time), Fancy, Genius, and Fame prepare for his arrival and characters from the plays dance across their creator's imagination. Brougham proved less capable in managing money than in earning it; in 1878 his friends had to rescue him from poverty with a testimonial at the Academy of Music which raised the then handsome sum of $10,000 for an annuity.

Shakspeare's Dream
(1858)

Cast of Characters
In the Allegory: Chronos, Fancy, Genius, Fame, Attendant Spirits
In the Vision: William Shakespeare

Scene I—A Wood
Chronos, Fancy, and Attendant Spirits

BALLET OF ACTION AND CHORUS—Fancy and the joyous hours
attempt to bind old Time in rosy chains.

Chorus—"Under Greenwood Trees."
Here in the greenwood, see
How happy, how happy are we
Old Time, if thou wilt stay,
We'll laugh thy cares away.
Come hither! come hither! come hither!
Here shalt thou see
No enemy,
No winter or rough weather.
Come hither, &e.

FANCY. Why look so angrily, old Father Time?
    Have we detained thee here against thy will?

CHRONOS. That have ye; and you know that time once lost—

FANCY. Oh, yes! we know that wise old saw full well.

CHRONOS. Respect it then, and keep me not aloof
    From the day's serious avocation.

[*All laugh*]

FANCY.   Hear him!
    And in such presence talk of seriousness!
    Thou wrinkled cheat! I know—so do we all—
    That in thy heart thou'dst rather linger here.

CHRONOS. That would I, truly—I deny it not,

And grieve most heartily the thought arose
So soon before me, I was playing truant;
For, when my brain and sense are all astir,
I must perforce plod on my weary way,
Treading the same dull mill-horse round forever!

FANCY. Ungrateful drudge! and is not from pity
   Of this, thy toll, that we, with merry laugh,
   With joyous song and jest from some wild nook,
   On life's broad highway, like freebooters rush,
   Crying, "Stand! and deliver up your cares!"

CHRONOS. And I am grateful to be so relieved,
   And with a lighter step pass on my way,
   As I must now; for thou hast not the power
   To stay me after the brief spell is broken.

FANCY. Well, let the churlish fellow pass; anon.
   He will be glad to be so well encountered.
   Heigh-day! What holds thee back? hast thou relented?
   Would'st thou with Fancy dream again?

CHRONOS.   Not so.
   In the full action of my waking thought,
   Am I now stayed; for lo! your sister comes—
   Your elder, heaven-born sister; first and rarest
   Of all the spirit-gifts on earth bestowed.
   To her I kneel, and heartened homage pay.

   Enter GENIUS, attended by FAME

   Hail mighty Genius! great Earth Goddess, hail!
   Of all world spirits, Time only bends to thee.

GENIUS. Thou hast displaced thy homage. Not to me
   Shouldst thou thus kneel in reverence; but here,
   To one much higher still—Immortal Fame!
   Who, unsought, honors thus my small desert,
   And my weak thought inspires by her bright presence.

CHRONOS. When Fame with Genius is on earth allied—
   As now I see it—each doth honor each;
   But in my day I've seen stark Impudence
   So oft bedeck itself in stolen robes
   From Genius filched; and Fame her brazen trump
   Sound just as loudly in the world's ear

Its praises, while the common herd took up
The lying shout, that I have small respect
For either; nor have I the power to check
The vile imposture, until the brief hour
Has passed of both the cheated and the cheater.

FANCY. Can this be so?

GENIUS.   Alas! I fear it is.
My children, brain-filled with inspiring thought,
Inhabit a weird-world of their own,
Dreaming amidst the very shock and strife
Of life's inevitable conflict;
They see not, heed not its unnumbered shares,
Its covert strategy or open warfare,
But all enrapt and heaven-communing, pass
Along, regardless of the battle's rage.
The wonder is, that in this busy world,
So many of my children—not so few—
Have been acknowledged; some like glorious stars
Have shone, while yet they lived, to all men's eyes,
A glowing wonder; and when from their spheres
They fell, wreaked heaven with their departing brightness.
But ah! how small their number when compared
With those whose destiny has been and, is—
Though only conscious of their equal power—
To run their shining race unseen, unknown,
Beyond the puny range of human vision!

CHRONOS. 'Tis well indeed thy children are so rare,
For, aloe-like, between each goodly blossom,
A century is counted—sometimes more,
Less never—to the world at least.

GENIUS.   One lives
To-day that shall outlive them all—the past
And the to-come—supreme throughout the earth;
Great Nature's Arch Magician, to whose spell
The varied passions of the human soul
Must quick obedience yield; a myriad minds
In one conjoined; a universe of thought
Within the compass of one mortal brain,
Holding dominion in his single hand;
Not all the sovereigns of the world can parallel,
The unchecked, undivided rule of heart!

CHRONOS. What eaglet amongst common birds is he?
What unhewn marble hides this peerless statue?
Has he a name?

GENIUS.   He has—unknown as yet;
Obscure, untitled—from the laboring million
The hand of Fate has lifted up this paragon
To overtop the highest; kings will pass away—
Nay, their whole lineage be forgotten dust;
Empires will rise and fall, new worlds be found
Where knowledge now declares a void; whole races
Disappear; and yet, amidst the general change,
While there exists one record of his land,
Or language and mankind would think of him
Who has pre-eminently honored both;
Spontaneous to their will come the name
Of WILLIAM SHAKESPEARE!

CHRONOS. Can we not see this new world-wonder?

GENIUS. You can; and also, dimly shadowed forth,
The mighty works that, through all future time,
Shall stand as his perpetual monument.
For, in a vision I shall feast his soul
With a slight foretaste of the great renown
That doth await him. Fancy and thy train,
I do invoke your aid!

CHORUS OF SPIRITS—"Witches' Chorus 'Macbeth.'"
Come away, come away, this wonder see;
At the sweet night-birds' gladsome voice,
We do not tremble, but rejoice.

Scene changes to another part of the wood—WILLIAM SHAKESPEARE
discovered on a bank, sleeping.

Solo—Fancy
Sleep, dreamer, sleep, while to thy gaze
We show thy fame of future days.

Solo—Tenor
What time, renown shall on the fall,
And in each cot or princely hall;
Men hail thee chief throughout the land,

Amidst the great thought-gifted baud;
The first and greatest that can come
From now until the final doom.

Solo—Soprano
What time, all nature's book to thee,
An easy page shall open be,
From first to last, where thou canst read,
Nor yet to slightest effort need;
For what, to others, only schools
Can teach, disdaining common rules
Inborn, to thee will come unsought,
And seem but the echo of thy thought.
[*Repeat chorus. They retire.* SHAKESPEARE *wakes.*]

SHAKS. Again those phantoms! Do they come in sleep
         To mock me for my wakeful hours that pass
         In dreamy indolence? within my soul,
         That seems as though it held a universe,
         Vast, shapless, and indefinite—through which
         Great aspirations struggle to find vent;
         A new-born world breathing thro' earthquakes .
         Oh! for one ray of heaven-perfecting light—
         The first faint glimmer of the morning dawn—
         To give me hope that day will shortly break
         Upon the ghost-like and fantastic night,
         So long, so weary, and so crowded full
         Of airy nothings—changeful fleeting forms,
         That, like embattled clouds, forever clash
         In huge gigantic warfare, hurtling forth,
         At intervals, electric bolts, that show,
         For a brief instant, the bright skies beyond,
         Only to quench the sense in blacker darkness!
         Glimpses I've had, within the great confusion,
         Of shapes majestic beckoning me on
         Towards gorgeous palaces; and once methought
         Grave History resigned to me her pen,
         Bidding me write the records of the past,
         And make familiar with the public mind
         The lore of schools, becoming thus immortal as herself;
         It cannot be that heaven designed
         This mighty maze of intermingled thought
         To rest unordered and unuseful here!

No, no; I have a sure abiding faith,
A certain prescience that the blessed sun
Will rise at last, and in that cheering hope,
Despair is lost! Impatient heart, be still
For inspiration comes but at His will!
I'll to my grassy couch once more and sleep;
Awake I'm but a man, in dreams a demi-god!

[SHAKESPEARE] *sleeps again, when ARIEL and her attendant sylphs appear, in a ballet of action, leading to a procession of all the principal characters in the Shakespearean plays.*

Scene changes to Temple of Fame, in which are grouped the various individualities immortalized by the pen of the "Poet Of All Time."

FINALE.

To the great Prince of Thought your heart's homage bring,
Loud let your voices swell, his praises to sing;
    Now, while each heart is glowing,
    Now, while delight is flowing,
    On him our love bestowing,
    Hail we the POET KING!

William Rendle
(1811–1893)

A Fellow of the Royal College of Surgeons and a devoted antiquarian, William Rendle spent much of his life studying the history of the borough of Southwark. During his research he discovered that in the late sixteenth century John and Isabel Mabb ran the Tabard Inn, the meeting place for Chaucer's pilgrims. This curious historical fact led to the *jeu d'esprit* "Shakespeare at the Tabard Inn: A Phantasy," published in the first volume of Edward Walford's *The Antiquarian Magazine & Bibliographer* (London: William Reeves, 1882). In addition to suggesting a bond between England's two greatest poets, Rendle offers a playful source for Mercutio's portrait of Queen Mab in "Romeo and Juliet."

"Shakespeare at the Tabard Inn: A Phantasy"
(1882)

Scene: The "Tabard" Inn, Southwark, about 1585. Seated inside the bar is Isabel Mabb, wife of the jolly host, and buxom mother of sundry little Mabbs, in full talk with guests and indroppers: among them is many a writer and player of "the Banke."

Enter Wm. Shakespeare

SHAKESPEARE: A little of the inspiring cordial, good Mistress Mabb— some sack, good Isabel? or as I would say, Queen Mabb, Queen of the Fairies. Why not? Was not old Geoffrey, whose spirit yet haunts the house, fond of the fairies? Without doubt, our Queen of the Tabard hath some of the jolie troop in pay, and might, if she chose, make them gambol on the green at the Bankside. There is no such queenly and comely Mabb in all Southwark as our Mistress here.

ISABEL MABB: Have done, sweet William; clever as you may be, I will not allow liberties with the name of John Mabb's honest wife, the mother of his boys. Perchance thou wilt be putting me in a play next for the laughter of the groundlings. There is your sack; take it, and be gone.

SHAKESPEARE: In a play, sayest thou, Isabel Mabb? A good thought, it shall be done; yes, I have something on the anvil: it shall take shape, and Mab, queen of the fairies, shall appear, if only in a phantasy—our buxom, lovely hostess in a dream! Ho, ho, ho! Good gentles all, fill your glasses. To Queen Mab, the fairies' midwife, the thrifty hostess.

> She who pinches country wenches,
> If they rub not clean their benches;
> And with sharper nails remembers,
> When they rake not up the embers.

See her face, her lips, do they not make us dream of kisses?

[*Lifting his glass to Queen Mab*]
(*All exeunt, fingers to lips, and blowing kisses to the Queen.*)

Franklin Harvey Head
(1832–1914)

Like many of his generation, Franklin Harvey Head decided to go west to find his fortune. The native New Yorker, who received bachelor's and master's degrees from Hamilton College, where he also studied law, first set up a law practice in Wisconsin. After a few years he moved further west to experiment with stock raising and mining in Utah, Nevada and California. Eventually settling in Chicago, he served at various times as the president of the Chicago Malleable Iron Works and the Chicago & Iowa Railway and as a director of various banks, railroads, and development companies, as well as the Columbian Exposition of 1893.

Head balanced his success as an industrialist with a passion for literature; he was especially proud of his service as president of the Chicago Literary Club. There he offered his lightly satirical readings of famous authors, readings which he called "unhistorical histories." One of these, *Shakespeare's Insomnia* (1886), begins with the assumption that "no man writes other than his own experiences." Head then traces in the play's descriptions of sleep, noting how "[r]arely is a blessing invoked which does not include the wish for tranquil sleep" and how "[c]onstantly also in anathemas throughout the plays are invoked, as the deadliest of curses, broken rest and its usual accompaniment of troubled dreams."

Shakespeare's interest in sleeplessness leads Head to search the playwright's own life for the causes of that interest. The second part of Head's work, the section included below, offers a collection of recently discovered letters by William Kempe, Sir Walter Raleigh, and the moneylender Mordecai Shylock. Their accounts of Shakespeare's investments, debts, and marital problems offer ample evidence for his preoccupation with insomnia.

Shakespeare's Insomnia and the Causes Thereof
(1886)

The meagre information we have as to the life and habits of Shakespeare would seem to make it an almost hopeless task now to discover the cause of his insomnia. He wrote a marvelous body of literature, and it might be thought this labor itself would suffice as an explanation: that the furnace heat in which the conceptions of Hamlet and Macbeth and Lear were wrought in the crucible of his brain would be fatal to repose. But his contemporaries speak of him as an easy and rapid writer; one whose imagination is only paralleled by the ease, the force and beauty of the phrase in which it is embodied. We are told, too, by Dr. H. A. Johnson, an eminent medical authority, in the second volume of his treatise on the pathology of the optic nerve, that it is not work, even heavy and continuous, but worry over this work, which drives away repose and shortens life.

I had observed, in collating the many passages in Shakespeare concerning sleep, that the greater number, and those bearing evidence of deepest earnestness, occurred in six plays: "Richard III," "Macbeth," "1 Henry IV," "Hamlet," "2 Henry IV," and "Henry V." The chronology of Shakespeare's plays seems almost hopeless, scarcely any two writers agreeing as to the order of the plays or the years in which they were written. Several of the most critical authorities, however—Dyce, White, Furnival, and Halliwell-Phillipps— are agreed that two of the plays above named were written in 1593, three in 1602, and one in 1609. This would seem to indicate that during these three years unusual perplexities or anxieties had surrounded our author; and on noting this, it occurred to me that on these points the series of papers recently discovered and called the Southampton manuscripts, which are not yet published, might give light. I accordingly addressed a letter to the Director of the British Museum, where the manuscripts are placed for safe keeping, and received the following reply:

British Museum, Office of the Chief Curator,
Department of Manuscripts, London, Feb. 14, 1886

Sir,—I am ... instructed by the curator to inform you that ... loaning to you all papers from the recently discovered Southampton Shakespeare Collection, bearing date in the years 1593, 1602, and 1609, is contrary to the regulations of this institution. If you cannot visit London to examine these interesting manuscripts, copies will be made and transmitted you for three halfpence per folio, payment by our rules invariably in advance. I note that you are evidently in error upon one point. The collection contains no letters or manuscripts of Shakespeare. It is composed principally of letters written to Shakespeare by various people, and which, after his death, in some way came into the possession of the Earl of Southampton. His death, so soon after that of Shakespeare, doubtless caused these letters to be lost sight of, and they were but last year discovered in the donjon of the castle. I have examined the letters for the years you name, and find that copies of the same can be made for 3 3s., exclusive of postage.

Very respectfully yours,

JOHN BARNACLE,

10th Ass't Sub-Secretary.

The money having been forwarded, I received in due time the copies. At the first date, 1593, Shakespeare was a young dramatist and actor struggling for recognition, poor and almost unknown; in 1602 he had won an assured position among his fellows, and, with the thrift which characterized him, had secured an interest in the Globe Theatre, where his plays were performed; in 1609 he was in the fullness of his contemporary fame, had bought valuable property in Stratford, and was contemplating retirement to his country home.

The following are the letters from the Southampton collection which serve to throw light upon the insomnia of Shakespeare. They are given in their chronological order, and verbatim, but not literatim, the orthography having been modernized. The first of the letters, dated in 1593, is from a firm of lawyers, Messrs. Shallow & Slender, and is as follows:

Inner Temple, London, Feb. 15, 1593.

To William Shakespeare:

Mr. Moses Solomons, an honored client of our firm, has placed with us, that payment may be straightway enforced, a bill drawn by John Heminge, for 10, due in two months from the date thereof, and the payment of which was assured by you in writing. This bill has been for some days overdue, and Mr. Solomons is constrained to call upon you for payment at once. Your prompt attention to this will save the costs and annoyance of an arrest.

The second letter is from the same parties, and bears date four days later than the first.

Inner Temple, Feb. 19, 1593.

Mr. William Shakespeare:

Reccuring to certain statements made by yourself at our chambers yesterday, we have considered the same, and have likewise the opinion thereon of our client, Mr. Solomons. As we do now recall them, you nominated three principal grounds why you should not be pressed to pay the bill drawn by

Mr. Heminge. First, that you received no value therefor, having put your name to the bill upon the assurance that it was a matter of form, and to oblige a friend.

To this we rejoin, that by the law of estoppel you are precluded to deny the consideration after the bill hath passed into the holding of a discounter unnotified of the facts.

Second, That, as our client paid but 1 for the bill, he should not exact 10 thereon. To which we reply, that, so a valuable consideration was passed for the bill, the law looketh not to its exact amount. It is also asserted by our client that, beyond actual coin given for the bill, he did further release to John Heminge certain tinsel crowns, swords, and apparel apurtenant to the representation of royalty, which had before then—to wit, two weeks before—been pledged to him for the sum of 8 shillings, borrowed by the said Heminge.

Third, That it was impossible for you to pay the bill, you having no money, and receiving no greater income than 22 shillings per week, all of which was necessary to the maintenance of yourself and family. We regret again to call to your notice the Statute of 16 Eliz., entitled, "Concerning the Imprisonment of Insolvent Debtors," which we trust you will not oblige us to invoke in aid of our suffering client's rights. To be lenient and merciful is his inclination, and we are happy to communicate to you this most favorable tender for an acquitance of his claim. You shall render to us an order on the Steward of the Globe Theatre for 20 shillings per week of your stipend therein. This will leave to you yet 2 shillings per week, which, with prudence, will yield to you the comforts, if not the luxuries, of substinence. In ten weeks the face of the bill will be thus repaid. For his forbearance in the matter of time, which hath most seriously inconvenienced him, he requires that you shall pay him the further sum of 2 as usury, and likewise that you do liquidate and save him harmless from the charges of us, his solicitors, which charges, from the number of grave and complicated questions which have become a part of this case and demanded solution, we are unable to make less than 4. We should say guineas, but your evident distress hath moved us to gentleness and mercy. These added sums are to be likewise embraced in the Steward's order, and paid at the same rate as the substance of the bill, and should you embrace this compassionate tender, in the brief period of sixteen weeks you will be at the end of this indebtedness.

The next letter is dated the following month, and is from Henry Howard, an apparent pawnbroker.

Queer Street, London, 10 March, 1593.

To William Shakespeare, Actor:

These presents are to warn you that the time has six days since passed in which you were to repay me 8 shillings, and thereby redeem the property in pledge to me; namely, one Henry VIII shirt of mail and visor, and Portia's law book, and the green bag therefor. Be warned that unless 8 shillings and the usance thereof be forthcoming, the town-crier shall notify the sale of the sundry articles named.

The next letter, and the last in this period of the poet's career (1693), is from Mordecai Shylock.

Fleet Street, Near the Sign of the
Hog in Armor, Nov. 22, 1593.

To William Shakespeare:
 I have been active in the way you some days since besought me; namely, the procuring for you of a loan of £5, that you might retire a bill upon which you were a garantor. As I then told you, I have no money myself, being very poor; but I have a friend who has money with which I can persuade him to relieve your wants. Had I myself the money, I should gladly meet your needs at a moderate usance, not more than twenty-five in the hundred; but my friend is a hard man, who exacts large returns for his means, and will be very urgent that repayment be made on the day named in the bill. He hath empowered me to take your bill at two months—for him, mind you—for £10, the payment to be assured, as you wished, by the pledge of your two new plays in manuscript—"Midsummer Night's Dream" and "Romeo and Juliet"—for which bill he will at my strong instance, and because you are a friend to me, give £5. My charge for services in this behalf, which hath consumed much time, will be 1, which I shall straightway pay out in the purchase of a new gown, much needed by my little daughter Jessica, who loves you and recalls often the pleasant tales you do repeat for her diversion.

The letters in the second period (1602) are nine years later than those just read. The first is from the same Mordecai Shylock, who, with the poet, seems to have prospered in worldly affairs, as his letters are dated in a more reputable portion of the city.

Threadneedle Street, London, April 17, 1602.

To William Shakespeare:
 In January last past you purchased of Richard Burbage four shares of the stock of the Globe Theatre for £100, and inasmuch as you had not available the whole means to pay therefor, borrowed from me the £60 wanting, paying yourself £40 of such purchase price, and giving me in pledge for my £60 such four shares of stock. Owing to special attractions at Blackfriar's Theatre, the stock of the Globe hath greatly declined in value, and I fear these four shares may no longer be salable at the price of even £60, and I therefore

must importune that you forthwith do make a payment of £20 on your said bill, or the four shares of stock will be sold at public vendue.

The next letter is from the same writer, and is dated nine days later.

Threadneedle Street, April 26, 1602.

To William Shakespeare:

I acknowledge to have received from you by the hand of Henry Condell £5, and two of your own shares in the stock of the Globe Theatre in further pledge of your bill of £60, as was engaged by us yesterday. It pains me make known to you that, owing to the great demands recently made upon the goldsmiths by her sacred Majesty, money hath become very dear; and as it was not my own lent you, I have been obliged to pay above the usance expected a further premium of seventeen in the hundred, which I pray you presently repay me. I am told that shares in the Globe can now be bought at £15; and inasmuch as yours were bought at £25, should you acquire other shares at £15, it would serve to equate your havings.

The next letter, from the same broker, is written but a few days later.

Threadneedle Street, May 12, 1602.

To William Shakespeare:

Acting as requested by you, I did one week ago buy for you three shares in the Globe Theatre for £15 each, using in such purchase the 15 given me by you, and 30, not of mine own, but which was furnished me by a goldsmith of repute. Yesterday I learned that shares were offered at £10 each, perchance from the efforts of forstallers, as also from the preaching of a dissenter, who fulminates that the end of the world is but three weeks away, which hath induced great seriousness among the people. Unless you can pay me, therefore, as much as £40, on the morrow I shall be constrained to offer such shares to the highest bidder at the meeting of the guild.

The next letter is also from the same Mordecai Shylock, and is dated four days later.

Threadneedle Street, May 16, 1602.

To William Shakespeare:

My earnest epistle to thee of four days since having elicited no response, I did on the following day offer at the meeting of the Brokers' Guild some of the shares of the stock in the Globe pledged to me, and three shares were bidden at £9 each by my brother, Nehemiah Shylock. As I offered next all the rest, one Henry Wriothsley, Earl of Southampton, did ask to whom the shares belonged, and when he was enlightened, did straightway take all the shares and pay me the whole balance owing, and called me divers opprobrious names. I answered not his railing with railing, for sufferance is the badge of all our tribe, but such slander is illy bestowed on one who has been your friend for long, and who was but striving to avert his own destruction.

The next letter in order is from one William Kempe, who would seem to be the business manager of the Globe Theatre, or the person having in charge the unskilled labor connected with the playhouse.

Globe Playhouse, Employment Bureau
May 25, 1602

William Shakespeare:

In much tribulation do I write thee as to the contention which hath arisen among our stock actors and supes of the Globe. Nicholas Bottom, whom you brought from the Parish workhouse in Stratford, is in ill humor with thee in especial. He says when he played with you in Ben Jonson's comedy, "Every Man in His Humor," he was by far the better actor and did receive the plaudits of all; despite which he now receives but 6 shillings each week, while you are become a man of great wealth, having gotten, as he verily believes, as much as £100. Vainly did I oppose to him that the reason that you had money when he had none was in verity that you had labored when he was drunken, and that this was to his profit, since, had not you and the other holders of shares in the Globe saved somewhat of money, unthrifty groundlings of his ilk would starve, as there would be none to hire them at wages; but he avers that he is ground in the dust by the greed of capital, and hath so much prated of this that he hath much following, and accounteth himself a martyr. I said to him that at your especial order he was paid 6 shillings per week, which was double his worth, and that he should go elsewhere if he was not content, as I could daily get a better man for half his wages; but he will not go hence, nor will he perform, and has persuaded others to join with him, his very worthlessness having made him their leader, and they threaten, unless they receive additional 4 shillings per week, and a groat each night for sack, they will have no plays performed, nor will they allow others to be hired in their stead. They do further demand that you shall write shorter plays; that you shall write no tragedies requiring them to labor more than three hours in the rendition; that you shall cut out as much as twelve pages each in "Richard III" and "Othello," and fifteen pages from "Hamlet," that they may not labor to weariness, and may have more hours to recreation and improvement at the alehouse. I know not what to do. If I yield to their demands, nothing will be left for the owners of shares in the Globe; and if I do not, I fear mobs and riots. Fain would I receive thy counsel, which shall have good heed.

The next letter is the last in the period under review, and bears date four days later than the one just quoted from William Kempe.

At the Elephant & Magpie Inn, London, May 29, 1602
To William Shakespeare:

This is written to thee by John Lely, a clerk, in behalf of Nicholas Bottom, who useth not the pen, and who says to me to tell William Shakespeare, fie upon him that he did order the aforesaid Bottom to be locked out of the Globe Playhouse. Hath he forgotten the first play he, William Shakespeare, did ever write, to wit, "Pyramus and Thisbe," when a boy at Stratford, which was played by himself and Nicholas Bottom and Peter Quince and others, in a barn, for the delectation of the townsmen? And is not this same play a part of his "Midsummer Night's Dream," which beggarly play he did sell for £10, and hath not Nicholas Bottom first and always been an ass therein? Doth he refuse to render to Nicholas Bottom 10 shillings per week when he can get £10 or even £11 for a beggarly play, which is nought unless it be acted? Many a time hath he paid me from a sponging house; often hath he given me groats for sack, and for purges when sack hath undone me; and did I ever insult him to offer to repay him a penny? Say to him, remembereth he not when the horses ridden by Duncan and Macbeth upon the stage did break though the floor, who, affrightened, did run howling away, whereby Burbage was aroused and did pick him, William Shakespeare, from among the horses' feet and save his life? And now, sweet Will, fie upon thee that thou didst frown upon thy townsman. Delay not to send me sundry shillings for the publican, who believes you will discharge, as often before, my reckoning. This, and much more of like tenor, said Nicholas Bottom to William Shakespeare by your worship's humble servant,

John Lely.

The letters in the third period bear date in 1609, seven years later than those last quoted. the first is from Rev. Walter Blaise, who appears to be the clergyman at Stratford-on-Avon.

Stratford, Feb. 23, 1609.
To William Shakespeare:

John Naps, of Greece, who did recently return to his home here from London, safely has delivered to Anne, your wife, the package entrusted to him for carriage. As your wife hath not the gift of writing, she does desire that I convey to you her thanks for the sundry contents of the hamper. She hath also confided to me as her spiritual adviser that she did diligently ply John Naps with questions as to his visit to you in London, and that said John Naps, under her interrogatories, has revealed to her much that doth make her sick at heart and weary of life.

Item. He doth report that you do pass among men as a bachelor, and, with sundry players and men of that ilk, do frequent a house of entertainment kept by one Doll Tearsheet, and do kiss the barmaid and call her your sweetheart.

Item. He doth also report that you did give to the daughter of the publican at whose house you now abide, a ring of fine gold, and did also write to her a sonnet in praise of her eyebrows and her lips, and did otherwise wickedly disport with the said damsel.

Item. He doth further report of you that you did visit, with one Ben Jonson, on the Sabbath-day, a place of disrepute, where were cock-fights and the baiting of a bear, and that with you were two brazen women, falsely called by you the wife and sister of Ben Jonson.

These things did overmuch to grieve Anne, who hath been to you a loyal wife and a true, and she desires that you do forthwith renounce your evil ways and return to the new house at Stratford, and in ashes and sackcloth repent of your wanderings from the straight and narrow way.

Thus far I have spoken to you as the mouthpiece and vice-regent of Anne, your wife, who is in sore affliction and deep grief by reason of your transgressions. But, beloved lamb of my flock, I should be unworthy my high and sacred calling did I not lift up also my rebuking voice as a pelican in the wilderness, and adjure you to beware of concupiscence and fleshy lust, which unceasingly do war upon the human soul. Thinkest thou to touch pitch and remain undefiled?

The next letter is from the firm of Coke & Dogberry, lawyers in London.

INNER TEMPLE, March 8, 1609.

To WILLIAM SHAKESPEARE:

We have been retained by mistress Anne Page as her solicitors to bring against you an action, for that you have not fulfilled and in sooth cannot fulfil with her a contract of marriage, and to seek against you under the laws of this realm heavy damages and an imprisonment of the body, in that you have in unholy ways trifled with her affections, contrary to the statute in such cases provided. She especially avers that you did, two days before Michaelmas, swear to her on a parcel gilt goblet that you did love her alone, and did give her a bracelet of price. But yesterday, as she was bargaining with a yeoman named Christopher Sly, from Stratford, for the purchase of a spotted pig of his own fattening, the said Sly did reveal to her that you were his friend, and that you had a wife and children in your native town where he dwelt. We beg you to straightaway name to us your solicitors, that we may confer with them and attend to the issuance of the writs.

I have aimed to select from the letters sent me only those bearing on some trouble tending to cause sleeplessness on the part of the poet, but make an exception in case of a letter of Sir Walter Raleigh, next in chronological order, which refers to matters of general interest.

THE MERMAID, March 20, 1609
TO WILLIAM SHAKESPEARE:

Full well do I know, my dearest Will, that often hast thou wondered of the fate of thy £50, which, with a hundred times as much of mine own, was adventured to found an empire in America. Great were our hopes, both of glory and of gold, in the kingdom of Powhatan. But it grieves me to say that all hath resulted in infelicity, misfortune, and an unhappy end. Our ships were wrecked, or captured by the knavish Spaniards. Our brave soldiers are perished. As I was blameworthy for thy risk, I send by the messenger your £50, which you shall not lose by my over-hopeful vision. For its usance I send a package of a new herb from the Chesapeake, called by the natives tobacco. Make it not into tea, as did one of my kinsmen, but kindle and smoke it in the little tube the messenger will bestow. Be not deterred if thy gorge at first rises against it, for, when thou art wonted, it is a balm for all sorrows and griefs, and as a dream of Paradise. And now, my sweet Will, whom my soul loveth, why comest thou not as of yore to the "Mermaid," that I may have speech with thee? Thou knowest that from my youth up I have adventured all for the welfare and glory of our Queen Elizabeth. On sea and on land and in many climes have I fought the accursed Spaniards, and am honored by our sovereign and among men, and have won both gold and fame; but all this would I give, and more, for a tithe of the honor which in the coming time shall assuredly be thine. Thy kingdom is of the imagination, and therefore hath no limit or end. Thy wise sayings are ever with me. Thou art the "immediate jewel of my soul," as thyself hast written. When I am bruised with adversity, I remember thy saying, "He fighteth as one weary of his life," and my courage comes; and even when I consider the solemn end of all, and that I do march the way to dusty death, still, in thy words, do I hope for grace "by Christ's dear blood, shed for our grievous sins."

The next, and the last letter in the collection which seems to have a bearing upon the sleeplessness of Shakespeare, is also from Rev. Walter Blaise.

STRATFORD, April 3, 1609.
TO WILLIAM SHAKESPEARE:

Sir Thomas Lucy, who is in her Majesty's commission as a Justice of the Peace in this bailiwick, yesterday did inform me that he had been questioned from London if you were a married man, and if yes, when and to whom you were wedded. As the parish records are in my keeping, I could but bestow the information sought, although with great sinking of heart, as a well-wisher to you, who, though given overmuch to worldly frivolities and revels, yet are

a worthy citizen, and a charitable and a just. Greatly did I fear this knowledge was sought to thy injury. Hast thou led a blameless life, the gates of hell
shall not prevail against thee; but the wicked stand on slippery ways. Anne,
thy wife, to whom I did unbosom my fears, is in much tribulation lest thou
art unfaithful to thy marriage vows, and again beseeches me to urge thee to
come forth from wicked Babylon and dwell in thy pleasant home at Stratford. Thou art become a man of substance, and hast moneys at usury. I have
read of thy verses and plays, which, albeit somewhat given to lewdness, and
addressed to gain the favor of the baser sort, yet reveal thee to be a man of
understanding. I cannot, as it is rumored do some of thy town associates,
award thee the title of poet, which title is reserved for the shining ones; but
thou hast parts. There are many parish clerks, and even some curates in this
realm, scarcely more liberally endowed in mind than thou. But greatly do I
fear that thou art little better than one of the wicked. How hast thou put to
use this talent entrusted thee by the Master of the vineyard? In the maintenance of the things which profit not; in seeking the applause of the unworthy; in the writing of vain plays, which, if of the follies of youth, may be for-
given and remembered not against thee, provided in riper years you put behind
you these frivolities, and atone for the mischief thou hast wrought by rendering acceptable service to the Master; by coming to the help of the Lord
against the mighty. Gladly would I take thy training in charge, and guide thy
tottering feet along the flowery paths of Homiletics. Who knoweth into what
vessels the All-seeing One may elect to pour his spirit? Perchance in mercy
I may be spared to behold thee a faithful though humble preacher of the
Word. Anne, thy wife, often hath likened me to the great light upon a high
hill-top, shining in the darkness far away. I would not magnify my powers,
but not to all is it given to be mighty captains of a host. Yet, according to thy
gifts might thy work be, and a little candle shining in a darkened room hath
its place.

In light of these letters, some passages in "Richard III" and the "Com-
edy of Errors," written in the same year (1609), have an added significance.
In "Richard III," Glouster says to Anne:
Your beauty was the cause of the effect:
Your beauty that did haunt me in my sleep,
To undertake the death of all the world,
So I might live one hour in thy sweet bosom.
In the "Comedy of Errors," the Abbess says to Adriana:-
The venom clamors of a jealous woman
Poison more deadly than a mad dog's tooth.
It seems his sleep was hindered by thy railing.
· · · · · · · ·
In food, in sport, and in life-preserving rest

> To be disturbed, would mad or man or beast.
> The consequence is, then, thy jealous fits
> Have scared thy husband from the use of wits.

Note, too, the kindred thought:-

> Love hath chased sleep from my enthralled eyes.

And again this passage, called forth possibly by the letters of the Rev. Walter Blaise:-

> Slander,
> Whose edge is sharper than the sword; whose
> Tongue
> Outvenoms all the worms of Nile; whose breath
> Rides on the posting winds and doth belie
> All corners of the world.

As also then:-

> Do not, as some ungracious pastors do,
> Show me the steep and thorny way to heaven,
> Whiles, like a puffed and reckless libertine,
> Himself the primrose path of dalliance treads,
> And recks not his own rede.

From these several letters sufficiently appear the causes for the insomnia of Shakespeare, which are some of the same causes resulting in its prevalence today. They illustrate anew that history repeats itself forever; that humanity is always the same; that like temptations and errors come to men with like results in all the centuries; that the sleeplessness of Shakespeare came, because, merely as a matter of form, he had indorsed for a friend,—because he had bought more stocks than he could pay for, and when his margins were absorbed, came forth a shorn and shivering lamb,—because of the turbulence of labor,—because, alas! he too had been dazzled and bewildered by

> The light that lies
> In a woman's eyes.

Marvelous as were the endowments of the master, yet was he human and as one of us.

Chicago, 1886

Richard Garnett
(1835–1906)

While working his way from an assistant copying titles to the keeper of printed books for the British Museum, Richard Garnett developed an impressive reputation as both a librarian and a man of letters. Perhaps his greatest professional achievement during the forty-nine years he spent with the museum was his work on editing and printing the general catalogue. At the same time he was a prolific translator and poet, a frequent contributor to general interest and professional journals and magazines, and the author of biographies, literary history, and introductions to a broad range of books.

Building on a series of legends about Shakespeare's early days— his poaching, schoolteaching, and early efforts as a playwright at Kenilworth—Garnett's *William Shakespeare: Pedagogue and Poacher* (1904) develops a witty, scholarly view of the playwright's early life. Much of the fun of the piece is the way Garnett weaves into his characters' speeches lines and phrases from the plays, some perfectly fitting, others wildly ironic. In this scene, the last of the play, the young schoolteacher, in front of his students and their parents, finally has an opportunity to attack Sir Thomas Lucy for his petty tyrannies against the citizens of Stratford. The desperately alliterating Sir Thomas, who suspects Shakespeare of poaching not only in his park but in his marriage chamber as well, seeks the strictest possible revenge for fancied wrongs. Only a *deus ex regina* can save the young writer from the knight's wrath.

William Shakespeare: Pedagogue and Poacher

(1904)

ACT II SCENE III

[Interior of the Court House, filled by the Public. Sir Thomas Lucy on the Bench, Lady Lucy and Ann Shakespeare near him. Shakespeare standing in the dock, handcuffed. The Scholars sitting together outside the dock. The Fathers and Mothers opposite. Clerk of the Court, Constable, Attendants, and ushers. Moles leaving the witness box.]

FIRST FATHER [*Aside to the Clerk of the court*].
　　Master, was this well howled?
THE CLERK OF THE COURT.　　　　　　Most wolfishly.
THE MOTHER. How was the weeping?
THE CLERK OF THE COURT.　　　　　　Very laudable.
　　So Niobe bewept herself to stone,
　　And Thisbe wailed by Ninny's monument.
　　Now silent sit and hopefully expect
　　The glad enlargement of your erring sons.
THE CONSTABLE. Hush! hush! Sir Thomas rises.
THE CLERK OF THE COURT.　　　　　　Hush!
THE ATTENDANT AND USHERS.　　　　　　Hush!
THE PUBLIC.　　　　　　　　　　　　Hush!
SIR THOMAS LUCY. Friends and admirers, burgesses of Stratford!
　　So crammed the Court is with particulars,
　　More to adduce were superfluity.
　　Thou chiefly, Moles, another Androclus,
　　Hast plucked the prickle from the lion's paw,
　　And limping Justice bounds and roars again.
　　The Court knows what it knows, and what it knows not
　　It knows is immaterial to be known.
　　Yet of our equity, though but for form's sake,
　　We'll hear what the defendant has to say,
　　And if his speech do aggravate his guilt,
　　Will mark the advantage. Come, thou serpent, if
　　Thou hast justification, hiss it forth!
SHAKESPEARE. Sir Thomas, I plead guilty.

SIR THOMAS LUCY.   Hast thou aught
    Meet to be urged in mitigation?
SHAKESPEARE. Much, would the magistrate so deem it, but
    'Twere faggot to the furnace of his wrath.
LADY LUCY. Take heed, then, heat not thou the furnace sevenfold.
ANN SHAKESPEARE. William, be ruled, petition for a whipping.
SHAKESPEARE. I thank your Ladyship for your good counsel,
    Which Prudence bids me hearken, yet should Truth
    Upbraid me, did I miss the rare occasion
    To bring her and Sir Thomas face to face
    For confirmation of their crescive love.
    She bids me say, Sir Thomas, that yourself
    Create the fault you would chastize in me,
    And keep yourself a poacher's school, your scholars
    Men goaded into wrong by righteous anger
    At small oppressions, petty grievances,
    Affronts, contumelies, scarce perceived by him
    Who gives, to him who takes esil and wormwood.
    These spring, I know, from no embosomed malice,
    But thoughtlessness and heady vanity,
    And pride so swollen that his pursed-up eyes
    Perceive not that the peasant is a man,—
    Praise him, he beams content; prick him, he bleeds;
    Feed him, he guards your substance; starved, he steals it.
    Deem you that I had robbed you of your deer
    If you had taken nought from me and mine?
    Wrongful the deed, I own, worse the example.
    'Tis said, the world subsists by thievery.
    The sun's an arrant spoiler of the ocean,
    The moon conveys her pallid fire from him,
    And earth and water plunder one another.
    But you, Sir Thomas, rob both earth and water,
    And would the sun and moon too, could you grasp them.
    How many commons have you not devoured?
    What paths not barred? where erst the villager
    Was used to trip, but now slinks sullen, conscious
    Both of his trespass and your injury,
    And all for your game's sake. Far worse I deem it
    That vices not your own, but by you planted,
    Do eat into our honest English nature.
    For frankness roguery, for truth evasion,
    For pleasure in his lord's prosperity
    Envy and grudge, for honourable dealing

A settled purpose by sly practices
The scale unfairly weighted to adjust,
The fiend expelling by another fiend.
These cankers prey upon our England's blood,
Pray Heaven they bring not palsy. Would'st thou hearken
My friendly suasion, some kind passages,
Some acres of filched common given back,
Some paths unstopped, a courteous mien, the pressure
Of hand by toil made honourably rough,
Some gifts dispersed as duty, not as dole,
Some genial largesse from thy parks and warrens,
Some boons to recompense the ravaged crops,
Some mingling with the people's sports and pastimes,
And on the seat of justice, should'st thou strain
The letter of the law at all, indulgence—
Trust me, Sir Thomas, such slight condescensions
Would make thee, in thy sphere, as England's Queen,
Whose throne is builded on her people's hearts.
Now, did I tell this populace I took
Thy deer for public cause, they would acclaim me,
Shakespeare, the Robin Hood of Warwickshire.
I shall not tell them, 'twere but half the truth.
I am the people's poet, not their tribune.
Sport pointed me the way with beechen spear,
And Youth, too young to know what conscience is.
This is the head and front of my offending,
And fault it is that Time is ever mending.
No exculpation plead I for my crime,
Save the most brisk and giddy-paced time
Of this my twentieth year, and overplus
Of spirit frolicsome and venturous,
And sick and sorry heart that bade me roam
To shun the hell of an unquiet home,
And love of the wild creatures in their lairs,
And joy to match my wiliness with theirs;
And if these pleas avail not, here I stand
Ready to take my sentence at thy hand:
But not upon my boys thy vengeance wreak,
Branding them miscreants for a youthful freak.
SIR THOMAS LUCY. A goodly speech, well studied and well spoken;
    Be sure it shall avail to shape thy sentence.
LADY LUCY [*aside*]. Alas! his bosom swells with pent-up fury.
    It tears him as fire tears a thunder-cloud.

ANN SHAKESPEARE [*aside*]. If he deliver sentence in this fluster
  I'll have to nurse my William for a month:
  Which for his blessing overrule, kind Heaven.
SIR THOMAS LUCY. Not much this cause demands of subtlety;
  It needeth but discrimination.
  To lack which were impossibility
  For me, by edict of forecasting heaven
  Ordained to be a county magistrate.
  But when the judge accedes to passing sentence
  Light doth he need, and to be done to wit
  Touching the wretched culprit at the bar,
  His dispositions and his antecedents,
  And who should know them better than his wife?
  Stand forth, Ann Shakespeare.
ANN SHAKESPEARE.   At your honour's bidding.
SIR THOMAS LUCY. Speak to thy husband's character.
ANN SHAKESPEARE.   Great Sir,
  A good youth were he, were he not a poet,
  And were we not too nearly of an age,
  As to the Court is plainly visible.
LADY LUCY [*aside*]. O brazen hussey!
ANN SHAKESPEARE. Had I caught him younger,
  Much had I made of him, much yet will make,
  Will you by my persuasion rule your doom,
  And yoke Law's lion with my lamb of love.
SIR THOMAS LUCY. What chastisement deem'st thou most meet for him?
ANN SHAKESPEARE. The lash, grave Sir, but with such love and wisdom
  Attempered, that it smite nor less nor more
  Than needful for his subjugation
  To his much injured and most loving wife,
  But lay him gently on a restful couch
  For profitable hours of penitence,
  And colloquy with me, continuous tasting
  The medicated honey of my speech
  Like time, as half renews the dwindled moon,
  Replenishing her lamp with chilly fire.
  But do not, with mistaking kindness, fix
  The thirsty leech on his poor family.
  I will attend him, for he is my husband;
  Diet his sickness, for it is my office;
  And will have no attorney but myself.
LADY LUCY. O good Sir Thomas, send the man a-packing,
  And be we rid and quit of him, and bar
  The gate of his return with penalty.

SIR THOMAS LUCY. Dames, to your service I am held and bounden,
　　Not as mere judge, but by devoir of knighthood
　　Therein most happy, may I stead you both.
　　　　　　　　　　　　　　　　　[*To the Public*]
　　The Court hath listened to these ladies, urging
　　One exile, one the scourge. Ere they had spoken,
　　I leaned to neither, but imprisonment.
　　But rapt audition of their eloquence
　　Hath shocked my purpose, and myself I liken
　　To Dardan Paris when the heavenly three
　　Sought the Idaean mountain all unrobed,
　　Contending for the apple*. Could the shepherd
　　Have shared it among all, what ravages
　　Of devastation he had spared the world!
　　Trojaque nunc stares, Priamique arx alta maneres.
　　What Paris might not do, Sir Thomas may:
　　And being, like him, confronted with the charms
　　Of three most beauteous competitors,
　　Banishment, flagellation, durrance vile,
　　And not like him, corrupted with a bribe,
　　Or violently in my proper person
　　Enamoured of their most divine embraces,
　　I do award the apple unto all.
　　That is to say, Shakespeare shall first be whipped,
　　Imprisoned then till healed, then for three years
　　Exiled to distant shires, there to propound,
　　With carriage apt and speech mellifluous,
　　Strange doctrines unto country gentlemen.
ANN SHAKESPEARE. Shall I have license to attend my lord,
　　And piteously beweep his horrid scars,
　　And soothe with opiates and leniments,
　　And reprehend him for his sinfulness,
　　And read him printed piety, and touch
　　His spirit to fine issues? Intercede,
　　I supplicate your Ladyship.
SHAKESPEARE.　　　　　　　　　　　　Alas
　　For blind Authority beating with his staff
　　The child that would have led him! Thou, Sir Thomas,

Priam and Hecuba, the parents of Paris, believing a prophecy that their son would cause Troy's destruction, sent him to be exposed on Mt. Ida, where he was saved and raised by a shepherd. Athena, Hera, and Aphrodite selected him as their judge in a quarrel over the Apple of Discord which was inscribed "to the fairest."

Thinking to shame me in thy lady's sight,
Sham'st but thyself in mine. Thou may'st not touch
My spirit that can suffer and be strong.
LADY LUCY. I doubt Sir Thomas sleeps not well to-night.
My tongue is shorter than thy Anna's, William,
By a good yard, but yet methinks 'twill serve.
SIR THOMAS LUCY. Relieve our presence of the knave's pollution.
THE CONSTABLE. Sir Thomas, I'm afeard to touch the man.
Thou heardest? he hath a familiar spirit,
Perchance an impish sootikin, but haply
Tail-switching Lucifer, Hell's emperor.
SHAKESPEARE. Aye, man, I hold in fee ten thousand spirits,
And more can summon from the vasty deep,
Who at my word shall seize thy knight and thee,
And set bemocked upon the public stage,
Stuff for the humorous world's derision.
THE CONSTABLE. What did I tell your honour?
THE PUBLIC [*from the lower end of the Court*]. Place! give place!
A messenger from her dread Majesty!
[*Enter Leicester, muffied in a horseman's cloak, much splashed.*]
LADY LUCY. Bespattered is he all from head to foot.
Urgent must be his errand.
SIR THOMAS LUCY.   To foul treason,
Belike, it hath respect, or Papistry.
THE CONSTABLE [*aside*]. I'll free me of the Pope and Devil together,
Getting me from the Court.   [*Exit hastily.*]
SIR THOMAS LUCY [*to Leicester*]. Our loves and duties,
Like greyhounds straining in the leashes, fret
To know the cause of thy commanded speed,
That the effect may follow.
LEICESTER.   I have charge
To claim the body of one William Shakespeare.
SIR THOMAS LUCY. Shakespeare! Hath rumour of the man's malfeasance
Reached then the royal ear? deems our liege Lady
Whipping too good for him? If so, our sentence
Admits recast.
LEICESTER.   Thou grossly errest, Lucy.
SIR THOMAS LUCY. Lucy! Thou Lucyest me! Knave malapert!
But for her state and grandeur who hath sent thee
(Most unadvisedly, if it be lawful
In aught her Grace's prudence to impeach),
I would commit thee.
LEICESTER.   Lucy, thou art blind.

Can mere disguisement of a horseman's cloak,
And travel-stains conceal the Lord of Leicester?
[*Throws off the cloak and appears dressed in a rich suit.*]
THE PUBLIC. Leicester! The Earl!
SIR THOMAS LUCY.   O good my lord-
LEICESTER.   Sir Thomas,
     Conceive all said on thy part and on mine.
     Time rushes on, upsetting Compliment.
     Excuse be hushed, and my commission speeded
     By sight of William Shakespeare.
SIR THOMAS LUCY.   There he stands
     Manacled in the dock.
LEICESTER.   What his offence?
SIR THOMAS LUCY. Heading a band of youthful desperadoes,
     He burst the barrier of my parked domain,
     Designing my deer's death, and if unhindered
     By vassal's vigilance, had questionless
     Broken my lodge and kissed my keeper's daughter.
LEICESTER. Thy deer, thou sayest, he slew but in intention,
     And thou hast in intention punished him.
     I deem you quits. Now hearken my award.
     Know all, I, Robert Dudley, Earl of Leicester,
     Knight of the Garter, Privy Counsellor,
     General, Lord Lieutenant of the county,
     Having well weighted the case of William Shakespeare,
     And of his six alleged accomplices,
     The doom of the inferior magistrate [*Aside*]
     (Not knowing and not caring what it was),
     Do quash, annul, and make of none effect,
     As also the indictment, and all process
     Past, present, or to come. [*Applause in court.*] His manacles
     Unrivet, and provide him with a horse,
     For with him I must hie to Kenilworth,
     To London then, where princely grace awaits him.
[*The Public throng around Shakespeare, vying in taking off his manacles. The
Father and the Mother caress their sons, who receive them unfilially.*]
SIR THOMAS LUCY. Are things turned inside out? or upside down?
     Or doth the earth, from Atlas' shoulder slipt,
     Tumble amain unto destruction?
     The beam of royal favour gild his brow
     Who would have antlered mine! whose felon hands
     Are ruddy with the blood of my fat bucks!
LEICESTER. The beam of royal grace, Sir Thomas Lucy,

Alighteth where it will, and willeth oft
Light, where eclipse were fitter. Yet, methinks,
It hath not this time lit upon a dunghill,
But on the goodliest man in thy court, whom
Authentic signatures of Jove and Venus
Do so commend, he greatly overlooks
Thy little brief authority. No wonder
He claimed the freedom of thy park.

                        [*To Shakespeare.*]
                        This argues

A generous strain in thee, and lordly instincts.
Deer-killing came in with the Conqueror.
Hast any record of thy lineage?

SHAKESPEARE. An ancestor of mine, so please your Lordship,
In our third Henry's reign was high exalted.   [*Aside.*]
Upon the gallows.

LEICESTER.   Like lot shall be thine.

SHAKESPEARE [*aside*]. The Lord forbid!

LEICESTER.   If thou do justify

Opinion by her Majesty conceived
Of thy facetious wit and parts. She hath heard
A little toy of thine, a comedy
('Tis called, I think, The Taming of a Shrew)
Read by a maid of honour, thereunto
Moved, as I gather, by one Master Field,
Late of this town, who further doth attest
Actor with bard met happily in thee.
Nought now will serve but thou must post to Court.
This charge is mine, which I, the more to blazon
My zeal, and happily countermine the workings
Of burrowing Intrigue, my credit sapping,
Perform in person. Take immediate leave
Of mates and kindred, and away with me.

SHAKESPEARE. Sir Thomas, I will stand your friend at Court:
On two conditions, one that presently
You do unclose the path you stopped last Christmas:
Next, that although the noble Earl of Leicester
Your sentence doth annul, yet, by his favour,
Two parts revoked, you amplify the third,
And banish me from Stratford for ten years.

LEICESTER. What moveth thee to this?

SHAKESPEARE.   My Lady Lucy
Surmiseth shrewdly, so doth Mistress Shakespeare.

And I myself would set division
Between my past and future, signifying
The new life to be led. Too long I've lingered
In my dark morning hours, but, now the sun
Of regal favour rises on my path,
Needs must I follow this to glorious noonday,
And then, unto my native place reverting,
Which ne'er was aught but dear to me, or shall be,
There slowly through the golden hours declining
Will set in splendour, like the westering sun,
But, unlike him, in the same zone and region
Where origin I had.

LEICESTER.　　　　　　　　　　　　　　'Tis nobly spoken,
And know the Earl of Leicester for thy friend
Not less than her great Majesty, and able
To ope yet wider worlds to thee. The quarrel
'Twixt Spain and England draweth to a head,
And soon the world shall ring with it, and then
The Hollander and we in union vanquish,
Or separate perish. This we know, and soon
The verdant level and the slow canal
Shall bristle with our pikes, throb with our drums,
Stream with our banners, and reverberate
The thunder of our cannon. I shall fill
The regent's seat, and my imperious truncheon
Shall beck thee to my retinue, to gather
Stuff for thy art by practice of the world.
What various shapes shall crowd the tented field!
Soldier and sutler, merchant, peasant, spy;
Captains courageous, English amazons,
Whom deaths of lovers slain most treacherously
Impel to hurl the Dons to Devildom;
Dicer and cut-purse, page, groom, beggar, minstrel;
Courtesans, fortune-tellers, desperadoes;
Armourers and devisers of strange engines;
And knights too corpulent to fight or fly.
And other matter shalt thou find, arrays
Of marching hosts, pent cities, trenched leaguers,
Sallies, alarms, encounters, skirmishes,
Duels and deaths, and, chief of all, examples
Most noble, in whose brightness thou may'st sit,
And as an eagle preen thee in the sun,
Purging all soilure haply gathered here;

> For know, my nephew Sidney tends my person,
> Mirror of courtesy and chivalry.

SHAKESPEARE. My Lord, the grace and bounty of your Lordship
> Leave me so rapt, I scarce find breath and boldness
> For one petition, 'tis most necessary.

LEICESTER. Say on.

SHAKESPEARE. I humbly crave that, their breadwinner
> Absent by Majesty's command, my wife
> And tender infants lack not sustenance.

LEICESTER. Be this thy care, Sir Thomas, and bestow
> Rather excess than insufficiency.

SIR THOMAS LUCY. Angels and ministers of grace defend us!
> This vixen queen, this dam of demi-bastards,
> Bedrenched like Danae with golden showers
> Whose drops distil from mine own treasury!

LEICESTER. Tush, Lucy, thou must be conformable,
> Or else abide her Grace's high displeasure.
> Thy lady, prone to offices of love,
> Shall seek the spouse forlorn, and soothe her sadness,
> Making a sunshine in the shady place.

ANN SHAKESPEARE [aside]. How best to bar my doorway?

LADY LUCY [aside].   I will tell her
> Rare passages of gallantry at Court.

THE SCHOLARS. Huzza! our master fares to Court addrest.

SHAKESPEARE. Bearing his boys for ever in his breast.

FIRST FATHER. Good Master Shakespeare, there is no unkindness?

SHAKESPEARE. No, not a grain. Myself should crave excuse.
> But the high ardour of your mettled sons
> To race the roads of learning, did demand
> Curb, more than spur.

THE MOTHER.   I ever knew my boy a
> A prodigy.

THE FATHERS.   And so say all of us.

SHAKESPEARE. Well, Anna, shall we change a world together?

ANN SHAKESPEARE. Perdition catch my soul, but I do love thee!

SHAKESPEARE. Deem'st thou I know not this? Wer't otherwise,
> Stratford and I had long ago been strangers.
> My good thou did'st intend, and had'st effected,
> Had'st thou not been,—but better 'twere to spare thee
> Thy faults' unlovely catalogue. Now listen.
> I am steeled 'gainst wrath and hate, and heaven forefend
> The one offence for ever unforgiven.
> If thou envenomest my childrens' bosoms

'Gainst me unseen, with crimes imaginary
Slurring my name, with a depicted devil
Scaring the innocent eye that should have seen
The Father's image in the earthly parent,
Then, and then only, take my malison.
ANN SHAKESPEARE. Of this nought apprehend.
SHAKESPEARE.   'Tis passing well
                              [*Kisses her.*]
Fix thou thy appetence on things supernal;
Guide our fair children in the paths of virtue;
Cherish the harmless necessary cat,
Who will for my departure wring her hands;
Speak of me sometimes, rail at me but seldom;
So for ten years farewell.
    [*An Attendant enters and whispers to Leicester.*]
LEICESTER.   To horse! to horse!
        [*Exit with Shakespeare. The curtain falls.*]

George Bernard Shaw
(1856–1950)

At the heart of George Bernard Shaw's response to Shakespeare was a lifelong sense of rivalry. The critic who coined the term "Bardolatry" saw in Shakespeare a figure whose reputation limited his own and whose popularity challenged what he considered his own revolutionary vision of the social and moral roles of the theater: "Shakespeare … is to me one of the towers of the Bastille, and down he must come." (*Ellen Terry and Bernard Shaw: A Correspondence*, ed. Christopher St. John [London, 1931], p. 149)

While defining the earlier poet's limits in the preface to his *Caesar and Cleopatra*, Shaw acknowledges his view of their relative merits: "It will be said that these remarks can bear no other construction than an offer of my Caesar to the public as an improvement on Shakespeare's, and in fact, that is their precise purport." Yet he does admit, "I do not profess to write better plays." The Irish-born playwright believed his claim to superiority lay in his ideas and his purpose. Such comments form a constant note from the beginning to the end of his career, from his earliest drama reviews to his last comments in the brief puppet play "Shakes vs. Shav," which ends with Shaw claiming at least a temporary victory.

Shaw's play "Dark Lady of the Sonnets" reflects his attempt to demysticize Shakespeare with a comic *menage à trois* of a gently conceited poet, a mysteriously regal woman, and a jealously self-centered dark lady. As Shakespeare madly tries to copy memorable lines on his tablets, the two women attempt to deal with his idiosyncracies. The end of the play shifts to the work's real purpose, an argument for establishing a national theater. The program for "The Dark Lady" at the Haymarket Theatre on 24 November 1910 included his brief sketch, "A Dressing Room Secret." In the story Shakespeare's bust admits to characters dressed for a Shakespeare Ball that Iago and Lady Macbeth were among his failures. As he describes the development of his plays, accident plays a far greater role than intention.

"The Dark Lady of the Sonnets"
(1910)

Fin de siecle 15-1600. Midsummer night on the terrace of the Palace at Whitehall, overlooking the Thames. The Palace clock chimes four quarters and strikes eleven.

A beefeater on guard. A Cloaked Man approaches.

THE BEEFEATER. Stand. Who goes there? Give the word.

THE MAN. Marry! I cannot. I have clean forgotten it.

THE BEEFEATER. Then you cannot pass here. What is your business? Who are you? Are you a true man?

THE MAN: Far from it, Master Warder. I am not the same man two days together: sometimes Adam, sometimes Benvolio, and anon the Ghost.

THE BEEFEATER. [*recoiling*] A ghost! Angels and ministers of grace defend us!

THE MAN. Well said, Master Warder. With your leave I will set that down in writing; for I have a very poor and unhappy brain for remembrance. [*He takes out his tablets and writes.*] Methinks this is a good scene, with you on your lonely watch, and I approaching like a ghost in the moonlight. Stare not so amazedly at me; but mark what I say. I keep tryst here tonight with a dark lady. She promised to bribe the warder. I gave her the wherewithal: four tickets for the Globe Theatre.

THE BEEFEATER. Plague on her! She gave me two only.

THE MAN. [*detaching a tablet*] My friend: present this tablet, and you will be welcomed at any time when the plays of Will Shakespear are in hand. Bring your wife. Bring your friends. Bring the whole garrison. There is ever plenty of room.

THE BEEFEATER. I care not for these new-fangled plays. No man can understand a word of them. They are all talk. Will you not give me a pass for The Spanish Tragedy?

THE MAN. To see The Spanish Tragedy one pays, my friend. Here are the means. [*He gives him a piece of gold.*]

THE BEEFEATER. [*overwhelmed*] Gold! Oh, sir, you are a better pay-master than your dark lady.

THE MAN. Women are thrifty, my friend.

THE BEEFEATER. 'Tis so, sir. And you have to consider that the most open-handed of us must e'en cheapen that which we buy every day. This lady has to make a present to a warder nigh every night of her life.

THE MAN. [*turning pale*] I'll not believe it.

THE BEEFEATER. Now you, sir, I dare be sworn, do not hath ever done thus before? that she maketh occasions to meet other men?

THE BEEFEATER. Now the Lord bless your innocence, sir, do you think you are the only pretty man in the world? A merry lady, sir: a warm bit of stuff. Go to: I'll not see her pass a deceit on a gentleman that hath given me the first piece of gold I ever handled.

THE MAN. Master Warder: is it not a strange thing that we, knowing that all women are false, should be amazed to find out own particular drab no better than the rest?

THE BEEFEATER. Not at all, sir. Decent bodies, many of them.

THE MAN. [*intolerantly*] No. All false. All. If thou deny it, thou liest.

THE BEEFEATER. You judge too much by the Court, sir. There, indeed, you may say of frailty that its name is woman.

THE MAN. [*pulling out his tablets again*] Prithee say that again: that about frailty: the strain of music.

THE BEEFEATER. What strain of music, sir? I'm no musician, God knows.

THE MAN. There is music in your soul: many of your degree have it very notably. [*Writing*] "Frailty: thy name is woman!" [*Repeating it affectionately*] "Thy name is woman."

THE BEEFEATER. Well, sir, it is but four words. Are you a snapper-up of such unconsidered trifles?

THE MAN. [*eagerly*] Snapper—up of- [*he gasps*] Oh! Immortal phrase! [*He writes it down*]. This man is greater than I.

THE BEEFEATER. You have my lord Pembroke's trick, sir.

THE MAN. Like enough: he is my near friend. But what call you this trick?

THE BEEFEATER. Making sonnets by moonlight. And to the same lady too.

THE MAN. No!

THE BEEFEATER. Last night he stood here on your errand, and in your shoes.

THE MAN. Thou, too, Brutus? And I called him a friend!

THE BEEFEATER. 'Tis ever so, sir.

THE MAN. 'Tis ever so. 'Twas ever so. [*He turns away, overcome*]. Two Gentlemen of Verona! Judas! Judas!!

THE BEEFEATER. Is he so bad as that, sir?

THE MAN. [*recovering his charity and self-possession*] Bad? O no. Human, Master Warder, human. We call one another names when we are offended, as children do. That is all.

THE BEEFEATER. Ay, sir: words, words, words. Mere wind, sir. We fill our bellies with the east wind, sir, as the Scripture hath it. You cannot feed capon so.

THE MAN. A good cadence. By your leave [*He makes a note of it*].

THE BEEFEATER. What manner of thing is a cadence, sir? I have not heard of it.

THE MAN. A thing to rule the world with, friend.

THE BEEFEATER. You speak strangely, sir: no offence. But, an't like you, you are a very civil gentleman, and a poor man feels drawn to you, you being, as twere, willing to share your thought with him.

THE MAN. 'Tis my trade. But alas! the world for the most part will none of my thoughts.

[*Lamplight streams from the palace door as it opens from within.*]

THE BEEFEATER. Here comes your lady, sir. I'll to t'other end of my ward. You may een take your time about your business: I shall not return too suddenly unless my sergeant comes prowling round. 'Tis a fell sergeant, sir: strict in his arrest. Good een, sir, and good luck! [*He goes*].

THE MAN. "Strict in his arrest"! "Fell sergeant"! [*As if tasting a ripe plum*]. O-o-o-h! [*He makes a note of them*].

[*A cloaked Lady gropes her way from the palace and wanders along the terrace, talking in her sleep.*]

THE LADY. [*rubbing her hands as if washing them*] Out, damned spot. You will mall her with these cosmetics. God made you one face; and you make yourself another. Think of your grave, woman, not ever of being beautified. All the perfumes of Arabia will not whiten this Tudor hand.

THE MAN. "All the perfumes of Arabia"! "Beautified"! "Beautified"! a poem in a single word. Can this be my Mary? [*To the Lady*]. Why do you speak in a strange voice, and utter poetry for the first time? Are you ailing? You walk like the dead. Mary! Mary!

THE LADY. [*echoing him*] Mary! Mary! Who would have thought that woman to have had so much blood in her! Is it my fault that my counsellors put deeds of blood on me? Fie! If you were women you would have more wit than to stain the floor so foully. Hold not up her head so: the hair is false. I tell you yet again, Mary's buried: she cannot come out of her grave. I fear her not: these cats that dare jump into thrones though they be fit only for men's laps must be put away. What's done cannot be undone. Out, I say. Fie! a queen, and freckled!

THE MAN. [*shaking her arm*] Mary, I say: art asleep?

[*The Lady wakes; starts; and nearly faints. He catches her on his arm.*]

THE LADY. Where am I? What art thou?

THE MAN. I cry your mercy. I have mistook your person all this while. Methought you were my Mary: my mistress.

THE LADY. [*outraged*] Profane fellow: how do you dare?

THE MAN. Be not wroth with me, lady. My mistress is a marvelous proper woman. But she does not speak so well as you. "All the perfumes of Arabia"! That was well said: spoken with good accent and excellent discretion.

THE LADY. Have I been in speech with you here?

THE MAN. Why, yes, fair lady. Have you forgot it?

THE LADY. I have walked in my sleep.

THE MAN. Walk ever in your sleep, fair one; for then your words drop like honey.

THE LADY. [*with cold majesty*] Know you to whom you speak, sir, that you dare express yourself so saucily?

THE MAN. [*unabashed*] Not I, nor care neither. You are some lady of the Court, belike. To me there are but two sorts of women: those with excellent voices, sweet and low, and cackling hens that cannot make me dream. Your voice has all manner of loveliness in it. Grudge me not a short hour of its music.

THE LADY. Sir: you are overbold. Season your admiration for a while with—

THE MAN. [*holding up his hand to stop her*] "Season your admiration for a while—"

THE LADY. Fellow: do you dare mimic me to my face?

THE MAN. Tis music. Can you not hear? When a good musician sings a song, do you not sing it and sing it again till you have caught and fixed its perfect melody? "Season your admiration for a while": God! the history of man's heart is in that one word admiration. Admiration! [*taking up his tablets*] What was it? "Suspend your admiration for a space—"

THE LADY. A very vile jingle of esses. I said "Season your—"

THE MAN. [*hastily*] Season: ay, season, season, season. Plague on my memory, my wretched memory! I must een write it down. [*He begins to write, but stops, his memory failing him*]. Yet tell me which has the vile jingle? You said very justly: mine own caught even as my false tongue said it.

THE LADY. You said "for a space." I said "for a while."

THE MAN. "For a while" [*he corrects it*]. Good! [*Ardently*] And now be mine neither for a space nor a while, but for ever.

THE LADY. Odds my life! Are you by chance making love to me, knave?

THE MAN. Nay: tis you who have made the love: I but pour it out at your feet. I cannot but love a lass that sets such store by an apt word. Therefore vouchsafe, divine perfection of a woman—no: I have said that before somewhere; and the wordy garment of my love for you must be fire-new—

THE LADY. You talk too much, sir. Let me warn you: I am more accustomed to be listened to than preached at.

THE MAN. The most are like that that do talk well. But though you spake with the tongues of angels, as indeed you do, yet know that I am the king of words—

THE LADY. A king, ha!

THE MAN. No less. We are poor things, we men and women-

THE LADY. Dare you call me woman?

THE MAN. What nobler name can I tender you? How else can I love you? Yet you may well shrink from the name: have I not said we are but poor things? Yet there is a power that can redeem us.

THE LADY. Gramercy for your sermon, sir. I hope I know my duty.

THE MAN. This is no sermon, but the living truth. The power I speak of is the power of immortal poesy. For know that vile as this world is, and worms as we are, you have but to invest all this vileness with a magical garment of words to transfigure us and uplift our souls til earth flowers into a million heavens.

THE LADY. You spoil your heaven with your million. You are extravagant. Observe some measure in your speech.

THE MAN. You speak now as Ben does.

THE LADY. And who, pray, is Ben?

THE MAN. A learned bricklayer who thinks that the sky is at the top of his ladder, and so takes it on him to rebuke me for flying. I tell you there is no word yet coined and no melody yet sung that is extravagant and majestical enough for the glory that lovely words can reveal. It is heresy to deny it: have you not been taught that in the beginning was the Word? that the Word was with God? nay, that the Word was God?

THE LADY. Beware, fellow, how you presume to speak of holy things. The Queen is the head of the Church.

THE MAN. You are the head of my Church when you speak as you did at first. "All the perfumes of Arabia"! Can the Queen speak thus? They say she playeth well upon the virginals. Let her play so to me; and I'll kiss her hands. But until then you are my Queen; and I'll kiss those lips that have dropt music on me heart. [*He puts his arms about her*].

THE LADY. Unmeasured impudence! On your life, take your hands from me.

[*The Dark Lady comes stooping along the terrace behind them like a running thrush. When she sees how they are employed, she rises angrily to her full height, and listens jealously.*]

THE MAN. [*unaware of the Dark Lady*] Then cease to make my hands tremble with the streams of life you pour through them. You hold me as the lodestar holds the iron: I cannot but cling to you. We are lost, you and I: nothing can separate us now.

THE DARK LADY. We shall see that, false lying hound, you and your filthy trull. [*With two vigorous cuffs, she knocks the pair asunder, sending the man, who is unlucky enough to receive the righthanded blow, sprawling on the flags*]. Take that, both of you!

THE CLOAKED LADY. [*in towering wrath, throwing off her cloak and turning in outraged majesty on her assailant*] High treason!

THE DARK LADY. [*recognizing her, and falling on her knees in abject terror*] Will: I am lost: I have struck the Queen.

THE MAN. [*sitting up as majestically as his ignominious posture allows*] Woman: you have struck WILLIAM SHAKESPEAR!!!!!!

QUEEN ELIZABETH. [*stupent*] Marry, come up!!! Struck William Shakespeare quotha! And who in the name of all the sluts and jades and light-o'-loves and fly-by-nights that infest this palace of mine, may William Shakespeare be?

THE DARK LADY. Madam: he is but a player. Oh, I could have my hand cut off—

QUEEN ELIZABETH. Belike you will, mistress. Have you bethought you that I am like to have your head cut off as well?

THE DARK LADY. Will: save me. Oh, save me.

ELIZABETH. Save you! A likely savior, on my royal word! I had thought this fellow at least an esquire; for I had hoped that even the vilest of my ladies would not have dishonored my Court by wantoning with a baseborn servant.

SHAKESPEAR. [*indignantly scrambling to his feet*] Baseborn! I, a Shakespear of Stratford! I, whose mother was Arden! baseborn! You forget yourself, madam.

ELIZABETH. [*furious*] S'blood! do I so? I will teach you-

THE DARK LADY. [*rising from her knees and throwing herself between them*] Will: in God's name anger her no further. It is death. Madam: do not listen to him.

SHAKESPEAR. Not were it e'en to save your life, Mary, not to mention my own, will I flatter a monarch who forgets what is due my family. I deny not that my father was brought down to be a poor bankrupt; but 'twas his gentle blood that was ever too generous for trade. Never did he disown his debts. 'Tis true he paid them not; but it is an attested truth that he gave bills for them; and 'twas those bills, in the hands of base hucksters, that were his undoing.

ELIZABETH. [*grimly*] The son of your father shall learn his place in the presence of the daughter of Harry the Eighth.

SHAKESPEAR. [*swelling with intolerant importance*] Name not that inordinate man in the same breath with Stratford's worthiest alderman. John Shakespear married but once: Harry Tudor was married six times. You should blush to utter his name.

THE DARK LADY. Will: for pity's sake-

(CRYING OUT TOGETHER)

ELIZABETH. Insolent dog-

SHAKESPEAR. [*cutting them short*] How know you that King Harry was indeed your father?

ELIZABETH. Zounds! Now by—[*she stops to grind her teeth with rage*].

THE DARK LADY. She will have me whipped through the streets. Oh God! Oh God!

SHAKESPEAR. Learn to know yourself better, madam. I am an honest gentleman of unquestioned parentage, and have already sent in my demand for the coat-of-arms that is lawfully mine. Can you say that much for yourself?

ELIZABETH. [*almost beside herself*] Another word; and I begin with my own hands the work the hangman shall finish.

SHAKESPEAR. You are no true Tudor: this baggage here has as good a right to your royal seat as you. What maintains you on the throne of England? Is it your renowned wit? your wisdom that sets at nought the craftiest statesmen of the Christian world? No. 'Tis the mere chance that might have happened to any milkmaid, the caprice of Nature that made you the most wondrous piece of beauty the age hath seen. [*Elizabeth's raised fists, on the point of striking him, fall to her side*]. That is what hath brought all men to your feet, and founded your throne on the impregnable rock of your proud heart, a stony island in a sea of desire. There, madam, is some wholesome blunt honest speaking of you. Now do your worst.

ELIZABETH. [*with dignity*] Master Shakespear: it is well for you that I am a merciful prince. I make allowance for your rustic ignorance. But remember that there are things which be true, and yet not seemly to be said (I will not say to a queen; for you will have it that I am none) but to a virgin.

SHAKESPEAR. [*bluntly*] It is no fault of mine that you are a virgin, madam, albeit tis my misfortune.

THE DARK LADY. [*terrified again*] In mercy, madam, hold no further discourse with him. He hath ever some lewd jest in his tongue. You hear how he useth me! calling me baggage and the like to your Majesty's face.

ELIZABETH. As for you, mistress, I have yet to demand what your business is at this hour in this place, and how you come to be so concerned with a player that you strike blindly at your sovereign in jealousy of him.

THE DARK LADY. Madam: as I live and hope for salvation-

SHAKESPEAR. [*sardonically*] Ha!

THE DARK LADY. [*angrily*]—ay, I'm as like to be saved as thou that believest naught save some black magic of words and verses—I say, madam, as I am a living woman I came here to break with him for ever. Oh, madam, if you would know what misery is, listen to this man that is more than man and less at the same time. He will tie you down to anatomize your very soul: he will wring tears of blood from your humiliation; and then he will heal the wound with flatteries that no woman can resist.

SHAKESPEAR. Flatteries! [*kneeling*] Oh, madam, I put my case at your royal feet. I confess to much. I have a rude tongue: I am unmannerly; I blaspheme against the holiness of anointed royalty; but oh, my royal mistress, AM I a flatterer?

ELIZABETH. I absolve you as to that. You are far too plain a dealer to please me. [*He rises gratefully*].

THE DARK LADY. Madam: he is flattering you even as he speaks.

ELIZABETH. [*a terrible flash in her eye*] Ha! Is it so?

SHAKESPEAR. Madam: she is jealous; and, heaven help me! not without reason. Oh, you say you are a merciful prince; but that was cruel of you, that hiding of your royal dignity when you found me here. For how can I ever be content with this black-haired, black-eyed, black-avised devil again now that I have looked upon real beauty and real majesty?

THE DARK LADY. [*wounded and desperate*] He hath sworn to me ten times over that the day shall come in England when black women, for all their foulness, shall be more thought on than fair ones. [*To Shakespear, scolding at him*] Deny it if thou canst. Oh, he is compact of lies and scorns. I am tired of being tossed up to heaven and dragged down to hell at every whim that takes him. I am ashamed to my very soul that I deemed him fit to hold my stirrup—one that will talk to all the world about me—that will put my love and my shame into his plays and make me blush for myself there—that will write sonnets about me that no man of gentle strain would put his hand to. I am disordered: I know not what I am saying to your Majesty: I am of all ladies most deject and wretched—

SHAKESPEAR. Ha! At last sorrow hath struck a note of music out of thee. "Of all ladies most deject and wretched." [*He makes a note of it*].

THE DARK LADY. Madam: I implore you give me leave to go. I am distracted with grief and shame. I—

ELIZABETH. Go [*The Dark Lady tries to kiss her hand*]. No more. Go. [*the Dark Lady goes, convulsed*]. You have been cruel to that poor fond wretch, Master Shakespear.

SHAKESPEAR. I am not cruel, madam; but you know the fable of Jupiter and Semele. I could not help my lightnings scorching her.

ELIZABETH. You have an overweening conceit of yourself, sir, that displeases your Queen.

SHAKESPEAR. Oh, madam, can I go about with the modest cough of a minor poet, belittling my inspiration and making the mightiest wonder of your reign a thing of nought? I have said that "not marble nor the gilded monuments of princes shall outlive" the words with which I make the world glorious or foolish at my will. Besides, I would have you think me great enough to grant me a boon.

ELIZABETH. I hope it is a boon that may be asked of a virgin Queen without offense, sir. I mistrust your forwardness; and I bid you remember that I do not suffer persons of your degree (if I may say so without offense to your father the alderman) to presume too far.

SHAKESPEAR. Oh, madam, I shall not forget myself again; though by my life, could I make you a serving wench, neither a queen nor a virgin should you be for so much longer as a flash of lightning might take to cross the river to the Bankside. But since you are a queen and will none of me, nor of Philip of Spain, nor of any other mortal man, I must een contain myself as best I may, and ask you only for a boon of State.

ELIZABETH. A boon of State already! You are becoming a courtier like the rest of them. You lack advancement.

SHAKESPEAR. "Lack advancement." By your Majesty's leave: a queenly phrase. [*He is about to write it down*].

ELIZABETH. [*striking the tablets from his hand*] Your tables begin to anger me, sir. I am not here to write your plays for you.

SHAKESPEAR. You are here to inspire them, madam. For this, among the rest, were you ordained. But the boon I crave is that you do endow a great playhouse, or, if I may make bold to coin a scholarly name for it, a National Theatre, for the better instruction and gracing of your Majesty's subjects.

ELIZABETH. Why, sir, are there not theatres enow on the Bankside and in Blackfriars?

SHAKESPEAR. Madam: these are the adventures of needy and desperate men that must, to save themselves from perishing of want, give the sillier sort of people what the best like; and what they best like, God knows, is not their own betterment and instruction, as we well see by the example of the churches, which must needs compel men to frequent them, though they be open to all without charge. Only when there is a matter of murder, or a plot, or a pretty youth in petticoats, or some naughty tale of wantonness, will your subjects pay the great cost of good players and their finery, with a little profit to boot. To prove this I will tell you that I have written two noble and excellent plays setting forth the advancement of women of high nature and fruitful industry even as your Majesty is: the one a skilful physician, the other a sister devoted to good works. I have also stole from a book of idle wanton tales two of the most damnable foolishnesses in the world, in the one of which a woman goeth in a man's attire and maketh impudent love to her swain, who pleaseth her wit by saying endless naughtinesses to a gentleman as lewd as herself. I have writ these to save my friends from penury, yet shewing my scorn for such follies and for them that praise them by calling the one "As You Like It," meaning that it is not as I like it, and the other "Much Ado About Nothing," as it truly is. And now these two filthy pieces drive their nobler fellows from the stage, where indeed I cannot have my lady physician presented at all, she being too honest a woman for the taste of the town. Wherefore I humbly beg your Majesty to give order that a theatre be endowed out of the public revenue for the playing of those pieces of mine which no merchant will touch, seeing that his gain is so much greater with the worse than with the better. Thereby you shall also encourage other men to undertake the writing of plays who do now despise it and leave it wholly to those whose counsels will work little good to your realm. For this writing of plays is a great matter, forming as it does the minds and affections of men in such sort that whatsoever they see done in show on the stage, they will presently be doing in earnest in the world, which is but a larger stage. Of late, as you know, the Church taught the people by means of plays; but the people flocked only to such as were full of superstitious miracles and bloody martyrdoms; and so the Church, which also was just then brought into straits by the policy of your royal father, did abandon and discountenance the art of playing; and thus it fell into the hands of poor players and greedy merchants that had their pockets to look to and not the greatness of this your kingdom. Therefore now must your Majesty take up that good work that your Church hath abandoned, and restore the art of playing to its former use and dignity.

ELIZABETH. Master Shakespear: I will speak of this matter to the Lord Treasurer.

SHAKESPEAR. Then am I undone, madam; for there was never yet a Lord Treasurer that could find a penny for anything over and above the necessary expenses of your government, save for a war or salary for his own nephew.

ELIZABETH. Master Shakespear: you speak sooth; yet cannot I in any wise mend it. I dare not offend my unruly Puritans by making so lewd a place as the playhouse a public charge; and there be a thousand things to be done in this London of mine before your poetry can have its penny from the general purse. I tell thee, Master Will, it will be three hundred years and more before my subjects learn that a man cannot live by bread alone, but every word that cometh from the mouth of those whom God inspires. By that time you and I will be dust beneath the feet of the horses, if indeed there be any horses then, and men be still riding instead of flying. Now it may be that by then your works will be dust also.

SHAKESPEAR. They will stand, madam: fear not for that.

ELIZABETH. It may prove so. But of this I am certain (for I know my countrymen) that until every other country in the Christian world, even to barbarian Muscovy and the hamlets of the boorish Germans, have its playhouse at the public charge, England will never adventure. And she will adventure then only because it is her desire to be ever in the fashion, and do humbly and dutifully whatso she seeth everybody else doing. In the meantime you must content yourself as best you can by the playing of those two pieces which you give out as the most damnable ever writ, but which your countrymen, I warn you, will swear are the best you have ever done. But this will I say, that if I could speak across the ages to our descendants, I should heartily recommend them to fulfil your wish; for the Scottish minstrel hath well said that he that maketh the songs of a nation is mightier than he that maketh its laws; and the same may well be true of plays and interludes. [*The clock chimes the first quarter. The warder returns on his round*]. And now, sir, we are upon the hour when it better beseems a virgin queen to be abed than to converse alone with the naughtiest of her subjects. Ho there! Who keeps ward on the queen's lodgings tonight?

THE WARDER. I do, an't please your majesty.

ELIZABETH. See that you keep it better in future. You have let pass a most dangerous gallant even to the very door of our royal chamber. Lead him forth; and bring me word when he is safely locked out; for I shall scarce dare disrobe until the palace gates are between us.

SHAKESPEAR. [*kissing her hand*] My body goes through the gate into the darkness, madam; but my thoughts follow you.

ELIZABETH. How! to my bed!

SHAKESPEAR. No, madam, to your prayers, in which I beg you to remember my theatre.

ELIZABETH. That is my prayer to posterity. Forget not your own to God; and so goodnight, Master Will.

SHAKESPEAR. Goodnight, great Elizabeth. God save the Queen!

ELIZABETH. Amen.

(*Exeunt severally: she to her chamber: he, in custody of the warder, to the gate nearest Blackfriars.*)

"A Dressing Room Secret"
(1910)

It was trying-on day; and the last touches were being given to the costumes for the Shakespear Ball as the wearers faced the looking-glass at the costumiers.

"It's no use," said Iago discontentedly. "I don't look right; and I don't feel right."

"I assure you, sir," said the costumier: "you are a perfect picture."

"I may look a picture," said Iago; "but I don't look the character."

"What character?" said the costumier.

"The character of Iago, of course. My character."

"Sir," said the costumier: "shall I tell you a secret that would ruin me if it became known that I betrayed it?"

"Has it anything to do with the dress?"

"It has everything to do with it, sir."

"Then fire away."

"Well, sir, the truth is, we cannot dress Iago in character, because he is not a character."

"Not a character! Iago not a character! Are you mad? Are you drunk? Are you hopelessly illiterate? Are you imbecile? Or are you simply blasphemous?"

"I know it seems presumptuous, sir, after so many great critics have written long chapters analyzing the character of Iago: that profound, complex, enigmatic creation of our greatest dramatic poet. But if you notice, sir, nobody has ever had to write long chapters about my character."

"Why on earth should they?"

"Why indeed, sir! No enigma about me. No profundity. If my character was much written about, you would be the first to suspect that I hadn't any."

"If that bust of Shakespear could speak," said Iago, severely, "it would ask to be removed at once to a suitable niche in the facade of the Shakespear Memorial National Theatre, instead of being left here to be insulted."

"Not a bit of it," said the bust of Shakespear. "As a matter of fact, I can speak. It is not easy for a bust to speak; but when I hear an honest man rebuked for talking common sense, even the stones would speak. And I am only plaster."

"This is a silly trick," gasped Iago, struggling with the effects of the start the Bard had given him. "You have a phonograph in that bust. You might at least have made it a blank verse phonograph."

"On my honor, sir," protested the pale costumier, all disordered "not a word has ever passed between me and that bust—I beg pardon, me and Mr. Shakespear—before this hour."

"The reason you cannot get the dress and the makeup right is very simple," said the bust. "I made a mess of Iago because villains are such infernally dull and disagreeable people that I never could go through with them. I can stand five minutes of a villain, like Don John in—in—oh, what's its name?—you know—that box office play with the comic constable in it. But if it had to spread a villain out and make his part a big one, I always ended, in spite of myself, by making him rather a pleasant sort of chap. I used to feel very bad about it. It was all right as long as they were doing reasonably pleasant things; but when it came to making them commit all sorts of murders and tell sorts of lies and do all sorts of mischief, I felt ashamed. I had no right to do it."

"Surely," said Iago, "you don't call Iago a pleasant sort of chap!"

"One of the most popular characters on stage," said the bust.

"Me!" said Iago, stupent.

The bust nodded, and immediately fell on the floor on its nose, as the sculptor had not balanced it for nodding.

The costumier rushed forward, and, with many apologies and solicitous expressions of regret, dusted the Bard and replaced him on his pedestal, fortunately unbroken.

"I remember the play you were in," said the bust, quite undisturbed by its misadventure. "I let myself go on the verse: thundering good stuff it was: you could hear the souls of the people crying out in the mere sound of the lines. I didn't bother about the sense—just flung about all the splendid words I could find. Oh, it was noble, I tell you: drums and trumpets; and the Propontick and the Hellespont; and a malignant and a turbaned Turk in Aleppo; and eyes that dropt tears as fast as the Arabian trees their medicinal gum: the most impossible, far-fetched nonsense; but such music! Well, I started that play with two frightful villains, one male and one female."

"Female!" said Iago. "You forget. There is no female villain in Othello."

"I tell you there's no villain at all in it," said the immortal William. "But I started with a female villain."

"Who?" said the costumier.

"Desdemona, of course," replied the Bard. "I had tremendous notion of a supersubtle and utterly corrupt Venetian lady who was to drive Othello to despair by betraying him. It's all in the first act. But I weakened on it. She turned amiable on my hands, in spite of me. Besides, I saw that it wasn't necessary—that I could get a far more smashing effect by making her quite innocent. I yielded to that temptation: I never could resist an effect. It was sin against human nature; and I was well paid out; for the change turned the play into a farce."

"A farce!" exclaimed Iago and the costumier simultaneously, unable to believe their ears. "Othello a farce!"

"Nothing else," said the bust dogmatically. "You think a farce is a play in which some funny rough-and-tumble makes the people laugh. That's only your ignorance. What I call a farce is a play in which the misunderstandings are not natural but mechanical. By making Desdemona a decent poor devil of an honest woman, and Othello a really superior sort of man, I took away all natural reason for his jealousy. To make the situation natural I must either have made her a bad woman as I originally intended, or him a jealous, treacherous, selfish man, like Leontes in The Tale. But I couldn't belittle Othello that way; so, like a fool, I belittled him the other way by making him the dupe of a farcical trick with a handerkerchief that wouldn't have held water off the stage for five minutes. That's why the play is no use with a thoughtful audience. It's nothing but wanton mischief and murder. I apologize for it; though, by Jingo! I should like to see any of your modern chaps write anything half so good."

"I always said that Emilia was the real part for the leading lady," said the costumier.

"But you didn't change your mind about me," pleaded Iago.

"Yes I did," said Shakespear. "I started on you with a quite clear notion of drawing the most detestable sort of man I know: a fellow who goes in for being frank and genial, unpretentious and second rate, content to be a satellite of men with more style, but who is loathsomely coarse, and has that stupid sort of selfishness that makes a man incapable of understanding the mischief his dirty tricks may do, or refraining from them if there is the most wretched trifle to be gained by them. But my contempt and loathing for the creature—what was worse, the intense boredom of him—beat me before I got to the second act. The really true and natural things he said were so sickeningly coarse that I couldn't go on fouling my play with them. He began to be witty and clever in spite of me. Then it was all up. It was "Richard III" over again. I made him a humorous dog. I went further: I gave him my own divine contempt for the follies of mankind and for himself, instead of his own proper infernal envy of man's divinity. That sort of thing was always happening to me. Some plays it improved; but it knocked the bottom out of "Othello." It doesn't amuse really sensitive people to see a woman strangled by mistake. Of course some people would go anywhere to see a woman strangled, mistake or no mistake; but such riff-raff are no use to me, though their money is as good as anyone else's."

The bust, whose powers of conversation were beginning to alarm the costumier, hard pressed as he was for time, was about to proceed when the door flew open and Lady Macbeth rushed in. As it happened, she was Iago's wife; so the costumier did not think it necessary to remind her that this was the gentlemen's dressing room. Besides she was a person of exalted social station;

and he was so afraid of her that he did not even venture to shut the door lest such an action might seem to imply a rebuke to her for leaving it open.

"I feel quite sure this dress is all wrong," she said. "They keep telling me I'm a perfect picture; but I don't feel a bit like Lady Macbeth."

"Heaven forbid you should, madam!" said the costumier. "We can change your appearance, but not your nature."

"Nonsense!" said the lady: "my nature changes with every new dress I put on. Goodness Gracious, what's that?" she exclaimed, as the bust chuckled approvingly.

"It's the bust," said Iago. "He talks like the one o'clock. I really believe it's the old man himself."

"Rubbish!" said the lady. "A bust can't talk."

"Yes it can," said Shakespear. "I am talking; and I am a bust."

"But I tell you you can't," said the lady: "it's not good sense."

"Well, stop me if you can," said Shakespeare. "Nobody ever could in Bess's time."

"Nothing will ever make me believe it," said the lady. "It's mere medieval superstition. But I put it to you, do I look in this dress as I could commit a murder?"

"Don't worry about it," said the Bard. "You are another of my failures. I meant Lady Mac to be something really awful; but she turned into my wife, who never committed a murder in her life—at least not a quick one."

"Your wife! Ann Hathaway! Was she like Lady Macbeth?"

"Very," said Shakespear, with conviction. "If you notice, Lady Macbeth had only one consistent characteristic, which is, that she thinks everything her husband does is wrong and that she can do it better. If I'd ever murdered anybody she'd have bullied me for making a mess and gone upstairs to improve it herself. Whenever we gave a party, she apologized to the company for my behavior. Apart from that, I defy you to find any sort of sense in Lady Macbeth. I couldn't conceive anybody murdering a man like that. All I could do when it came to the point was just to brazen it out that she did it, and then give her a little touch of nature or two—from Ann—to make people believe she was real."

"I am disillusioned, disenchanted, disgusted," said the lady. "You might at least held your tongue about it until after the Ball."

"You ought to think the better of me for it," said the bust. "I was really a gentle creature. It was so awful to be born about ten times as clever as anyone else—to like people and yet to have to despise their vanities and illusions. People are such fools, even the most likeable ones, as far as brains go. I wasn't cruel enough to enjoy my superiority."

"Such conceit!" said the lady, turning her nose.

"What's a man to do?" said the Bard. "Do you suppose I could go round pretending to be an ordinary person?"

"I believe you have no conscience," said the lady. "It has often been noticed."

"Conscience!" cried the bust. "Why, it spoilt my best character. I started to write a play about Henry V. I wanted to show him in his dissolute youth; and I planned a very remarkable character, a sort of Hamlet sowing his wild oats, to be always with the Prince, pointing the moral and adorning the tale— excuse the anachronism: Dr. Johnson, I believe: the only man that ever wrote anything sensible about me. Poins was the name of this paragon. Well, if you'll believe me, I had hardly got well into the play when a wretched super whom I intended for a cowardly footpad just to come on in a couple of scenes to rob some merchant and then to be robbed himself by the Prince an Poins— a creature of absolutely no importance—suddenly turned into a magnificent reincarnation of Silenus, a monumental comic part. He killed Poins; he killed the whole plan of the play. I revelled in him, wallowed in him; made a delightful little circle of disreputable people for him to move and shine in. I felt sure that no matter how many other characters might go back on me, he never would. But I reckoned with my conscience. One evening, as I was walking through Eastcheap with a young friend (a young man with his life before him), I passed a fat old man, half drunk, leering at a woman who ought to have been young but wasn't. The next moment my conscience was saying in my ear: 'William: is this funny?' I preached at my young friend until he pretended he had an appointment and left me. Then I went home and spoilt the end of the play. I didn't do it well. I couldn't do it right. But I had to make that old man perish miserably; and I had to hang his wretched parasites or throw them into the gutter and the hospital. One should think before one begins things of this sort. By the way, would you mind shutting the door? I am catching cold."

"So sorry," said the lady. "My fault." And she ran to the door and shut it before the costumier could anticipate her.

Too late.

"I am going to sneeze," said the bust; "and I don't know that I can."

With an effort it succeeded just a little in retracting its nostrils and screwing up its eyes. A fearful explosion followed. Then the bust lay in fragments on the floor.

It never spoke again.

Maurice Baring
(1874–1945)

When Maurice Baring published "The Rehearsal" as one of his
gently satiric *Diminutive Dramas* in 1911, he had already established
a distinguished reputation as a foreign correspondent after a brief
career in England's foreign service. During the next three decades he
continued as a correspondent and playwright, served as an officer in
the Royal Air Force, and became a popular translator, poet, biographer and novelist. All of his works reflect his broad but unpretentious learning, deep awareness of and sympathy for human foibles,
and light touches of humor.

Baring's military service during the First World War earned
him an O.B.E., an honorary commission as an Air Force Wing Com-
mander, and an appointment to the Legion of Honour. After the war
his poems about it proved popular, as did such novels as *C* (1924),
Cat's Cradle (1926), and *In My End Is My Beginning* (1931). A friend
of Gilbert Keith Chesterton and Hillaire Belloc, he shared their interest in religion and history and their concern with moral and social
values. "The Rehearsal," with its comic insights into the psychology
of the theater, reflects his awareness of both the possibilities of language and the dynamics of human relationships.

"The Rehearsal"
(1911)

Characters

Mr. William Shakespeare

The Producer

The Stage Manager

Mr. Burbage (Macbeth)

Mr. Hughes (Lady Macbeth)

Mr. Kydd (Banquo)

Mr. Foote (Macduff)

Mr. Thomas (The Doctor)

Mr. Lyle (First Witch)

Second Witch

Third Witch

SCENE. The Globe Theater, 1606. On the stage the Author, the Producer, and the Stage Manager are standing. A rehearsal of "Macbeth" is about to begin. Waiting in the wings are the actors who are playing the Witches, Banquo, Macduff, etc. They are all men.

THE STAGE MANAGER. We'd better begin with the last act.

THE PRODUCER. I think we'll begin with the first act. We've never done it all through yet.

THE STAGE MANAGER. Mr. Colman isn't here. It's no good doing the first act without Duncan.

THE PRODUCER. Where is Mr. Colman? Did you let him know about rehearsal?

THE STAGE MANAGER. I sent a messenger to his house at Gray's Inn.

THE FIRST WITCH. Mr. Colman is playing Psyche in a masque at Kenilworth. He won't be back until the day after tomorrow.

THE PRODUCER. That settles it. We'll begin at the fifth act.

THE FIRST WITCH. Then I suppose I can go.

THE SECOND & THIRD WITCHES. And I suppose we needn't wait.

THE STAGE MANAGER. Certainly not. We're going on to the fourth act as soon as we've done the fifth.

BANQUO. But I suppose you don't want me.

THE STAGE MANAGER. And what about your ghost entrance in Act Four? We must get the business right this time; besides, we'll do the second act if we have time. Now, Act Five, Mr. Thomas and Mr. Bowles please.

THE FIRST WITCH. Mr. Bowles can't come to-day. He told me to tell you. He's having a tooth pulled out.

THE STAGE MANAGER. Then you will read the waiting gentlewoman's part, Mr. Lyle. You can take this script. [*The First Witch takes the script.*] Where is Mr. Thomas?

THE FIRST WITCH. He said he was coming.

THE STAGE MANAGER. We can't wait. I'll read his part. We'll leave out the beginning and just give Mr. Hughes his cue.

THE FIRST WITCH. [*reading*] "Having no witness to confirm my speech."

THE STAGE MANAGER. Mr. Hughes.

THE FIRST WITCH. He was here a moment ago.

THE STAGE MANAGER. [*louder*] Mr. Hughes.

> *Enter* Lady Macbeth (*Mr. Hughes, a young man about twenty-four.*)

LADY MACBETH. Sorry.

> [*He comes on down some steps L.C.*]

THE PRODUCER. That will never do, Mr. Hughes; there's no necessity to sway as if you were intoxicated, and you mustn't look at your feet.

LADY MACBETH. It's the steps. They're so rickety.

THE PRODUCER. We'll begin again from "speech."

> [*Lady Macbeth comes on again. He looks straight in front of him and falls heavily on the ground.*]

I said those steps were to be mended yesterday.

> [*The First Witch is convulsed with laughter*]

LADY MACBETH. There's nothing to laugh at.

THE PRODUCER. Are you hurt Mr. Hughes?

LADY MACBETH. Not much.

> [*The steps are replaced by two supers.*]

THE PRODUCER. Now, from "speech."

> [*Mr. Hughes comes on again*]

THE PRODUCER. You must not hold the taper upside down.

LADY MACBETH. How can I rub my hands and hold a taper too? What's the use of this taper?

THE PRODUCER. You can rub the back of your hand. You needn't wash your hands in the air. That's better.

GENTLEWOMAN. "Neither to you or anyone; having no witness to confirm my speech. Lo you, here she comes!" [*Enter Lady Macbeth*]

GENTLEWOMAN. "This is her very guise; and, upon my life, fast asleep. Observe her! stand close."

THE DOCTOR. "How came she by that light?"

GENTLEWOMAN. "Why, it stood by her: she has light by her continually; 'tis her command."

THE DOCTOR. "You see, her eyes are open."

GENTLEWOMAN. "Ay, but their sense is shut."

THE DOCTOR. "What is it she does now? Look, how she rubs her hands."

GENTLEWOMAN. "It is an accustomed action with her to seem thus washing her hands: I have known her continue in this quarter of an hour."

Enter the Doctor (Mr. Thomas). He waits R.

LADY MACBETH. "Here's a damned spot."

THE STAGE MANAGER. No, no, Mr. Hughes, "Yet here's a spot."

THE PRODUCER. Begin again from "hands".

GENTLEWOMAN. "It is an accustomed action with her to seem thus washing her hands: I have known her continue in this quarter of an hour."

LADY MACBETH. "Yet here's a damned spot."

THE STAGE MANAGER. It's not "damned" at all. That come later.

LADY MACBETH. It's catchy. Couldn't I say "mark" instead of "spot" in the first line?

THE DOCTOR. [*coming forward*] That would entirely spoil the effect of my "Hark". You see "mark" rhymes with "Hark". It's impossible.

THE PRODUCER. Oh! It's you, Mr. Thomas. Will you go straight on. We'll do the whole scene over presently. Now from "hour."

LADY MACBETH. "Yes, here's a spot."

THE DOCTOR. [*at the top of his voice*] "Hark!"

THE PRODUCER. Not so loud, Mr. Thomas, that would wake her up.

THE DOCTOR. [*in a high falsetto*] "Har-r-rk! She spe-e-eaks. I will… set…down."

THE PRODUCER. You needn't bleat that "speaks," Mr. Thomas, and the second part of that line is cut.

THE DOCTOR. It's not cut in my part. "Hark, she speaks."

LADY MACBETH. "Yet here's a spot."

THE STAGE MANAGER. No, Mr Hughes; "out, damned spot."

LADY MACBETH. Sorry.

THE PRODUCER. We must get that right. Now from "hour."

LADY MACBETH. "Yet here's a spot."

THE DOCTOR. "Hark! she speaks."

LADY MACBETH. "Get out, damned spot! Get out, I say! One, two, three, four: why there's plenty of time to do't. Oh! Hell! fie, fie, my Lord! a soldier and a beard! What have we got to fear when none can call our murky power to swift account withal? You'd never have thought the old man had so much blood in him!"

THE AUTHOR. I don't think you've got those lines quite right yet, Mr Hughes.

LADY MACBETH. What's wrong?

THE STAGE MANAGER. There's no "get." It's "one; two": and not "one, two, three, four." Then it's "Hell is murky." And there's no "plenty." And it's "a soldier and afeared," and not "a soldier and a beard."

THE AUTHOR. And after that you made two lines into rhymed verse.

MR. HUGHES. Yes, I know I did. I thought it wanted it.

THE PRODUCER. Please try to speak your lines as they are written, Mr. Hughes.

[*Enter Mr. Burbage, who plays Macbeth.*]

MR. BURBAGE. That scene doesn't go. Now don't you think Macbeth had better walk in his sleep instead of Lady Macbeth?

THE STAGE MANAGER. That's an idea.

THE PRODUCER. I think the whole scene might be cut. It's quite unnecessary.

LADY MACBETH. Then I shan't come on in the whole of the fifth act. If that scene's cut I shan't play at all.

THE STAGE MANAGER. We're thinking of transferring the scene to Macbeth. [*To the Author*] It wouldn't need much altering. Would you mind rewriting that scene, Mr. Shakespeare? It wouldn't want much alteration. You'd have to change that line about Arabia. Instead of "this little hand," you might say: "All the perfumes of Arabia will not sweeten this horny hand." I'm not sure it isn't more effective.

THE AUTHOR. I'm afraid it might get a laugh.

MR. BURBAGE. Not if I play it.

THE AUTHOR. I think it's more likely that Lady Macbeth would walk in her sleep, but—

MR. BURBAGE. That doesn't signify. I can make a great hit in that scene.

LADY MACBETH. If you take that scene from me, I shan't play Juliet tonight.

THE STAGE MANAGER. [*aside to Producer*] We can't possibly get another Juliet.

THE PRODUCER. On the whole, I think we must leave the scene as it is.

MR. BURBAGE. I've got nothing to do in the last act. What's the use of my coming to rehearsal when there's nothing for me to rehearse?

THE PRODUCER. Very well, Mr. Burbage. We'll go on to the Third scene at once. We'll go through your scene again later, Mr. Hughes.

MR. BURBAGE. Before we do this scene, there's a point I wish to settle. In Scene Five, when Seyton tells me the Queen's dead, I say: "She should have died hereafter. There would have been time for such a word"; and then the messenger enters. I should like a soliloquy here, about twenty or thirty lines, if possible in rhyme, in any case ending with a tag. I should like it to be about Lady Macbeth. Macbeth might have something touching to say about their happy domestic life, and the early days of their marriage. He might refer to their courtship. I must have something to make Macbeth sympathetic, otherwise the public won't stand it. He might say his better-half left him, and then he might refer to her beauty. The speech might begin:

> O dearest chuck, it is unkind indeed
> To leave me in the midst of my sore need.

Or something of the kind. In any case it ought to rhyme. Could I have that written at once, and then we could rehearse it?

THE PRODUCER. Let me see; I forget what is your part.

THE STAGE MANAGER. Mr. Shakespeare is playing Seyton. [*aside*] We cast him for Duncan, but he wasn't up to it.

THE PRODUCER. Mr. Kydd, will you read Mr. Shakespeare's part?

BANQUO. Certainly.

THE PRODUCER. Please let us have that speech, Mr. Shakespeare, as quickly as possible. [*aside*] Don't make it too long. Ten lines at the most.

THE AUTHOR. [*aside*] Is it absolutely necessary that it should rhyme?

THE PRODUCER. [*aside*] No, of course not; that's Burbage's fad. [*exit the Author in the wings*]

MR. BURBAGE. I should like to go through the fight first.

THE PRODUCER. Very well, Mr. Burbage

THE STAGE MANAGER. Macduff—Mr Foote—

MACDUFF. I'm here.

MR. BURBAGE. I'll give you the cue: "Why should I play the fool and like a Roman die on my sword: while there is life, there's hope. The gashes are for them."

MACDUFF. "Turn, hell-hound, turn."

MR. BURBAGE. I should suggest: "False monarch, turn." It's more dignified.

MACDUFF. I would rather say "hell hound."

THE PRODUCER. Supposing we made it "King of Hell."

MR. BURBAGE. I don't think that would do.

THE PRODUCER. Then we must leave it for the present.

MACDUFF. "Turn, hell-hound, turn."

> [*They begin to fight with wooden swords*]

THE STAGE MANAGER. You don't begin to fight until Macduff says: "Give thee out."

MR. BURBAGE. I think we might run those speeches into one, and I might say:

> "Of all men I would have avoided thee,
> But come on now, although my soul is charged
> With blood of thine, I'll have no further words.
> My voice is in my sword."

Then Macduff could say:

> "O bloodier villan than terms can well express."

THE PRODUCER. We must consult the Author about that.

MR. BURBAGE. We'll do fencing without words first.

[*They begin to fight again. Macduff gives Mr. Burbage
a tremendous blow on the shoulder.*]

MR. BURBAGE. Oh! Oh! That's my rheumatic shoulder. Please be a little more careful, Mr. Foote. You know I've got no padding. I can't go on rehearsing now. I am very seriously hurt indeed.

MACDUFF. I'm sure I'm very sorry. It was entirely an accident.

MR. BURBAGE. I'm afraid I must go home. I don't feel up to it.

THE STAGE MANAGER. I'll send for some ointment. Please be more careful, Mr. Foote. Couldn't you possibly see your way to take Scene Three, Mr. Burbage?

MR. BURBAGE. I know Scene Three backwards. However, I'll just run through my speech.

THE STAGE MANAGER. What? "This push will cheer me ever?"

MR. BURBAGE. [*peevishly*] No, not that one. You know that's all right. The tricky speech about the medicine. Give me that cue.

THE STAGE MANAGER. "That keep her from her rest."

MR. BURBAGE.   "Cure her of that:
Canst thou not minister to a sickly mind,
Pull from the memory a booted sorrow,
Rub out the troubles of a busy brain,
And with a sweet and soothing antidote
Clean the stiff bosom of that dangerous poison
Which weighs upon the heart?"
There, you see, word-perfect. What did I say?

THE STAGE MANAGER. No, no, Mr. Burbage. It's not a booted sorrow, but a rooted sorrow. It's not a stiff bosom but a stuff bosom—but here's Mr. Shakespeare.

THE AUTHOR. I've written that speech.

THE PRODUCER. Please.

MR. SHAKESPEARE. [*reads*] "To-morrow, and to-morrow, and to-morrow,
Creeps in this petty pace from day to day,
To the last syllable of recorded time;
And all our yesterdays have lighted fools
The way to dusty death. Out, out, brief candle!
Life's but a walking shadow, a poor player
That struts and frets his hour upon the stage,
And then is heard no more: it is a tale
Told by an idiot, full of sound and fury,
Signifying nothing."

MR. BURBAGE. Well, you don't expect me to say that, I suppose. It's a third too short. There's not a single rhyme in it. It's got nothing to do with the situation, and it's an insult to the stage. "Struts and frets" indeed! I see there's nothing left for me but to throw up the part. You can get any one you please to play Macbeth. One thing is quite certain, I won't.

[*Exit Mr Burbage in a passion.*]

THE STAGE MANAGER. [*to the Author*] Now you've done it.

THE AUTHOR. [*to the Producer*] You said it needn't rhyme.

THE PRODUCER. It's Macduff. It was all your fault Mr. Foote.

LADY MACBETH. Am I to wear a fair wig or a dark wig?

THE PRODUCER. Oh! I don't know.

THE AUTHOR. Dark, if you please. People are always saying I'm making portraits. So, if you're dark, nobody can say I meant the character for the Queen or for Mistress Mary Fritton.

THE STAGE MANAGER. It's no good going on now. It's all up—it's all up.

CURTAIN

Charles Walter Stansby Williams (1886–1945)

In a typically self-deprecating introductory note, Charles Williams claims that the purpose of *A Myth of Shakespeare* (1928) "is only to provide a momently credible framework for representative scenes and speeches from the Plays." As usual, Williams is modest about his contribution. Much of his play's value stems from an opportunity to see a gifted reader and a fine poet musing about Shakespeare's creative process. From the time he joined the Oxford University Press as a reader in 1908, Williams helped shape literary values and tastes as an editor, poet, novelist, critic, and lecturer on English poetry at Oxford. A prominent member of the group of writers known as the Oxford Christians, or Inklings, a group which included C.S. Lewis, J.R.R. Tolkien, and the philosopher Owen Barfield, he shared his friends' interest in both religion and myth.

Like the following excerpt set in the Mermaid Tavern, the legendary haunt of adventurers and writers, each of the *Myth*'s scenes mixes passages from Shakespeare's plays with Williams' musings on the playwright's relationships and ideas. After an opening passage from *Twelfth Night* (II.iii), featuring those curious exemplars of chivalry, Sir Toby Belch and Sir Andrew Aguecheek, Williams offers Shakespeare, Ben Jonson, and Dick Burbage discussing playmaking, creativity, theology and history. Their discussion focuses on both Jonson's concerns (his rival's work habits and education) and Williams' (our ability to discover the divine in nature and our responsibility to each other).

A Myth of Shakespeare
(1928)

ACT II, SCENE II
A ROOM AT THE MERMAID

[*Shakespeare, Jonson, Burbage at one table. Sir Toby Belch and Sir Andrew Ague-cheek at another.*]

SIR TOBY BELCH. Marian, I say! a stoup of wine!

[*Enter Clown*]

SIR ANDREW AGUECHEEK. Here comes the fool, i' faith.

CLOWN. How now, my hearts! Did you never see the picture of 'we three'?

SIR TOBY BELCH. Welcome, ass. Now let's have a catch.

SIR ANDREW AGUECHEEK. By my troth, the fool has an excellent breast. I had rather than forty shillings I had such a leg, and so sweet a breath to sing, as the fool has. In sooth, thou wast in very gracious fooling last night, when thou spokest of Pigrogromitus, of the Vapians passing the equinoctial of Queubus: 'twas very good, i' faith. I sent thee sixpence for thy leman: hadst it?

CLOWN. I did impeticos thy gratillity; for Malvolio's nose is no whipstock: my lady has a white hand, and the Myrmidons are no bottle-ale houses.

SIR ANDREW AGUECHEEK. Excellent! why, this is the best fooling, when all is done. Now, a song.

SIR TOBY BELCH. Come on; there is sixpence for you: let's have a song.

SIR ANDREW AGUECHEEK. There's a testril of me too: if one knight give a—

CLOWN. Would you have a love-song, or a song of good life?

SIR TOBY BELCH. A love-song, a love-song.

SIR ANDREW AGUECHEEK. Ay, ay; I care not for good life.

CLOWN.   O mistress mine! where are you roaming?
               O! stay and hear; your true love's coming,
                   That can sing both high and low.
                   Trip no further, pretty sweeting;
                   Journeys end in lovers meeting,
                   Every wise man's son doth know.

SIR ANDREW AGUECHEEK. Excellent good, i' faith.

SIR TOBY BELCH. Good, good.

CLOWN.   What is love? 'tis not hereafter;
                          Present mirth hath present laughter;
                          What's to come is still unsure:
                          In delay there lies no plenty;
                          Then come kiss me, sweet and twenty,
                          Youth's a stuff will not endure.

SIR ANDREW AGUECHEEK. A mellifluous voice, as I am true knight.

SIR TOBY BELCH. A contagious breath.

SIR ANDREW AGUECHEEK. Very sweet and contagious, i' faith.

SIR TOBY BELCH. To hear by the nose, it is dulcet in contagion. But shall
we make the welkin dance indeed? Shall we rouse the night-owl in a catch
that will draw three souls out of one weaver? Shall we do that?

SIR ANDREW AGUECHEEK. An you love me, let's do 't: I am dog at a catch.

CLOWN. By'r lady, sir, and some dogs will catch well.

SIR ANDREW AGUECHEEK. Most certain. Let our catch be, 'Thou knave.'

CLOWN. 'Hold thy peace, thou knave,' knight? I shall be constrain'd in't to
call thee knave, knight.

SIR ANDREW AGUECHEEK. 'Tis not the first time I have constrain'd one to
call me knave. Begin, fool: it begins, 'Hold thy peace.'

CLOWN. I shall never begin if I hold my peace.

SIR ANDREW AGUECHEEK. Good, i' faith. Come, begin.
                                    [*They sing a catch*

CLOWN. Beshrew me, the knight's in admirable fooling.

SIR ANDREW AGUECHEEK. Ay, he does well enough if he be disposed, and
so do I too; he does it with a better grace, but I do it more natural.

                                        [*They drift out*

BURBAGE [*looking at Shakespeare and quoting*]. O God! that men should put
an enemy in their mouths to steal away their brains; that we should, with
joy, pleasance, revel, and applause, transform ourselves into beasts.

JONSON.   That's true too; but a man should take his drink
                     Most like, as all could do, a man whose mind
                     Uses his habits to his profit, skims

The cream o' the milk, and lets the jug stand by
For thirsty neighbours.

SHAKESPEARE.   'Should.' Ben, you were made
For a wise pulpiter.

JONSON. So were not you.

SHAKESPEARE. I thank God for it.

JONSON.   Do you so—thank God
That you have never tried to turn a man
From his foul ways, and what he loves too well,
To cleaner? Honest men must needs be clean.

SHAKESPEARE. The only thing I have against you, Ben,
Isn't your doing; you've the rarest touch
Of old moralities in your humours—aye,
I almost see the Vice jump out at last
Scolding the devil to hell.

JONSON.   That's the Old Faith
That works in me—you've neither the old nor new,
Good Catholic nor good Puritan.

SHAKESPEARE.   Why no,
I learned my craft upon another bench
From quite another master, than your bluff,
Honest, broad-shouldered Master Right-and-Wrong.

JONSON. Meaning—

SHAKESPEARE. Even now I cannot think of him
But with a secret melancholy, him,
I mean, who was a greater then than I,
And might be greater now, had he been met
By no two surly ruffians; who still kept
His eager eyes on knowledge, his swift feet
Spurning the paltry pavements for the air
They loved so—Marlowe.

BURBAGE.   Aye; he died the year
Before we went to Greenwich first.

SHAKESPEARE.   He was
All excellency, he was my sole friend
When I was young, and my great master. Now
There are moments when my heart beats through my veins

Those unkind tidings as if all were new—
Marlowe is dead, and as one dazed by the moon
I stagger at it.

JONSON.   He died in a brawl?

SHAKESPEARE.   He died—
Let it rest there.... He died of that excess
Wherein his mighty heart, beating its way
About the weakness of the thinning air
Beyond the stars, plunged like a falling star
Through the great void that took him.

BURBAGE.   All's a void
Beyond our natural shutting-up of eyes.
Neither of you two, you the Catholic
Or you the poet, can instruct me there.

JONSON.   Go to a priest—if you can find a priest
Hid in a cellar; go to the Spanish lord's
New chaplain.

SHAKESPEARE.   All ends somehow. I would have
No huddled-up and scrabbling end of life,
Leaving all things off to the last, as some
Schoolboy sits gabbling i' the morning o'er
His book ere yet he gets himself to school
Half-knowing it. Week's work, week's pay, week's end.
                [Singers heard without]
By your leave, my friends. Maria, bring them in.
                [They enter]
Well met, good fellows. What, can you sing a verse
After a glance at it?

FIRST SINGER.   Master, if it go
Tunefully—is there music?

SHAKESPEARE.   No, not yet.
[He gives them a paper. They gather round, examining and whispering.]
        Well, can you do it? or hath learning now
        Stolen the natural instinct from our hearts
        To make a song of any likely words?

FIRST SINGER. Why, aye, we'll try it.

SHAKESPEARE. On then; you'll do well.
                [They sing]

> Fear no more the heat o' the sun,
>   Nor the furious winter's rages;
> Thou thy worldly task has done,
>   Home art gone, and ta'en thy wages;
>   Golden lads and girls all must,
>   As chimney-sweepers, come to dust.
>
> Fear no more then from o' the great,
>   Thou art past the tyrant's stroke:
> Care no more to clothe and eat;
>   To thee the reed is as the oak:
>   The sceptre, learning, physic, must
>   All follow this, and come to dust.
> [*Shakespeare gives them money and they go out.*]

BURBAGE.   That's a new song?

SHAKESPEARE.   Aye.

JONSON.   An old song, I think.
          All men have known it.

BURBAGE.   No man has known more.
          But there's a speech, Will, in another play,
          Your Measure for Measure, that I got by heart
          Not for the acting but for the mere dread,
          A thing I keep to love and shudder at—
                    [*He rises and speaks it.*]
              Ay, but to die, and go we know not where;
              To lie in cold obstruction and to rot;
              This sensible warm motion to become
              A kneaded clod; and the delighted spirit
              To bathe in fiery floods, or to reside
              In thrilling region of thick-ribbed ice;
              To be imprison'd in the viewless winds,
              And blown with restless violence round about
              The pendant world; or to be worse than worst
              Of those that lawless and incertain thoughts
              Imagine howling: 'tis too horrible!
              The weariest and most loathed worldly life
              That age, ache, penury and imprisonment
              Can lay on nature is a paradise
              To what we fear of death.

JONSON.   A young fool in a dungeon whining out
          That his dear body, which is all he knows,

Having no hint of the victorious mind,
And lesser as a Christian man than souls
Such as great Seneca and wise Plutarch were:
That this most cherished body, which the stews,
And well-served victuals, and warm sheets by night,
Made him enjoy, should go into the dark
Sobbing for all the good it leaves behind!
Will, your young heroes are the loathliest crew.

SHAKESPEARE. Take them for what they are—heroes; naught else.

JONSON. You take no trouble with your plays.

SHAKESPEARE.   My god!
I take no trouble! I—who spend more time
Coaxing a vicious troublesome little noun
Into its place between two adjectives
Than you did over all your comedies—
At least to hear them grunt the verse out.

JONSON. Grunt!

SHAKESPEARE. Grunt. O your prose—that's well, but poetry—
Ben, you have hit it once or twice by chance,
You don't know what it is.

JONSON.   At least, I keep
A decent line with history.

SHAKESPEARE.   So do I
If I remember and have time enough.
But it's not so that plays are written.

BURBAGE.   Not yours.

SHAKESPEARE. Well, no—not mine then.

BURBAGE.   How do you write your plays?

SHAKESPEARE. Sometimes because a pretty story cries
In my ear for telling on a gay bright stage;
And sometimes for some notion that has crept
Into my brain by night of how a man
Might be or do this, that, or the other, and show
What happens to the mind when that is done;
And sometimes—to put other people right.

BURBAGE. Will!

JONSON.   Doubtless! Me, now?

SHAKESPEARE.   O no, Ben, not you.
   You know that play that came out t'other day—
   "King Leir"?—there's chances gone a-begging; there
   The fellow got an old deserted king
   Out in the country, in a thunderstorm,
   With a murderer after him; where all he did
   Was to cry out on hell and brimstone, how
   It wasn't right to kill a man—boom, boom,
   Goes thunder; wouldn't you like to go to heaven?
   Boom, boom; but kill me if you must—boom, boom,
   Till honest murderer thinks that thunder's sent
   To damn him past redemption and runs off.—
   I'll show him how to write.

BURBAGE.   What will you do?

SHAKESPEARE. It was a window opened; think—he goes,
   An outspurned royalty, from his daughter's hearth,
   Swelling, high-vexed, and nigh to madness; think—
   Not madness only, but all things at once
   Dissolving in a general horror; think—
   This very being, this manhood, that we are,
   Breaking; our beating centres dispossest
   And all our voices and concerns of life
   Eccentric, underivable, dismayed,
   Till they have changed past knowing; to which end—
   As which of you has not feared madness once,
   However staunch you sit?—I will have one
   On either side of kingship's toppling brain:
   One—a poor-born fool, a mad innocent,
   A world without direction; one a world
   Of fierceness, nakedness, and dancing rags—
   And all three worlds sent spinning in a sky
   Wherethrough the greater elements dissolve
   Even as the lesser. O and all around
   High and incestuous and possessive thoughts
   And some few steady fools amid the storm
   Blundering to shelter. You have known it then,
   How near the pit we are?

BURBAGE.   Go not too near.

SHAKESPEARE. Then the bare heart should crack; then the full main

Of being, in an uncanonical haste,
Crawling with greedy, rash, and mountainous waves,
Pre-empt upon the mind's occasion, thwart
The type of manhood, and there force in him,
Behind the ungovernable tricks of speech,
Such blinding fracture of intelligence
As makes the play. But that's for evening time.
I'm for the theatre now. You're coming, Dick?

BURBAGE. You're early, aren't you?

SHAKESPEARE.   Yes—you'll come on?

BURBAGE.   Yes,
          In another quarter of an hour.

SHAKESPEARE.   Good. Farewell,
          My learned Ben!

JONSON.   Farewell, my unschooled Will:
                    [*Shakespeare goes out*]
          What is it goes there?

BURBAGE.   That's what I ask myself
          When I've been sitting with him.

JONSON.   Indolent
          But alert if need shall call him; full of jest,
          But if one gives, as talk runs, a glance back
          To find his silence out, there sits a dim
          Shadow of melancholy on his face;
          No learning, no philosophy, yet a knack
          For bringing all a philosophic school
          Into a phrase.

BURBAGE.   It is his poetry
          Searches our hearts out. Do you know the play
          He goes down to rehearse this afternoon
          Ere it's presented at the Inns of Court?

JONSON. "Macbeth"? no.

BURBAGE.   Ben, I think sometimes this man,
          Will Shakespeare, is not all so much a man
          As the wise earth speaking aloud; so fair,
          In such a supernatural wonder, come
          His utterances, and with so deep a sound
          As if they had beaten down the corridors
          Without us and within us, the mid-world

With our mid-hearts mingled in passages
Where only the great music that is he
Goes echoing on for ever.

JONSON.   But "Macbeth"?—
Holinshed's story is it? the Scotch thane?

BURBAGE. Aye, that. The murder of Duncan—not alone
              Murder itself treading with ghastly foot
              The crimson and revolted house of life;
              But afterwards—Macbeth and Macbeth's Queen,
              Both in their separate ways cut off and poisoned
              Within the changeless horror of a sleep
              That dreams of naught but Duncan. She who held
              The imperial queendom of the active world,
              As quick, as vigilant, as physical
              As the round earth's self, in her slumber goes
              About the astonished palace, and heaves up
              Her slender hands to all men's terror; he,
              Being apt in meditation and in dreams,
              Finds all his dreams grow round him till they close
              All ways between him and material things,
              Immense and incorporeal, and he treads,
              His mind sleepwalking, and his heart—no sound,
              None, but its solitary beating—through
              Clefts of futility and helplessness,
              Himself most futile.

JONSON.   And he laughs at me
For being moral!

BURBAGE.   But this doom is none
Of our inventions and predicaments
To stay man in from evil. These last years
He has neighboured with old Nature, and gone in
To the world's bottom; he has been made one
With the metaphysical principle of things;
He is made that primal necessary voice
Proclaiming its vast being. If he turn,
Now, for a fit of craftsmanship, a sting
Thrust in him by some folly of this bad play,
That first necessity against itself,
And bring man's topmost struggle into the hid
Cradle and sepulchre of our common life—
I promise you I fear it.

JONSON.   He's a great man;
          But never was a poet yet who took
          The last step into madness—all but that;
          That's held from them. Well, Dick, maybe you're right.
          And yet—for all this largeness—he's a friend
          To the common people.

BURBAGE [*rising*].   Aye, to a point; but if
          Your common people try to cheat him, click!
          There's the law shut on them. Ben, do you know
          He's never lost a law case yet?

JONSON [*rising*].   Well done;
          Praise to the poet who can beat the world
          At its own game.
[*As they pay the reckoning*]
                    Well, child, and what do you think
          Of Master Shakespeare?

MARIA.   O sir, I don't think
          Of the gentlemen who come here; only this—
          He's got the pleasantest voice in London.

JONSON.   Aye,
          But it never talked Greek to you.

MARIA.   Mayhap, sir,
          His mouth has said a better thing than Greek.

JONSON. Mayhap. Godden.   [*To Burbage*]:
                    It seems this voice that sounds—
          Where did you say?—in the caverns where Etna's fuelled
          By giants—hasn't lost its keenness yet
          For wrangling with a lawyer or its sweet
          Persuasiveness for wheedling friends and maids.

Edward Henry Warren
(1873–1942)

There is some appropriateness in the fact that it was a professor at the Harvard Law School—one who specialized in corporations, equity, and property—who located Shakespeare on Wall Street during the boom and bust year of 1929. Even Edward H. Warren's connection with the literary world was legal. After helping to incorporate the *Atlantic Monthly*, he represented George H. Mifflin, head of Houghton Mifflin, when labor troubles arose at the Riverside Press, and acted as New England counsel for the Author's League of America. Warren's memoirs, *Spartan Education* (Houghton Mifflin, 1942), reveal a man more comfortable with libraries than people ("books are my intimate friends"). His primary passion was the literary style of jurists.

If all of this suggests that *Shakespeare on Wall Street* (1929) might be a ponderous piece, it would be misleading. Warren's play creates a comically poetic world of investors, where the "eternal question" is "whether to go long or short."* A brooding Hamlet tries to sell bonds to a world mad only for stocks. A timid Macbeth, urged to greater daring by a wife who cannot understand his caution ("He's balmy in the bean"), goes to the witches for market tips. The witches themselves count margins, prophesy the Federal Reserve's actions, and consult Hecate's raven which warns, "The market now is out of joint."

Underlying the entire play is Warren's cautionary message that investing is fundamentally a game which calls for more sense than most people are willing to bring to it. Looking to the future often means expecting change. For Warren, the great Wall Street herds of bears (those who expect stock prices to fall) and bulls (those who expect stock prices to rise) should be seen as reflections of a fluid economy rather than a moral commentary on society.

---

*Going long and short is part of the arcane lexicon of finance which Warren uses mostly for comic effect. Going long involves accumulating stocks or commodities, often on margin, in the belief that prices will rise. Going or selling short is a bit more tricky. It involves selling stocks or commodities without owning them. A person who sells short expects prices to fall, so that he (or she) can buy those stocks or commodities at a lower price by the date he (or she) must deliver them to the buyer.

Shakespeare on Wall Street
(1929)

DRAMATIS PERSONAE

SHAKESPEARE
MRS. SHAKESPEARE
SHAKESPEARE'S SONS
　　　HAMLET, a bond salesman
　　　MACBETH, a timid bull
　　　FALSTAFF, an anti-prohibitionist
LADY MACBETH, always bullish
BANQUO
BARDOLPH, valet to Falstaff
POLONIUS, secretary to Shakespeare
SHYLOCK, a stock-broker
THREE TRADERS
THREE WITCHES
HECATE

ACT I

SCENE I

Near a Blast Furnace in New Jersey
Enter Three Witches

FIRST WITCH. The sky is blue, the weather fair,
　　　And business prospers everywhere.
SECOND WITCH. I'm looking here, and looking there,
　　　I do not find a prosperous bear.
THIRD WITCH. There is a Turn to every fate.
　　　Who buys them now, buys far too late.
FIRST WITCH. That's not what I heard.
SECOND WITCH. What did you hear?
FIRST WITCH. What all the speculators say:
　　　The market wings its upward way,
　　　That Radio will sell more high
　　　Than eagle's flight across the sky.
THIRD WITCH. There'll be an end to all this winning;
　　　The bears will play the final inning.

FIRST WITCH. When Radio is thirty-two
   What the Hell will people do?
THIRD WITCH. Come, sisters, we shall meet again
   When prices fall like showers of rain.
ALL. When the market's set to crack,
   To this foul spot we'll all come back.

           (*Exeunt*)

SCENE II

New York. The Library of Shakespeare's House
Shakespeare and Mrs. Shakespeare

SHAKESPEARE. The bitter toil of years is mine, yet I am poor.
   My neighbors all are rich. The market's rising star
   Hath clearly shown the road to easy fortune's grasp,
   But I, consummate ass, have stumbled through the dark.
   Now I am weary, pushing on and on my impecunious pen.
   I'll quit and now. There is no stroke of pen can touch
   A market stroke of luck. And still there's time.
   The bullish tide still rolls, why should it end?
   There is no end to dreams. Together with the world I'll ride
   The glory while it lasts.
MRS. SHAKESPEARE. Such stuff as this from you, my lord,
     seems strange.
SHAKESPEARE. Strange it may be, but not more strange
   Than you should cry for hats and clothes
   I cannot buy. You'll get them now, or else go broke!
MRS. SHAKESPEARE. 'Tis sleep you need, my lord; the morning's
     cold appraisal
   Will give you second thought.
SHAKESPEARE. Not I. My dumbest years are done.
MRS. SHAKESPEARE. It seems they just begin.
SHAKESPEARE. The market is the nation's fever, deep-seated in
     its blood.
   Now who am I to be so strong I can escape the germ?
   Fond mothers flock the brokers' rooms, and grandma holds
     a chair.
   Then soon will come the time when babes do cry for stocks.
   Wouldst have it said that I was last? It shall not be.
   The die is cast, the fun begins. Lead on, you bulls,
   And strong be he who first shall scent a bear.

     (*Curtain*)

SCENE III

New York. Macbeth's Apartment on Park Avenue
Enter Macbeth and Lady Macbeth

LADY MACBETH. Did you buy Chrysler, as I asked?
MACBETH. No. I thought better of it.
LADY MACBETH. Did you buy Auburn, then?
MACBETH. I dared not.
LADY MACBETH. What have you done?
MACBETH. I bought a hundred Overland.
LADY MACBETH. O perfect ass! There's not a profit in a thousand
   Overland to buy the baby shoes.
MACBETH. But Overland is safe.
LADY MACBETH. Safe! Who wishes to be safe?
   Better be Perfection's fool than someone medium done.
MACBETH. There are many in Overland.
LADY MACBETH. I know of one who has forsworn to shave
   Till Overland shall rise. Now are his whiskers grown
   Far longer than a mermaid's hair. Forever they will grow!
MACBETH. My broker recommends.
LADY MACBETH. Who cares? Give me a stock with a rocket's rush,
   A shooter for the stars.
MACBETH. Too risky that.
LADY MACBETH. Had you but shown the coward temper of your mind
   When you did ask my hand in marriage.
   Do you suppose that now you'd call me wife?
   My great mistake! Alas! The fervent ardor of your suit
   Swept through me like a prairie fire, unhinged my
     common sense,
   And made me fail to see the weak and watered soul of you
   Who calls himself a man; and yet who dares to say,
   I do not dare to take a chance.
   This life is filled with people pale and pallid,
   Content to graze on life's prosaic way, as pastured cows
   Do munch and munch their everlasting cud. The world has
     many tails,
   And I do fear that you are one, to follow on behind,
   To droop with woe, to wag again, to droop, impotent silly
     tail,
   A signpost on the desert road to nowhere.
MACBETH. I'll take the plunge. It may be deep,
   But better far than face the torment of your nagging.
LADY MACBETH. Good news! Now watch the profits roll!

We'll break out such a limousine, my boy,
'Twill star the streets, cause passers-by to stand and gape,
Pop-eyed with its wonder.
MACBETH. But if we lose?
LADY MACBETH. Why, then, we lose. What matter's it?
We walk, and we have walked before.

(*Curtain*)

ACT II

SCENE I

New York. The Top of the Singer Building
Hamlet, Looking Out Over New York

HAMLET. Here on this lofty tower I feel once more
The world's romance far out beyond the smoky air
To the distant shore of dreams. Here in this reach of space
My spirit lifts, and for the moment dares regain
The spice and charm of life, so rudely lost
When I from college plucked, by quick financial need,
Was forced to knock the rich man's door
And beg him buy a bond.
O what a weary world, and what a job is mine!
Had I but half a lion's nerve, I'd jump,
But I do fear the drop and squash
Upon the pavement far below. That gives me pause,
And makes me bear my task accursed of selling bonds.
A million bonds to sell, and none to buy!
When I parade my wares, why, even widows laugh,
And point their broker's balance sheet to show
The brilliance of their stocks.
Would that I had never known the sidewalks of New York,
That I might live again bright college years at Yale,
My philosophic nights, and days of Kelly pool.
There was a glamour then, a joy I have forgot,
In bonds, bonds, bonds, filthy unsalable bonds!
Nor am I fitted with a salesman's gall,
And day of bonds is done. Far down the canyoned street
The muffled clock strikes ten. The Stock Exchange moves on,
Its stocks renew their climb, to reach the skies,
To touch the sun, perhaps. And yet the sun shines short
In Wall Street's cleft, its many-windowed walls are dark.
The gambler makes his play, but none can read reflected there

What way the spots will roll.
If to-day might be to-morrow, the crystal ball reveal
The future trend of ups and downs, why, then we'd know
Whether to go long or short, the eternal question never
    answered yet,
And never will but by the hand of chance.

SCENE II

New York. Shakespeare's Study
Enter Shakespeare and Polonius

SHAKESPEARE. What news, Polonius?
POLONIUS. The brokers' loans increase.
SHAKESPEARE. What? Again? Great gods, it cannot be!
POLONIUS. The figures here do state. Look, my lord.
SHAKESPEARE. It cannot be, but still it is.
    My eyes do read, yet scarce believe.
    Sound reason tells, when stocks are down,
    The loans should not be up.
    This strange benighted paradox doth fuddle up my brain.
POLONIUS. Not yours alone, my lord.
SHAKESPEARE. The world is thinking far too much of these damned
    brokers' loans.
    Greater than the wide world's work, their headline stars
      the page
    A record high, the nation gasps, the timid traders quake,
    Strong statisticians rush to print the country's gone to Hell.
POLONIUS. They'll never see the day, but still there's danger
    in the wind.
         (*Enter Lady Macbeth*)
SHAKESPEARE. I know no poison in the loans,
    Now why should these things be?
LADY MACBETH. You ask him why? Go to, and ask the Sphinx.
    There's none alive can answer. These loans
    Will drive me mad, as they have done Macbeth.
SHAKESPEARE. What is't you say?
LADY MACBETH. Not wholly mad, perhaps, but at the rate he goes,
    'Twill not be long. These sad statistics have o'ercome
    What feeble brain he had. He's balmy in the bean.
POLONIUS. What? From thinking on the loans?
LADY MACBETH. Forever that, each waking hour and more,
    'Tis even through the night,
    The mutters of his sleep repeat the total brokers' loans.

POLONIUS. Such constant thinking would wear away
          The mind of genius even.
LADY MACBETH. And who would call my husband that
          Is duller than a fool.
SHAKESPEARE. He lacks perspective. Come, take the man abroad,
          Where is no end to lans and loans, yet no one cares
          A continental damn. That's what he needs.
          The change will cure him quick.
LADY MACBETH. How shall we go? As stowaways?
SHAKESPEARE. Take money from the bank. Take principal.
          In this essential cause, what matters which you take?
LADY MACBETH. There's nothing in the bank. The all we have
          Our broker holds, with iron in his clutch.
          He'll not let loose, nor is content with what he has;
          The villain calls for more.
SHAKESPEARE. So that is why you came.
LADY MACBETH. Exactly that.
SHAKESPEARE. Then are you not ashamed to come to me?
LADY MACBETH. Why so? You are my husband's father.
SHAKESPEARE. You are the cause of this.
          Without your whisper in his ear, he never would have sold
          His prosperous oyster farms to General Foods,
          And sunk substantial fortune in the market's chance,
          For what? To exercise your greed for more,
          When then you had enough.
LADY MACBETH. I am at fault, but I am human like the rest.
SHAKESPEARE. Too true!
LADY MACBETH. Who could resist the market's thrall? Know you one?
          Unless it be the deaf, the dumb, and blind.
SHAKESPEARE. I know of none. I could not.
LADY MACBETH. You of all the world! And yet you censure me.
SHAKESPEARE. I shall not. My censure is withdrawn.
LADY MACBETH. Accept my thanks.
SHAKESPEARE. How could you lose? The market's close to top,
          It rather seems not you, your broker is the fool.
LADY MACBETH. Blame not my broker's foul advice, but mine.
          I told Macbeth the motor stocks would rise.
SHAKESPEARE. The motor stocks! Immortal gods!
          Lie down my tongue, and do not speak,
          I dare not be so harsh.
LADY MACBETH. Speak out!
SHAKESPEARE. Why, babes could see the motor stocks would crash.
          Inflated like balloons they stood, far out beyond the pack,

For bears to single out, fat targets in their drive.
LADY MACBETH. No more than others were.
SHAKESPEARE. Not so, you know it. Financial experts spread abroad
    The saturation point is reached. Beware the motors' fall!
LADY MACBETH. So often heard, I listened not at all.
    The cry was false ten years ago.
    It will be ten years hence.
SHAKESPEARE. But it has proven true.
LADY MACBETH. A technical reaction, that is all.
SHAKESPEARE. You should have bought in power and gas.
LADY MACBETH. Why bring that up? I did not.
SHAKESPEARE. It's not too late to shift.
LADY MACBETH. If I do shift, wilt carry my account?
SHAKESPEARE. I will; there is no chance in that.
    Utilities will rise and rise and rise and rise.
                (Enter Falstaff)
FALSTAFF. Now did I hear some mention of a rise?
    But give me back the price I paid, then you can have
        them all.
SHAKESPEARE. May God have mercy! You, too.
FALSTAFF. I'm loaded to the ears.
LADY MACBETH. With what, utilities?
FALSTAFF. And they are twice too much.
SHAKESPEARE. Too little, rather. The writing on the wall is clear.
    The nation grows on power, electric is the home.
FALSTAFF. The ancient fireside long is dead, the housewife works no more.
LADY MACBETH. Dream on, there'll be electric babies yet.
FALSTAFF. A rotten scheme, but if they bring my money back,
    I'll sacrifice the cause.

(Curtain)

ACT III

SCENE I

Macbeth's Apartment in New York
Macbeth and Lady Macbeth

MACBETH. Grown weary of the market strain
    The courage from my faltering heart is oozing bit by bit.
    How gladly would I sell! I cannot. This dreadful business
        will go on,
    There's no escape! When winter comes and folds the land
        in snow,

The shaggy forest bears will seek their lairs under ground;
Stange irony of fate, the Wall Street bears will still parade,
To terrorize my nerves, already frayed from watching tape unroll
Disaster to the stocks I hold, while up the market moves.
To lose, when all the world has lost, is bitter dreg enough;
To lose and lose, when wins the world, is double star of woe.
But had I vision of the path they trod, I'd be a millionaire.

LADY MACBETH. So say we all! Our fretful hours of might have been
Do clog the forward way to fortune and success.
But yesterday is yesterday, it never can be more.
To-morrow is another day. It may be ours, who knows?

MACBETH. The shadows by the wall take shape
In multitudes of bears to drive me mad. Uneasy is my sleep.
Wakeful through the night's long hours, I dread the morning
news.
Calamity's rumor on the wind foreruns the storm
I know must break to topple o'er the pyramid of stocks,
Grown tall beyond the bounds of sense, and will destroy,
As surely as before, the dream of man, built weakly in the air,
On slender threads of hope, too fragile far to hold.

LADY MACBETH. Man's dream, that you now hold to scorn,
Has conquered worlds, and still has far to go.
The fabric that you hold so weak is built of solid stuff.
Beyond your poor imagining, the nation grows, and fast.
Brilliant is the future's promise, unmistakable and clear to
wise men,
Yet dim to one whose nose has clouded up his sight.

MACBETH. What noise is that?

LADY MACBETH. What noise, my lord? You are unnerved.
Some newsboy cries his "Extra" down the street.

MACBETH. Methought I heard a voice cry, "The brokers' loans are up."

LADY MACBETH. Do not disturb yourself, my lord.
I heard his cry, "Another murder in Chicago."

(*Curtain*)

SCENE II

Falstaff's Apartment
The Bedroom, Falstaff in Bed
Enter Bardolph

BARDOLPH. Good-morning, my lord.

FALSTAFF. 'Twere better had you said good-night.

BARDOLPH. You look not well.

FALSTAFF. Wow, what a head have I!
        The cobwebs in my brain do stop my ears.
        My tongue, last night a wagging piece of wit,
        Recumbent lies, a sodden pad of cotton waste
        To swell the bitter desert of my mouth.
BARDOLPH. I have always said, my lord, you had better stick to gin.
FALSTAFF. Gin, you fool! 'Twas gin hath made me thus.
BARDOLPH. Far too strong, I fear.
FALSTAFF. I will forswear this drinking from a flask.
        Too treacherous that by far.
        Such devil's power is hid in Prohibition's flask
        If poured on Tutankhamen's antique tomb, 'twould bring
        The distant dead to wake, break through their mummy wraps,
        Dissolve their centuries of death, to stride the world, alive.
BARDOLPH. As I have said, my lord, none but a camel
        Can drink a gallon's fill, and none but an owl is made
        To wander all the night.
FALSTAFF. Then, Bardolph, I should have been an owl.
        I long for the twilight hour, I grow with the rising moon.
        When lights are out, and the moon has set, my twinkle lives
        To answer the midnight stars. Then I am I, Falstaff,
        The inner man revealed, stripped clear of inhibition's stuff,
        Forgetful of mankind's prepared opinion. Dictator of the world
            asleep,
        I hold a million shares.
        Too brief the hour! The morning star winks out,
        And with the star the better part of me.
BARDOLPH. So sad, my lord!
FALSTAFF. Have at me, Bardolph. Make havoc with your play
        Of dull ironic jest. I am too weak for answer.
BARDOLPH. Not irony, but truth, my lord.
FALSTAFF. Come, my pretty, let her loose!
        Call me what you will, clodpole, ass, and purple goat!
        Say anything you like, 'twill not be half I feel.
BARDOLPH. A cup of coffee and an egg will put you right, my lord.
FALSTAFF. An egg, a yellow, woozy egg! I cannot face the beast.
BARDOLPH. A cup of coffee, then.
FALSTAFF. Begone! And have a double care lest you disturb me.
        The bears make whoopee with my bank account. Watch out!
        One move that's false, and you are done.

(*Curtain*)

SCENE III

The Blast Furnaces
Enter the Witches

FIRST WITCH. Where hast thou been, sister?
SECOND WITCH. Peeking in the brokers' books, counting margins.
FIRST WITCH. How have you found them?
SECOND WITCH. I found them margined well.
THIRD WITCH. Well, but not too well.
FIRST WITCH. What climbs to Heaven now
        Some day will fall to Hell.
THIRD WITCH. Such horrid news I hold
        I am on fire with joy. Come closer, sisters,
        That I may breathe the hellish word
        Will send iced shivers down your spines.
ALL. Tell, tell! Suspense will make us numb!
THIRD WITCH. The Federal Reserve in secret conclave ponders
        Means to cure the nation's cloudy state o'ercast
        By stormy speculation. To-morrow morning's news proclaims
        The fury of their warning. Such dismal stuff will shake
        The Wall Street world to marrow of its gambling bones;
        Will make the poor man more than poor, the bloated rich
          disgorge
        Their profits piled, their fortunes drop like shooting stars.
SECOND WITCH. Say Au Revoir to bulls; the gaunt and hungry bears
        Have finished with the long, lean years. At last, at last!
ALL. At last, at last, a man without a margin!
FIRST WITCH. To-morrow is a day of days. I cannot wait,
        I burst within, to keep the news I hold.
SECOND WITCH. The little gamblers are in bed, asleep,
        Their dreams content.
THIRD WITCH. O, to ride the murmur of the night wind,
        To breathe the ghastly news in every nook, in every sleeping
          ear,
        Awake the world to know disaster stalks. What utter joy!
           (*Enter Hecate, dragging a cauldron*)
ALL. What have you in the pot?
HECATE. One of the great American public.
FIRST WITCH. Is he cooked?
HECATE. Not yet, but soon he will be.
ALL. Prepare the brew, and cook the goose.
FIRST WITCH. Throw in the horns of bulls, and mix
        The entrails of a margin speculator mangled.

SECOND WITCH. Pour in the brains of fools, and mix
　　　　Unwary feet, the optimist's fond wish,
　　　　The smiles that were, the last of hope,
　　　　And all that was, and never will.
THIRD WITCH. Pour and pour and pour, till all the cauldron's filled,
　　　　Then kindle fast the flame with paper profits heaped,
　　　　Till up they go, in clouds of murky smoke.
HECATE. Hold still, you hags! Here comes a likely sheep,
　　　　With wool grown ripe for fleecing.
　　　　　　　　(Enter Macbeth and Banquo)
ALL. A tip, a tip! Now who will give
　　　　A farthing for a tip?
MACBETH. That will I, a golden eagle even.
FIRST WITCH. Beware the tips, Macbeth,
　　　　That turn out to be but whispers of despair.
BANQUO. That much is clear, but tells us nothing.
MACBETH. Speak out, you hags!
　　　　Unroll the future from your tongue
　　　　And I will pay you rich.
SECOND WITCH. The top is near, Macbeth, the bottom far away.
MACBETH. What is't you mean?
THIRD WITCH. Sell at the top, buy at the bottom.
　　　　Take that path, Macbeth, then you are sure to win.
　　　　　　　　(The witches vanish)
MACBETH. Now any ass could tell me that!
BANQUO. Not so, my lord,
　　　　There is a reading in the lines
　　　　That makes me think 'tis time to duck.
MACBETH. What say you?
BANQUO. You heard as well as I,
　　　　The top is near, they said. Methinks I'll sell
　　　　The paltry shares I hold before it is too late.
MACBETH. Your guess, good Banquo, strikes the nail!
　　　　From this prophetic fog the answer comes so clear
　　　　That I am dumb I could not see. The hour has come
　　　　To sell, yet I dare not. For I do fear my wife.
　　　　Her words do echo in my brain, "Stand fast, Macbeth,
　　　　This rise has just begun."
BANQUO. Stuff cotton in your ears,
　　　　Let not your listening impede your firm resolve to sell.
MACBETH. You do not know my wife.
　　　　If I do sell the stocks I hold, and after comes a rise,
　　　　My home were such a fury then, that Hell itself seems mild!

BANQUO. Are you not a man?
MACBETH. I know not sometimes. Make haste and sell your stocks,
        I follow on in thought.

(*Curtain*)

ACT IV

SCENE I

Falstaff's Apartment in New York
Falstaff, Hamlet, and Lady Macbeth

LADY MACBETH. This bond business is the bunk. Get out!
FALSTAFF. I told you, Hamlet, long ago. Play stocks.
HAMLET. No stock ever has flown so high but some colossal ass
        Would buy it at the top.
FALSTAFF. Buy Bond and Share and Foreign Power.
LADY MACBETH. Buy Auburn Motor Car. Two hundred points is mild.
HAMLET. My country has a love for gold I do not share,
        Nor can I face the turmoil and the bitter strife
        That men profess to hate, yet, deep within their hearts, adore.
        But never I! For I am one, built hermit-like
        To live and think apart, unravel from my cloudy mind
        Strange riddle of life's perplexity, that has no answer,
        But is sport withal, to test ingenious cunning of the brain.
LADY MACBETH. Thou art as cuckoo as the bird
        That peeps from out the clock.
FALSTAFF. There's nothing wrong with him
        But too much damned philosophy. The trouble with these
            thinkers is
        An overdose of thought. To think and think without a whit
            of common sense,
        What profits it? Our brother here has muddled up his
            thinking-piece
        Until he knows not bulls from bears. His thoughts, confused,
        Like peas in pods do wabble to and fro.
LADY MACBETH. The man's miscast in selling bonds. The Senate is
        his role.
HAMLET. Had I but money of my own, no hand could hold me here.
FALSTAFF. Tell me, bird! Now where wouldst thou wander?
HAMLET. Far to a Southern shore, where warm winds blow;
        Some distant land from life apart, no sound but wind and sea.
FALSTAFF. And what do there, you duffer head?
        Make faces at the moon?

HAMLET. I've had too much of doing.
>This constant push drives on beyond me. I cannot hold the pace.

LADY MACBETH. How strange!
>New York hath gathered up my heart, strong holds me in its thrill.
>The city's many millioned voice is dear, is parcel of my life.
>The lights of Broadway are my eyes: I should be blind without.

HAMLET. Then you can have it all. My share is yours, and free.

LADY MACBETH. What think you, Falstaff?
>A little liquor, very strong, would stir this Hamlet's gullet
>To speak some normal sense?

FALSTAFF. The gin's not mixed.

LADY MACBETH. Then mix it, fool!
>The camel's virtue is not mine. I rattle in my throat.

FALSTAFF. I fear this Hamlet.
>You know the man, he's worse when drunk.
>His vaporings are mild, but gentle stuff, until he has a drink,
>Then does he ooze from all his pores such damned philosophy
>Compared to him old Socrates is dumb.

LADY MACBETH. A pity that, but can't be helped.
>Some artificial aid my being craves; my nerves are twittered with
>the fear
>The market opens down so low that snakes will sit on top.
>Some villain whispers in my ear, the discount rate is raised.

FALSTAFF. Dost know that?
>Or is it but a fair excuse to make the evening wild?

LADY MACBETH. The source whence comes the news too often has been
>right.

FALSTAFF. Then Hell prepares!
>I'll set the stage before. The dawn's not yet,
>The night still lives, and what a night!
>Play on, play fast, until the waking cock shall crow
>How dismal is the morn.

LADY MACBETH. You could not hit more apt my present mood. Lead on!

FALSTAFF. Come on, you hermit fool. Before I'm done I'll make you yet
>A roaring night-club hound. (*Exeunt*)

SCENE II

The Blast Furnace
Enter Three Witches

FIRST WITCH. The Reserve did strike a warning bell.
>The note was clear, yet, strange to tell,
>The market failed to go to Hell.

SECOND WITCH. I've stirred and stirred a pot of trouble.
   It will not boil, nor will it bubble.
THIRD WITCH. You ninny! Know you not the reason why?
   The potion sleeps by stirring, nor will it boil
   Until the mixture's ripe. And 'tis not yet.
FIRST WITCH. Stand off and wait. The time will come.
    (*Enter Hecate, with a bird on her shoulder*)
THE WITCHES. What have you there, a woodpecker?
HECATE. No woodpecker this. A fine young raven.
FIRST WITCH. Prophet of evil from a distant land.
HECATE. Not this bird. Straight from Babson Park.
FIRST WITCH. What, a Puritan bird!
SECOND WITCH. What else? Hast ever seen a look more black?
THIRD WITCH. What ails you, bird? Dost think the market too extravagant?
THE RAVEN. The market's sick. I think it well
   To sell and sell and sell and sell.
FIRST WITCH. If that's your cue, old bird, pipe down!
   We've heard that stuff before.
SECOND WITCH. Old stuff, it smells.
THIRD WITCH. Old? Antique, you mean.
FIRST WITCH. I hear the horse's laugh,
   The donkey's hee-haw in the fields.
SECOND WITCH. Be silent, bird; some more like that
   And mules will crack their lips.
THIRD WITCH. Why have you brought this bird?
   Dost think this buoyant land will heed such dismal croaking?
HECATE. It will, and now's the hour!
FIRST WITCH. Stand still, my blackened heart!
   If this be true, then Santa Claus is dead.
SECOND WITCH. Dead as the desert dust.
THIRD WITCH. Buy Woolworth, sisters.
   There'll be treasure in a ten-cent piece.
FIRST WITCH. If this be true, I'll drive the buzzards from the bulls.
   This bird shall feed alone.
THE RAVEN. This market now is out of joint.
    'Twill dribble, dribble, point by point,
    Down and down, till dismal day
    When eighty points have fled away.
HECATE. Hear! Hear!
THE WITCHES. We hear, but dare not heed.
   There's something whispers in our ear
   This bird's been wrong before.
          (*Exeunt*)

SCENE III

Shylock's Offices on Broadway
Shylock and Three Traders

SHYLOCK. Well, gentlemen, bullish as ever?

FIRST TRADER. No. Put me down as bearish.

SECOND TRADER. For shame! A bear to-day, and yesterday's bull!
        Has all your courage oozed that you do cast aside your horns
        And now forsake the cause? No man is man who falls in step
        With cowards' flying feet.

THIRD TRADER. Do not blame him. The herd has turned,
        And he, like any worthy sheep, must follow on.

SECOND TRADER. The Trans-Lux screen has glued his eyes. He cannot see
        beyond.

FIRST TRADER. The Wall Street mind is never fixed, but, lightning like, its
        temper shifts.
        To fit the temper's gauge.

THIRD TRADER. A broad outlook, that!

FIRST TRADER. 'Tis yours, you fool!

SECOND TRADER. And mine, I do admit.

SHYLOCK. As prices go, so goes the Street.

                (*Enter Falstaff*)

FALSTAFF. How, now, you fat commission hound!
        What think you of the market?

SHYLOCK. The tone was better at the close.

FALSTAFF. The tone? What mean you by the tone?
        Never was a broker yet who did not speak as if he thought
        The market were a music piece. And so it is,
        For goats to play on. Come on, speak out!
        What is't you think, if anything? If not,
        For mercy hold your peace.

SHYLOCK. My opinion is, the market opens up.

FALSTAFF. I thank you much for that.
        The brokers' damned equivocating would gall the patience of a
        duck,
        And ducks are patient beasts.

                (*Clerk hands Shylock a wire*)

SHYLOCK. I am surprised at this.

FALSTAFF. I am surprised at nothing. The news is bad, I'll wager.
        Come, read it out.

SHYLOCK. "Sellers all around the floor."

FALSTAFF. There they go again! Some more of this, and I shall be as naked
        as a babe.

(Enter Hamlet)

HAMLET. Bonds for widows, bonds for grandmothers.
       Bonds for tottering trustees, bonds for damned fools.
       Bonds, bonds, beautiful bonds! Gilt-edged bonds!
       Now who will buy a bond?

FALSTAFF. Who could if he would? Not I.

SHYLOCK (*looking at the ticker*). The opening is off, quite off.

FALSTAFF. And so I might have known, when first I heard you say
       The opening would be up. Another rotten guess, friend Shylock,
       Nor will it be the last.

FIRST TRADER. There's none can guess.

SECOND TRADER. Morgan and Rockefeller, they know.

THIRD TRADER. And Mellon, too; he knows.

FIRST TRADER. No more than you or I. The cards are spread too wide
       For one man's knowing. He is a fool who tries.

FALSTAFF. A worse than fool, an utter nincompoop.

FIRST TRADER. Long, short, short, long! Which to be or both?
       Once right to-day, thrice wrong to-morrow.
       What profits that, and yet we do not quit!

FALSTAFF. Nor will, until we're broke. Methinks it won't be long.
                   (*Shylock hands Falstaff a paper*)
       So that's it, more margin!
       Let loose the leech who's written that, and if he cling to me
       I will unseat the lizard from his brains, and pull his tonsils off.

SHYLOCK. Be calm! Dost think we make this call for sport?
       We must protect ourselves.

FALSTAFF. Indeed! 'Twas you, none other, who is responsible for this.

SHYLOCK. How so?

FALSTAFF. Was it not you who said,
       To buy and buy and buy. The market's on the wing, climb on?
       I climbed, you held the ladder's rung. Now get me out.

THE TRADERS. A cheer for Falstaff, noble soul!
       He speaks from out our hearts. We did not dare.
       Come, Shylock, get us out. Once we are even on the books,
       Our dust will smoke the world.

SHYLOCK. A common statement that,
       And like the most, without a word of truth.
       I'll wait until eleven. If margin's not forthcoming then,
       I sell. I have no other choice.

FALSTAFF. Eleven, is it? There's magic in the time.
       The hour the Armistice was signed. Propitious hour!
       Mayhap some kindly relative of mine will pass this life
       And leave his wherewithal to me.

SHYLOCK. I doubt it much.

FALSTAFF. And so do I. O Shylock, let me dream,
>   While dreams are good. To spur them on, it might be well
>   To take a little drink.

TRADERS. So say we all!

(Exeunt)

SCENE IV

Shakespeare's Home. The Library
Enter Shakespeare and Polonius

SHAKESPEARE. Have you heard from Falstaff?

POLONIUS. He has just telephoned.

SHAKESPEARE. Has he lost everything, or are there rags to save?

POLONIUS. My lord, I do suspect.

SHAKESPEARE. Out with it, you ninny-nanny!
>   Your hesitation waltz of thought doth get my goat.
>   Hast ever had an opinion?

POLONIUS. I think, my lord, he's broke.

SHAKESPEARE. Well, there's one in the family gone. Count him out.

POLONIUS. Let not your courage wilt, my lord.
>   There's hope in this idea to pool our resources.

SHAKESPEARE. I doubt we raise enough to buy canaries meals.

POLONIUS. Macbeth has also telephoned.

SHAKESPEARE. Will he be here?

POLONIUS. He will, but, begging your pardon, my lord,
>   I think no good will come of it.

SHAKESPEARE. I never thought so. Still, had he an opinion?

POLONIUS. He said, referring to Lady Macbeth's jewelry, it was already
>   hocked.
>   Also, if I would wire the Federal Reserve, they might think
>   of something.

SHAKESPEARE. Think of something?

POLONIUS. He said, they thought so much on the way up,
>   They might, mayhap, think of something on the way down.

SHAKESPEARE. At times like this such foolery is bitter stuff.
>   It seems that he's gone, too. Count him out.
>   There's only Hamlet left.

POLONIUS. Now, there you've hit the mainstay of our hope.
>   I've heard him say he would not buy—that stocks were up
>   too far.

SHAKESPEARE. The cry was sour grapes. He bought the bonds he could not sell,
>   And had no money left.

POLONIUS. Then is his fortune near intact. I pray it be enough.
SHAKESPEARE. He's here.
(Enter Hamlet)

HAMLET. What would you, Father?
        Your call so urgent seemed, I have foregone
        Some pressing business elsewhere. On that account, be brief.
SHAKESPEARE. I called you, Hamlet, in the hope your aid
        May help recoup the family fortune fading fast
        With each new market crash. Your brother Falstaff, myself, Macbeth,
        Are on the rocks. You are our single hope.
HAMLET. Then bid good-bye to hope!
        The seventh crash before the last I thought that stocks were cheap.
        I sold the bonds I held, and doubled up in stocks.
        And such a slender grip I hold, one kiss will let me fall.
(Enter Falstaff)

SHAKESPEARE. Farewell, a long farewell to all my profits.
(Enter Macbeth and Lady Macbeth)

FALSTAFF. Now here's the whole damned crew, with all our feathers plucked.
HAMLET. We only lack the mother of the brood. Where's she?
SHAKESPEARE. She is in bed, thank God.
HAMLET. The pressure of our cause demands her presence here;
        Her aid may save our skin.
SHAKESPEARE. Enough of that! But let me hear one word
        To show our present state, then you are damned.
        Lay off! Some weeks ago I told her that I sold.
HAMLET. But she will have to know; why fend the issue off?
        If we go down, then she goes too.
SHAKESPEARE. I never thought of that. This market cracks our brain.
(Enter Mrs. Shakespeare)

MRS. SHAKESPEARE. What do you up so late, my chicks?
        Out forming up a pool, to stave your broker's call?
SHAKESPEARE. What? You know?
MRS. SHAKESPEARE. Yes, I know.
SHAKESPEARE. You know, yet there you stand
        All silent like the clam. How strange! No sound of fury
        From your tongue, no single word of blame.
        Am I grown deaf, or is this but the calm precedes
        The terror of the storm?
MRS. SHAKESPEARE. The germ that bit the world bit me. I, too, am in.
FALSTAFF. In and all in! O perfect home, your record is sublime!
SHAKESPEARE. Now comes the end of pleasure, the beginning of my work.
MRS. SHAKESPEARE. Be not alarmed. I sold the market short.

SHAKESPEARE. You! The pillar of our home, model of our life,
       Are sunk so low as to sell the country short!
MACBETH. To think that you, our mother,
       Should be in league with these foul bears, whose rumors vile
       Cried down their country's worth, set panic in the land,
       Drove down the best of stocks to naked zero's reach,
       To hang us all on ruin's limb, gaunt specters of the past!
       Here is a tale incredible! The crocodiles will weep!
HAMLET. You idiot dolts! What temper of mind is this
       That you do moralize on things you would have done
       Had you but thought you'd win?
FALSTAFF. The boy is right. These damned philosophers have a use
       I never knew could be.
HAMLET. What she has made may cancel all our loss.
FALSTAFF. Good boy! The point you make blows morals to the winds.
       Our Hamlet scores again. Now were he less the fool,
       He might be very bright.
SHAKESPEARE. We can forgive her, don't you think?
MRS. SHAKESPEARE. Forgive? For what? I have not sold the country short,
       Nor ever will. The stocks you bought, in like amount I sold.
LADY MACBETH. How have you known, to let you do this?
MRS. SHAKESPEARE. Lest you forget, my child, you babble in your sleep.
MACBETH. Now do I live again! Lead on, you bulls,
       And damned be he who first shall turn a bear!

           (*Curtain*)

Joseph Rudyard Kipling
(1865–1936)

As praised for his craftsmanship as he has been condemned for his politics, Rudyard Kipling reigned as Great Britain's apologist of empire, invoking the spirit of the raj and the camraderie of the barracks. Despite his reputation as an outspoken nationalist, he refused England's Poet Laureateship in 1896. Works like *The Jungle Book* (1894) and *Kim* (1901) brought him vast popularity and, in 1907, a Nobel Prize for Literature, while his poetry came to be admired by critics as demanding as W.H Auden and T.S. Eliot. Kipling's later stories occasionally move back in time and touch on more philosophical issues.

"Proofs of Holy Writ" (1932) combines Kipling's lifelong interests in the King James Version of the Bible and Shakespeare. Although Kipling was born in India, his parents brought him back to England in 1871 to ensure a solid British upbringing while they returned to India. During the six years he spent living in Southsea with a strict, religious couple in a household he would later characterize as the "House of Desolation," his Sunday reading was restricted to the King James Bible and Cranmer's Collects. His detailed interest in the language of the King James, which was to help shape his own prose, becomes apparent in his dialogue between Shakespeare and Jonson.

After exchanging opinions and insults about each other's art, learning, and values, the two writers use their talents to help with a new translation of Isaiah as part of the King James Version of the Bible. Will's ear for English clearly comes to prove more valuable than Ben's memory of Latin. An early poem, "The Craftsman," also shows the two playwrights together, but here Shakespeare spends the night at the Mermaid Tavern describing how he found material for his female characters:

> How at Bankside, a boy drowning kittens
> Winced at the business; whereupon his sister—
> Lady Macbeth aged seven—thrust 'em under,
>   Somberly scornful.

"Proofs of Holy Writ"
(1932)

Arise, shine; for thy light is come, and the glory of the Lord is risen upon thee.

2. For, behold, the darkness shall cover the earth, and gross darkness the people: but the Lord shall arise upon thee, and his glory shall be seen upon thee.

3. And the Gentiles shall come to thy light, and kings to the brightness of thy rising.

. . . .

19. The sun shall be no more thy light by day; neither for brightness shall the moon give light unto thee: but the Lord shall be unto thee an everlasting light, and thy God thy glory.

20.Thy sun shall no more go down; neither shall thy moon withdraw itself: for the Lord shall be thine everlasting light, and the days of thy mourning shall be ended.

Isaiah LX. Authorized Version

They seated themselves in the heavy chairs on the pebbled floor beneath the eaves of the summer-house by the orchard. A table between them carried wine and glasses, and a packet of papers, with pen and ink. The larger man of the two, his doublet unbuttoned, his broad face blotched and scarred, puffed a little as he came to rest. The other picked an apple from the grass, bit it, and went on with the thread of the talk that they must have carried out of doors with them.

"But why waste time fighting atomies who do not come up to your belly-button, Ben?" he asked.

"It breathes me—it breathes me, between bouts! You'd be better for a tussle or two."

"But not to spend mind or verse on 'em. What was Dekker to you? Ye knew he'd strike back—and hard."

"He and Marston had been baiting me like dogs … about my trade as they called it, though it was only my cursed step-father's. 'Bricks and mortar,' Dekker said, and 'hodman.' And he mocked my face. 'Twas clean as curds in my youth. This humour has come on me since."

"Ah! 'Every man and his humour'? But why did ye not have at Dekker in peace—over the sack as you do at me?"

"Because I'd have drawn on him—and he's no more worth a hanging than Gabriel. Setting aside what he wrote of me, too, the hireling dog has merit, of a sort. His Shoemaker's Holiday. Hey? Though my Bartlemy Fari, when 'tis presented, will furnish out three of it and—"

"Ride all the easier. I have suffered two readings of it already. It creaks like an overloaded hay-wain," the other cut in. "You give too much."

Ben smiled loftily, and went on. "But I'm glad I lashed him in my Poetaster, for all I've worked with him since. How comes it that I've never fought with thee, Will?"

"First, Behemoth," the other drawled, "it needs two to engender any sort of iniquity. Second, the betterment of this present age—and the next maybe—lies, in chief, on our four shoulders. If the Pillars of the Temple fall out, Nature, Art, and Learning come to a stand. Last, I am not yet ass enough to hawk up my private spites before the groundlings. What do the Court, citizens, or 'prentices give for thy fallings-out or fallings-in with Dekker—or the Grand Devil?"

"They should be taught, then—taught."

"Always that? What's your commission to enlighten us?"

"My own learning which I have heaped up, lifelong, at my own pains. My assured knowledge, also, of my craft and art. I'll suffer no man's mock or malice on it."

"The one sure road to mockery."

"I deny nothing of my brain-store to my lines. I—I build up my own works throughout."

"Yet when Dekker cries 'hodman' y'are not content."

Ben half heaved in his chair. "I'll owe you a beating for that when I'm thinner. Meantime, here's on account. I say, I build up my own foundations; devising and perfecting my own plots; adorning 'em justly as fits time, place, and action. In all of which you sin damnably. I set no landward principalities on sea-beaches."

"They pay their penny for pleasure—not learning," Will answered above the apple-core.

"Penny or tester, you owe 'em justice. In the facture of plays—nay, listen, Will—at all points they must be dressed historically—*teres atque rotundus*—in ornament and temper. As my 'Sejanus,' of which the mob was unworthy."

Her Will made a doleful face, and echoed, "Unworthy! I was—what did I play, Ben, in that long weariness? Some most grievous ass."

"The part of Caius Silius," said Ben stiffly.

Will laughed aloud. "True. 'Indeed that place was not my sphere.'"

It must have been a quotation, for Ben winced a little, ere he recovered himself and went on: "Also my 'Alchemist' which the world in part apprehends. The main of its learning is necessarily yet hid from 'em. To come to your works, Will—"

"I am a sinner on all sides. The drink's at your elbow."

"Confession shall not save ye—nor bribery." Ben filled his glass. "Sooner than labour the right cold heat to devise your own plots you filch, botch, and clap 'em together out o' ballads, broadsheets, old wives' tales, chap-books—"

Will nodded with complete satisfaction. "Say on," quoth he.

"'Tis so with nigh all yours. I've known honester jackdaws. And whom among the learned do ye deceive? Reckoning up those—forty, is it?—your plays you've misbegot, there's not six, which have not plots common as Moorditch."

"Ye're out, Ben. There's not one. My 'Love's Labour' (how I came to write it, I know not) is nearest to lawful issue. My 'Tempest' (how I came to write that, I know) is, in some part, my own stuff. Of the rest, I stand guilty. Bastards all!"

"And no shame."

"None! Our business must be fitted with parts hot and hot—and the boys are more trouble than the men. Give me the bones of any stuff, I'll cover 'em as quickly as any. But to hatch new plots is to waste God's unreturning time like a—"—he chuckled—"like a hen."

"Yet see what ye miss! Invention next to knowledge, whence it proceeds, being the chief glory of Art—"

"Miss, say you? Dick Burbage—in my 'Hamlet' that I botched for him when he had staled of our Kings? (Nobly he played it.) Was he a miss?"

Ere Ben could speak, Will overbore him.

"And when poor Dick was at odds with the world in general and womenkind in special, I clapped him up my 'Lear' for a vomit."

"An hotch-potch of passion, outrunning reason," was the verdict.

"Not altogether. Cast in a mould too large for any boards to bear. (My fault!) Yet Dick evened it. And when he'd come out of his whoremongering aftermaths of repentance, I served him my 'Macbeth' to toughen him. Was that a miss?"

"I grant you your 'Macbeth' as nearest in spirit to my 'Sejanus'; showing for example: 'How fortune plies her sports when she begins To practise 'em.' We'll see which of the two lives longest."

"Amen! I'll bear no malice among the worms."

A liveried serving-man, booted and spurred, led a saddle-horse through the gate into the orchard. At a sign from Will he tethered the beast to a tree, lurched aside and stretched on the grass. Ben, curious as a lizard, for all his bulk, wanted to know what it meant.

"There's a nosing Justice of the Peace lost in thee," Will returned. "Yon's a business I've neglected all this day for thy fat sake—and he by so much the drunker.... Patience! It's all set out on the table. Have a care with the ink!"

Ben reached unsteadily for the packet of papers and read the superscription: "'To William Shakespeare, Gentleman, at his house of New Place in the town of Stratford, these—with diligence from M.S.' Why does the fellow withhold his name? Or is it one of your women? I'll look."

Muzzy as he was, he opened and unfolded a mass of printed papers expertly enough.

"From the most learned divine, Miles Smith of Brazen Nose College," Will explained. "You know this business as well as I. The King has set all the scholars of England to make one Bible, which the Church shall be bound to, out of all the Bibles that men use."

"I knew." Ben could not lift his eyes from the printed page. "I'm more about Court than you think. The learning of Oxford and Cambridge—'most noble and most equal,' as I have said—and Westminster, to sit upon a clutch of Bibles. Those 'ud be Geneva (my mother read to me out of it at her knee), Douai, Rheims, Coverdale, Matthew's, the Bishops', The Great, and so forth."

"They are all set down on the page there—text against text. And you call me a botcher of old clothes?"

"Justly. But what's your concern with this botchery? To keep peace among the Divines? There's fifty of 'em at it as I've heard."

"I deal with but one. He came to know me when we played at Oxford—when the plague was too hot in London."

"I remember this Miles Smith now. Son of a butcher? Hey?" Ben grunted.

"Is it so?" was the quiet answer. "He was moved, he said, with some lines of mine in Dick's part. He said they were, to his godly apprehension, a parable as it might be, of his reverend self, going down darkling to his tomb 'twixt cliffs of ice and iron."

"What lines? I know none of thine of that power. But in my 'Sejanus'—"

"These were in my 'Macbeth.' They lost nothing at Dick's mouth:—

> To-morrow, and to-morrow, and to-morrow
> Creeps in this petty pace from day to day
> To the last syllable of recorded time,
> And all our yesterdays have lighted fools
> The way to dusty death—

or something in that sort. Condell writes 'em out fair for him, and tells him I am Justice of the Peace (wherein he lied) and armiger, which brings me within the pale of God's creatures and the Church. Little and little, then, this very reverend Miles Smith opens his mind to me. He and a half-score others, his cloth, are cast to furbish up the Prophets—Isaiah to Malachi. In his opinion by what he'd heard, I had some skill in words, and he'd condescend—"

"How?" Ben barked. "Condescend?"

"Why not? He'd condescend to inquire o' me privily, when direct illumination lacked, for a tricking-out of his words or the turn of some figure. For example"—Will pointed to the papers—"here be the first three verses of the sixtieth of Isaiah, and the nineteenth and twentieth of that same. Miles has been at a stand over 'em a week or more."

"They never called on me." Ben caressed lovingly the handpressed proofs on their lavish linen paper. "Here's the Latin atop and"—his thick forefinger ran down the slip—"some three—four—Englishings out of the other Bibles. They spare 'emselves nothing. Let's to it together. Will you have the Latin first?"

"Could I choke ye from that, Holofernes?"

Ben rolled forth, richly: "'*Surge, illumare, Jerusalem, quia venit lumen tuum, et gloria Domini super te orta est. Quia ecce tenebrae operient terram et caligo populos. Super te autem orietur Dominus, et gloria ejus in te videbitur. Et ambulabunt gentes in lumine tuo, et reges in splendore ortus tui.*' Er-hum? Think you to better that?"

"How have Smith's crew gone about it?"

"Thus." Ben read from the paper. "'Get thee up, O Jerusalem, and be bright, for thy light is at hand, and the glory of God has risen up upon thee.'"

"Up-pup-up!" Will stuttered profanely.

Ben held on. "'See how darkness is upon the earth and the peoples thereof.'"

"That's no great stuff to put into Isaiah's mouth. And further, Ben?"

"'But on thee God shall shew light and on——' or 'in,' is it?" (Ben held the proof closer to the deep furrow at the bridge of his nose.) "'On thee shall His glory be manifest. So that all peoples shall walk in thy light and the Kings in the glory of thy morning.'"

"It may be mended. Read me the Coverdale of it now. 'Tis on the same sheet—to the right, Ben."

"Umm—umm! Coverdale saith, 'And therefore get thee up betimes, for thy light cometh, and the glory of the Lord shall rise up upon thee. For lo! while the darkness and cloud covereth the earth and the people, the Lord shall shew thee light, and His glory shall be seen in thee. The Gentiles shall come to thy light, and kings to the brightness that springeth forth upon thee.' But 'gentes' is, for the most part, 'peoples,'" Ben concluded.

"Eh?" said Will indifferently. "Art sure?"

This loosed an avalanche of instances from Ovid, Quintilian, Terence, Columella, Seneca, and others. Will took no heed till the rush ceased, but stared into the orchard, through the September haze. "Now give me the Douai and Geneva for this 'Get thee up, O Jerusalem,'" said he at last. "They'll be all there."

Ben referred to the proofs. "'Tis 'arise' in both," said he. "'Arise and be bright' in Geneva. In the Douai 'tis 'Arise and be illuminated.'"

"So? Give me the paper now." Will took it from his companion, rose, and paced towards a tree in the orchard, turning again, when he had reached it, by a well-worn track through the grass. Ben leaned forward in his chair. The other's free hand went up warningly.

"Quiet, man!" said he. "I wait on my Demon!" He fell into the stage-stride of his art at that time, speaking to the air.

"How shall this open? 'Arise?' No! 'Rise!' Yes. And we'll have no weak coupling. 'Tis a call to a City! 'Rise—shine'... Nor yet any schoolmaster's 'because'—because Isaiah is not Holofernes. 'Rise—shine; for thy light is come, and—!'" He refreshed himself from the apple and the proofs as he strode. "'And—and the glory of God!'—No! 'God''s over short. We need the long roll here. 'And the glory of the Lord is risen on thee.' (Isaiah speaks the part. We'll have it from his own lips.) What's next in Smith's stuff? ... 'See how?' Oh, vile—vile! ... And Geneva hath 'Lo'? (Still, Ben! Still!) 'Lo' is better by all odds: but to match the long roll of 'the Lord' we'll have it 'Behold.' How goes it now? 'For, behold, darkness clokes the earth and—and—' What's the colour and use of this cursed caligo, Ben?—'*Et caligo populos.*'"

"'Mistiness' or, as in Pliny, 'blindness.' And further—"

"No—o ... Maybe, though, *caligo* will piece out *tenebrae*. '*Quia ecce tenebrae operient terram et caligo populos.*' Nay! 'Shadow' and 'mist' are not men enough for this work.... Blindness, did ye say, Ben? ... The blackness of blindness atop of mere darkness? ... By God, I've used it in my own stuff many times! 'Gross' searches it to the hilts! 'Darkness covers'—no—'clokes' (short always). 'Darkness clokes the earth, and gross—gross darkness the people!' (But Isaiah's prophesying, with the storm behind him. Can ye not feel it, Ben? It must be 'shall')—'Shall cloke the earth' ... The rest comes clearer.... 'But on thee God shall arise' ... (Nay, that's sacrificing the Creator to the Creature!) 'But the Lord shall arise on thee,' and—yes, we'll sound that 'thee' again—'and on thee shall'—No! ... 'And His glory shall be seen on thee.' Good!" He walked his beat a little in silence, mumbling the two verses before he mouthed them.

"I have it! Hark, Ben! 'Rise—shine; for thy light is come, and the glory of the Lord is risen on thee. For, behold, darkness shall cloke the earth, and gross darkness the people. But the Lord shall arise on thee, and His glory shall be seen upon thee.'"

"There's something not all amiss there," Ben conceded.

"My Demon never betrayed me yet, while I trusted him. Now for the verse that runs to the blast of rams'-horns. '*Et ambulabunt gentes in lumine tuo, et reges in splendore ortus tui.*' How goes that in the smithy? 'The Gentiles shall come to thy light, and kings to the brightness that springs forth upon thee?' The same in Coverdale and the Bishops'—eh? We'll keep 'Gentiles,' Ben, for the sake of the indraught of the last syllable. But it might be 'And the Gentiles shall draw.' No! The plainer the better! 'The Gentiles shall come to thy light, and kings to the splendour of——' (Smith's out here! We'll need something that shall lift the trumpet anew.) 'Kings shall—shall—Kings to—' (Listen, Ben, but on your life speak not!) 'Gentiles shall come to thy light, and kings to thy brightness'—No! 'Kings to the brightness that springeth—' Serves not! ... One trumpet must answer another. And the blast of a trumpet is always ai-ai. 'The brightness of'—'Ortus' signifies 'rising,' Ben—or what?"

"Ay, or 'birth,' or the East in general."

"Ass! 'Tis the one word that answers to 'light.' 'Kings to the brightness of thy rising.' Look! The thing shines now within and without. God! That so much should lie on a word!' He repeated the verse—"'And the Gentiles shall come to thy light, and kings to the brightness of thy rising.'"

He walked to the table and wrote rapidly on the proof margin all three verses as he had spoken them. "If they hold by this," said he, raising his head, "they'll not go far astray. Now for the nineteenth and twentieth verses. On the other sheet, Ben. What? What? Smith says he has held back his rendering till he hath seen mine? Then we'll botch 'em as they stand. Read me first the Latin; next the Coverdale, and last the Bishops'. There's a contagion of sleep in the air." He handed back the proofs, yawned, and took up his walk.

Obedient, Ben began: "*Non erit tibi amplius Sol ad lucendum per diem, nec splendor Lunae illuminabit te.* Which Coverdale rendereth, 'The Sun shall never be thy daylight, and the light of the Moon shall never shine unto thee.' The Bishops read: 'Thy sun shall never be thy daylight and the light of the moon shall never shine on thee.'"

"Coverdale is the better," said Will, and, wrinkling his nose a little, "the Bishops put out their lights clumsily. Have at it, Ben."

Ben pursed his lips and knit his brow. "The two verses are in the same mode, changing a hand's-breadth in the second. By so much, therefore, the more difficult."

"Ye see that, then?" said the other, staring past him, and muttering as he paced, concerning suns and moons. Presently he took back the proof, chose him another apple, and grunted. "Umm-umm! 'Thy Sun shall never be—-' No! Flat as a split viol. '*Non erit tibi amplius Sol—*' That *amplius* must give tongue. Ah! ... 'Thy Sun shall not—shall not—shall no more be thy light by day' ... A fair entry. 'Nor?'—No! Not on the heels of 'day.' 'Neither' it must be—'Neither the Moon'—but here's splendor and the rams'-horns again. (Therefore—ai—ai!) 'Neither for brightness shall the Moon—' (Pest! It is the Lord who is taking the Moon's place over Israel. It must be 'thy Moon.') 'Neither for brightness shall thy Moon light—give—make—give light unto thee.' Ah! ... Listen here! ... 'The Sun shall no more be thy light by day: neither for brightness shall thy Moon give light unto thee.' That serves, and more, for the first entry. What next, Ben?"

Ben nodded magisterially as Will neared him, reached out his hand for the proofs, and read: "'*Sed erit tibi Dominus in lucem sempiternam et Deus tuus in gloriam tuam.*' Here is a jewel of Coverdale's that the Bishops have wisely stolen whole. Hear! 'But the Lord Himself shall be thy everlasting light, and thy God shall be thy glory.'" Ben paused. "There's a hand's-breadth of spendour for a simple man to gather!"

"Both hands rather. He's swept the strings as divinely as David before

Saul," Will assented. "We'll convey it whole, too.... What's amiss now, Holofernes?"

For Ben was regarding him with a scholar's cold pity. "Both hands! Will, hast thou ever troubled to master any shape or sort of prosody—the mere names of the measures and pulses of strung words?"

"I beget some such stuff and send it to you to christen. What's your wisdomhood in labour of?"

"Naught. Naught. But not to know the names of the tools of his trade!" Ben half muttered and pronounced some Greek word or other which conveyed nothing to the listener, who replied: "Pardon, then, for whatever sin it was. I do but know words for my need of 'em, Ben. Hold still awhile!"

He went back to his pacings and mutterings. "'For the Lord Himself shall be thy—or thine?—everlasting light.' Yes. We'll convey that." He repeated it twice. "Nay! Can be bettered. Hark ye, Ben. Here is the Sun going up to overrun and possess all Heaven for evermore. Therefore (Still, man!) we'll harness the horses of the dawn. Hear their hooves? 'The Lord Himself shall be unto thee thy everlasting light, and—' Hold again! After that climbing thunder must be some smooth check—like great wings gliding. Therefore we'll not have 'shall be thy glory,' but 'And thy God thy glory!' Ay—even as an eagle alighteth! Good—good! Now again, the sun and moon of that twentieth verse, Ben."

Ben read: "'*Non occidet ultra Sol tuus et Luna tua non minuetur: quia erit tibi Dominus in lucem sempiternam et complebuntur dies luctus tui.*'"

Will snatched the paper and read aloud from the Coverdale version. "'Thy Sun shall never go down, and thy Moon shall not be taken away....' What a plague's Coverdale doing with his blocking ets and urs, Ben? What's minuetur? ... I'll have it all anon."

"Minish—make less—appease—abate, as in—"

"So?" ... Will threw the proofs back. "Then 'Wane' is good, but overweak for place next to 'moon'" ... He swore softly. "Isaiah hath abolished both earthly sun and moon. Exeunt ambo. Aha! I begin to see! ... Sol, the man, goes down—down stairs or trap—as needs be. Therefore 'Go down' shall stand. 'Set' would have been better—as a sword sent home in the scabbard—but it jars—it jars. Now Luna must retire herself in some simple fashion.... Which? Ass that I be! 'Tis common talk in all the plays.... 'Withdrawn' ... 'Favour withdrawn' ... 'Countenance withdrawn.' 'The Queen withdraws herself' ... 'Withdraw' it shall be! 'Neither shall the moon withdraw herself.' (Hear her silver train rasp the boards, Ben?) 'Thy sun shall no more go down—neither shall thy moon withdraw herself. For the Lord ...'—ay, the Lord, simple of Himself—'shall be thine'—yes, 'thine' here—'everlasting light, and' ... How goes the ending, Ben?"

"'*Et complebuntur dies luctus tui.*'" Ben read. "'And thy sorrowful days shall be rewarded thee,' says Coverdale."

"And the Bishops?"

"'And thy sorrowful days shall be ended.'"

"By no means. And Douai?"

"'Thy sorrow shall be ended.'"

"And Geneva?"

"'And the days of thy mourning shall be ended.'"

"The Switzers have it! Lay the tail of Geneva to the head of Coverdale and the last is without flaw." He began to thump Ben on the shoulder. "We have it! I have it all, Boanerges! Blessed be my Demon! Hear! 'The sun shall no more be thy light by day, neither for brightness the moon by night. But the Lord Himself shall be unto thee thy everlasting light, and thy God thy glory.'" He drew a deep breath and went on. "'Thy sun shall no more go down; neither shall thy moon withdraw herself, for the Lord shall be thine everlasting light, and the days of thy mourning shall be ended.'" The rain of triumphant blows began again. "If those other seven devils in London let it stand on this sort, it serves. But God knows what they can not turn upsee-dejee!"

Ben wriggled. "Let be!" he protested. "Ye are more moved by this jugglery than if the Globe were burned."

"Thatch—old thatch! And full of fleas! ... But, Ben, ye should have heard my Ezekiel making mock of fallen Tyrus in his twenty-seventh chapter. Miles sent me the whole, for, he said, some small touches. I took it to the Bank—four o'clock of a summer morn; stretched out in one of our wherries—and watched London, Port and Town, up and down the river, waking all arrayed to heap more upon evident excess. Ay! 'A merchant for the people of many isles' ... 'The ships of Tarshish did sing of thee in thy markets'? Yes! I saw all Tyre before me neighing her pride against lifted heaven.... But what will they let stand of mine at long last? Which? I'll never know."

He had set himself neatly and quickly to refolding and cording the packet while he talked. "That's secret enough," he said at the finish.

"He'll lose it by the way." Ben pointed to the sleeper beneath the tree. "He's owl-drunk."

"But not his horse," said Will. He crossed the orchard, roused the man; slid the packet into an holster which he carefully rebuckled; saw him out of the gate, and returned to his chair.

"Who will know we had a part in it?" Ben asked.

"God, maybe—if He ever lay ear to earth. I've gained and lost enough—lost enough." He lay back and sighed. There was long silence till he spoke half aloud. "And Kit that was my master in the beginning, he died when all the world was young."

"Knifed on a tavern reckoning—not even for a wench!" Ben nodded.

"Ay. But if he lived he'd have breathed me! 'Fore God, he'd have breathed me!"

"Was Marlowe, or any man, ever thy master, Will?"

"He alone. Very he. I envied Kit. Ye do not know that envy, Ben?"

"Not as touching my own works. When the mob is led to prefer a baser Muse, I have felt the hurt, and paid home. Ye know that—as ye know my doctrine of play-writing."

"Nay—not wholly—tell it at large," said Will, relaxing in his seat, for virtue had gone out of him. He put a few drowsy questions. In three minutes Ben had launched full-flood on the decayed state of the drama, which he was born to correct; on cabals and intrigues against him which he had fought without cease; and on the inveterate muddle-headedness of the mob unless duly scourged into approbation by his magisterial hand.

It was very still in the orchard now that the horse had gone. The heat of the day held though the sun sloped, and the wine had done its work. Presently, Ben's discourse was broken by a snort from the other chair.

"I was listening, Ben! Missed not a word—missed not a word." Will sat up and rubbed his eyes. "Ye held me throughout." His head dropped again before he had done speaking.

Ben looked at him with a chuckle and quoted from one of his own plays:—

Mine earnest vehement botcher
And deacon also, Will, I cannot dispute with you.

He drew out flint, steel, and tinder, pipe and tobacco-bag from somewhere around his waist, lit and puffed against the midges till he, too, dozed.

Thomas Edward Bond
(b. 1934)

The appearance of Edward Bond's *Saved* at the Royal Court Theatre on November 3, 1965 established a distinctive new voice on the British stage and provoked an uproar in theatrical, critical, legal and political circles. The last play to be prosecuted by the Lord Chamberlain under England's then licensing laws, *Saved*'s portrayal of violence, especially the stoning of a baby in its pram, outraged those who felt that Bond had gone too far in politicizing drama. But it also inspired many younger writers, critics and activists who agreed with his view that the roots of violence lie in the corrosive effect of corrupt social and economic structures on human relationships.

Shakespeare's influence on Bond began in 1946 when the young working-class student at Crouch End Secondary Modern School saw a production of "Macbeth" at the Bedford Theatre, Camden. Bond's reaction to the experience was as much political as aesthetic: "for the first time in my life … I met somebody who was actually talking about my problems, about the life I'd been living, the political society around me." Throughout his career Bond has treated Shakespeare as a mentor, turning to his plays for inspiration, ideas, and images that he could reshape to meet his vision of contemporary society. Traces of "Timon of Athens," thus, appear in *The Worlds* (1979), "The Tempest" in *Summer: A European Play* (1982), and "King Lear" in the opera libretto *For We Come to the River* (1976), on which he collaborated with the composer Hans-Werner Henze. His clearest homage is his revised *Lear* (1971), which features a more actively committed protagonist.

Bond's Shakespeare in *Bingo: Scenes of Money and Death* suffers from a sense of guilt over his silent assent in a plan by his neighbor William Combe to enclose Stratford's common fields. The plan was part of the enclosure movement which profoundly disrupted the lives of the poor. In this scene from the play (Part Two, Scene Four), a hostile Ben Jonson, who has come to visit, and Shakespeare, who only wants to withdraw from all responsibilities, meet for a drink at the Golden Cross Inn. As the economic problems of Stratford begin to intrude on them, Shakespeare moves towards the despair which will lead him to commit suicide at the end of the play.

Bingo
(1974)

[The Golden Cross. A large, irregular shaped room. Stone floor. Left, a few tables and benches, Right, a table and three chairs. A large open fire between them. Burning wood. Night. Lamps. Shakespeare and Jonson are at the table right. Bottles and two glasses on the table. No one else in the room.]

SHAKESPEARE. How long did the theatre burn?

JONSON. Two hours.

SHAKESPEARE (*tapping the table*): When I was buying my house the owner was poisoned. By his son. A half-wit. They hanged him. Legal complications with the contract. My father was robbed by my mother's side of the family. That was property too.

JONSON. Coincidences.

SHAKESPEARE. But that such coincidences are possible.... Jokes about my play setting the house on fire?

JONSON. What are you writing?

SHAKESPEARE. Nothing.

[*They drink*]

JONSON. Not writing?

SHAKESPEARE. No.

JONSON. Why not?

SHAKESPEARE. Nothing to say.

JONSON. Doesn't stop others. Written out?

SHAKESPEARE. Yes.

[*They drink*]

JONSON. Now, what are you writing?

SHAKESPEARE. Nothing.

JONSON. Down here for the peace and quiet? Find inspiration, look for it, anyway. Work up something spiritual. Refined. Can't get by with scrabbling it off in noisy corners any more. New young men. Competition. Your recent stuff's been pretty peculiar. What was the Winter's Tale about? I ask to be polite.

SHAKESPEARE. What are you writing?

JONSON. They say you've come down to study grammar. Or history. Have you read my English Grammar? Let me sell you a copy. I've got a few in my room.

[*Silence. Shakespeare pours drinks.*]

What am I writing? You've never shown any interest before.

SHAKESPEARE. Untrue.

JONSON. O, how many characters, enough big parts for the leads, a bit of comedy to bring them in—usual theatre-owner's questions. Trying to pick my brains now? Run out of ideas?

[*They drink.*]

Nice to see you again. I'm off to Scotland soon. Walking. Alone. Well, no one would come with me. Might be a book in it. Eat out on London gossip. The Scots are very credulous—common sense people are always superstitious, aren't they? Can't imagine you walking to Scotland. That sort of research is too real!

SHAKESPEARE (*smiles. Starts to stand*): Well.

JONSON. Don't go. Sit down. Would you like to read my new play? It's up in my room. Won't take a minute.

SHAKESPEARE. No.

JONSON. Nice to see you again. Honest William.

SHAKESPEARE. I wouldn't read it. It would lie there.

JONSON. What is it? Tired? Not well? [*Shakespeare starts to stand*] Sit down. [*He pours drinks*] Wife better?

SHAKESPEARE. No.

JONSON. Wrong subject. D'you like the quiet?

SHAKESPEARE. What quiet?

[*They drink.*]

JONSON. What are you writing? [*Slight pause*] The theatre told me to ask.

SHAKESPEARE (*shakes his head*): Sorry.

JONSON. What d'you do?

SHAKESPEARE. There's the house. People I'm responsible for. The garden's too big. Time goes. I'm surprised how old I've got.

JONSON. You always kept yourself to yourself. Well, you certainly didn't like me. Or what I wrote. Sit down. I hate writing. Fat white fingers excreting dirty black ink. Smudges. Shadows. Shit. Silence.

SHAKESPEARE. You're a very good writer.

JONSON. Patronizing bastard.

[*Slight pause. They drink*]

You don't want to quarrel with me. I killed one once. Fellow writer. Only way to end a literary quarrel. Put my sword in him. Like a new one. He flowed as if inspired. Then the Old Bailey. I was going to hang. That's carrying research too far. I could read, so they let me off. Proper respect for learning. Branded my thumb. A child's alphabet: T for Tyburn. I've been in prison four times. Dark smelly places. No gardens. Sorry yours is too big. They kept coming in and taking people out to cut bits off them. Their hands. Take off their noses. Cut their stomachs open. Rummage round inside with a dirty fist and drag everything out. The law. Little men going out through the door. White. Shaking. Even staggering. I ask, is it prison? Four times? Don't go, don't go. I want to touch you for a loan. I know I'm not human. My father died before I was born. That desperate to avoid me. My eyes are too close together. Look. A well known fact. I used to have so much good will when I was young. That's what's necessary, isn't it? Good will. In the end. O God.

[*Silence. They drink.*]

Yes.

[*Silence.*]

What are you writing?

SHAKESPEARE. I think you're a very good writer. I made them put on your first play.

JONSON. God, am I that bad? In prison they threatened to cut off my nose. And ears. They didn't offer to work on my eyes. Life doesn't touch you, I mean soil you. You walk by on the clean pavement. I climb tall towers to show I'm clever. Others do tricks in the gutter. You are serene. Serene. I'm going to make you drunk and watch you spew. You aren't well, I can see that! Something's happening to your will. You're being sapped. I think you're dying. What a laugh! Are you getting hollow? Why don't you get up? Walk out? Why are you listening to my hysterical crap? Don't worry about me. I'll survive. I've lived through two religious conversions. I thrive on tearing myself into bits. I even bought enough poison. Once. In a moment of strength. [*He takes a small bottle from his collar. It hangs round his neck on a chain*] I was too weak to take it. Hung the cross here in my Catholic period. [*He takes the top off the bottle*] Look: coated in sugar. Like to lick my poison? I licked it once to try. [*Shakespeare doesn't react*] Well, it's not the best. All I could afford. Little corner shop in London.

SHAKESPEARE. Give it to me.

JONSON. Sentimental whiner. You wouldn't uncross your legs if I ate the lot. You're upset I might give it to someone else. [*He puts the bottle back in his collar*] I should live in the country. No—I'd hear myself talk. When I went sight-seeing in the mad house there was a young man who spent all his time stamping on his shadow. Punched it. Went for it with a knife. Tried to cut the head off. Anything to be free. The knife on the stone. The noise. Sparks.

[*They drink.*]

I helped to uncover the gunpowder plot. Keep in with the top.

[*They drink.*]

Your health. I'm always saying nice things about you, Serenity. Of course, I touch on your lack of education, or as I put it, genuine ignorance. But you can't ignore an elephant when it waves at you with its trunk, can you? You taking this down? Base something on me. A minor character who comes on for five minutes while the lead's off changing his clothes or making a last effort to learn his lines? Shall I tell you something about me? I hate. Yes— isn't that interesting! I keep it well hidden, but it's true: I hate. A short hard word. Begins with a hiss and ends with a spit: hate. I hate you, for example. For preference actually. Hate's far more jealous than love. You can't satisfy it by the gut or the groin. A terrible appetite. Interrupt me. Speak. Sob. Nothing? I'm not afraid to let myself be insulted.

[*The Son, Wally, Jerome, and Joan come in right.*]

SON (*pointing left*): Over there.

[*The Son goes out right again. The others sit.*]

WALLY. They'm followed us.

JEROME. No matter. They'll know who t'was.

WALLY. They'm followed us. I were neigh on slaughtered. One a Combe's men heaved a rock at us when I were scramblin' out the ditch. I'm certain—sure they'm followed us. Where's us shovels?

JEROME. I hid they in the hedge out back.

JOAN (*looking across at Shakespeare and Jonson*): Careful, there's gen'men in here.

JEROME. Too drunk t' hear if yo' shouted.

WALLY. Git the mud off yo'. That show what us bin up to. Us don't ought-a done it. That'll only start more row.

JEROME. That's us land. Shall us sit down an' let 'em rob it? How I live then? How I feed my wife an' little-uns?

JOAN. Hush.

JEROME. I'll break Combe's neck.

JONSON. Where was I? Yes: hate. I hate you because you smile right up to under your eyes. Which are set the right distance apart. O I've wiped the smile off now. I hate your health. I'm sure you'll die in a healthy way. Well at least you're dying. That's incense to scatter on these burning coals. I hate your long country limbs. I've seen you walking along the city streets like a man going over his fields. So simple stride. So beautiful and simple. You see why I hate you. How have they made you so simple? Tell me, Will? Please. How have they made you good? You even know when it's time to die. Come down here to die quietly in your garden or an upstairs room. My death will be terrible. I'll linger on in people's way, poor, sick, dirty, empty, a mess. I go on and on, why can't I stop? I even talk shit now. To know the seasons of life and death and walk quietly on the path between them. No tears, no tears. Hate is like a clown armed with a knife. He must draw blood to cap the joke, you know? Well, have you got a new play, it has to be a comedy, rebuilding is expensive, they'd like you to invest. Think about it. You may come up with an idea. Or manage to steal one. But it must be in time for next season.

[*Silence.*]

My life's been one long self-insult. It came on with puberty.

[*Silence.* Jonson *drinks.*]

Teach me something.

> [Shakespeare *falls across table and spills his glass.*
> *Jonson tries to dry Shakespeare with a napkin. He sets him*
> *up in his chair. Shakespeare slumps forward again. The Son*
> *comes on with a bottle and glasses. Joan pours.*]

SON. They won't give up.

JOAN. No more'll us. [*She hands him a drink. He waves it aside.*]

SON (*Rocking slightly*): Rich thieves plunderin' the earth. Think on the
poor trees an' grass an' beasts, all neglect an' stood in the absence of God.
One year no harvest'll come, no seed'll grow in the plants, no green, no
cattle won't leave their stall, stand huddled-to in the hovel, no hand'll turn
water into their trough, the earth'll die an' be covered with scars: the mark
a dust where a beast rot in the sand. Where there's no Lord God there's
wilderness.

WALLY. Don't go forth in it now, brother. [*To the others*] He's allus close
t' tears. [*To the Son*] Don't git took up.

JOAN (*offers the Son the drink again*): Yo' hev this. That's cold out there
t'night. [*The Son doesn't take it*]

WALLY. The waters of Babylon run by his door.

SON (*rocking slightly*): The absence of God, the wilderness... neglect....

[*Combe comes in. He goes to the Son.*]

COMBE. You've been here all evening.

SON (*nods*): Even', Mr. Combe.

COMBE (*to Jonson*): How long have they been there?

JONSON. When I drink my eyes swim closer together. One, two, nine, ten
peasants....

[*Shakespeare is still slumped forward on the table.*]

COMBE (*to the Son*): I thought the brothers didn't swill.

SON. We may quench thirst in an orderly 'oust.

COMBE. After labour.

> [*Jonson gets up and goes out right. As he goes he talks. The others*
> *ignore him. He is drunk but controlled.*]

COMBE. Every time you fill my ditches I'll dig them out. Every time you pull down my fence I'll put it back. There'll be more broken fences.

SON (*To Wally*): Note that.

COMBE. Be very careful on Sunday. Wear the right cap and go to the parish church—not some holy hovel out in the fields. Keep to the law. Don't come up in front of me.

JONSON. To spend my life wandering through quiet fields. Charm fish from the water with a song. Gather simple eggs. Muse with my reflection in quiet water having Wear the right cap and go to the parish church—not some holy hovel out in the fields. Keep to the law. the accents of philosophy. And lie at last in some cool mossy grave where maidens come to make vows over my corpse. [*He goes.*]

SON. Whose interest's that protectin'? Public or yourn?

COMBE. You trespass on my land. Fight my men. Trample my crop. Now you turn me into the devil. The town will benefit from what I'm doing. So will the poor.

JEROME (*quietly*): S'long's they'm still alive.

COMBE. What? [*Jerome doesn't answer. Combe turns to the Son*] There's a division in this country. We're not just fighting for land. Listen. I've been suffering, I've caused some of it-and I try to stop it. But I know this: there'll always be real suffering, real stupidity and greed and violence. And there can be no civilization till you've learned to live with it. I live in the real world and try to make it work. There's nothing more moral than that. But you live in a world of dreams! Well, what happened when you have to wake up? You find that real people can't live in your dreams. They don't fit, they're not good, sane or noble enough. So you turn to common violence and begin to destroy them. [*He stops*] Why should I talk to you? You can't listen. [*To Jerome*] You hold your farm on a lease. When you die your son has to pay a fee before he inherits it. That fee isn't fixed—it's decided by the landlord, my brother-in-law. We work with anyone who shows good will. But there can only be one master.

[*Jonson comes back. He carries a bottle.*]

SON. A sexton's diggin' your ditches, Combe.

WALLY. Amen.

SON. An' yo'll be buried in 'em.

JOAN. So dig 'em deep.

Israel.

JONSON. Where can you buy a good spade? I'm sure there's a book on it. Should find a sale. Sound practical manual in a good, simple, craftsman's style.

WALLY. Israel. Israel. Israel.

COMBE. Grown men acting like children.

> [*Combe goes out.*]

SON. God take us on a long journey. That man's prophetical. We see the same truth from odd sides but us both know tis the truth.

WALLY (*softly*): Glory. Glory.

SON. I looked cross a great plane into his eyes. A sword were put into my hand. The lord god a peace arm us. We must go back an' fill up they ditches agin' t'night.

JEROME. T'night?

SON. Whenever he turn his back. Every time.

JEROME. Us'll come.

JOAN. No.

JEROME. Ah! There's only one master. When yo' put your hand in your pocket now yo' find another hand there.

> [*The Son and Wally go towards the door.*]

JONSON. Shepards?

> [*The Son and Wally ignore him and go out.*]

JONSON. (*to Joan and Jerome*) Fill your bowls.

JOAN. (*to Jerome*) That's a full bottle. Wasted on them in that state.

JEROME. While us wait.

> [*Jerome and Joan go to Jonson's table. Shakespeare still slumped forward. Jerome recognizes him.*]

JONSON (*shaking Shakespeare*): The pilgrims have come.

JEROME. We yont better sit with the gen'man.

SHAKESPEARE. Sit down.

> [*Jonson starts to fill their glasses.*]

JONSON. Was that man your enemy? Call him back and let me kill him for you.

SHAKESPEARE. You've been filling the ditches.

JEROME. No.

SHAKESPEARE. Lie to me. Lie. Lie. You have to lie to me now.

[*Wally runs in. He has a shovel.*]

WALLY. Snow! Snow!

JOAN. Snow!

WALLY. Late snow! A portent! A sign!

JEROME (*seeing the shovel*) Git that shovel out!

JOAN. Snow! Shall us still go?

JEROME (*pushing Wally*): Git that out! Yo' fool!

WALLY. What? Snow! Snow!

SHAKESPEARE. Lie to me. Lie to me.

[*Wally and Jerome go out. Joan follows them.*]

JONSON. They went? Was it my talk? I talk too much. [*He sits. They drink*] I hope you're paying. I certainly can't afford drink like this. You said something about a loan. [*Shakespeare puts money on the table*] I thought it was just drink talking. [*He counts the money*] In paradise there'll be a cash tree, and the sages will sit under it. You can't manage anything better? You won't notice it. I had to borrow to bury my little boy. I still owe on the grave. [*He puts the money in his pocket.*] I suppose you buried your boy in the best oak. Sit down, sit down.

John Clifford Mortimer (b. 1923)

A modern Proteus, John Mortimer has achieved success in a broad range of fields. The son of a barrister and a product of Harrow and Oxford, his distinguished legal career, which include representing the defense in significant freedom-of-speech trials and helping abolish censorship in the British theater, led him to be named Master of the Bench for the Inner Temple in 1975. He is even better known, however, as a writer. A dramatist, novelist, scriptwriter, critic, translator, travel writer and journalist, he has created Rumpole of the Bailey, adapted *I, Claudius* and *Brideshead Revisited* for television, and even authored a script for the Son et Lumiere show at Hampton Court.

Mortimer's *Will Shakespeare* (1977) is an enthusiastic account of Shakespeare's theatrical career as seen by a young actor. The novel follows Shakespeare's rivalry with Marlowe, his friendship with Hal the Horse Thief (who metamorphoses into Henry Wriothesley, Third Earl of Southampton), his attempts to reach an autistic son, his affair with the self-centered Mary Fleminge, and his involvement in Robin Essex's tragicomic rebellion. But, above all, the story focuses on politics and change at the Globe, as Jack Rice, the narrator, becomes the chief female lead, displacing that "pallid, thin streak of a Puritan" Alex Cooke, only to age and see the younger Nathan Field take over his roles.

This excerpt from the novel recounts Shakespeare's early life on the edge of the theater world. Jack Rice, born to the stage but now, in a Puritan age, serving as sexton for the Church of St. Barnaby ("no coloured glass, no graven saints, no hassocks nor kneelers and a whipping for any child who sleeps or whispers"), writes in secret his memoirs of a brighter age. Fueled by Communion wine, Jack mixes history and commentary, Shakespeare's life and his own, in recalling what he titles, "The Tragical, Comical History of King William, with an Account of His Conquests, Loves, Struggles, Jealousies, Hatreds, and Final Reconciliation with the She-Dragon."

Will Shakespeare
(1977)

Of How Shakespeare Lied About
His Life At The Rose Theatre,
And How An Honest Man
Lost A Capon

When I first knew Shakespeare, he tended the horses outside the old Rose Theatre.

We didn't know he was Shakespeare or where he came from, we didn't even know that he was eaten up with a longing to be inside the Theatre and not at the gate with a load of hay and a spade for gathering dung so it would not foul the red heels of the Lordlings on their way to their seats on the stage. All we knew, he was called "Will" and for a ha'penny he would tend a man's horse while he was at the play.

It was also known that he did his work with commendable efficiency.

At this time I was also working at the Rose. How did the two of us get there, Will, who was twenty-six years old and little Jack Rice, who was then a kind of starveling, under-developed twelve, having not yet come to my full tide of beauty and blossomed into a girl? I will tell you shortly.

What had been his history before he appeared wearing an old red hat and a leather jerkin to tend the horses outside the theatre? Sure he was not born as I was, in the shadow of the gallows and the players' cart. His father was a glove-maker of Stratford, nicely prosperous before debt began to gnaw away his horde. And Will Shakespeare must have been comfortable enough in the country, stuffing his head with all the books he could lay his hand to, and tumbling whatever wench would go with him "primrose-picking," as he called it, on the long walk to Shottery. There when he was but eighteen he tumbled a big-boned, butter-hair Anne, who was eight years his senior. "Let still the woman take an elder than herself," Shakespeare wrote in a play where I did act the breeches part. Perhaps if Anne had been a few years younger she wouldn't have put the fear of God into Shakespeare to make him marry her. Or perhaps it was her family that drove him to the altar; but marry they did in haste one cold November and his wife had a girl, Susanna, in the following May. And then she bore him twins, a girl, Judith, and a son Hamnet, who lived to be ... well, you shall hear what he lived to be.

Now, family life, they tell me, is not the easiest of conditions. I know not truly because although I have had boy-lovers and girl-lovers, men-lovers and women-lovers pass through my long life for a while, yet I have never had one face to stare at from breakfast time to supper and my only family was my mother who, in spite of her gypsy temper, was a credulous old soul who gave no trouble. Some men solve their family difficulties by being meek and complaisant, some by cuffing the children, kicking the cat and generally terrorising the homestead. Shakespeare's way was the simplest; he moved himself off. Some say the actors came to Stratford, he saw a play and the next day he was gone; but it is my belief he had his plans in head years before that and the getting of his family came only as an enforced interruption.

Now here comes the mystery: and it's only the first one we shall meet in tracing the Comical, Tragical History of William Shakespeare. After he left Stratford, Will vanished.... Where exactly? Some say he went for a schoolmaster, but I have never heard him speak in the tedious tone of a pedagogue. Some say he worked in an Attorney's office, and there gained his knowledge of bills, leases and feestail, and his tight grasp on a handful of money. Dick Burbage once told me Will went for a soldier in the Low Countries, but that was a night of Claret wine and partridges and Dick would remember anything. From time to time I heard Shakespeare swear in the Lingua Italia, and some have said he travelled as far as Verona and Venice where his scenes be set: though I think he got no nearer those hot cities than the sweating pages of Boccaccio.

There was a day when I asked Shakespeare where he spent those years after he left home, and his face went dark and there was silence which told you that if he gave you an answer it would be a lie, or even a warning to learn your part or mind your acting and not his business. They say the old Knights went into retreat in certain dark monasteries before venturing to battle, and all I can think is that Shakespeare retired into the shadows before assaulting the old Rose Theatre and arriving there as horse-tender. But whether his monastic retreat was a soldier's camp, or lawyer's clerk's office, or even an Italian bordello or stew house by St. Paul's I am not able to tell you. All I know is he came from thence with his head full of the rough ends of a great knowledge of men, women, and books and powerful determination to leap from the dung pile outside the door to the stage inside it.

Now his wife Anne, and two girls, and even his son Hamnet when he began to totter, must have been greatly perplexed to know if they had a father or no. But now and then the sums of money would be brought to them by travellers or sent in a pedlar's sack from an address unknown. At last Anne got a letter from her husband containing a gold coin he had earned by holding the horses. I have been told of this self-same letter by many parties so I can now repeat it to you, and you may see that whatever skills William had learned in his dark years, he had now become a past-master in the art of telling lies.

To my dear wife Anne at Stratford. Wish me well, sweetness.

[The letter was somewhat tattered and had a smell of dung which his wife attributed to the Irish pedlar who carried it.] I have been so long silent as my whole strength has been turned on one Object, that of making your Fortune and my Immortality. [With such times off as he turned his strength to making the night beautiful with a pot-girl or a boy lute-player.] Now I have news which will gladden your heart and that of our little family. [When the infant heard it they say he vomited in disbelief, the others were more credulous.] Anne, my dear Anne. I am become a voice in a cry of players. We are set in comfort at the Theatre in the old Rose Garden at Maiden Lane and every night we make the rafters ring with the boasts of Tamburlaine the Great. [A fine bloodthirsty piece by one Marlowe whom you shall hear more of presently. True it did make the rafters ring but not with any voice of Shakespeare's.] The groundlings cheer at the terrible tale of the Tyrant and his captive Queens. [A bad habit of alliteration which he improved later, but it was a phrase to stir the blood in Stratford.] I must leave writing for I am called for to the Great Battle scene. [He meant someone had summoned him to hold a horse's head.] Today I act but for you, and in memory of your beauty which with God's Grace I shall behold again when I am given leave of absence by my audience. Kiss the dear children for me.

Trusting you will share this delight with me and spend on strong ale and good cheer all of this gold piece:

> Yr. loving husband,
> Will. S.

God knows how these appalling falsehoods did not blister his hand and burn the paper! And God knows why he should have chosen such a time, when he was about as close to the stage as the lad who cleaned a Privy Councillor's boots was to the Government of England, to suddenly boast of his alleged success. Perhaps he was lonely and bethought him of a big-boned, soft-bodied woman with primrose-coloured hair and a smell of milk in a warm bed in Stratford. Perhaps he thought that by writing down his dreams they might come true by magic. I can tell you the facts only and what went on behind the locked doors of that skull, Shakespeare only knows.

Now the letter was read and re-read by Anne and told to the children and shown to her brothers, who were openly scornful and secretly impressed, and to her old Uncle Hathaway, who had once seen a burgomask danced in the courtyard of Warwick Castle at Christmas and held himself out to be connoisseur of all matters theatrical. And the neighbours were called in, good Master Hamnet Sadler and his wife Judith. Hamnet Sadler, godfather to the children, after whom young Hamnet Shakespeare was named, was as honest as the skin between his brows and a wool merchant in a small way of business, excellent at the grading of sheep-shearings and knowing the price of flax, but he was a slow scholar and the letter had to be read to him a number of times before he gathered in the news that his old school-fellow and neighbour was now a Great Actor in the city. But when this sunk into his honest skull he was quick with his decision. "When I go into London next month on the wool cart," he promised, "I will call on neighbour William and to celebrate his triumph I will take him a fat Stratford capon reared in my own yard." So then a part of the gold piece was spent on small ale, and Uncle Hathaway brought apricot wine and tried to dance a burgomask, and Judith Sadler grew so warm at the thought of having a neighbour in the Theatre that that night she pulled her hulking husband on top of her and so got their child Francis, him that is now a snivelling Justice of the Peace and devoted to silence on the Sabbath and the flogging of actors.

So it came about that on a warm fine Spring day Hamnet Sadler came to London on the wool cart carrying with him a corn-fed capon to the great actor or minor ostler, depending on whether you look at the matter with Hamnet's eye or the eye of God.

First he went to the Widow Braxton's house at Southwark, an accommodation address where Will had often been accommodated either by that energetic widow woman or her three handsome "daughters," who were related only in their enthusiasm for pressing sheets without a flat iron and their interest in the chinks to be earned by such labour. Shakespeare used this place, among other things, for the writing of letters.

"Master Shakespeare!" Hamnet Sadler stood in the street and called up at the window of Mother Braxton's evil-smelling dwelling at the sign of the Grasshopper.

A shutter opened stealthily. A female face of somewhat tarnished nobility showed itself: behind in the shadows Hamnet glimpsed younger, creamier countenances and heard a giggle of laughter.

"I seek Master Shakespeare. The great actor. Famous in this town."

"Shake who? I'll shake you, my fine caterwauler." Widow Braxton was not so bold or so foolish as to ask the names of her visiting gentry, so all this babble of Shakespeare meant nothing to her.

"His wife sends me with messages from the country, and I have a fine capon. Is Master Shakespeare gone to his work at the Theatre?" Hamnet was puzzled; although it was on the hop of midday the figures at the window appeared to him dressed for the night. He was also tired.

"Do but let me step inside and rest my capon. It's a heavy bird to carry."

At which Hamnet stepped forward to the door and stepped back quickly and covered his capon as a good half gallon of slops dropped on him like that gold rainstorm which the Ancients believed concealed Jupiter the Thunderer. London folk, Hamnet Sadler had discovered, are nothing near so friendly as Stratford folk.

So Hamnet Sadler set out to find the Rose Theatre.

Now London was a different sort of place then. If you pass along the Surrey Bank now, you may find an outdoor prayer meeting, or one hanging for an offence to Parliament, to entertain you, but then it was all amusement and jollity. Hamnet had not gone five yards before he was solicited to see the Bear-Bait, and apes torn to pieces by dogs, or the wonderful living Mermaid from Gravesend, or the monstrous Blue Giant of Wapping. He was offered the sight of an old soldier's wound for a penny, and then told that if he did not pay a penny he would be shown the self-same wound without mercy. He was offered half an hour with a certain Lucy Negro, Abbess de Clerkenwell and a promise he'd never be hurried for sixpence, and for a shilling he might see a Virgin from Waltham Cross marry with an ass. At last Hamnet found a snarling Puritan fellow, father, as I believe, to our own dear Rector here, who told him, as neighbour Sadler had no reason to doubt, that the Day of Judgment was at hand. So he asked the way to the Rose Theatre.

"The theatre is a plague-spot, sir. A wen! A boil which runs puss and poison, infecting us with Idle Dreams of Vanity and Lust. It is a congregation of rogues and harlots," the Puritan piped in a high moan of doom and added more quietly, "Take that lane on the right hand. By London Bridge. You may nose the actors as you come towards the river." So Hamnet Sadler went on his way, sniffing like a fox-hound.

Hamnet Sadler told me, many years after, how he walked through Southwark Market something discouraged. His capon was weighing extremely heavy and he set it down by a horse-trough to sluice his hot face and drink a little. And when he emerged and shook the water from his eyes, lo and behold the capon was gone! And all he saw was a figure in a red hat running swiftly away through the crowds.

By Christ, this London, where a man may not even set down a capon for half a minute whilst he takes a drink!

"Stop thief! Call the Constable! Stop thief!" cried Hamnet, pursuing the red hat like hounds after a scent. The Constable was pleasuring himself up an alley with a whore he had lately arrested and was taking in for a whipping, and the citizens of Southwark paid scant attention.

So through piled apples and between hanging sides of beef and under cartwheels the chase continued, till Hamnet grabbed the red-hat in a little stinking court by the fish market.

"Got you! You thieving London knave!" said Hamnet and shook his prey as if he were indeed an old hunting dog with Reynardo between his teeth.

And the red hat fell off, revealing none other than the great self-styled actor of the Rose Theatre and Hamnet Sadler's neighbour.

"Will! Will Shakespeare!" Hamnet was astonished. "As large as life!"

"Is this yours? Forgive me, Neighbour Hamnet. It's not often a man finds a dinner, abandoned by a Southwark horse-trough."

So Shakespeare bowed and formally handed back the capon, and Hamnet bowed and formally handed it back to him. And, having discovered that his neighbour Sadler was well provided with money, Shakespeare suggested they repair at once to the Dagger Inn in Holborn to have that capon cooked and eaten before worse befell it.

Leon Rooke
(b. 1934)

On the evidence of his plays, Shakespeare had little fondness for dogs. When his characters are not demeaning each other as "Whoreson dog," "inhuman dog," "mangy dog," "rascal dogs," unpeaceable dog," "hellish dog," "egregious dog," "cut-throat dog," "unmanner'd dog," and "You bawling, blasphemous, uncharitable dog," they are dropping observations like "Hope is a curtal dog in some affairs" or "Truth's a dog must to kennel; he must be whipped out." The consistency of the playwright's hostility has inspired the writer Leon Rooke to seek its source. His energetically witty *Shakespeare's Dog* (1983) offers an account of Shakespeare's life in Stratford during the 1580's as told by his dog, Mr. Hooker. The novel traces both pet and master's frustrations with an increasingly restrictive world.

Born in North Carolina, Rooke moved to Canada in 1969 and has since become a Canadian citizen. His carefully detailed short stories and novels focus firmly on characters whose often painful stories reveal a slightly surreal vision of ordinary life. These works have won him the Canada/Australia Literary Prize in 1981, an award for Best Paperback Novel of 1981 for *Fat Woman*, and the Governor General's Award for Fiction for *Shakespeare's Dog*.

In the following excerpt from the first section of the novel, Hooker describes life among the peculiar "Two Foots" or humans. A dog of venomous sensuality, Hooker has just finished mauling his chief rival, Wolfsleach, for making advances to the seductive bitch, Marr. The other dogs believe Hooker has become too much like the humans, especially the Shakespeares Senior (John and Mary) and Junior (Will and Anne). Hooker's powers of observation, which at times approach the telepathic, reveal not only the major characters, human and canine, but a broad range of others, including Will's "brats"—Susanna and the twins Judith and Hamnet—and his siblings—Gilbert the prance, Joan the addled, and Edmund the squirt. All of the forces which will drive Will from Stratford appear through the questioning, challenging eyes and ears of Shakespeare's dog.

Shakespeare's Dog
(1983)

We were making quite the whoobug when my master Two Foot's kicksy-wicksy, the noxious Hathaway, still stiff and pudged from laying eggs, howled in her drone's eminence from the back door. I slowed down some, thinking she might come with her cold water pots to splash down on us, or with sticks hot as lightning bolts, not to mention epithets so randomly obscene they'd cross my eyes. But she was for the moment oblivious to dog, her voice besotted with tender wooing, crafty appeal, wifely caresses to soothe the swarthy air. Putting timid inquiry to Will's shuttered scribbler's room above and standing drab and pottled on her flat wide feet, as if the whole of the world was to be shouldered by her wits alone. By her hips' girth and tits' swell.

"There's no penny in the goose mug, my Will!" she called.

"Oh, Willum, Susanna's got the chokes!"

"Oh, Will, my poke, your old Da is at his ale mumblings again!"

"Will? Will?"

But my Two Foot was master of her subterfuge and wisely kept his visage clear. Acute with reason, warder's law, he kept his throat muscles squelched.

"Oh, Mr. Shake, my peat!"

My peat, my pet, what a false snit this jailer was.

I could hear his deep-thought dropping down draughts of fumy hebenon, juice of hemlock, thorny relish-of-pire, that her tongue-wag might be scalded shut and her curdled wifer's sauces be rat-licked away.

"Perish, hag!" I heard him say. But growled down through breeze that only a canine could catch, for the calf had his natural fear of her. More than once she'd throttled him.

"Get thee a pitchfork and ride, ignominious witch."

"Will, your old mother needs buckets from the mere! Needs it now, my Will."

"Scat, Hathaway."

"And your honey needs her honey, sweet. One kiss? Open up, my saint."

Will stayed silent, the mouse.

She chunked a pebble or two at his shuttered sightway, called twice and three times more. Then the dolorous wench heaved a resentful sigh. She struck up a snarly curse and finally went slug-footed back indoors.

My Two Foot's nose instantly snuckered forth.

"Has the drab biscuit gone?" he whispered to me. "The viper's got her sweetness," he growled to my nodding, "yet she's still the viper Hathaway. Let's boil the slut in oil."

I barked my feeling passion for his tune. But the scribbler's nose was already back at work.

The stooge. He'd been up there all day, minting rhyme, scratching dandruff from his empty head.

Words. How I hated them. (It ain't words, he'd say, but how they're shook.) As if words, his or mine, would ever have their day. Yet sight of the rogue made my humours lift. I could see some merit in the ghoulish English sky, in the clouds fermenting above us like a black gang of ticks....

And stood foolishly wagging tail, whining my degree of wanted fellowship up at him: Hooker awaits without, my liege. Let's for a man-and-dog walk along the Avon's shore or take a fast tumble through Arden Wood. I'll give good ear to your mush and sprinkle on it a syllable or two of form.

My pause had given Wolfsleach the faint hope of slithering free. I lifted a claw from his belly further to encourage him in this view. And spat out his limp, salivered, half-devoured ear. Let the humper think what he wished. Let the scab think I was done with him. That Hooker's gorge was filled. Hope, even for a cur like him, is always there. I could feel under my pads his gross heart begin to swell. Let it, I thought. When he's idling in grass, ears laid back to snooze, I'll fry him in the true Hooker fat. I'll tear the sludge limb from limb.

Then, out of need mortifying to my self-image, I lifted leg and piddled over leaf and on head of some addled, brain-jerking bug and—dumb beast that I was—arightly and with arrogant aplomb loped off to lick my clack-dish. Oh, for supper! I thought. Oh, for a rack of bacon to confirm me on my do-gooder's path. Oh, for meated bone. Oh, for a carcass or two of whale.

Well, piss, I'd as soon pray to Sirius the Dogstar, for my clack-dish lacked even a smell. Not a tinge. Empty again. These Two Foots, including my wordy Shagsbier, couldn't be bothered with feeding dog. Better the dog should go on feeding them. My insides rumbled. Diet-of-Nothing's what I had. It had been three weeks since I'd had a bone between my paws, and that only one up-rooted that had been chawed on a thousand times. Some knee's joint, some Pope's gristle, peasant's toe left over from the Middle Ages (on the whole, a friendlier period). Bleached by the mindless energy of a hundred gloppy years. ("Chew it pointy," Will had said. "I'll stab the witch with it as she sleeps.")

Dog wants more, I tell you. A field of hares, all boxed in, nowhere to run. To ride the backs of Sir Lucy's deers.

And more yet. Wants quitting of this corn-shucking town.

Marr was stretched out on the boards across the old tanning pit. Eyes at blinker on the world, or such, from her closed web, that she wished to see of it. I gave the harlot a shriveling stare. She took it with a pouty, maddening grin. "I don't like you," she glomped. "You've changed. You get more like the Two Foots every day."

Piddle on the cur.

Wolf limped over to lay his head down on her, whining like a bowlegged toad complaining how I'd broke his leg. To lift a hooded glance at me, saying, "Marr's right, Mr. Hooker. You've gone round the bend. You've turned against dog. Next, we know, you'll be wearing pants. You'll be scribbling too." Though he wouldn't say it out loud. But it would be what he'd go drumming into another dog's ear: "Pzzzzt.... Hooker thinks he's Two Foot.... Watch out for Hooker."

Piddle, piddle. I'd as soon be lowing cow for all the change in dog I wrought.

My scop's mother, old Mary, came out and beat a rag against the steps. Then flopped it over her shoulders, said, "Don't I look pretty? Don't you dogs have nothing to do?" and stomped back inside, weary as a load of coal.

A rat came up from the bowels of the house and gnawed down to glom on whatever it was he thought he saw. A spot of blood bedezined his chin, and I wondered what it was he'd found to be chewing on. Another rat was my guess. Or maybe he'd nipped a bite of nose from one of the sleeping twins. Human meat was gruel to such filth as him. I skittered up, silent as an eel, but when I pounced, his smelly spot was bare.

Old monotony, the stunted, web-flowing day, had me shackled to my toes. I let my head hang between my legs, my tongue hanging too, thinking what's the use? Why struggle on? This day counts for nothing, as has every other. Time, I told myself, to wedge myself up to a tree and sleep. There was hope for some tickle there.

I let out a yowl, a long, goose-bumping, arching flight of woe (pure bravado), just to show the world I still knew how. No one noticed. No one, for all I knelled, even heard.

I dropped down and dozed.

Or was about to when my bloodmate Terry, unhinged sister of mine and half-cousin to a sow, came bleaping through a break in the mud wall, her long snout smeared with bear paw from putting it where snout had no right to be—and now putting it there again with all insistence, blathering as though she had lost all hold on intellect and more as though she were kin to a creaking quarry cart.

"Oh, Mr. Hooker," she cried, "you've been fighting again. Is violence all you know?" Then heard Wolf's sobs and toe-stepped her way over to him, laying warm drool over his flanks. "What right have you?" she exclaimed. "You've hurt my liefest one, Wolfsleach, you hotbreath pooch!" And let loose a string of livid abuse, tying up my head and the air around me with her prassy talk, when here she was in her harlotry bloom, shame as far away from her hanging belly as cart horse could run or lickety be split, and the whole wide world from Shottery to Snitterfield to see what she'd let that snaggle-tooth do to her.

"Swallow a tod of wool next time," I told this grass-roller. "Oh, Terry, what's to be done with you, what would our own Mam and bloodspit say?" For truly her wantonness made me blush; she made me wish I'd shared my birthing with a needle-eyed snake.

"Poor Wolf," she said to the freak and commenced licking him from head to tail.

Inside the house, one of the babies began to squall, and then the other, and much caterwauling from the three women there, and next was the Hathaway at the door kicking up her skirts and throwing up a swirl of fists at Will's shuttered aperture, crying in her shrillest: "You there, rhymer, in your swaddling clothes, come down and change a diaper!"

A hex moved over the house like a savage wand. I melted down inside a pile of leaves, soul-weary and purposeless as a thing reduced to lead. My former cock-stomping was now all fencepost and briar, a honey's drip; I was deep in my humors and under my Two Foot master's unmasterly hood, as nothing had been going right for us of late, there being naught but woe and more woe heaped on through all of our long moons. I felt as some swooning, mooching bear must feel when the full weight of his cave has come down on him.

Madness, I thought, what's the use? My Two Foot Will was sore in the thumbs from brooding at nasty fate, while the geck's wife was sick with fury at his nothingness—"You'd take meaningful employment," she kept telling him, "if you cared about me or your brats. But, nay, you're all lit up by prince and princess, king and queen, you don't care snit about the real world!" The whole house naught but a stinkpodge of mood, of hurts big and small. Gilbert was a prance. Joan addled. Edmund a squirt. And the goose jar eternally empty, as empty as my clack-dish eternally was. Bubble, bubble, toil and trouble. My master's sire, the white-haired John, had the dropsy in his features and ever trembled now in wait of debtor's prison or the stocks, whichever grinning justice snared him first. This arch mentor, blacker in outlook than a chimney pot, spun out his daily hours sucking the marrow of mutton bone carried for luck in his oiled unrattling purse, the Geneva Bible to mumble over spread open on his lap. As he dared not venture of Sundays to Holy Trinity Church, the book's thick pages were speckled with puke spewed up by his grief and rage or what was spilled from his dented pewter tankard that was ever deep with his and Warwickshire's best brown ale—which brew the young shortlegs Edmund, his last brat, was faithful fetcher for. No and nay, he could give up his senses, John Two Foot could, and pay off owed shillings as the turtle ran, but he would never the sweet mercy of ale so long as there was secret barley in the rafters and grey day didn't flaunt herself to final black.

"You're a tosspot, John," old Mary would entreat. "No more, no more."

But the sour keg would go on drinking it down all the faster, weighing venom against the double-dealing law that allowed slagheaps on the street for some but not for others, bellyaching that between his loutish brother Henry and Mary's crop-sucking, swindling relatives, not to mention assorted thieves by name of Ralph Cawdrey and the like, he had not pot to pee in nor hardly cause to stand upright. From moment to nasty moment, he'd hight instructions to hapless Gilbert, close by in the glover's shop, although Gilbert, more fop than son, scarcely had wit to hold a paring knife and longed only to invest finery up to his brow, pirouette in puffed sleeves through the Bankcroft to Avon's mist-burning shore, there to sketch with other lazy swans the river's blue sweep or doltish archers at practice on the green.

But Will was the rub. That devious firstborn son was first to drive in the parental blade, and foremost one to keep it there. "Oh, he's for art," the gentle Mary would say. And stick her sweetened finger into the squalling mouths of what his art had done, for sure enough the duo's own mother lacked the spit. Will had no mind for wool-bending, for cutting and tanning, for whittawing sheep's pelt, goat hide, or cheverel, any more than he had for schoolmastering or articling with Henry Rogers, clerk to the borough. Shucked from that contraction now. Shucked for quilling doggerel in the book when he should have been keeping leets and law days and attending the assizes. The rogue. Ardent verse begetter, book forager, perishing between Stratford visits of ass-laden players, content merely to war with the Hathaway bitch, bounce his babies on his knees, carouse with that Sadler bunch, theorize on history, thunder at parchment, weigh the bait and line of Londontown.

"This Avon's a pimple!" Will would rail, croaking his fury at the unbending Hathaway, his face blazing as the great actor Alleyn's would, rapping her with sauce pots to show that his rage matched her ire and that a Henley Street son could better a Shottery wench even on the worst of days. "You twilight hump" he'd screech. "Old woman! Cradle snatcherr! Apple-john, Barbary hen, you drumbling, letharged pizzle-minder. To become the laced mutton, you'd have betrothed your patch even to the wheelwright's crass boy."

"Oh, thee!" she'd rant back. "Enough of your flattery. Don't think you can gloze me with your mindless stammer."

"Bate-breeder, bed-swerver, thou imperseverent, rancid mome!"

"Codpole!" she'd answer. "Thou woodcock, what stick is it grows between your legs that makes you think you can take a merry bride and quit her before the nighttime falls?"

"Ah, me," he'd moan, "I'd as lief stumble over a precipice under dark moon or sleep in a quagmire with hooting frogs as ever again fall myself in love!"

"Love!" she'd croak. "You call this love!" And she'd potch him one and potch him another and take her claws to his sneering face and whap at him with her stickbroom.

"Hag!"

"Word-blower! Thou shitted stool!"

So toe to toe they'd push and pull, kick and blather, swing-buckling the very hour down to its rawest nubs, and quell all hope of sleep, leaving the Henley Street citizenry to think Doomsday's great foot was stomping down, that murder and mayhem were aprowl, with earthquake next ... until at last the tethered pair apoplexed down.

"Avon's the pimple, Anne, and thou art the blot that holds me here."

"Snecke up!" she'd say. "Snecke up!"—which meant "Go hang yourself, wretch born to lead apes and women into hell!"

And this when—behold!—a fig's turn later they'd be all dovecote-trundled, honey-bucketed, cooing love notes cheek to cheek and chirp for chirp.

"Ahh, buss me, Will!"

"Ahh, my back's hot for thee, Anne!"

"Stoke me, Will!"

"Thou art a moist one, thou art!"

It would be "my alderliefest this" and "my alderliefest that," enough to make even a dog's toes curl.

Aye.

Aye, John would think, hearing his proud walls one minute shake from riotous argument and next steam up like a Ludd's town brothel from lip-smacking and what else? Gods forbot, he'd think, the plague should have got us all! Him married to that sack of hip and tit and three foaled before I could shake a stick. Now five here to nest, crowding me out of house and home!

Woe, woe.

So the pater would stare down at his wasted glover's hands at scratch over his woolen crotch, and at his legs gone spindley from what the physician said was disuse and nothing more—else he wanted the cure of frog's spawn to wrap his tongue around—and with bemused, unbalanced eye he'd thus follow the unwelcome oar and paddle of the world. His grief so thick he hacked it up in hacking cough, he'd wetly contemplate this cargo of troubles descended on him—humans of every age, drift, and treacherous scope, some two or three with mustard enough to capsize the walls even of a double house—and try to blink back what the world had done to him, ambitious yeoman's son seven years apprenticed to that daft Dickson scoundrel, cutter of white gloves, and then risen to be ale-taster, constable, alderman, and finally boss-man bailiff (a good Lord Mayor, eh what? and privileged to wear the town's scarlet gown). A burgess of uncommon esteem. Not bad for a farmer's boy. And graced in the bargain with an Arden heiress for bride. "Since spring fifty-eight it was," he'd remind himself in a mumble, ale aflow down his chin, "the year a mule throwed poor Timothy Fox and broke his neck." Precious Mary, his nightingale, his hopemate, his nightly tonic. "My bosom," he'd say, "my chuck, my soul's breath, Mary."

Yea, and autumn the year before—"Or fifty-six, maybe it was, what's time to a sticklehead like me?"—his hand in Mary's as they approached her enfeebled old pa, swimming through seven sisters to have their pull on him. But no worry. Mary being the favorite. "What? Marriage? To this slackjaw? You want him? A rusty sharecropper's son when there's gentry chasing all round your heels? You'd corrupt our noble flow? What would old Turchillus of Arden say? Roll over in his grave, the bugger would. You do? You will? You want him anyway? Well, bugger old Turchill, if you say we must. But hold off a year or two. Wait till after I'm aged and impotent and dead. Then you can hawk down with him."

A fine, mellowy old ram, despite his talk. One of the best.

But what Robert Arden didn't know that day as they stood before him with clasped hands, begging leave to marry, was that the airy Warwickshire hills had made their brains to dance and already they were hawking down. That they'd stole their secret cups more than once. And Mary worried lest her tummy heave up and betray the stumbling. Yet eager to hawk again each chance she got. "My hitching post," is what she called his stick, and wriggled in so tight and creamy he spent his courtship wrapped up in a sweat.

Now cart had got before horse again and history was repeating itself. As he was to his precious Mary, so was Will to his precious slut. Something in the Shokespit blood, he reckoned, that had to fatten a woman. Like father, like son, Mary would say. Oh, that the Hathaway was sluttish was part of her stamp on character and no point on heaping blame on what was only being true to its nature. A bossy hamper. Willful where Will was clottish. But sluttish, yes. The taint of pigsty was on her. You had only to look at her bare feet and sturdy legs, at her hip roll, how she flounced, the way her eyes could make juice jump out of cherry, to know what she'd look like naked on a sheet and stir a boy's hot vinegar. Making no bones about it, lasciviousness was rooted deeper in her than the Puritan tunes she prattled. "Head goes one way, heart another," as Mary said. "Faith yes, we've known from the start she was shallow."

Aye, Mary had spotted where Hathaway was charm and where she was affliction. Poor Mary. One wondered about Mary: how she kept afloat a household spirit in these ragged times. Such a sweet thumper, so sweet-tempered, was Mary. Thirty long years his bedwarmer now and ripe for the tranquillity of gratified age after bearing five to reach this mean season, and losing three only to Holy Trinity's blessed ground there, where lime trees give halt to rain.

Aye. Aye and double aye. Now the Devil take it. The Queen, with all her rubies, could take it. Let the bishops have it. Stuff it all up Sir Lucifer's roomy rump. More ale, he'd think. Where's my ale? My flagon of beeswax, my stoup of courage. The stomach's rancid, my ears flop. Wet my whistle, how else to survive the gawdy hour? Time hangs like a stinking fish. "Ale!

Another ale!" Aye. For Hell's upper shelf had opened forth to send its gale, and you couldn't so much as raise a fire for warmth without having your chimney taxed.

Why me? he'd think.

And for the humpteenth time ask it of the harried air: "Why me, when it was only a gentleman I wanted to be, and swain to my sweetheart, with as many prideful children to staunch up my Shakespoot's name as there are arches in Clopton Bridge."

Then likely as not the debtserver's fist would swoop down on the Henley Street door, and his Wilmcote prize—the same Arden, forty-plus now and ragged as her broom, yet sterner in the discipline than he—would scuttle his reveries by way of whispered shake ("Wake up, wake up, you sot, you sweated hog!") and hasten him off to root nose in trunk or chicken shed or in crawl space between walls until the coastway cleared.

John Anthony Burgess Wilson
(b. 1917)

One of the most popular and visible of contemporary novelists, the prolific Anthony Burgess began his writing career as a teacher in Malaya during the 1950s with the Malayan Trilogy. In 1962 *A Clockwork Orange*, with its Nadsat slang and dystopian vision of a violent, gang-ridden, behaviorist-dominated future, established him as a major cultural figure, a reputation that Stanley Kubrick's brilliant film adaptation in 1971 only enhanced. Burgess' interest in the possibilities of language, the nature of time, and the moral influence of art continued in his later novels, including his fictional biography of Shakespeare, *Nothing Like the Sun* (1964), and his series of novels about the eccentric writer F. X. Enderby.

Although Enderby died of a heart attack in *The Clockwork Testament*, or *Enderby's End* (1974) after seeing his screenplay of Hopkins' *The Wreck of the Deutschland* transformed into a pornographic movie about Nazis and nuns, Burgess resurrected him ten years later in *Enderby's Dark Lady; Or No End to Enderby* (1984). Most of *Enderby's Dark Lady* centers on Enderby's work on a musical about Shakespeare's life, but the book begins and ends with short stories, allegedly by the fitfully talented Enderby. The first story, "Will and Testament," was actually written by Burgess as a part of an American bicentennial tribute to Shakespeare in 1976 and, like Kipling's "Proofs of Holy Writ," plays on the relationship between Jonson, Shakespeare, and the King James translation of the Bible. The second, "The Muse" (reproduced here), offers a science fiction adventure into multiple worlds. In it, a literary historian crosses time and space only to find a Shakespeare with all the legendary character flaws but little of the talent of the original.

"The Muse"
(1984)

The hands of Swenson ranged over the five manuals of the instrument console and, in cross rhythm, his feet danced on the pedals. He was a very old man, waxed over with the veneer of rejuvenation chemicals. Very wise, with a century of experience behind him, he yet looked much of an age with Paley, the twenty-five-year-old literary historian by his side. Paley grinned nervously when Swenson said:

"It won't be quite what you think. It can't be absolutely identical. You may get shocks when you least expect them. I remember taking Wheeler that time, you know. Poor devil, he thought it was going to be the fourteenth century he knew from his books. But it was a very different fourteenth century. Thatched cottages and churches and manors and so on, and lovely cathedrals. But there were polycephalic monsters running the feudal system, with tentacles too. Speaking the most exquisite Norman French, he said."

"How long was he there?"

"He was sending signals through within three days. But he had to wait a year, poor devil, before we could get him out. He was in a dungeon, you know. They got suspicious of his Middle English or something. White-haired and gibbering when we got him aboard. His jailers had been a sort of tripodic ectoplasm."

"That wasn't in System B303, though, was it?"

"Obviously not." The old man came out in Swenson's snappishness. "It was a couple of years ago. A couple of years ago System B303, or at least the K2 part of it, was enjoying the doubtful benefits of proto–Elizabethan rule. As it still is."

"Sorry. Stupid of me."

"Some of you young men," Swenson said, going over to the bank of monitor screens, "expect too much of Time. You expect historical Time to be as plastic as the other kinds. Because the microchronic and macrochronic flows can be played with, you consider you ought to be able to do the same thing with—"

"Sorry, sorry, sorry. I just wasn't thinking." With so much else on his mind, was it surprising that he should be temporarily ungeared to the dull realities of clockwork time, solar time?

"That's the trouble with you young—Ah," said Swenson with satisfaction, "that was a beautiful changeover." With the smoothness of the tongue gliding from one phonemic area to another, the temporal path had become a spatial one. The uncountable megamiles between Earth and System B303 had been no more to their ship than, say, a two-way trans–Atlantic flipover. And now, in reach of this other Earth—so dizzyingly far away that it was the same as their own, though at an earlier stage of history—the substance vedmum had slid them, as from one dream to another, into a world where solid objects might exist that were so alien as to be familiar, fulfilling the bow-bent laws of the cosmos. Swenson, who had been brought up on the interchangeability of time and space, could yet never cease to marvel at the miracle of the almost yawning casualness with which the nacheinander turned into the nebeneinander (there was no doubt, the old German words caught it best). So far the monitor screens showed nothing, but tape began to whir out from the crystalline corignon machine in the dead center of the control turret—coldly accurate information about the solar system they were now entering. Swenson read it off, nodding, a Nordic spruce of a man glimmering with chemical youth. Paley looked at him, leaning against the parferate bulk-head, envying the tallness, the knotty strength. But, he thought, Swenson could never disguise himself as an inhabitant of a less well-nourished era. He, Paley, small and dark as one of those far distant Silurians of the dawn of Britain, could creep into the proto–Elizabethan England they would soon be approaching and never be remarked as an alien.

"Amazing how insignificant the variants are," Swenson said. "How finite the cosmos is, how shamefully incapable of formal renewals—"

"Oh, come," Paley smiled.

"When you consider what the old musicians could do with a mere twelve notes—"

"The human mind," Paley said, "is straight. Thought travels to infinity. The cosmos is curved."

Swenson turned away from the billowing mounds of tape, saw that the five-manual console was flicking lights smoothly and happily, then went over to an instrument panel whose levers called for muscle, for the blacksmith rather than the organist. "Starboard," he said. "15.8. Now we play with grav-ities." He pulled hard. The monitor screen showed band after band of turquoise light, moving steadily upwards. "This, I think, should be—" He twirled a couple of corrective dials on a shoulder-high panel about the levers. "Now," he said. "Free fall."

"So," Paley said, "we're being pulled by—"

"Exactly." And then: "I trust the situation has been presented to you in its perilous entirety. The dangers, you know, are considerable."

"Scholarship," Paley smiled patiently. "My reputation."

"Reputation," Swenson snorted. Then, looking towards the monitors, he said: "Ah. Something coming through."

Mist, cloudswirl, a solid shape peeping intermittently out of vapor por-ridge. Paley came over to look. "It's the Earth," he said in wonder.

"It's their Earth."

"The same as ours. America, Africa—"

"The configuration's slightly different, see, down there at the southern tip of—"

"Madagascar's a good deal smaller. And, see, no Falklands."

"The cloud's come over again." Paley looked and looked. It was unbelievable.

"Think," Swenson said kindly, "how many absolutely incomputable systems there have to be before you can see the pattern of creation starting all over again. This seems wonderful to you because you just can't conceive how many myriads upon myriads of other worlds are not like our own."

"And the stars," Paley said, a thought striking him. "I mean, the stars they can actually see from there, from their London, say—are they the same stars as ours?"

Swenson shrugged at that. "Roughly," he said. "There's a rough kinship. But," he explained, "we don't properly know yet. Yours is only the tenth or eleventh trip, remember. To be exact about it all, you're the first to go to B303 England. What is it, when all's said and done, but the past? Why go to the past when you can go to the future?" His nostrils widened with complacency. "G91," he said. "I've done that trip a few times. It's pleasant to know one can look forward to another thirty years of life. I saw it there, quite clearly, a little plaque set up in Rostron Place: To the memory of G.F. Swenson, 1963–2094."

"We have to check up on history," Paley said, mumbling a little. His own quest seemed piddling: all this machinery, organization, expertise in the service of a rather mean inquiry. "I have to know whether William Shakespeare really wrote those plays."

Swenson, as Paley expected, snorted. "A nice sort of thing to want to find out," he said. "He's been dead six hundred and fifty years, is it, and you want to prove that there's nothing to celebrate. Not," he added, "that that sort of thing is much my line. I've never had much time for poetry. Aaaah." He interposed his own head between Paley's and the screen, peering. The pages of the atlas had been turned; now Europe alone swam towards them. "Now," Swenson said, "I must set the exactest course of all." He worked at dials, frowning but humming happily, then beetled at Paley, saying: "Oughtn't you to be getting ready?"

Paley blushed that, with so huge a swathe of the cosmos spent in near idleness, he should have to rush things as they approached their port. He took off his single boilersuit of a garment and drew from the locker his Elizabethan fancy dress. Shirt, trunks, codpiece, doublet, feathered French hat, slashed shoes—clothes of synthetic cloth that was an exact simulacrum of old-time weaving, the shoes of good leather handmade. And then there was the scrip with its false bottom: hidden therein was a tiny two-way signaller. Not that, if he got into difficulties, it would be of much use: Swenson was (and these were strict orders) to come back for him in a year's time. The signaller was to show where he was and that he was still there, a guest of the past, really a stowaway. Swenson had to move on to yet farther into timespace: Professor Shimmins had to be picked up on FH78, Dr. Guan Moh Chan in G210, Paley collected on the way back. Paley tested the signaller, then checked the open and honest contents of his scrip: chief among these was a collection of the works of William Shakespeare. The plays had been copied from a facsimile of the First Folio in fairly accurate Elizabethan script; the paper too was an acid-free imitation of the coarse stuff Elizabethan dramatists had been said to use. For the rest, Paley had powdered prophylactics in little bags and, most important, gold—angels firenew, the odd portague, ecus.

"Well," Swenson said with the faintest tinge of excitement, "England, here we come." Paley looked down on familiar river shapes—Tees, Humber, Thames. He gulped, running through his drill swiftly. "Countdown starts now," Swenson said. A synthegott in the port bulkhead began ticking off cold seconds from 300. "I'd better say goodbye then," Paley gulped, opening the trap in the deck which led to the tiny jetpowered very-much-one-man aircraft. "You should come down in the Thames estuary," Swenson said. "Au revoir, not goodbye. I hope you prove whatever it is you want to prove." 200-199-198. Paley went down, settled himself in the seat, checked the simple controls. Waiting took, it seemed, an age. He smiled wryly, seeing himself, an Elizabethan, with his hands on the controls of a twenty-third century miniature aircraft. 60-59-58. He checked his Elizabethan vowels. He went over his fictitious provenance: a young man from Norwhich with stage ambitions ("I have writ a play and a goodly one"). The syntheglott, booming here in the small cabin, counted to its limit. 4-3-2-1.

Zero. Paley zeroed out of the mothership, suddenly calm, then elated. It was moonlight, the green countryside slept. The river was a glory of silver. His course had been preset by Swenson; the control available to him was limited, but he came down smoothly on the water. What he had to do now was ease himself to the shore. The little engine purred as he steered in moonlight. The river was broad here, so that he seemed to be in a world of water and sky. The moon was odd, bigger than it should by rights have been, with straight markings like fabled Martian canals. The shore neared—it was all trees, sedge, thicket; there was no sign of habitation, not even another craft. What would another craft have thought, sighting him? He had no fears about that: with its wings folded, the little airboat looked, from a distance, like some nondescript barge, so well had it been camouflaged. And now, to be safe, he had to hide it, cover it with elmboughs and sedge greenery. But first, before disembarking, he must set the timeswitch that would, when he was safe ashore, render the metal of the fuselage high-charged, lethally repellent of all would-be boarders. It was a pity, but there it was. It would switch off automatically in a year's time, in twelve months to a day. Meanwhile, what myths, what madness would the curious examiner, the chance finder generate, tales uncredited by sophisticated London.

Launched on his night's walk upriver, Paley found the going easy enough. The moon lighted fieldpaths, stiles. Here and there a small farmhouse slept. Once he thought he heard a distant whistled tune. He had no idea of the month or day or time of night, but he guessed that it was late spring and some three hours or so off dawn. The year 1595 was certain, according to Swenson. Time functioned here as true on Earth, and two years before Swenson had taken a man to Muscovy, where they computed according to the Christian calendar, and the year had been 1953. That man had never come back, eaten by bears or something. Paley, walking, found the air gave good rich breathing, but from time to time he was made uneasy by the unfamiliar configurations of the heavens. There was Cassiopeia's Chair, Shakespeare's first name's drunken initial, but there were constellations he had not seen before. Could the stars, as the Elizabethans themselves believed, modify history? Could this Elizabethan London, because it looked up at stars unknown on true Earth, be identical with that other one which was known only from books? Well, he would soon know.

London did not burst upon him, a monster of grey stone and black and white wood. It came upon him gradually and gently, houses set in the fields and amid trees, the cool suburbs of the wealthy. And then, a muffed trumpet under the sinking moon, the Tower and its sleeping ravens. Then came the crammed crooked houses, all at rest. Paley breathed in the smell of this late spring London, and he did not like what he smelled. It was a complex of old rags and fat dirt, but it was also a smell he knew from a time when he flipped over to Borneo and timidly touched the periphery of the jungle: it was, somehow, a jungle smell. As if to corroborate this, a howl arose in the distance, but it was a dog's howl. Dogs, dogges, man's best friend, here in outer space; dog howling to dog across the inconceivable vastness of the cosmos. And then came a human voice and the sound of boots on cobbles. "Four of the clock and a fine morning." He instinctively flattened himself in an alleyway, crucified against a dampish wall. The time for his disclosure was not yet. He tasted the vowel sounds of the bellman's call—nearer to the English of Dublin than of his own London. "Four vth cluck." And then, knowing the hour at last and automatically feeling for a stopped wristwatch that was not there, he wondered what he should do till day started. Here were no hotels with clerks on allnight duty. He tugged at his dark beard (a three month's growth) and then decided that, as the sooner he started on his scholar's quest the better, he would walk to Shoreditch where the Theatre was. Outside the City's boundaries, where the play-hating City Council could not reach, it was at this time, so the history said, a new and handsome structure. A scholar's zest, the itch to know, came over him and made him forget the cold morning wind that was rising. His knowledge of the London of his own day gave him little help in the the orientation of the streets. He walked north—the Minories, Houndsditch, Bishopsgate—and, as he walked, he retched once or twice involuntarily at the stench from the kennel. There was a bigger, richer, filthier, obscener smell beyond this, and this he thought must come from Fleet Ditch. He dug into his scrip and produced a pinch of powder; this he placed on his tongue to quieten his stomach.

Not a mouse stirring as he walked, and there, under rolling cloud all besilvered, he saw it, the Theatre, with something like disappointment. It was mean wood rising above a wooden paling, its roof shaggily thatched. Things were always smaller and more ordinary than one expected. He wondered if it might be possible to enter. There seemed to be no protective night watchman. Before approaching the entrance (a door for an outside privy rather than a gate to the temple of the Muses) he took in the whole moonlit scene, the mean houses, the cobbles, the astonishing and unexpected greenery all about. And then he saw his first living creatures.

Not a mouse stirring, had he thought? But those creatures with long tails were surely rats, a trio of them nibbling at some dump of rubbish not far from the way into the Theatre. He went warily nearer, and the rats at once scampered off, each filament of whisker clear in the light. They were rats as he knew rats—though he had seen them only in cages in the laboratories of the university—with mean bright eyes and thick meaty tails. But then he saw what they had been eating.

Dragged out from the mound of trash was a human forearm. In some ways Paley was not unprepared for this. He had soaked in images of traitor heads stuck up on Temple Bar, bodies washed by three tides left to rot on Thames shore, limbs hacked off at Tyburn and carelessly left for the scavenging. Kites, of course, kites. But now the kites would all be roosting. Clinically, his stomach calm from its medicine, he examined the raw gnawed thing. There was not much flesh off it yet: the feast had been interrupted at its very beginning. On the wrist was a torn and pulpy patch which made Paley frown—something anatomically familiar but, surely, not referable to a normal human arm. It occurred to him for just a second that this was rather like an eye-socket, the eye wrenched out but the soft bed left, still not completely ravaged. And then he smiled that away, though it was difficult to smile.

He turned his back on the poor human remnant and made straight for the entrance door. To his surprise it was not locked. It creaked as he opened it, a sort of harsh voice of welcome to this world of 1595 and its strange familiarity. There it was—tamped earth for the groundlings to tamp down yet further; the side boxes; the jutting apron; the study uncurtained; the tarrass; the tower with its flagstaff. He breathed deeply, reverently. This was the Theatre. And then—

"Arrr, catched y'at it!" Paley's heart seemed about to leap from his mouth like a badly fitting denture. He turned to meet his first Elizabethan. Thank

God, he looked normal enough, though filthy. He was in clumsy boots, goose-turd-coloured hose, and a rancid jerkin. He tottered somewhat as though drunk, and, as he came closer to peer into Paley's face, Paley caught a frightful blast of ale breath. The man's eyes were glazed and he sniffed deeply and long at Paley as though trying to place him by scent. Intoxicated, unfocused, thought Paley with contempt, and as for having the nerve to sniff…. Paley spoke up, watching his words with care.

"I am a gentleman from Norwich, but newly arrived. Stand some way off, fellow. Know you not your betters when you see them?"

"I know not thee, nor why tha should be here at dead of night." But he stood away. Paley glowed with small triumph, the triumph of one who has, say, spoken home-learnt Russian for the first time in Moscow and has found himself perfectly understood. He said:

"Thee? Thee? I will not be thee-and-thou'd so, fellow. I would speak with Master Burbage, though mayhap I am somewhat early for't."

"The young un or th'old?"

"Either. I have writ plays and fain would show them about." The watchman sniffed Paley again. "Genlmn you may be, but you smell not like a Christian. Nor do you keep Christian hours."

"As I say, I am but newly arrived."

"I see not your horse. Nor your traveller's cloak."

"They are—I ha' left 'em at mine inn."

The watchman muttered. "And yet he saith he is but newly arrived. Go to." Then he chuckled and, at the same time, delicately advanced his right hand towards Paley as though about to bless him. "I know what 'tis," he said, chuckling. "'Tis some naughtiness, th'hast trysted ringading with some wench, nay, some wife rather, nor has she belled out the morn." Paley could make little of this. "Come," the man said, "chill make for 'ee an th'hast the needful." Paley looked blank. "An tha wants beddn'," the man said loudly. Paley caught that, he caught also the meaning of the open palm and wiggling fingers. Gold. He felt in his scrip and produced an angel. The man's jaw dropped as he took it. "Sir," he said, hat-touching.

"Truth to tell," Paley said, "I am shut out of mine inn, late returning from a visit and not able to make mine host hear with e'en the loudest knocking."

"Arrr," and the watchman put his finger by his nose, he scratched his cheek with the angel, finally, before stowing it in a little purse at his girdle, passing it a few times in front of his chest. "With me, sir, come."

He waddled speedily out, Paley following him with pulse fast abeat. "Where go we then?" he asked. He received no answer. The moon was almost down and there were the first intimations of early summer dawn. Paley shivered in the wind; he wished he had brought a cloak with him instead of the mere intention of buying one here. If it was really a bed he was to be taken to, he was glad. An hour or so's sleep in the warmth of blankets and never mind whether or not there would be fleas. On the streets nobody was astir, though Paley thought he heard a distant cat's concert—a painful courtship, just as on true Earth. Paley followed the watchman down a narrow lane off Bishopsgate, dark and stinking. The effects of the medicine had worn off; he felt his gorge rise as before. But the stink, his nose noticed, was subtly different from what it had been: it was, he thought in a kind of small madness, somehow swirling, redistributing its elements as though capable of autonomous action. He did not like this. Looking up at the paling stars he felt sure they too had done a sly job of refiguration, forming fresh patterns like a sand tray on top of a thumped piano.

"Here 'tis," the watchman said, arriving at a door and knocking without further ado. "Croshabels," he winked. But the eyelid winked on nothing but glazed emptiness. He knocked again, and Paley said:

"'Tis no matter. It is late, or early, to drag folk from their beds." A young cock crowed near, brokenly, a prentice cock.

"Never one nor t'other. 'Tis in the way of a body's trade, aye." Before he could knock again, the door opened. A cross and sleepy-looking woman appeared. She wore a filthy nightgown and, from its bosom, what seemed like an arum lily peered out. She thrust it back in irritably. She was an old Elizabethan woman, greyhaired, about thirty. She cried:

"Ah?"

"One for one. A genlman, he saith." He took his angel from its nest and held it up. She raised a candle the better to see. The arum lily peeped out again. All smiles now, she curtseyed Paley in. Paley said:

"'Tis but a matter of a bed, madam." The other two laughed at that 'madam'. "A long and wearisome journey from Norwich," he added. She gave a deeper curtsey, more mocking than before, and said, in a sort of a croak:

"A bed it shall be and no pallet nor the floor neither. For the gentleman from Norwich where the cows eat porridge." The watchman grinned. He was blind, Paley was sure he was blind. On his right thumb something winked richly. The door closed on him, and Paley and the madam were together in the rancid hallway.

"Follow, follow," she said, and she creaked first up the stairs. The shadows her candle cast were not deep; from the east grey was filling the world. On the wall of the stairwell were framed pictures. One was a crude woodcut showing a martyr hanging from a tree, a fire burning under him. Out of the smiling mouth words ballooned: AND YETTE I SAYE THAT MOGRADON GIUETH LYFE. Another picture showed a king with a crown, orb and sceptre and third eye set in his forehead. "What king is that?" asked Paley. She turned to look at him in some amazement. "Ye know naught in Norwich," she said. "God rest ye and keep ye all." Paley asked no further questions and kept his wonder to himself at another picture they passed: "Q. Horat. Flaccus" it said, but the portrait was of a turbaned Arab.

The madam knocked loudly on a door at the top of the stairs. "Bess, Bess," she cried. "Here's gold, lass. A cleanly and a pretty man withal." She turned to smile with black teeth at Paley. "Anon will she come. She must deck herself like unto a bride." From the bosom of her nightgown the lily again poked out and Paley thought he saw a blinking eye enfolded in its head. He began to feel the tremors of a very special sort of fear, not a terror of the unknown so much as of the known. He had rendered his flying boat invulnerable; this world could not touch it. Supposing it was possible that this world was in some manner rendered invulnerable by a different process? A voice in his head seemed to say, with great clarity: "Not with impunity may one disturb thee." And then the door opened and the girl called Bess appeared, smiling professionally. The madam said, smiling also:

"There then, as a pretty mutton slice as was e'er sauced o'er." And she held out her hand for money. Confused, Paley dipped into his scrip and pulled out a dull-gleaming handful. He told one coin into her hand and she still waited. He told another, then another. "We ha' wine," she said. "Wouldst?" Paley thanked her: no wine. The grey hair on her head grew erect. She mockcurtseyed off.

Paley followed Bess into the bedchamber, on his guard now. The ceiling bent like a pulse; "Piggesnie," Bess croaked, pulling her single garment down from her bosom. The breasts swung and the nipples ogled him. They were, as he had expected, eyes. He nodded in something like satisfaction. There was, of course, no question of going to bed now. "Honeycake," gurgled Bess, and the breast-eyes rolled, the long black lashes swept up and down coquettishly. Paley clutched his scrip tightlier to him. If this distortion— likely, as far as he could be the judge—were to grow progressively worse—if this scrambling of sense data were a regular barrier against intrusion, why was there not more information about it on Earth? Other time-travellers had ventured forth and come back unharmed and laden with sensible records. Wait, though: had they? How did one know? There was Swenson's mention of Wheeler, jailed in the Middle Ages by chunks of tripodic ectoplasm. "White-haired and gibbering when we got him aboard." Swenson's own words. How about Swenson's own vision of the future—a plaque showing his own birth and death dates? Perhaps the future did not object to intrusion from the past, since it was made of the same substance. But (Paley shook his head as though he were drunk, beating back sense into it) it was not a question of past and future, it was a matter of other worlds existing now. The now-past was completed, the now-future was completed. Perhaps that plaque in Rostron Place, Brighton, showing Swenson's death some thirty years off, perhaps that was an illusion, a device to engender satisfaction with the pattern. "My time is short," Paley said suddenly, using urgent twenty-third-century phonemes, not Elizabethan ones. "I will give you gold if you will take me to the house of Master Shakespeare."

"Maister-?"

"Shairkespeyr."

Bess, her ears growing larger, stared at Paley with a growing montage of film battle scenes playing away on the wall behind her. "Th'art not that kind. Women tha likes. That I see in tha face."

"This is urgent. This is business. Quick. He lives, I think, in Bishopsgate." He could find out something before the epistemological enemies took over. And then what? Try to live. Keep sane with signals in some quiet spot till a year was past. Signal Swenson, receive his reassurances in the reply; perhaps—who knew?—hear from far time-space that he was to be taken home before the scheduled date, instructions from Earth, arrangements changed—

"Thou knowest," Paley said, "what man I mean. Master Shakespeare the player at the Theatre."

"Aye aye." The voice was thickening fast. Paley himself: It is up to me to take in what I wish to take in; this girl has no eyes on her breasts, that mouth new-formed under her chin is not really there. Thus checked, the hallucinations wobbled and were pushed back temporarily. But their strength was great. Bess pulled on a simple smock over her nakedness, took a worn cloak from a closet. "Gorled maintwise," she said. Paley pushed like mad; the words unscrambled. "Give me money now," she said. He gave her a portague.

They tiptoed downstairs. Paley tried to look steadily at the pictures in the stairwell, but there was no time to force them into telling the truth. The stairs caught him off guard and changed to a primitive escalator. He whipped them back to trembling stairhood. Bess, he was sure, would melt into some monster capable of turning his heart to stone if he let her. Quick. He held the point-of-day in the sky by a great effort. There were a few people in the street. He durst not look on them. "Is it far?" he asked. Cocks crowed, many and near, mature cocks.

"Not far." But nothing could be far from anything in this crammed and toppling London. Paley strained to keep his sanity. Sweat dripped from his forehead and a drop caught on the scrip which he hugged to himself like a stomachache. He examined the drop as he walked, stumbling often on the cobbles. A drop of salty water from his pores. Was it out of alien world or of his own? If he cut off his hair and left it lying, if he dunged in that foul jakes there from which a three-headed woman now appeared, would this B303 London reject it, as a human body will reject a grafted kidney? Was it perhaps not a matter of natural law but of some God of the system, a God against Whom, the devil on one's side, one could prevail? Was it God's club rules he was pushing against, not some deeper inbuilt necessity? Anyway, he pushed, and Elizabethan London, in its silver dawn, steadied, rocked, steadied, held. But the strain was terrific.

"Here, sir." She had brought him to a mean door which warned Paley that it was going to turn into water and flow down cobbles did he not hold

his form fast. "Money," she said. But Paley had given enough. He scowled
and shook his head. She held out a fist which turned into a winking bearded
man's face, threatening with chattering mouth. He raised his own hand, flat,
to slap her. She ran off, whimpering, and he turned the raised hand to a fist
that knocked. His knock was slow to be answered. He wondered how much
longer he could maintain this desperate holding of the world in position. If
he slept, what would happen? Would it all dissolve and leave him howling
in cold space when he awoke?

"Aye, what is't, then?" It was a mishapen ugly man with a row of bright
blinking eyes across his chest, a chest left bare by his buttonless shirt. It was
not, it could not be, William Shakespeare. Paley said, wondering at his own
ability to enunciate the sounds with such exact care:

"Oi ud see Maister Shairkespeyr." He was surlily shown in, a shoulder-
thrust indicating which door he must knock at. This, this, then, at last. He
knocked. The door was firm oak, threatening no liquefaction.

"Aye?" A light voice, a pleasant voice, no early morning displeasure in
it. Paley gulped and opened the door and went in. Bewildered, he looked
about him. A bedchamber, the clothes on the bed in disorder, a table with
papers on it, a chair, morning light framed by the tight-shut casement. He
went over to the papers; he read the top sheet ("...giue it to him lest he rayse
al helle again with his factuousness"), wondering if perhaps there was a room
adjoining whence came that voice. Then he heard that voice again, behind
him:

"'Tis not seemly to read a gentleman's private papers lacking his permission." Paley spun round to see, dancing in the air, a reproduction of the
Droeshout portrait of Shakespeare, square in a frame, the lips moving but the
eyes unanimated. Paley tried to call but could not. The talking woodcut
advanced on him—"Rude, mannerless, or art thou some Privy Council spy?"—
and then the straight sides of the frame bulged and bulged, the woodcut features dissolved, and a circle of black lines and spaces tried to grow a solid
body. Paley could do nothing; his paralysis would not even permit him to
shut his eyes. The solid body became an animal shape, indescribably gross
and ugly—some spiked sea-urchin, very large, nodding and smiling with hor-
rible intelligence. Paley forced it into becoming a more nearly human shape.
his heart sank in depression totally untinged by fear to see standing before
him a fictional character called "William Shakespeare," an actor acting the
part. Why could he not get in touch with the *Ding an sich*, the Kantian
noumenon? But that was the trouble—the thing-in-itself was changed by the
observer into whatsoever phenomenon the categories of time and space sense
imposed. He took courage and said:

"What plays have you writ to date?"

Shakespeare looked surprised. "Who asks this?"

Paley said: "What I say you will hardly believe. I come from another world that knows and reveres the name of Shakespeare. I come, for safety's sake, in disguise as a man from Norwich who seeks his fortune in the theatre and has brought plays of his own. I believe that there was, or is, an actor named William Shakespeare. That Shakespeare wrote the plays that carry his name— this is the thing I must prove."

"So," said Shakespeare, tending to melt into a blob of tallow badly sculpted into the likeness of Shakespeare, "you speak of what I will hardly believe. For my part, I will believe anything. You will be a sort of ghost from this other world you speak of. By rights you should have dissolved at cock-crow."

"My time may be as short as a ghost's. What plays do you claim to have written up to this moment?" Paley spoke the English of his own day. Though the figure before him shifted and softened, tugged towards other shapes, the eyes changed little, shrewd and intelligent eyes, modern. Paley noticed now a small fireplace, in which a meagre newlit fire struggled to live. The hands of Shakespeare moved to their warming through the easy process of elongation of the arms. The voice said:

"Claim? 'Heliogabalus.' A Word to Fright Whoremaster. 'The Sad Reign of Harold First and Last.' 'The Devil in Dulwich.' Oh, many and many more."

"Please." Paley was distressed. Was this truth or teasing, truth or teasing of this man or of his own mind, a mind desperate to control the sense data and make them make sense? On the table there, the mass of papers. "Show me," he said. "Show me somewhat," he pleaded.

"Show me your credentials," Shakespeare said, "if we are to talk of showing. Nay," and he advanced merrily towards Paley, "I will see for myself." The eyes were very bright now and shot with oddly sinister flecks. "A pretty boy," Shakespeare said. "Not so pretty as some, as one, I would say, but apt for a brief tumble of a summer's morning before day warms."

"Nay," Paley protested, "nay," backing and feeling the archaism to be strangely frivolous, "touch me not." The advancing figure became horribly ugly, the neck swelled, eyes glinted on the hairy backs of the approaching hands. The face grew an elephantine proboscis, wreathing, feeling; two or three suckers sprouted from its end and blindly waved towards Paley. Paley dropped his scrip the better to struggle. The words of this monster were thick, they turned into grunts and lallings. Pushed into the corner near the table, Paley saw a sheet of paper much blotted ("Never blotted a line," did they say?):

> I haue bin struggling striuing seeking how I may compair
> This jailhouse prison? where I liue unto the earth world
> And that and for because

The scholar was still alive in Paley, the questioning spirit clear while the body fought off those huge hands, each ten-fingered. The scholar cried:

"'Richard II'? You are writing 'Richard II'?"

It seemed to him, literary history's Claude Bernard, that he should risk all to get that message through to Swenson, that "Richard II" was, in 1595, being written by Shakespeare. He suddenly dipped to the floor, grabbed his scrip and began to tap through the lining at the key of the transmitter. Shakespeare seemed taken by surprise by his sudden cessation of resistance; he put out forks of hands that grasped nothing. Paley, blind with sweat, panting hard, tapped: "UNDOUBTED PROOF THAT." Then the door opened.

"I did hear a noise." It was the misshapen ugly man with eyes across his bare chest, uglier now, his shape changing constantly though abruptly, as though set upon by silent and invisible hammers. "He did attack tha?"

"Not for money, Tomkin. He hath gold enow of's own. See." The scrip, set down so hurriedly, had spilt gold onto the floor. Paley had not noticed; he should have transferred that gold to his—

"Aye, gold." The creature called Tomkin gazed on it greedily. "The others that came so brought not gold."

"Take the gold and him," Shakespeare said carelessly. "Do what thou wilt with both." Tomkin oozed toward Paley. Paley screamed, attacking feebly with the hand that now held the scrip. Tomkin's claw snatched it without trouble.

"There's more within," he drooled.

"Did I not say thou wouldst do well in my service?" said Shakespeare.

"And here is papers." He looked towards the fire with a sheaf of them. Then he went to the grate and offered them. The fire read them hurriedly and converted them into itself. There was a transitory blaze which played music for shawms.

"Not all the papers." Shakespeare took the rest. "Carry him to the Queen's Marshal. The stranger within our gates. He talks foolishly, like the Aleman that came before. Wildly, I would say. Of other worlds, like a madman. The Marshal will know what to do."

"But," screamed Paley, grabbed by strong shovels of hands, "I am a gentleman. I am from Norwich. I am a playwright, like yourself. See, you hold what I have written."

"First a ghost, now from Norwich," Shakespeare smiled. He hovered in the air like his portrait again, a portrait holding papers. "Go to. Are there not other worlds, like unto our own, that sorcery can make men leave to visit this? I have such stories before. There was one came from High Germany–"

"It's true, true, I tell you." Paley clung to that, clinging also to the chamber door with his nails, the while Tomkin pulled at him.

"You are the most intelligent man of these times! You can conceive of it!"

"And of poets yet unborn also? Drythen, or some such name, and Lord Tennisballs, and Infra Penny Infra Pound? You will be taken care of like that other."

"But it's true, true!"

"Come your ways," growled Tomkin. "You are a Bedlam natural." And he dragged Paley out, Paley collapsing, frothing, raving. Paley raved: "You are not real, any of you. It's you who are the ghosts! I'm real, it's all a mistake, let me go, let me explain."

"'Tis strange he talks," growled Tomkin. And he dragged him out.

"Shut the door," said Shakespeare. Tomkin kicked it to. The screaming voice went, over thumping feet, down the passageway without. Soon it was quiet enough to sit and read.

These were, Shakespeare thought, good plays. A pity the rest was consumed in that fire that now, glutted, settled again to sleep. Too hot today for a fire anyway. Strange that the play he now read was about, so far as he could judge, a usurious Jew. This Norwich man had evidently read Marlowe and seen the dramatic possibilities of an evil Lopez kind of character. Shakespeare had toyed with the idea of a play like this himself. And here it was, ready done for him, though it required copying into his own hand that questions about its provenance be not asked. And there were a promising couple of histories here, both about King Henry IV. And here a comedy with its final pages missing in the fire, its title "Much Ado About Nothing." Gifts, godsends! He smiled. He remembered that Aleman, Doctor Schleyer or some such name, who had come with a story like this madman (mad? Could madmen do work like this? "The lunatic, the lover and the poet": a good line in that play about fairies Schleyer had brought. Poor Schleyer had died of the plague). Those plays Schleyer had brought had been good plays, but not, perhaps, quite so good as these.

Shakespeare furtively, though he was alone, crossed himself. When poets had talked of the Muse had they perhaps meant visitants like this, now screaming feebly in the street, and the German Schleyer and that one who swore, under torture, that he was from Virginia in America, and that in America they had universities as good as Oxford or Leyden or Wittenberg, nay better? Well, whoever they were, they were heartily welcome so long as they brought plays. The "Richard II" of Schleyer's was, perhaps, in need of the amendments he was now engaged upon, but the earlier work untouched, from "Henry VI" on, had been popular. He read the top sheet of this new batch, stroking his auburn beard finely silvered, a fine grey eye reading. He sighed and, before crumpling a sheet of his own work on the table, he reread it. Not good, it limped, there was too much magic in it. Ingenio the Duke of Parma said:

> Consider gentleman as in the sea
> All earthly life finds like and parallel
> So in far distant skies our lives be aped
> Each hath a twin each action hath a twin
> And twins galore and infinite
> And een these stars be twinn'd

Too fantastic, it would not do. He threw it into the rubbish box which Tomkin would later empty. Humming a new song of the street entitled "Leave well alone", he took a clean sheet and began to copy in fair hand:

"The Merchant of Venice, A Comedy"

Then on he went, not blotting a line.

Jorge Luis Borges
(1899–1986)

Known for his precisely crafted, richly allusive, and surrealistic stories and poems, Jorge Luis Borges has helped shape twentieth-century Latin American literature. Born in Buenos Aires to a distinguished family, Borges quickly developed the fascination with English and American literature which would lead to his appointment as a professor of English Literature at the University of Buenos Aires and a Norton Lecturer at Harvard. His intellectual interests expanded even further when his family became stranded in Geneva during World War I, and he spent his teenage years mastering German and French. After the war, he visited Spain with his family and studied in England before returning to Argentina.

In Madrid Borges associated with a group of young poets influenced by such artistic movements as Imagism and Vorticism and associated with the magazine Ultra, a journal committed to moving beyond conventional literary boundaries. Bringing the Ultraist movement home to Buenos Aires, Borges gathered a group of writers to develop a national literature emphasizing metaphor and simplicity. In 1935 his *A Universal History of Infamy* offered the first model of magic realism. Strongly opposed to the Perón regime, Borges developed a conservative political philosophy which separated him from many of the young writers whose works he profoundly influenced. In 1955, at the end of the Perónista period, Borges became Director of the National Library.

"Everything and Nothing" reflects Borges' belief that characterization is the essence of Shakespeare's plays: "[I]n the case of Shakespeare, you believe in the characters, you don't believe in the plots." (*Borges at Eighty: A Conversation*, ed Willis Barnstone [Bloomington: Indiana University Press]). In Borges' story, those characters come to form a labyrinth in which Shakespeare both loses and finds himself. The story characteristically reflects its author's sensitivity to language (the play on "no one" in the opening sentence), his easy mixture of fact and fancy, and his deceptive simplicity. The following translation is by Anthony Kerrigan.

"Everything and Nothing"
(1961)

There was no one in him: behind his face (even the poor paintings of the epoch show it to be unlike any other) and behind his words (which were copious, fantastic, and agitated) there was nothing but a bit of cold, a dream not dreamed by anyone. At first he thought that everyone was like himself. But the dismay shown by a comrade to whom he mentioned this vacuity revealed his error to him and made him realize forever that an individual should not differ from the species. At one time it occurred to him that he might find a remedy for his difficulty in books, and so he learned the "small Latin, and less Greek," of which a contemporary spoke. Later, he considered he might find what he sought in carrying out one of the elemental rites of humanity, and so he let himself be initiated by Anne Hathaway in the long siesta hour of an afternoon in June. In his twenties, he went to London. Instinctively, he had already trained himself in the habit of pretending he was someone, so it should not be discovered that he was no one. In London, he found the profession to which he had been predestined, that of actor: someone who, on a stage, plays at being someone else, before a concourse of people who pretend to take him for that other one. His histrionic work taught him a singular satisfaction, perhaps the first he had ever known. And yet, once the last line of verse had been acclaimed and the last dead man dragged off stage, he tasted the hateful taste of unreality. He would leave off being Ferrex or Tamburlaine and become no one again. Thus beset, he took to imagining other heroes and other tragic tales. And so, while his body complied with its bodily destiny in London bawdyhouses and taverns, the soul inhabiting that body was Caesar unheeding the augur's warnings, and Juliet detesting the lark, and Macbeth talking on the heath with the witches who are also the Fates. No one was ever so many men as that man: like the Egyptian Proteus he was able to exhaust all the appearances of being. From time to time, he left, in some obscure corner of his work, a confession he was sure would never be deciphered: Richard states that in his one person he plays many parts, and Iago curiously says "I am not what I am." The fundamental oneness of existing, dreaming, and acting inspired in him several famous passages.

He persisted in this directed hallucination for twenty years. But one morning he was overcome by a surfeit and horror of being all those kings who die by the sword and all those unfortunate lovers who converge, diverge, and melodiously expire. That same day he settled on the sale of his theater. Before a week was out he had gone back to his native village, where he recuperated the trees and the river of his boyhood, without relating them at all to the trees and rivers—illustrious with mythological allusion and Latin phrase—which his Muse had celebrated. He had to be someone: he became a retired impresario who has made his fortune and who is interested in making loans, in lawsuits, and in petty usury. It was in character, then, in this character, that he dictated the arid last will and testament we know, from which he deliberately excluded the any note of pathos or trace of literature. Friends from London used to visit him in his retreat, and for them he would once more play the part of poet.

History adds that before or after his death he found himself facing God and said: *I, who have been so many men in vain, want to be one man, myself alone.* From out of a whirlwind the voice of God replied: *I am not, either. I dreamed the world the way you dreamed your work, my Shakespeare: one of the forms of my dream was you, who, like me, are many and no one.*

APPENDIX I

THE VISITATION
or, an Interview Between
the Ghost of
SHAKESPEAR
and
D-V-D G-RR--K, Esq.

Now Morpheus had, his Mace of Lead
Strok'd o'er each sober, prudent Head;
Time seem'd to stop, and this great Town,
In a lethargic State was thrown;
Save drousy Watchmen, here and there,
Of Libertines, and Thieves, the Care;
And some few Women of the Town,
By Name of (Pleasure Ladies) known,
(Of whom there's those, who still maintain
They deal in Pleasure, less than Pain)
The Streets were clear, nor Man nor Beast,
That had a Home, but was at Rest.

   The Night was silent and serene,
Illumin'd by its silver Queen,
Diana, peerless may she boast,
Compar'd with all the starry Host.

   Let this suffice—'twas such a Night
As might a guilty Soul affright,
When the busy Ghosts, as we have read,

Stalk round the Curtains of a Bed,
Or lay a cold Hand o'er a Face
And cause a fearful, smelling Case.

In Country Villages it's found,
That Sprites and Goblins most abound,
There Ghosts are made of Stocks and Stones,
And nothing's heard save dismal Groans;
In every Bush, and every Grove,
Utter'd by Spirits cross'd in Love,
Who sometimes chuse the Shape to wear,
Of an old Post, or white neck'd Mare.

On such a Night great Shakespear's Shade,
Appear'd to G-rr-k, as he laid
Involv'd in serious Contemplation,
Of his late dang'rous Situation.

The little Hero struck with Fear,
Like Richard look'd, or mad like Lear,
Like Romeo in the Pangs of Death,
Or like sleep murdering Macbeth,
Each several Passion seiz'd the Play'r,
Rage, Sorrow, Terror and Despair;
Thrice he essay'd—I dauntless dare,
The Shade as often cry'd "Beware!
To clear thy Conduct ne'er pretend,
Nor vile Ingratitude defend;
For know to thee I can impart,
The closest Secrets of the Heart.
(Perhaps, you have forgot the Day,
When in Obscurity you lay,
For Favours past, I have been told.
May be forgotten e're we're old)
Could'st thou, with base ignoble Mind,
To Fortune, and my Favours blind,
Forget I chose thee out, and fought,
To teach thee all, e're nature taught?
Taught thee to feel, each nice Sensation,
And reign unrival'd in a Nation?
Rais'd thee from nothing to high Glory,
Making all Actors bow before ye,
Acknowledging themselves unequal

To equal you?—now mark the Sequel,
You have of late, why best you know,
Deserted those, that serv'd you so;
Contemn'd that Pow'r, you lately priz'd,
And follow'd Arts you once despis'd;
O'erbearing all, with haughty Spirit,
Buoy'd up by self-sufficient Merit;
Preferr'd Toll Loll, and what's akin,
Compar'd with Drama—Harlequin;
Aids that the Grecian Stage ne'er knew,
Aids that Dame Nature never drew;
Besides you late brought on a Dance,
Perform'd by servile Slaves from France,
(Slaves whose chief Worth, whoe'er reveals,
Must own it center'd in their Heels)
But that, my Sons by me inspir'd,
With noble Indignation fir'd,
Condemn'd—
Enrag'd they join'd with one Accord,
Nor fear'd they Officer, or Lord,
They storm'd your House, and clearly prov'd
Without me you'd ne'er been belov'd."

  The British Roscius thus reply'd,
"Dread Sir, I own you for my Guide,
Acknowledge you, and you alone,
Could make me shine as I have shone;
But, Sir, 'twas not in my Ability
To stem the Will of our Nobility,
Whose Appetites are quite deprav'd,
By foreign Foppery enslav'd,
They in the Drama find no Joys,
But doat on Mimickry and Toys.
Thus when a Dance is in my Bill,
Nobility my Boxes fill;
Or send three Days before the Time
To croud a new made Pantomime.
Int'rest, dread Sir, will often cause
A Man to spurn at Reason's Laws,
And holding all Things else as Light,
Prove right is wrong, or wrong is right
Howe'er for Time to come I swear,
No Dance, nor Pantomime, nor Air:

Will I exhibit on the Stage,
Tho' Ladies fume or nobles rage,
Let them when next they want a Dance
Repair to Italy, or France;
I'll henceforth rest on you alone,
As chief Supporter of my Throne."

The Bard afflicted pensive grew,
And wept as Spirits us'd to do:
Then thus he cry'd in moving Sort,
"Are these the Sinews of a C—rt?
These who no Spark of Worth retain,
But prove a Star may hide a Stain,
These Moths in Honour's sacred Flame,
Noble in nothing, but in Name,
Ah! how the Times are alter'd quite,
Since last my Eyes beheld the Light?
Then Nobles strove with noble Deeds,
To cleanse the Land of all such Weeds.
They danc'd, it's true, from Night to Noon,
They danc'd—but 'twas another Tune,
They danc'd at Agincourt one Day,
And took in bloody Crowns their Pay;
But Needless 'tis to tell you more,
You've often read my Works before.

"Now as I fancy, 'tis confest
You strove to please a vicious Taste,
And thence, perhaps, might think it due,
To pleasure those that profit you.
To give you Pardon, I incline,
If you'll revive a Work of mine;
You need not fear it will miscarry."
"What Play d'ye mean Sir?"—"My fifth Harry."
The Bard now snuff'd the Morning Air,
And found 'twas time to disappear—
Then seal'd a Pardon (on Condition)
Error was cancell'd by Contrition.
As G-rr--k mus'd (the Shade retir'd)
Reflecting what was late requir'd;
He thought to acquiesce with Speed,
Would in his Favour intercede;
So now you'll see in little Space,

Shakespear's fifth Harry show his Face.
Oh may the Scene each Bosom fire,
With martial Rage, and vengeful Ire!
Once more our Flags shall then advance,
And quell the haughty Pride of France;
Who urg'd by Envy, and Ambition,
By Poverty and superstition,
Seeks to disturb our State of Peace,
And rob all Europe of its Ease.

   Of stern Adversity a Child,
On whom kind Fortune never smil'd;
Who Peace or War must be the same,
Too low to hope to grasp at Fame.
Thus prays, that Providence may pour,
Bliss without End on Briton's Shore!
May her triumphant matchless Fleet,
Where'er it moves, fresh Conquests meet,
And, oh! blest Pow'rs indulgent shine,
On George and his illustrious Line,
And grant that Line may never cease,
(Under whose Sway we live at Ease)
Till Time shall feel a near Decay,
And Nature's self shall melt away.

—Anonymous

FINIS

APPENDIX II

FAMILIAR VERSES FROM THE GHOST OF WILLY SHAKSPEARE TO SAMMY IRELAND

George Moutard Woodward (?1760-1809)

Ah Sammy! Sammy! why call forth a ghost?
Rather of Critics summon up an host!
They—luckless wights! indite for daily bread;
But you disturb the ashes of the dead!
Peaceful I lay in Stratford's hallowed fane,
And, but for thee, might yet enshrined remain:
"Blest were the man" I said, "who spar'd the stones;
But curs'd be he, who dared to move my bones!"
'Tis true, my bones lie unmolested there,
Yet still my spirit's dragg'd to open air.
Rich in your prize, of praise, you take your fill,
But *Spectres yet may speak,—and speak* I will!

Oft have I conjured, from the vasty deep,
Myriads of spirits at one magic sweep!
And shalt thou dare, with weak unnervate arm,
To bind Will Shakespeare with a cobweb charm?
His genius unconfin'd with fancy plays
Where Avon's stream through fertile meadows strays;
Laughs with the loves, the flitting sunbeam rides,
And through the boundless paths of Nature glides.
Not lock'd in trunks,—in *auncient dirtie* scrolls,
Long shreds of parchment, deeds, and *mustie* rolls;

210

Receipts for candles, bills and notes of hand,
Some that you may—but more not understand.
Samples of hair, love songs, and sonnets meete,
Together meet by *chaunce* in *Norfolk-street*;
Where, fruitful as the vine, the tiny elves
Produce *young manuscripts* for Sammy's shelves.
Dramas in embrio leave their lurking holes,
And little Vortigerns* start fprth in shoals.
To work, ye Lawyers! ransack all your deeds,
The bait is swallowed, and the Public bleeds.
Freely the Cash comes down,—lead boldly on,
The Book† complete:—Four Guineas!—*Presto!*—gone!
More papers found!!! a neighbor here hard by—
An antiquarian wight, of curious eye,
Deep skill'd in pedigrees, well known to Fame—
Has found some writings in an hand the same—
Has found some writings in an hand the fame,
The very dots, the stops,—the self-same *Shak*,
That soon must lay each quibbler on his back:
None shall their sanction to the truth refuse;
For, if they'll not believe, they must be Jews.

    Long fam'd for *finding*, Sammy, art thou known,
With steady perserverance,—all thy own;
E'en Hogarth§ could not 'scape thy prying eye,
Lo! at thy beck, new beauties we descry!
Tobacco prints, and legendary tales,
Engraved on porter-pots with crocked nails;
Impressions scarce, long hidden from the light,
And comic wonders bursting on the sight.

    When late to Stratford you incog. came down,
Peeping for relics through each lane in town,
I guess'd that something fresh was in the wind,
And thus to Davy Garrick spoke my mind:
"Since you call'd forth the wond'ring nobles round
"To see my Jubilee on Fairy ground,
"To chaunt my praises in harmonious strain,
"And strut in Pageants through a shower of rain,

The "lost" Shakespeare play William discovered.
†*Samuel Ireland's edition of the newly discovered papers.*
§*Ireland's Graphic Illustrations of Hogarth.*

"Ne'er has mine eye in Warwick's county scann'd
"So learn'd a wight as Sammy Ireland!"
　　The chair, the kitchen, room where I was born,
All from old Time's mysterious veil were torn;
I often thought—so steady were his pains,
And from his work*, so certain were his gains—
He'd never give his deep researchers up,
Until he found my spoon and christ'ning cup:
Some curious remnants of my mother's spinning;
My little shoes, and all the child-bed linen!
—So have I seen a *Jack-daw* in a yard,
With head askaunt, some chosen spot regard,
Where, deep enearthed, some dainty morsels lay,—
Wisely laid there against a rainy day:
When hunger pinches, to the ground he hies,
Now cheerful hops, and elated flies;
But not contented with his well known store,
He whets his bill, and greedy pecks for more.

　　But turn we now again to Norfolk-Street,†
Where Authors sage and Commentators meet;
To that fam'd spot where Dramatists repair,
And Antiquarians darken all the air:
There Mister Kemble§ struts with solemn pace,
Then takes the chair; with academic grace
Pronounces all are genuine, true, and rare;
While none to contradict the Actor dare.
That wond'rous man,—the Brother, in right line,
To wond'rous Siddons,**—names well-known as mine!
Who shall persume his judgement to disown,
Who makes my choicest dramas half his own?
He, Mohawk like, unfeeling cuts and lops,
That Shakepeare's Plays appear like *modern Crops*!
Then from the press comes forth *editions* true,
And John's *additions* meet the public view:
No faults throughout the title page we spy,
And J.P. Kemble strikes the wond'ring eye!!!
Next mount sublime, upon the critic throne,

*Ireland's engravings of Avon landscapes.
†The Irelands' home.
§John Philip Kemble of the acting family.
**Sarah Siddons, the actress.

A trusty blade, and true yclep'd *Malone*.
He scorns complying sentiments to sham,
And, 'spite of Kemble, states the whole a flam.
Though some declare he never saw a line,
And 'gainst his judgement all their strength combine;
Other's attempt his doubting course to steer,
And *Mifter* Stevens*, marches in the rear.
Burke *Sammy* aids, and Sheridan the same;
The latter, right or wrong, is not to blame;
For well he knows, "*All's grist that comes to mill!*"
And Vortigern can't fail the house to fill.
Boydell† looks grave, and wisely holds his peace;
For, true or false, they can't his fame decrease:
His grand edition still will stand the test,
And Ireland's *Cayan* gives the whole a zest.
    Now Sammy, you of course, will wish to know
The Ghost's opinion, farther light to throw;
For Shakespeare's sanction must have lasting weight,
And fix for ever thy depending fate;
Give thee entire the Antiquarian rule,
Or spurn thee forth indignant from thy stool:—
Then, know, my Friend, to ease thy troubled mind,
Thy Willy's Ghost, to thee was always kind;
And, far from judging the old writings found,
Said to be mine, so long in darkness bound,
I'll not pretend thy mystic veil to draw—
Pronounce them forg'd, or pass them into law:
To speak the truth, I give it on my word;
For years long past, my Muse has felt the sword,—
Such hacking, slashing, cutting here and there,
Some parts press'd down, and others puff'd to air;
I know not what is mine, nor what is not.
If true,—thy envied fame will quickly spread,
And Britain's honours play around thy head:
If forg'd,—be prudent, vigilant, and wise;
Keep thy own counsel, and each threat despise.
    But hold!—Methinks I scent the morning air;
Abrupt we part, nor can I more declare:
Lo! in the East, the glowing tints I see.
Sammy, adieu!—Farewell!—remember me!

*George Stevens, an editor of the plays.
†John Boydell, politician and engraver.

BIBLIOGRAPHY

Adee, David Graham. "Bacon and Shakespeare. A Study." *The United Service: A Monthly Review of Military and Naval Affairs*, ns 15, No. 6 (June 1896), 512–36, and continued in ns 16, No. 1 (July 1896), 48–66.

Alexander, Louis C. *The Autobiography of Shakespeare: A Fragment.* London: Headley Brothers, 1911.

Anderson, H.M. *Golden Lads: A Tale.* London: William Blackwood, 1928.

Baring, Maurice. "The Rehearsal." In *Diminutive Dramas.* London: Constable and Company, 1911.

Bennett, John. *Master Skylark: A Story of Shakspere's Time.* New York: The Century Company, 1898.

Black, William. *Judith Shakespeare: A Romance.* London: Sampson Low, Marston, 1884.

Blair, Wilford. *The Death of Shakespeare.* Oxford: Blackwell, 1916.

Bond, Edward. *Bingo: Scenes of Money and Death.* London: Eyre Methuen, 1974.

Borges, Jorge Luis. "Everything and Nothing." Translated by Anthony Kerrigan. In *A Personal Anthology.* New York: Grove Press, 1967.

Bradshaw, Christopher Brooke. *Shakspere and Company.* London, 1845.

Brahms, Caryl and S.J. Simon. *No Bed for Bacon.* 1941. Rpt. London: New English Library, 1964.

Brougham, John. *Shakspere's Dream: An Historical Pageant.* New York: Samuel French, 1858.

Burgess, Anthony. "The Muse." In *Enderby's Dark Lady.* New York: McGraw-Hill, 1984, pp. 142–60.

_____. *Nothing Like the Sun.* London: Heinemann, 1964.

_____. "Will and Testament." In *Shakespeare: Patterns of Excelling Nature.* Eds. David Bevington and Jay L. Halio. Newark, Del.: Univ. of Delaware Press, 1976, pp. 46–65.

Campbell, Lawton. *Shakespeare Smiles.* London: Appleton, 1924.

Carlton, Grace. *The Wooing of Anne Hathaway.* London: The Mitre Press, 1938.

Chariton, Morris. *Conversations with Shakespeare.* Toronto: privately printed, 1969.

Chute, Marchette. *The Wonderful Winter.* London: Phoenix House, 1956.

Clare, Maurice [Byron, May Clarissa (Gillington)]. *A Day with Shakespeare.* London: Hodder and Stoughton [191–].

Clark, Imogen. *Will Shakespeare's Little Lad.* New York: Charles Scribner, 1897.

Cooper, Stanley. *Nine Fancy Pictures of Events in Shakspere's Country, Town, and Court Life.* London: F. Norgate, 1893.

Cox, Samuel Alfred. *Shakespeare Converted into Bacon: An Extravaganza in Two Acts.* Dublin: Sealy, Bryers, and Walker, 1899.

Curling, Henry. *The Forest Youth: or, Shakspere As He Lived: An Historical Tale.* London: Eli Charles Eginton, 1853.

_____. *The Merry Wags of Warwickshire: or The Early Days of Shakspere*. London: George Wright, 1854.

_____. *Shakspere; The Poet, The Lover, The Actor, The Man: A Romance*. 3 vols. in 1. London: Richard Bentley, 1848.

Dane, Clemence. *Will Shakespeare: An Invention in Four Acts*. London: William Heinemann, 1921.

"A Day with England's Greatest Man." *My Magazine* [192–], pp. 115–29, 209–12.

Dennis, John. Prologue to Julius Caesar. In *A Collection and Selection of English Prologues and Epilogues*. Vol. III. London, 1779, 1–2. 4 vols.

Drake, Nathan. "Montchesney, A Tale of the Days of Shakspere." In *Noontide Leisure or, Sketches in Summer*. London: T. Cadell, 1824. Vol. I, 18–100, 155–241, and continued in Vol. II, 74–140, 173–214, 274–327.

Duval, Alexandre-Vincent Pineu. *Shakespeare Amoureaux*. Paris, 1812.

Emerson, Ralph Waldo. "Shakspere, or the Poet." In *Collected Works*, ed. Wallace E. Williams and Douglas Emory Wilson. Vol. IV. Representative Men: Seven Lectures. Cambridge, Mass.: Belknap Press, 1987.

_____. "Intellect." *Collected Works*, ed. Joseph Slater, Alfred R. Ferguson, and Jean Ferguson Carr. Vol II. *Essays: First Series*. Cambridge, Mass: Belknap Press, 1979

Fisher, Edward. *The Best House in Stratford*. New York: Abelard-Schuman, 1965.

_____. *Love's Labour Won: A Novel About Shakespeare's Lost Years*. New York: Abelard-Schuman, 1963.

_____. *Shakespeare & Son*. New York: Abelard-Schuman, 1962.

Fruehe, D.H. "Swan of Avon: A Non–Historic Dialogue in One Act." MS from Vienna, 1924. Shakespeare Centre Library.

Garnett, Richard. *William Shakespeare: Pedagogue and Poacher*. London: John Lane, 1905.

Garrick in the Shades; or A Peep into Elysium, A Farce. London: J. Southern, 1779.

Gregg, Tresham D. *Queen Elizabeth; or the Origin of Shakespeare*. London: Wm. MacIntosh, 1872.

Gruner, E. Hamilton. *With Golden Quill: A Cavalcade, Depicting Shakespeare's Life and Times*. Stratford-on-Avon: The Shakespeare Press, 1936.

Halidom, M.Y. *The Poet's Curse*. London: Greening, 1911.

Hamley, Major General E. B. "Shakespeare's Funeral." In *Tales from Blackwood*, ns 2. London: William Blackwood, 1878, 1–65.

Harris, Frank. *Shakespeare and His Love*. London: Frank Palmer, 1910.

Head, Franklin H. *Shakespeare's Insomnia and the Causes Thereof*. Cambridge: Riverside Press, 1886.

Holmes, Martin. "Shakespeare at Whitehall." *The Sketch* (Christmas Number 1957), 22–23, 54.

Howells, W[illiam] D[ean]. *The Seen and Unseen at Stratford-on-Avon: A Fantasy*. New York: Harper, 1914.

James, Henry. "The Birthplace." *The Complete Tales of Henry James*. Ed. Leon Edel. Philadelphia: J. B. Lippincott, 1964. XI, 403–65.

Jerrold, Douglas. "Shakespeare in China." *The New Monthly Magazine and Humorist* (1837), 233–39.

Jordan, William. *Elizabeth's Immortal Son: Part Three: His Autobiography*. Brighton: The Southern Publishing Company, 1960.

Kingsmill, Hugh. *The Return of William Shakespeare*. London: Duckworth, 1929.

Kipling, Rudyard. "Proofs of Holy Writ." *Uncollected Prose*. Vol XXIII of *The Burwash Edition of the Complete Works in Prose and Verse*. 1941. Rpt. New York: AMS, 1970, 663–78.

Krieger, Norbert. *Prologue to Shakespeare's Hamlet.* Jerusalem, 1942.

[Landor, Walter Savage]. *Citation and Examination of William Shakspeare, Euseby Treen, Joseph Carnaby, and Silas Gough, Clerk, before the Worshipful Sir Thomas Lucy, Knight, Touching Deer-Stealing, on the 19th Day of September in the Year of Grace 1582; Now First Published from Original Papers.* London: Saunders and Otley, 1834.

[Langston, C. J.]. "How Shakespeare's Skull Was Stolen." *The Argosy,* 28, No. 167 (October 1879), 268–77.

Lawrence, C. E. *The Hour of Prospero.* London: Gowans and Gray, 1927.

Lengyel, Cornel Adam. "Will of Stratford." MS [196–]. Shakespeare Centre Library.

Loessel, G. A. *A Midnight Vision in Westminster Abbey as a "Lever de Rideau" to Scenes from Shakespeare's Plays.* MS [?1930]. Shakespeare Centre Library.

Longworth, Clara (Comtesse de Chabrun). *My Shakespeare Rise! Recollections of John Lacy, One of His Majesty's Players.* Stratford-on-Avon: Shakespeare Press, 1935.

Lord, Katherine. "The Day Will Shakspere Went to Kenilworth: A Pageant Play." In *The Little Playbook.* New York: Duffield, 1926.

Malpass, Eric. *Sweet Will.* London: Macmillan, 1973.

Martin, Mrs. George Madden. *A Warwickshire Lad: The Story of the Boyhood of William Shakespeare.* New York: Appleton, 1916.

Messner, Rhoda Henry. *Absent Thee from Felicity: The Story of Edward de Vere, Seventeenth Earl of Oxford.* Shaker Heights, Ohio: Corinthian Press, 1975.

Mortimer, John. *Will Shakespeare.* New York: Delacorte Press, 1977.

O'Riordan, Conal [Norreys Connell]. "Shakespeare's End." In *Shakespeare's End and Other Irish Plays.* London, Stephen Swift, 1912, pp. 85–167.

Phelps, C. E. D. and Leigh North. *The Bailiff of Tewkesbury.* Chicago: A. C. McClurg, 1893.

Porter, T. H. *A Maid of the Malverns: A Romance of the Blackfriar's Theatre.* London: Lynwood, 1912.

Rendle, W. "Shakespeare at the Tabard Inn: A Phantasy." *The Antiquarian Magazine.* London: Reeves, Unwin, and Redway, 1882, p. 32.

Rooke, Leon. *Shakespeare's Dog.* New York: Alfred A. Knopf, 1983. (arranged by) Rose, Mrs. C[onstance]. *Shakespeare's Day.* Cheltenham, 1927.

Rubinstein, H[arold] F[rederick] and Clifford Bax. *Shakespeare: A Play in Five Episodes.* London: Benn Brothers, 1921.

Rubinstein, H.F. *Bernard Shaw in Heaven.* London: William Heinemann, 1954.

_____. "Shakespeare's Globe." *The Amateur Theatre and Playwright's Journal,* 4, No. 75 (June 1937), 369–73, 379.

_____. *Unearthly Gentleman: A Trilogy of One Act Plays About Shakespeare* ["Night of Errors," "One Afternoon in Henley Street," and "Gentleman of Stratford"]. London: Victor Gollancz, 1965.

Saward, William T. *William Shakespeare: A Play in Four Acts.* London: Elkin Matthews, 1907.

Schoenbaum, Samuel. *Shakespeare's Lives.* New York and Oxford: Oxford University Press, 1970.

Sensabaugh, Roy S. *The Favor of the Queen: A Play in Four Acts.* Birmingham, Alabama, 1929.

Severn, Emma. *Anne Hathaway; Or Shakspeare in Love.* 3 vols. London: Richard Bentley, 1845.

"Shakespeare's Ghost." *The London Magazine,* 19 (June 1750), 278–9.

Shaw, George Bernard. "The Dark Lady of the Sonnets." *The English Review,* January 1911, pp. 258–69.

_____. "A Dressing Room Secret." 1910. Rpt. in *Shaw on Shakespeare*. Ed. Edwin Wilson. New York: E. P. Dutton, 1961, pp. 243–49.

_____. *Shakes vs. Shav: A Puppet Play*. The Arts Bulletin Council, 113 (September 1949).

Sisson, Rosemary Anne. *The Young Shakespeare*. London: Max Parrish, 1959.

Somerset, C. A. *Shakspeare's Early Days: An Historical Play*. London: John Cumberland [1830?].

Sterling, Sarah. *Shakespeare's Sweetheart*. London: Chatto and Windus, 1905.

Taylor, Gary. *Reinventing Shakespeare*. New York: Weidenfield & Nicolson, 1989.

Vandervell, W. F. *The Tercentenary; or, A Night with Shakespeare*. London: Charles Jeffreys, 1864.

The Visitation; or an Interview Between the Ghost of Shakespear and D-V-D G-RR--K, Esq. London, 1755.

Warren, Edward H. *Shakespeare on Wall Street*. Cambridge: Riverside Press, 1929.

Williams, Charles. *A Myth of Shakespeare*. Oxford: Oxford Univ. Press, 1928.

Williams, Robert Folkstone. *The Secret Passion*. 3 vols. London: Henry Colburn, 1844.

_____. *Shakspeare and His Friends; Or "The Golden Age" of Merry England*. 3 vols. London: Henry Colburn, 1938.

_____. *The Youth of Shakspeare*. Paris: Baudry's European Library, 1839.

Wood, Alan. "Playing Days at Stratford." MS [1964]. Shakespeare Centre Library.

[Woodward, George M]. *Familiar Verses from the Ghost of Willy Shakspeare to Sammy Ireland*. London: Richard White, 1796.

INDEX